PRAISE FOR G

"Astonishing and totally uniq[...] fearlessly that it feels as if she [...] Immersion. An intricately crafted and superbly rendered vision of horror-fantasy from one of the genre's most brilliant and devastating voices."

Eric LaRocca, Bram Stoker Award nominated author of Things Have Gotten Worse Since We Last Spoke

"A deep dive into the horrors of depression, *Full Immersion* takes readers on a harrowing journey into the character of Magpie, a woman grappling with a horrifying history she can barely remember, now lost within herself. There, a host of terrors play out in unexpected, gruesome ways. Told through duelling POVs, Ms. Amor's writing is tense and sharp, reminiscent of Kealan Patrick Burke, Jeanette Winterson and Charlotte Perkins Gilman. Fans of both psychological and body horror will find much to enjoy here!"

D.K. Stone, author of *Fall Of Night*

"Powered by dread from the very beginning, *Full Immersion* is a full-throated scream in the heart. Gemma Amor wields an ever-tightening emotional vice, constantly questioning and challenging the malevolent unreality we accept as our lives. A harrowing inward odyssey."

Hailey Piper, Bram Stoker Award winning author of Queen of Teeth

"Raw, personal, confrontational, and timely, Gemma Amor bares her soul in full for a book that will rock you to your core. Charting a metaphysical landscape of pain and real suffering, *Full Immersion* is nothing less than a klaxon call confirming one of the most daring and fearless voices in contemporary fiction."

Kealan Patrick Burke, Bram Stoker Award-winning author of Kin *and* Sour Candy

"With *Full Immersion*, Gemma Amor offers you an incredible journey into the dangers and possibilities of the human mind. It's shocking and unnerving and heartbreaking and, ultimately, hopeful in a way that makes you want to jump for joy. It will reawaken you to the possibilities – and depths – of our souls."

Nick Kolakowski, author of Absolute Unit *and* Boise Longpig Hunting Club

"Gemma Amor's raw, dreamlike novel, *Full Immersion*, crept under my skin in the most delicious way. A modern-day fairy tale where the princess must save herself, this book will unnerve you and break your heart. An important, timely story."

Meagan Jennett, author of You Know Her

"All of Gemma's work is vivid and visceral, but *Full Immersion* will invade every space of your heart and mind. The hurt is terrifying as it jumps off the page to create haunting images of catastrophic proportions. If you are not a Gemma fan already then you will be after this one. I felt every word."

V. Castro, Bram Stoker Award nominated author of Goddess of Filth

"The bravest book you'll read all year. Harrowing, yes, but necessarily so. As empowering as it is powerful. Not only does the book benefit a crucial cause, the stories are extraordinary, written by more than a dozen paramount voices in horror. Sometimes a book illuminates as it entertains; *We Are Wolves* is that rare find."

Josh Malerman, New York Times best selling author of Bird Box *and* Malorie, *on* We Are Wolves

"It pulls no punches, asks for no quarter, and will leave you breathless. I loved it."

Brian Keene, best-selling author and World Horror Grandmaster Award-winner, on We Are Wolves

Gemma Amor

FULL IMMERSION

ANGRY
ROBOT

ANGRY ROBOT
An imprint of Watkins Media Ltd

Unit 11, Shepperton House
89 Shepperton Road
London N1 3DF
UK

angryrobotbooks.com
twitter.com/angryrobotbooks
Life after Life

An Angry Robot paperback original, 2022

Cover by Francesca Corsini
Edited by Eleanor Teasdale and Andrew Hook
Set in Meridien

ISBN 978 0 85766 981 0
Ebook ISBN 978 0 85766 984 1

Printed and bound in the United Kingdom by TJ Books Ltd.

9 8 7 6 5 4 3 2 1

This book is for those who kept me here when I wanted to leave, and for those who gave me a reason to stay. For those who fought alongside me, dragged me up the mountain, helped me draw a line in the sand. Thank you.

It is also for those who solved their own mysteries, but most especially, this book is for those who could not.

It is for The Kid, who I love, eternally, without bounds.

And lastly, this book is for me.

FOREWORD

How much is a woman's life worth, when you think about it? When it comes down to the nuts and bolts, the cowrie shells, the leather bank notes. I think about this a lot, for reasons that will be clearer once you've read this book. I think about the value we place on human life. I think about how willing we are sometimes to let that life fall to the wayside, as if it were no more important than a broken-down car. When we malfunction, our value decreases in the eyes of society. Our peers, colleagues, government, and even sometimes our friends and lovers struggle to see our substance beneath the cracks. Never was this made more apparent than when I gave birth to my son, and later became quite unwell, mentally. I felt people around me withdraw as if stung. I felt like dirty goods, not to be touched. In turn, this made me feel doubly unqualified and unfit to be a mother, which was silly, when you think about it, because the only opinion I should have cared about was my son's. 'We just want you to get better,' people said, as if the 'un-better' version of me was now untenable. I think in hindsight many of them were genuine about this, and equally afraid of saying or doing something that might make me worse, but still. It felt like a strange, cosmic punishment, the loneliness that ensued. As if I was suddenly invisible to many who had seen me clearly before. I became staggeringly obscure. Like a ghost pounding on the walls. Yet my shine was still there. All it took was for someone to understand that a broken state need not be permanent, need not be repulsive, and maybe help a little, thumb some of the dirt away, expose my natural hue.

That person, first and foremost, had to be me. I'm not saying I didn't need help. I did, but I found it difficult to ask for. In time, I was able to lean upon my husband. My therapist. My doctor, who didn't dismiss my concerns out of hand (what a world, where I feel grateful for the simple act of being taken seriously). But my true champion, my white knight, my hero, in the end, turned out to be myself. I had to figure out how much my own life was worth, flaws and all. It was a slow process. A large part of it revolved around me sitting in a café after the school run, writing this novel. I wrote it, and it saved my life. I wrote it, and hoped that in the future, my son would know me better. I don't want him to feel responsible for anything that happened while I was sick, but I know that children take a lot upon themselves. I thought long and hard about whether or not I wanted to expose myself by getting this book published, but anyone who knows me knows that I am not ashamed or afraid of writing painful truths. I'm aware that judgement often follows. But by putting it all down like this, I become more real in my own eyes, remind myself of my worth. The value of a woman's life, measured by her bodyweight in words. And writing this story showed me something. It showed me that broken, chipped, scarred, cracked, flawed… none of this means less valuable. Coins minted with mistakes are often more valued by collectors. Inclusions in gemstones remind us that nature puts her own, unique signature into something: individuality. Michelangelo's statue of David is missing a muscle between his spine and shoulder blade, owing to an imperfection in the marble. Being broken didn't make me less valuable. If you're feeling cracked down the middle, I would like you to remember that.

Anyway, for readers who are new here: I like to write forewords. Partly in defiance of the foreword naysayers, but mostly because I like to let folks know what they are in for when it comes to certain topics, themes and content they might find distressing. I feel strongly about letting people decide for themselves whether or not to engage with this stuff, so here goes: this novel deals heavily with themes of suicidal ideation, intrusive thoughts, post-natal depression, implied harm to a child, and descriptions of childbirth that some of you may find a little challenging. I shall say no more than this: *Full Immersion* was my first completed novel, and it remains, to date, my most raw, my most painful, and yet my most hopeful.

At the back of this book I've included a list of charities and organisations that may be helpful to anyone fighting a similar battle. There are some brilliant people and resources out there who can help you see your incredible worth through the fog of despair.

In the meantime, I want you to know: I see you, too. I see that shine. You aren't broken, not to me. You're brimming with potential, with hope, with wonderful things to come. You're riddled with wonderful cracks, anomalies, quirks, idiosyncrasies. Your babies love you, and I think you're incredible, and your worth simply too great to quantify.

1

Words on a Page

To: The Department of Virtual and Experimental Therapy
University of Bristol
One Cathedral Square
College Green
Bristol

June 26th, 2019

Dear Sirs,

It has taken me six months to write this letter.

You should know I have tried everything else. I have tried medication, counselling, cognitive reprogramming exercises. I do yoga, and I paint. I take long walks. I sleep for eight hours a day, read self-help books, listen to soothing podcasts and ambient, lyric-less music. I have a therapy app on my phone, in fact I have three. I masturbate frequently and stay hydrated.

None of it works.

Because I still wake up every single day without exception and think about throwing myself off the Bristol suspension bridge.

It's not an idle thought, nor a romantic one. I don't wake up and wonder what it feels like to fly, or how the cold metal suspender cables will feel in my hands as I climb up above the bridge deck, or whether the impact of hitting the river will kill me before I drown, pushing my bones out through my skin, snapping my neck. It isn't a dramatic response to stress, or a morbid fascination, or an indeterminate sense of melancholy, or even a cry for help (unlike this letter).

It's a compulsion. It's like I am being called. It's relentless.

And I just don't know *why*.

That's why I need your help.

I know about your department and your Virtual Experimental Therapy programme. My husband keeps up with that sort of thing – he has a vested interest now, I imagine. I first read about you in a magazine of his, then did some digging. I understand that you are widely considered "unorthodox".

Well, maybe unorthodox is exactly what I need, because Christ knows nothing else is working.

I understand you accept a limited number of patients on a deferred payment plan basis. I need you to consider this letter as my application to be one of those patients. You see, the thing about my condition is that I can't hold down a steady job. This means I have no money. I can't ask my husband for any more help; I have taken enough from him already.

But without money, I can't afford your services.

So again, these words:

Help me.

Words are funny, aren't they? They're like little pieces of yourself, given away. Like the words in this letter. Are they persuasive enough? I hope so. I was a writer, in my better days. I don't really know what I am anymore. A shadow, perhaps. An echo. An impression of a person, rather than the whole.

I'm drunk, writing this. Ten minutes before putting pen to paper I chased the booze with some of those pills various doctors keep giving me, the ones that don't help much at all. I keep telling them, *these don't help,* but all I end up with is a fresh prescription, a different type of pill. If you listen carefully enough, you might hear me rattle, I am so full.

But you don't want to hear all that.

There is a point to this.

The point is "The Question".

And "The Question" is always the same. People always want to know the same thing.

"Why do you want to kill yourself?" they ask.

And I never know how to answer.

Because leaving everything behind would only make sense if there was a *reason* for me to want to do so, surely.

"Did something happen to you?"

This is The Other Question that people always ask. They're also looking for "A Reason", an exposition. Maybe a trauma, an event, as described, something that perverts my brain away from its vital task of the everyday, and makes it weaker, and tired, and colours everything grey.

And this question is actually a "Good Question".

Because, sure, lots of things have happened to me. Things I can consciously recall. Bad things. Good things. Awful things, surmountable things, shameful things.

But what if something happened to me that I *can't* recall? My memory feels like a beach bathed in fog.

Or worse, what if I did something? Something wrong? Something bad? Something I've forgotten. What if there is a dark secret lurking in my head?

And if there were, could you help me uncover it? Your programme seems ideally placed to do so.

If there *is* no grand, insidious secret, if it turns out that life is just a steady trickle of events, a slow and creeping succession of little traumas, a collection of hurt, if you will, then your treatment may also help me come to terms with that.

Either way, my mind is being eaten away steadily. In the better hours, I can just about remember my name, and that I am married, and that I used to be a Mother, have a life. Other times, the words escape me. Because words are tricky, aren't they? In the time it has taken you to read this far, I have told you that I no longer want to live. Perhaps I'm already dead. Who knows? You can't see me, you can only see my words, like footprints left behind in the sand.

Do you believe me? Why would you? If I was serious, then I wouldn't be sending this letter, would I?

God, I'm tired of myself.

I'm writing with no expectations, only desperation. Words, marching quickly across the white page like dutiful ants going about their business, and that business is this: alive, or dead.

Heads, or tails. Black, or white.

Seems simple, doesn't it?

It isn't.

Please help me.

Yours, with hope,

M

2

Voyeurs

In a dark, modestly furnished room that smells of hot coffee and hot metal and hot plastic, two technicians sit side by side, crammed up against the far wall. They are pinned in place by a vast array of electronics and equipment: wires, screens of varying sizes, VR headsets, headset base stations, a projector, routers, laptops, a scanner or two, mounted panels with flashing, multi-coloured LEDs, keyboards, speakers, wireless controllers, a strange, square, multi-parameter monitor with a built-in printer, and other things that are difficult to make out in the low light. It's a mess, but one the pair seem comfortable with. On three walls of the room, polished whiteboards hang, graffitied with scribbles and doodles. On the last wall, closest to where the Techs and their equipment huddle, a large expanse of glass stretches from corner to corner: a window, or, more precisely, a reciprocal mirror, reflective on one side, transparent on the other.

The team of two speak in a hushed, absent-minded way to each other as they fiddle with their gear, fully absorbed in their work, wiring themselves up, slotting headphones over their ears, plugging themselves in with the practiced seriousness of astronauts preparing for launch. They have an important task to perform. A new project. They are the watchers. The moderators, the Behind the Scenes team.

They are the Control Room.

They have been doing this for some time now, spying out in the open like this. It is as legitimate as voyeurism will ever get. They have letters after their names and paperwork that gives them agency to do so, day in, day out, and get paid for the pleasure. Infiltration in the name of science. A rum job, but someone has to do it. At least, that's what they say to each other, jokingly, but the reality is much more serious. They are not spies, not really. They are an intervention. A rescue team. White knights, of a sort.

Before them, that tinted glass window yawns. They can see perfectly well into the neighbouring room through it, but no-one can see them from the other side.

Not that the occupant of the adjoining room is in any condition to try.

She hangs in a hypnagogic state, hovering somewhere between wakefulness and sleep, thin steel wires, pulleys and cables keeping her form amply suspended in the air about four feet above the ground. Her limbs are supported at the joints by soft fabric cuffs attached to the wires. Her body (thinly clothed in paper pyjamas), neck and the back of her head is braced by a strong silicon cradle, articulated and moulded to fit the contours of her spine closely. The cradle is held up by more steel cables that are mounted to a moveable track on the ceiling. She looks like a dangling marionette in storage, waiting for a performance to start, which is precisely what she is. Tubes of varying sizes crawl into her mouth and nostrils and other hidden parts of her body, and there is an IV drip plugged into a vein on one thin, bruised arm. A forest of wires protrudes from her shaved scalp, attached to dozens of biomedical sensor pads held in place around her skull by an elaborate headband. A wide curved visor covers her eyes, which are blue in colour and held open by tiny eyelid retainers and special adhesive strips to keep the eyelashes clear. Small white buds nestle into the hollows of her ears: wireless headphones. Her hands, which hang loosely by her sides, are sheathed in fingerless gesture control gloves, and her feet are clad in thin, membranous boots wired to a massive unit standing off to one side. There are several of these large black units positioned around the edges of the room, monumental things that hum as they process, emitting a low, keen non-sound that can only be heard if a person were to focus on it, a white rush of noise that is as absorbent as it is abrasive. The patient will not be able to hear it beyond the ambient sounds trickling into her brain through the headphones.

The Observation Room in which the patient hangs feels cavernous: a large, clinical space that has been kept purposefully clear so she can move about, enact things freely at the end of her wires. Being able to do so will reduce the cognitive dissonance between a sleeping, immobile version of herself and the notion that she is free to move, explore, react. More headsets dangle from the ceiling behind her like strange redundant vines, not needed for this scenario, and an organised mass of colour-coded cables snake around fluorescent strip lights that are currently switched off. The floor is black vinyl, easy to clean and sanitise. Patients in this room often secrete fluids: vomit, piss, sweat, it's all been thought about and catered for.

A nurse in a crisp white uniform makes herself busy attending to the patient, reapplying anaesthetic eye drops so she doesn't feel the subconscious need to blink, adjusting wires and cuffs, checking pulse rates and blood pressure, smearing barrier cream onto any parts of her body that can chafe, gently rubbing at hands and feet to keep the circulation flowing. It is tricky to manoeuvre around the wires and tubes, but she knows what she is doing. This is not her first rodeo. She notes things down on a tablet with a stylus as she works, her handwriting neat and precise. The notes pop up onto a small monitor in the Control Room next door. The team within ignore them. The patient is stable. If there was something wrong with her vitals, they would know about it. The system has been designed to panic at the first sign of physical instability. Lawsuits are an ever-present threat to experimental medicine, so they are taking no risks. Not that the woman could sue if she *did* die. Angry relatives on the other hand, are a different kettle of expensive fish.

The patient breathes softly in and out, unaware of her surroundings and the gentle bustle of the Nurse. Unaware of anything much, except a deep, dull ache in her heart, an ache that straddles both the sleeping and wakeful parts of her. Luckily, the people behind the glass claim to be adept at administering to aches. The patient is here for that reason, and because she wrote them a long, painful letter that rambled and ended with three devastatingly simple words:

Please help me.

And so, the techs will endeavour to do so.

It is not a completely selfless act: these are salaried heroes who are encouraged to maintain a professional distance from the patient herself. Boundaries are important in this industry – their efficient, business-like demeanour is therefore not due to a lack of sympathy. As technicians, they are encouraged to see the disease, rather than the host, as many doctors are encouraged to triage and treat symptoms before delving into causality.

Still. It is hard for them to not feel some pity for the woman who hangs, lightly drooling, before them. Her thin, bruised state acts as an incentive. The most desired outcome is, of course, a long, happy continued life for the patient. After that, words like "Fellowship" and "Royal Society" and "research award" and "pay rise" flit through the technicians' respective minds.

Around them, monitors display a variety of scenes from what looks like a live video feed, cycling through high-definition snapshots of the world outside the darkened room in quick succession: a river, over which a vast, curved bridge hangs suspended, a meadow, an island, a huge, colonnaded space like that of a museum, or an art gallery. A small laptop resting on one of the tech's knees shows strings of code moving up and down, living digits that crawl across the screen like insects, like ants. Not words, but cipher. Soul cipher, although the techs don't know that, not yet.

Eventually, with all routine checks completed, the pair lean back in their chairs, stretch out sore arms and roll their heads around uncomfortably on stiff necks. Then, in unspoken agreement, they turn to one another.

"Ready?" says the first into a small microphone mounted on her desktop. She is dressed in a pinstriped shirt that pulls a bit around her shoulders, and brown corduroys. In her late fifties, she is ageing well, skin still smooth, at odds with her thick silver hair. She speaks to her colleagues as a Boss speaks to a subordinate: gently commanding, professional, but pulling rank with every syllable.

The Nurse in the next room completes her last check, adds a final note to her tablet, smiles, rearranges a wire or two, then makes a thumbs-up gesture.

"Thank you," the Boss says.

The Nurse leaves the room quietly and the sleeping-yet-awake patient is alone, at last. She sways gently as the wires settle; a human pendulum headed for equilibrium.

"Ready?" The silver-haired woman repeats the question for the man sitting next to her, who wears a security tag on a lanyard about his neck on which the name "Evans" can be read.

Evans takes a deep breath, reaching out a single finger and letting it hover it over a large red button anchored to a Perspex safe-box on his desk.

"As I ever will be," the younger man replies, and, with that, his finger descends and he pushes the button.

A loud, long beep fills the air between them. The woman suspended mid-air twitches, just once, and then settles.

The session has begun.

3

MY BODY

I found my body early on a Tuesday.

I had been walking, as was my habit, without purpose along the Portway. In a melancholic state, vision turned inwards, I felt as if I drifted in this manner most mornings. Looking for what, I could not recall. I wandered alone, my hands firmly plunged into my pockets, my fingers twitching rhythmically in forgotten arrangements, remembering the ghostly movements of some old functionality long since dissolved. What was it I had used to do, before I had begun to walk here every day? What had I used my hands for? *(Mummy, can you pick me up? I can't see!)*. I could never remember. My shoulders hunched against the chill. Every now and then, I managed to drag my eyes away from the beautiful bridge that hung above me, a bridge I stared at without really seeing, trying and failing to block out its insistent, persuasive calls. I would look away, struggling to reconnect my feet and my body to the ground beneath me, but my gaze always drifted back. The bridge was magnetic.

Every day it was like this, every day the same, walking, walking along the Portway under the suspension bridge, following the river, sliding in and out of my own skin, fingers trembling with echoes of past use. Aimless, searching.

Pretty fucking useless.

The day I found my body was no different, only it was a

particularly beautiful morning, and promised to be a particularly beautiful day. It was quiet, unusually so. Mist hung all around. The air was freezing and fresh. Occasionally, a car would pass by, but the engine noise was muted, its rude hum swallowed quickly by cold fog.

And the bridge called to me, as was its way.

In the Control Room, Evans fiddles with various settings on various panels, turning his attention to a large, central monitor upon which the patient is visible. Only not as she really is, dangling from wires in the next room, her fingers spasming, her legs cycling gently as if she is walking upright, enmeshed in a sprouting nest of wires. Instead, the monitor displays a river, and the limestone gorge it cuts through, and a beautiful iron suspension bridge spanning that gorge, underneath which the virtual version of the patient ambles slowly, as if sleepwalking.

"The graphics are looking bloody good," Evans says, whistling through his teeth. "Even if I do say so myself."

"I'll admit, this is some of your best work yet."

"Thanks, Boss. To be fair, we had great source material to work with."

"Even so. I'm having a hard time distinguishing it from the real thing. I jog along that path most weekends, right where she is now. Consider me impressed."

"Thank you. This is full VR, not augmented photos or footage. I'm proud of our team. Full Immersion, Boss, that's what the doctor ordered."

"Full Immersion is a myth, Evans, we both know that."

"Fine, fine. But close enough, right?"

The Boss laughs. "Maybe."

"One day."

"Not in our lifetime, Evans. But, seriously, well done. I really am impressed. There is so much detail! I don't know where to look first."

Evans snorts. "To be honest, it's better than even I remember. Maybe a few of the team did some post sign-off polishing. Not really process, but I'll let them off if it makes me look good."

"Anything that makes the transition smoother, eh? It all works in our favour."

"She does seem to be taking to it well. Even if she has spent the last ten minutes wandering about staring into space."

"She's world building, is all. You know those with a creative bent respond better to the visuals."

"Writer, isn't she?"

"Yes."

"She doesn't fit our usual profile."

"You're not wrong. But you should have seen the letter she sent us, Evans. I had a hard time rejecting her application. Until, well, you know. The bursary board changes its mind every five minutes."

"Do you think she looks comfortable? Should we adjust the visor? It's a bit low down on her head."

"No, leave her be, it doesn't seem to be bothering her much. We can't fiddle with her without calling the Nurse back in anyway, and she's on break. Are we recording okay?"

"Seems fine." Evans leans across his desk to type something into one of the laptops. "We'll never get Full Immersion, like you said. But one day, we won't just be able to see everything she can, hear everything she hears. We'll be able to hear what she's, you know... *thinking*."

"And you'd be out of a job." The older woman grins, waving at the hanging system next door, the equipment in the control room. Evans blinks, not sure how he feels about this comment.

His Boss sighs, then sits up straight, attentive, focussed, her mind switching to the next task on the list.

"Now, shhhh," she says, flapping a hand impatiently. "The Introduction is often one of the hardest parts, we need to be ready to react if she doesn't take to it."

"Right you are, Boss."

More keys are tapped on a keyboard.

The woman walking beneath the bridge blinks, hesitates, then continues on her way.

Where was I?

Oh, yeah, walking. Always walking, never seeming to quite get anywhere.

The river that ran beside me that day was wide, and brown. It worked its way sluggishly along between two large banks of mud that nestled at the bottom of a wide gorge. Hence the bridge. An old, decrepit landing stage thrust its rotten teeth out of the mud to the left of me: wormy, stricken pegs that had no business still standing, but clung to their positions regardless.

I stopped to lean on the wall that banked the river and stared down at the remains of the stage. Someone had spray-painted a crude stickman onto the rotting wood in neon pink, and I didn't like it. My wrist burned when I looked at the graffiti, so I dragged my sleeve down, to cover it. I was feeling nauseous, dizzy, but I didn't know why. My stomach had begun to lurch wildly, as if I were sea-sick. I hoped I hadn't eaten anything bad, and tried to distract myself with local trivia. The landing stage below used to take the weight of wealthy passengers who came by ferry to visit a long shuttered hot spring and spa nestled into the cliff above my head, part of a Victorian hotel complex. I had read somewhere that the spring waters that fed the spa were found to be poisonous, full of mercury, but in reality I think the rich folk of the city simply lost faith in its healing powers, and drifted away, as people do, hungry for the next diversion.

I leaned further over the wall and scrutinised the thick swells of mud, licking my lips as hot saliva built up in my cheeks. A pair of magpies flew past, flashes of white and black against the brown. I was used to feeling disconnected from my surroundings, used to feeling disoriented, but today... today I felt as if I were moving about in a dream, a dream where the ground felt weirdly insubstantial, spongey and inadequate under my feet. I looked back up to the perfect arc of the bridge for some reassurance.

And for a while, I could see nothing else.

A sigh rolls around the Control Room.

"What's wrong?"

Evans wrinkles his nose. "I know the bridge looks good and all, but Christ, I wish she'd get on with it. This is a bit like watching paint dry!"

"She's just settling in Evans, that's all. It's a good thing. The more time she spends getting comfortable in her surroundings, the better. Besides, you should be happy she's enjoying your wonderful graphics."

"If she spends the next three days staring at mud banks and mooning over individual blades of grass, I'm voluntarily looking for another job."

The Boss shoots her colleague a look with a wink.

"Good luck with that," she laughs.

I blinked, shaking myself free of inertia. I was cold, I needed to start walking again, but this had always been my favourite part of the city, here, beneath the bridge, an ostentatious symbol of industry and vision and daring. It captivated me. Something so simple, in principle. A means of getting from one side of a river to the other. And yet it wasn't simple. Beneath the rock, the anchored cables of the bridge stretched down into the earth like the roots of great teeth; every link, every shape, every part of it planned and calculated and assembled in an incomprehensibly complex, yet beautiful design. It is the engineers that raise us up to become civilised, I always said. Or had someone else said that? I couldn't remember. Regardless, it was both inspiring and depressing to think about. I knew that in all the life that was left to me, I would never build anything or create anything to match the worth of that bridge. My legacy would disappear after I died, and my children died, and my children's children died. Nothing I did would ever be as permanent, as lasting as that perfect iron span, as significant as...

I swallowed again, then once more.

(Children)

The word triggered a sudden, roiling bout of nausea. I felt immediately both hot, and cold. My skin prickled. My mind's eye conjured an image of blonde hair, kissed by sunlight. Instead of a bridge, I saw a curl, perfect, soft, spun in gold. The image dissolved, but the damage was done. My belly cramped. Hot liquid surged in my throat.

I puked over the wall, violently.

In the Observation Room, the suspended woman groans, twitches and jerks about uncomfortably. Then she lurches forward, eyes wide open, bulging but still only seeing what plays out on her visor. She promptly vomits, spraying herself, the cradle, her visor and everything else with a small fountain of brownish-yellow bile. It splatters onto the floor below her as the woman continues to gag and retch and heave.

"Oh, great," Evans moans, as the woman sinks back into her wires, purged. Drool leaks down her chin and makes a bid for the ground beneath. "VR sickness already?"

"It's no big deal," his Boss replies calmly. She presses a comms button nearby, summoning the Nurse, hoping she is not still on break. "Clean up in the O.R.," she orders, and a small, exasperated noise comes back to her as the Nurse registers the call. Minutes later, the uniformed woman is back in the room behind the glass window, wrinkling her nose a little as she mops up foul-smelling liquid, reattaches loose cables and tubes and a sensor pad that ripped off during the violent motion of the patient purging herself. She cleans and rearranges the visor, peels off the patient's loose, stained paper pyjamas and redresses her with new paper clothes kept sterile in a shrink-wrapped packet from a nearby shelf. The pyjamas are cut-out garments fitted by a series of plastic press-studs, allowing the Nurse to dress the woman without interfering with her hanging system or any of her tubes. Evans catches a glimpse of the patient's skin before she is re-clothed. Stretch marks, deep yet faded, stripe the patient's belly, the tops of her thighs, the sides of her breasts. The Nurse, perhaps sensing his scrutiny, moves to shield the patient from view with her own body.

The techs continue to watch her work, Evans twitching his leg nervously. A digital clock app counts the seconds passing on his desktop.

"If she doesn't hurry up, we'll have to reset. We can't keep the patient out of flow long without messing everything up."

"I'm doing the best that I can," the Nurse replies tartly, from behind the glass. The Boss has forgotten to switch off her desk mic. The older woman rolls her eyes at Evans and placates the Nurse.

"Thank you, you're doing a brilliant job," she soothes, before switching her comms off.

Evans jiggles some more in his chair. "We've not had a puker for a while," he says.

His Boss shrugs. "It happens. Some are more sensitive than others. Tiny inaccuracies in the visuals…"

"How very dare you."

"…her personal simulation threshold… all sorts of factors can affect it. The longer she spends in there, the easier it'll get, I hope. Can't be easy, lying suspended and semi-unconscious whilst, you know, walking around in your mind. Gravity feels different, everything at odds with everything else. She'll get used to it."

"It's not that easy sitting in *here*, waiting to get the fuck on with things." Evans screws up his face, peeved.

His Boss sighs again. She feels like she is doing that a lot, lately.

"Cheer up Evans, would you? Go make the coffee if you're bored."

"Fine." Evans is tired already. "Coffee it is."

"Milk, no sugar please. And be snappy – the Nurse is almost done."

"Milk, no sugar. Right you are."

I wiped my mouth, feeling better. A small puddle of yellowish-brown bile had been deposited onto the mud bank beneath me.

I looked down at it, froze.

And saw a slender, female hand sticking out of the mud.

Fuck, I thought. *Fuck!*

Had it had been there all along, for me to see it only now? Elegantly beckoning: *Come here*, it said.

I remained fixed to the spot. Fear and indecision took hold of me. I felt blood pounding against my ear drums. I looked about for some help. There was none; it was not long after dawn. The city still slept.

I thought about calling someone, but then I remembered I had no phone, and no money with me. That realisation hit me in all the wrong places. Why would I have left the house without money? Did I even have my keys? I patted myself down. No. That didn't make any sense. I always took my keys with me when I left the house. Why would I have…

Does it matter? I cried, silently. *There's a fucking hand sticking out of the mud bank not ten feet away!*

I looked at the hand again. It was a good job I had already been sick.

What the fuck was I supposed to do about this? I couldn't call anyone, so common sense dictated I should go and get help. But I couldn't just leave the hand sticking out of the bank like that, unattended. It felt wrong, to my core. There was, presumably, a body attached to the hand, lying down there in the sludge, and leaving it alone felt cruel, for reasons I didn't understand completely.

Carefully, I climbed over the wall and hopped down onto the rickety landing station. It creaked and moaned underneath my weight, but held. I inched across to the edge of the station, so I was directly above where the arm poked out of the mud. I lay flat on my belly, threaded my feet through the gaps in between the timbers. Reached out.

The hand was too far away.

"Wait!" a voice cried, and I nearly fell headlong off the station and into the riverbank. There was a thud, and a jolt. Another person landed on the jetty next to me. A man.

He spread himself out beside me. I looked at him in shock and grateful surprise.

"Let me help," he said. I was in no position to refuse.

I let him hold my legs as I shuffled further forward, allowing my upper body to hinge and hang down from the waist, straining, reaching, until finally, my fingers brushed the cold, wet fingers protruding from the bank.

"Got it!" I gasped.

Together, we braced ourselves, and pulled.

The body resisted at first, then, like a babe from the womb, slid free from the mud. The noise was indescribable. Excruciating. I knew I would never forget it. Between us, with huge effort, we hauled the corpse up onto the jetty. I don't know how, exactly, but we did. I then lay on my belly for several minutes, spent, panting, covered in slimy filth. It felt as if I'd given birth once again.

(Given birth once again never again not after last time I'm sorry, I know you're disappointed but–)

Suddenly it was hard to breathe. I pushed up onto my knees, dry heaving.

What the fuck was wrong with me?

There was nothing left in my belly to vomit out.

"Is she going to hurl again?"

"She's got barely anything left in her stomach, so I hope not."

"It's going to be really, *really* difficult to implement anything if she spends this whole scenario blowing chunks."

The Boss squeezes a fold of skin between her eyebrows, feeling faintly stressed. Evans has always been a complainer, and the Boss knows it is mostly harmless bluster, but he is starting to grate on her.

"Evans," she says, as patiently as she can, "I know we don't hire you for your bedside manner, but do you think you can at least try to have some sympathy for the poor girl? She's clearly having a rough old time of it. How about a bit more patience for the patient?"

Evans snorts, folding his arms.

"Fine," he says, eventually. "But it's putting me right off my lunch, I'll tell you that much."

I heaved a few more times, got a hold of myself. Eventually, I sat back on my heels, looked across to my helper. He was a youngish man with a short, dark beard, longish hair and pale green or blue eyes, I couldn't tell which colour, exactly.

We acknowledged each other silently, and turned our attention to the body.

It was female, of average height and weight, and she had long wavy hair coated in gelatinous mud. Her skin was cold, livid. A thick, dirt-flecked film of mucus glazed her unseeing eyes. She was well and truly dead, and reminded me of a jellyfish washed up on a beach: spent, limp.

Tentatively, I scooped the dirt away from her eyes, her

mouth, her nostrils, hoping in vain that she would perhaps find herself able to breathe, wake up.

She did not.

And the more I cleaned her, the more I began to tremble. My own skin grew cold. *Shock,* I thought, remotely. *I'm in shock.*

Because I realised, as she emerged from underneath the filth, that I knew her.

I found a handkerchief in my pocket, spat on it as best I could with my now very dry mouth. Wiped her lips so that the colour could seep back through: it did not, they remained pale, blueish. I slicked the hair back from her forehead, removed the clay from her eyelashes, wiped every finger clean. Tears ran down my face. A few of them dropped, left wet clean trails on her skin. She didn't flinch. She remained cold, motionless, uncaring. It might have been mistaken for poise, were it not for the lividity.

I stopped when I knew I could do no more.

She was dead, gone.

My new friend placed a hand on my shoulder. It was warm, a welcome contrast to the hand that I now held.

"Do you know her?" he asked, his voice kind.

"I do," I said, for the body I was looking at was my own.

My own.

My lifeless face, staring back uncomprehendingly.

Mirror, mirror, on the wall, who is…?

Dead?

You are, my dear.

4

DEBT

"How's she doing?" The Boss returns from a bathroom break, rubbing sanitizer into the dry skin of her hands as she carefully re-seats herself at the control deck.

"Better. Sickness seems to have abated. She's not pregnant, is she? Just a thought."

The Boss shakes her head. An odd look paints her face. "Definitely not," she says, in a curt tone.

Awkward silence prevails for a moment. Evans, not oblivious to tonal shifts, tries to lighten the mood.

"Well, she's running with it just fine now. That's the beauty of this method. It gives her back some control. Or the illusion of it, at least."

"*All is illusion…*" The Boss mutters, to herself.

Evans rummages around in his nose with the tip of a pen.

"Although if you ask me, this scenario is a bit brutal. Finding her own dead body like that. It's… downright morbid."

"Don't you ever read the script properly, Evans?"

"Nah. Too busy, you know, working. The beat sheets work just fine for me. I always was an edited highlight sort of guy."

The Boss shakes her head. "I swear you are the sole reason I have gone so grey. But okay, yes, it is a touch dramatic, I suppose. But that's what the Psych ordered, so that's what we've delivered. He's obviously decided a more extreme approach is necessary this time."

"Shouldn't we be worried about triggering her?"

"To do what? She can't harm herself now, not the way we have her restrained. She's safer here than anywhere else." The older woman gestures to the Observation Room. Inside, the patient is leaning forward, her knees drawn up beneath her as far as the wires will allow. Her mouth hangs open beneath the visor. She is crying. It looks highly uncomfortable.

"Besides, we know she's in denial over previous suicide attempts."

"All three of them, too. Talk about selective memory."

"Trauma response. Unusual for her to have blanked each attempt so completely from her mind, but everyone is different. Memory loss, delusions… maybe it's better that she doesn't remember."

"Can you imagine? Throwing yourself off a bridge that high? I can't." Evans shudders.

The Boss sighs. "I don't want to imagine. I want to help her. And so does the Psych. Perhaps he thinks that shock tactics will help… shift things around a bit, so to speak."

"Epiphany."

There is a pause as the techs take a moment to think. Eventually, Evans clears his throat.

"It is… you know. For her." He stumbles with his words.

"Sad?" The Boss sighs. "Yes, yes it is. Hopefully, we can put a stop to some of her more dangerous compulsions. I guess only time will tell. How do you think she's responding to our guy?"

"What's his name again?"

"Oh, this is one of our Anonymous Psychs. He's been on our books for a while. I've never worked with him directly before, but I've heard good things."

"Anonymous Psychs. Pfft… Fucking hubris, if you ask me."

"The opposite of hubris, surely? Being Anonymous. Means you can't claim the credit for anything that comes after."

"Or blame. Fine, not hubris, but still a bit dramatic. Regardless, the Introduction seems to have gone well, I think."

"Well, it's early days yet. Is the text-to-speech bot working okay? I'm having a hard time figuring out if he's getting my messages." It was unreliable on the best of days, but the easiest way of communicating with the Psych when he was otherwise occupied. The Boss texted a two-way inbox that converted her directions to speech and fed them into his earpiece where he received them at a time that was convenient for him. It felt convoluted, but it enabled the Psych to interact with Tech when he was ready, without the distraction of anyone chattering directly into his ear mid-session. Easier to listen to a pending message than constantly mute and unmute an active dialogue, the thinking being.

"I think so. I'll add it to my ever-growing list of things to keep an eye on. Fancy another coffee?"

"Thought you'd never ask."

Once I'd gotten over the shock of finding myself dead, I began to turn my mind to the important questions.

How?

How did I die?

Well, that much was obvious. I'd jumped off the bridge and into the river.

Hadn't I?

It made sense. It was, after all, a wholly impractical way to go. And I did love the bridge. Maybe that was why I walked here every day. Maybe I was supposed to find myself, quite literally. After I'd jumped, fallen the two hundred and forty-five feet into the water, my broken form had bobbed to the surface like a cork, and the current had carried me along a little ways. I'd ended up here in the mud bank, like a fossil in the making, an ammonite in slow bloom.

When?

Did it matter? I seemed to be dressed in the same clothes that the alive version of me was wearing. I was missing my shoes, but I suppose that was to be expected. The force of impact alone would have torn them off easily, and if not that, the insistent pull of the current.

No, when it had happened didn't matter, not one bit. Time had lost all meaning for me lately, and on reflection, I realised that it had been that way for a long while: hours, days, minutes, seconds, markers, meaningless ways of dividing time into digestible little chunks, like dicing a steak before we chew on it and swallow.

And the more I thought about it, *how* it happened also didn't seem to distress me as much as it perhaps should. I was remarkably accepting of the idea that I had done this to myself, rather than been pushed, or simply fallen by accident. I couldn't explain it, but jumping just felt like something I might do.

Why, though?

Aha. *That* was the big question.

(*"The Question", why do they always want to know why, if I knew that I wouldn't–*)

I reached down and gripped my own chin between my numb fingers, searching for answers, and finding only mud in the familiar lines of my face.

I drew a horrible blank.

And then, without warning, everything flickered, and stopped.

In the Control Room, the monitors suddenly snap and blink in a rippled wave of distortion, and then each one in turn goes black.

At the same time, a faint but marked tremor runs through the room, sharply jangling and rattling the equipment around the techs for a split second, like a tiny earthquake flexing its muscles.

The Boss pushes up, half-out of her chair.

"What was that?"

"Uhh, just a glitch, I think?" replies Evans, furiously tapping at some keys. "Hang on just a sec..."

"No, I mean the tremor."

"What tremor?"

"You didn't feel that?" The Boss looks at Evans incredulously.

"Feel what?" He avoids eye contact.

Confused, the Boss looks to the patient in the OR. She is still in a kneeling position mid-air, but swaying a little more vigorously than her motion allows for. Something has disturbed that room the same as this one. A small commotion, but a marked one.

The Boss looks back at Evans. "I think we just had a miniature earthquake," she says, eyes wide.

"In Bristol?" Evans scoffs, still markedly preoccupied with the tech blackout. "Don't be daft!"

"I swear to God! I have no idea how you didn't feel that. The whole room just...vibrated."

"I honestly think it was just a glitch, Boss, I..."

The screens pop back into life as if nothing at all has happened, and Evans breathes a huge sigh of relief.

The older woman lowers herself slowly back into her seat, a little ashamed of how quickly she lost her cool.

"Just a glitch," both techs murmur, as they wait for their heart rates to return to normal.

On the screen, the patient still stares at her own muddy corpse.

"That's you, isn't it?" My companion said, over my shoulder.

I shuddered back into the moment. An internal voice whispered:

What just happened?

The man, who knelt beside me, gently touched the little brown mole that lived under my left eye, and then touched the corresponding mole on the dead woman's face.

I flinched, then nodded my head mutely.

"That's a shame," the man sighed. "Don't you have any family? People who will... miss you?"

"I do." I bit my lip, thinking furiously. "At least I think I do." *(Wanna know a secret? You love me? I know. I know you know, but I'll never stop saying it.)*

"I'm married, maybe. There is... something..."

My mind was a basket full of holes.

"This just doesn't make any sense," I burst out, exasperated.

"You can't remember? Why you did it?"

"What makes you think I did anything?" I reared back from him, angry. "I could have fallen, you know. Who even are you?"

"Just a friendly stranger," he replied, holding his hands up in a placatory gesture. "I think the situation is sad, that's all."

I couldn't argue with that. It was sad, terribly so. I looked down at my corpse again.

Why?

Something nudged at my mind. A sound. A... cry? *(Please stop please stop please)* Was that a memory? A child crying, or was it a woman? I couldn't make it out.

I sensed, although I had no idea what his motivations were for doing so, that my new friend was trying to keep me talking, distract me from something. Maybe from the awful truth of myself as a corpse. Perhaps he *was* only an innocent bystander, trying to help, but there was something off about his expression, as if he were not really concentrating, as if he were half-listening to me, and half-listening to someone else. My hackles rose, just a little. I took a moment to newly examine this new person, his shifting eye-colour, subtly changing facial contours, thick brown hair that sometimes appeared longer than it was. I really saw him, and re-appraised.

"Is this my George Bailey moment?" I asked suddenly, noting how complicated the look in his eyes was, how resolute the set of his mouth. It was the only thing that seemed to make sense to me. I was in a movie, or a novel, perhaps, and my character was about to be taught an important metaphysical lesson.

He shook his head and his attention snapped fully back to me and my dead counterpart.

"Sadly not." He picked up the dead woman's hand – *my* dead hand – and let it drop back down to the jetty, which it did with a very final sounding thump. I flinched again.

"Get off," I muttered, batting him away. It suddenly struck me how absurd this all was. "That's my body."

"It's a little late to get protective over it now, wouldn't you say?"

He was right, but I didn't appreciate the truth.

"Anyway it doesn't much matter why I did it," I continued, getting to my feet. "Dead is dead, as you say."

As the words came out of my mouth, a faint breeze picked up around me, carrying a sweet, fresh smell with it. Colours seemed to deepen a little and noises began to filter through the mist and trickle into my ears. Birdsong, faint. Water, gently splash-splashing. It was significant, because it made me realise that those things had, somehow, been missing before. The smells, the sounds. As if I'd been walking around without two of my senses. Only that wasn't quite right. No, it was more like... those things had just been absent, before, and now, were not.

I found myself faced with an awful and immediate practicality: what to do with my dead body.

Out loud, I said: "So what should we do with this corpse?" It felt difficult to say, the words mealy in my mouth.

My new friend lowered his gaze. "I don't think that's my call," he said, gently. "Like you said. It's your body."

I chewed upon my lip, thinking. "The best thing is to roll her back into the river," I replied, eventually. "Let her float. Perhaps I could roll myself in with her. Me. Whatever." It was hard keeping track of the different versions of myself.

My new friend shook his head sympathetically. "Nope. You can't kill yourself twice, I'm afraid."

"Either way, I just want to get rid of her. I'm tired."

"Doesn't she deserve more than that? Don't *you* deserve more than that? Aren't you even remotely curious as to why you died?"

I shrugged, unapologetic. "Not really." It was a lie. I did want to know, but for some reason, I didn't want *him* to know that I wanted to know.

"But everyone wants to know *why* something happens."

I shrugged again. "I don't."

"Really?"

"Really." Bored of the conversation, I began to push at my dead body. It was heavy.

My friend tried a different tack, moderating his tone.

"Wait, please. Just a moment."

"Why?"

He made another placatory gesture with his hands. He had nice hands, I noticed. Long fingers. Strong palms. Nice nails.

"Maybe... maybe you could look at it like... a debt. You *could* argue that you owe it to yourself, perhaps. To get some closure on all this."

I shook my head. What he was saying sounded suspiciously like blackmail, manipulation.

"You think a woman who kills herself when she probably has everything left to live for owes herself anything? Good riddance, more like. That's what people say, isn't it? Plenty of other people on this planet... why not make more room for someone who actually wants to be here?"

He exhaled loudly; the sound tinged with the tiniest flash of thinly veiled frustration.

"Well, put it this way." He went to place both hands on my shoulders, but stopped himself at the last moment. The attempt gave me pause, and I considered him. I hated people touching me, and was glad that he had exercised restraint. Glad, but also curious about him, his motivations. Why was he so familiar with me? Did I know this person, somehow, outside of this situation?

"Well?" I prompted.

"What else are you going to do with yourself?" he said, with a shrug.

"Walk." I sniffed, gestured to the road beneath the bridge. "Just keep walking."

"You just told me you were tired. Wouldn't it be nice to rest, for a while?"

I rolled my eyes, but then I thought about it. I looked at my poor, dead, bloated body, so cold and spent, mottled, bruised, rotting, a discarded banana skin person. For a second, the air shimmered, and I blinked. Something about the body had changed, but it happened so quickly I had no idea what, or why. And then the shimmer was gone, and there was only a body.

I realised I *was* tired, dreadfully tired, tired of drifting, tired of having no purpose.

I shook my head. "The problem is... I can't remember anything. Anything at all. I don't even know where to begin."

He smiled, gently. "Generally, people begin at the beginning, and end at the end."

"That is an infuriating thing to say, and supremely unhelpful."

"Quite." The man, whose name I had forgotten to ask for, rubbed his nice hands together, blowing into them to stave off the cold. "Either way, it's fucking freezing out here, so let's get moving, shall we?"

I thought about it. The longer I stood here and stared at my own corpse, the more depressed I felt. I realised that I had never been particularly kind about my own face, but the more I looked, the more I felt a slow sense of longing as my eyes wandered over well-known features. The mole underneath my eye, which I'd always hated, *(Mummy is that your beauty spot?)*, seemed now less ugly and more distinctive than I'd imagined when alive. My hair, greased and muddy, was long and thick, and I reached out and ran a strand of it through my fingers. It left a gritty residue on my fingertips. I rubbed it into my living skin. My eyes, upturned, milky, unseeing, were fine eyes, eyes I should have looked at the world more hopefully with. Should. Should.

Should?

(You know you shouldn't talk to me like that, don't you? You know, right? It's not how people who love each other–)

Maybe my companion was right. I suppose I did owe it to myself. Maybe.

I stopped pushing at my corpse and decided to leave it there on the jetty, because pushing it into the river felt callous, and made me feel guilty, as if I were trying to cover up a crime. Instead, I rearranged my limbs so that I looked less like a drowned woman and more like a woman lying on her back, gazing at the sky. I crossed my cold hands upon my abdomen, arranged my hair in a slick, wet wreath around my face, straightened out my arms and legs. My friend watched me work without intervening.

Then, I turned away from my body and edged towards the wall next to the jetty. I had to be careful. The wooden structure groaned beneath our collective weight.

"Give me a boost, would you?"

My new friend obliged, hoisting me up so I could reach the lip of the wall above.

"That's more like it. So where are we going?" my friend asked, grunting a little under my bulk. Although oddly, I didn't feel like I weighed anything. I felt strangely light, as if my weight were, somehow, already being supported. Realising that made me feel nauseous again, but I focused on what he was asking me instead of the sensation, and the sickness retreated after a moment or two.

"Back to my house," I said over my shoulder, now back up on the road, pumping my arms and legs in an effort to regain some body warmth and leave the other cold body behind as quickly as possible. I held a hand down for him, so he could climb up after me.

"At least, if nothing else, I think I can remember where I live."

"Well, that was close."

"Yep."

"I mean, no harm done, but what the hell *happened* there, Evans?"

"Just a glitch, I told you."

"You really didn't feel the... that tremor?"

Evans swallows, shoulders lowering in defeat. "Fine, fine. Yes, I did. But I'm thinking instead of an earthquake... which is absurd, by the way... I think it was some sort of feedback glitch, a somatosensory error, something that triggered the haptic tech and it all went off at once, causing the tremor... maybe. I don't know. First time I've ever seen it happen. But it was only a minor thing. No biggie smalls. Everything is back online, working as it should."

"What would cause an error that large?"

Evans shakes his head, typing into a small diagnostic window on a laptop.

"Could be a number of things, I wish I could give you a definitive answer. This whole environment is affected by her brain activity, so maybe... if there's a break in the connection with her, it could, in theory, interfere with the sequencing. It's never happened before, but... Maybe we spent too long with her on pause while the nurse cleaned up the puke. I dunno." His voice took on the tone of a person being harassed.

"I don't like theory, Evans, not when I am responsible for a multi-million pound, privately funded project that depends on us not fucking anything up and making our benefactor accountable."

"I wish I knew what to tell you. Do you want to stop?"

The Boss scoffs at the idea. "And start all over again? We'd have to wait weeks before we could, you know that. No, I do not want to stop. Rescheduling would be a nightmare of epic administrative proportions."

"I still think her visor is in the wrong position, by the way. It looks too low down."

The older woman frowns. "I sincerely doubt that has anything to do with the haptics, but let's get it checked anyway, if it bothers you so much. I don't want any more distractions, Evans, this job is hard enough without dicking around with this sort of nonsense every five minutes. Can we scene-transition her now? Get her to the Gallery, before anything else goes haywire."

"Yes, Boss." Evans says, in a conciliatory tone.

The Boss makes a note in her work pad, and goes back to staring at the screen, her mood verging on belligerent. Evans is quiet for a moment, and then a question occurs to him, something the patient had said earlier.

"Who the fuck is George Bailey, anyway?"

There is silence. The older woman blinks. Then:

"Are you kidding me?"

"Don't shake your head at me like that, I have a life you know."

"One devoid of anything culturally worthwhile, apparently. It's from a film, Evans, a very famous, very good film. About not killing oneself. And Christmas. I can't believe you asked me that. What do you kids do for fun these days, anyway?"

"I'm thirty-seven years old Boss, and you already know the answer to that. I don't."

"Don't what?"

"Have fun."

5

COLLECTION

I found myself standing in front of my house in no time at all, which was odd, because the walk from the bridge to where I lived should have taken a good, solid hour, and yet when I arrived, I found I had no actual memory of traveling across town with my new friend. My feet should have felt tired, but they weren't. It was as if someone had snapped their fingers and teleported me there, and I didn't like it. I still felt off, peculiar, but then I reminded myself that I'd just discovered my own dead body, and perhaps I should try to redraw my boundaries when it came to what I felt was "normal", and what wasn't.

As I pulled my keys from my pocket *(wait, wait, hadn't my keys been missing before? I couldn't remember, why could I never remember anything for longer than a moment or two?)* and moved to unlock my front door, I felt a growing sense of trepidation. A change had occurred within my house, I could feel it. Something had been disturbed inside, altered. When you know a place so well, when you know every detail and line and angle, any change at all is jarring, and it made me deeply uncomfortable, even though I could not tell what that change was yet. I just knew that things behind the door were not going to be as they had been when I left them early this morning.

Nervous, I turned to the man who waited patiently behind me. "Before we go in. What do I call you, again?"

"Oh no, you first. What should I call *you?*" Deflected, and not for the first time.

"Do you always have to answer a question with another question?"

He smiled.

"What's your interest in all this, anyway?" I persisted, folding my arms and barring the way into my house.

He shrugged, noncommittally. "I'm just trying to be a good friend."

I stared at him, wrinkling my nose. He *was* familiar, and it bothered me. His face, his speech patterns, his gestures. Familiar, and yet not. This was evidenced by the fact that I couldn't bring myself to send him away, although I had every right to. Or perhaps it was just nice to have the company, and dead people couldn't afford to be too picky when it came to their friends. It seemed like it had been a long while since I'd had anyone around to talk to. I wish I could actually remember how long.

An idea hit me as I dithered on my doorstep. I smiled.

"I get it. You're the ghost of all my boyfriends past," I said, tilting my head back and staring down my nose at him. "You're annoying enough."

His blue-green eyes twinkled. "Shall we go in?"

"Yes," I said, for no other reason than to take back some control, and I pushed my key, which was suddenly in my hand, into the Yale lock, and turned it to the right. The door opened. We stepped inside, and at the exact same moment as my left foot crossed the threshold, there was a little "click" inside my head, like a man flicking a switch, or snapping a twig, or perhaps his fingers. I blinked, froze for a second, and then let the right foot follow.

I was committed now.

"Thank God for that," Evans breathes, as the subject slides her front door key into the lock. "I thought she was never going to get there. This is, without a doubt, the longest Prologue we've ever run."

"It's been a bit of a rollercoaster, I'll give you that. Still, she's had a tough few days."

"Pfft. She should try doing this job for a day or two, then she'd understand true misery."

The Boss smiles indulgently. "You'll never get a pay rise like that, you know. Professional conduct, etcetera."

"I wouldn't get a pay rise if I got down on my knees and kissed my own dick, no offence, Boss. I've been doing this for five years, I should know."

Evan's boss shakes her head but says nothing, watching the screen rather than indulge in her colleague's nonsense.

Evans broods for a second, then his face lights up.

"She's going in! Hal-ley-fucking-lujah, and thank the Lord." He spins around in his swivel chair, almost garrotting himself with his headphone wires in the process. He coughs and untangles himself and flicks a few switches on a switchboard mounted to his left, swigging from a cup as he does so, grimacing.

His Boss raises an eyebrow, calm and composed, the opposite of her report.

"You aren't remotely religious Evans; I do wish you'd stop invoking the heavens on work time."

"I'm just keen to get on with things, is all. I rather like the scenario she's about to enter."

"Is that enthusiasm I smell? Surely not."

"Ugh, no. What you can probably smell is this coffee. Which tastes like shit."

"It always does, when you make it."

"By the way… how come the Psych is being so squirrely with the name thing?"

The Boss scratches her chin. "They have their reasons. He's allowed to give her a name, but they don't usually like to at this stage. It has to feel… what's the word they use? *Earned*."

"I see." His tone implies otherwise.

"Anyway, we're about to go in. You ready?"

"Yup." Evans fingers one last switch, and it makes a distinct "click", the noise coinciding almost exactly with the patient's first step across her threshold.

A green light blinks on in the darkness, and both techs grow quiet, leaning forward.

The programme transitions.

My house was an ordinary terraced house, in an ordinary suburb, the kind you move to when you have children *(stop thinking about children stop thinking about blonde hair stop thinking about it stop)*, the kind that has a playground and a supermarket and a good school right on its doorstep. It had an ordinary pebbledashed exterior, ordinary, greying double-glazed windows, an ordinary bedroom and bathroom layout, and an ordinary garden filled with all the ordinary plants you'd expect: rhubarb, ferns, red hot pokers, ivy, that sort of thing. Completely and utterly unremarkable, indistinguishable from the house to the left of it, and from the house on the right.

Except that when we entered it, it was no longer my ordinary, utterly unremarkable house.

Instead, there was light, bright and warm and overwhelming. It poured out of the door to greet us, blinding me momentarily as I moved across the threshold.

And when my vision cleared, I found myself somewhere that wasn't my home.

I found myself in a vast and colonnaded gallery instead.

I gaped, let my head fall back and my eyes drift to the ceiling high above, which was plain, un-frescoed, undecorated, made from a pale grey stone that captured the sunlight pouring in from windows set high up on either side, captured it, played with it, bounced it around, so that everything was coated in it. The floor, by contrast, was tiled with a black and white diamond pattern, each slate bordered with Greek scrolls. The overall effect was one of simple grandeur: stone and tile, sunlight and space, the design elegant and ornate, without being oppressive. I was reminded of a postcard, or a scene from a video game. It was so perfectly built, so pleasing to the eye. There wasn't a line or tile out of place. This was both unnerving and compelling, in equal measure.

"Well," I breathed, unsure of how to proceed.

"I like what you've done with the place," said my friend, moving past me to study an alcove set into the gallery wall. I watched him go, and realised that there were alcoves all along the gallery, lining both sides of the space.

"What's... what's going on here?" I could feel a sense of something shifting, thinning out, like the rules of reality were soft taffy being pulled tight around me as I tried to apply my brain to this new puzzle.

He ignored me.

I cast a look behind. My front door, still open, revealed my street, my front garden, my car parked on the curb. I turned back. The gallery greeted me again, huge, unmoving, impossible. I looked back over my shoulder once more. My car was now gone, as was the street outside. In its place, a strange sort of dark blankness hung like a curtain, punctuated with tiny, weakly sparkling motes of light.

I felt fiercely afraid. That dark space outside was *too* dark, too open. I peered at it. Was there something moving in the black? Something that obscured some of the light motes? A jerky, juddery sort of thing, a thing that interrupted the darkest dark? I stared until my eyes watered. The more I tried to make it out, the less I could actually see, as if the darkness was eating up my vision.

I realised I had no idea where I was, or what was happening to me. I just knew that I'd wanted to go home, and even that small thing had been denied to me.

I moved, stumbling over myself to be closer to my new

friend, the only other living being in this unfamiliar landscape. He waited for me next to the nearest alcove.

"Okay?" he asked, kindly.

"Not really," I replied. "I wish I knew what the fuck was going on."

The man said nothing, but gestured for me to look. Reluctantly, I did so.

Inside the alcove stood a pedestal, carved from marble. Upon this, rested a domed glass display case, which in turn rested upon a little turned wooden mahogany platform. It was the sort of display case you found in museums, populated with poorly taxidermied animals or birds. Victorian in the way that all things produced in that era were: imposing, forbidding, well-crafted. It gleamed in the sun. *No dust*, I wondered silently.

A little brass plaque with the Roman numeral "I" was attached to the base.

"Well?" I said, nervous, unsure of what I was staring at.

"Look," my friend said, patiently.

"At what?"

"Inside," he insisted, gently, and I peered through the glass. It took me a moment, but then I recognised the item on display within the case.

It was a single, golden, curling lock of *(stop brushing, it hurts!)* hair.

I recoiled as if punched in the gut, my mouth filling up with that sour, thick saliva once again. Red lay upon the curl like a kiss. I could see every tiny strand, picked out in minute detail, every wondrous filament clumped together.

My heart flooded with immense pain, and longing, and regret, and shame.

And I remembered, as violently and clearly as a slap.

The lock of hair belonged to my son.

For I had been a Mother, once.

I had kept the lock of hair folded in tissue, laid to rest inside a special memory box, from the day of his first haircut to this day, where I found it in this case, in this Gallery.

"Get rid of that!" I gasped, turning my back on it. I realised I could no longer breathe, and spat, rather than letting myself vomit, spat like an old man spitting tobacco in a saloon bar from times long past. A small, thick gobbet of something brown and viscous plopped onto the perfectly tiled floor by my feet, landing dead centre in the middle of a white diamond slate, and I peered at it unsteadily, relieved and revolted at the same time. The blob was thick and glossy, like mud, and it reminded me of my own dead corpse, mud-slick and useless as it lay on the dock. I gulped, blinked, reeling from the impact of seeing the lock of hair. What was it doing here, under the glass like that? What *was* this place, even? Where had my house gone? Why had I not questioned this before now?

Was I drugged?

Was I dreaming?

I wiped my mouth with the back of my hand. The dizziness had returned, so the walls and vertices of the Gallery swam, ducked and dived. I groaned, feeling sweat pop out on my brow. I felt awful, feverish.

"Are you alright?"

"Is it gone?!"

"It's gone, I promise. Breathe through it," my friend said, gently. "Take your time." I sensed he meant for me to look at the rest of the Gallery, and I was trying my best, but it was hard when it felt like the world was made of marshmallow.

Eventually I got a hold of myself, saw that the other alcoves set along the length of the Gallery also held domed glass cases. I didn't want to know what was inside those domes. I couldn't bear the thought of any more artefacts like the lock of hair resting under the glass.

Despite my reluctance to go over to each alcove and confirm for myself, it dawned on me what exactly this space was. I could tell, without having to get close, that every single case displayed something I would recognise. An item that belonged to me, or to someone I valued. A keepsake, a memory, a dearly prized possession.

"Someone has made an exhibition out of my life," I muttered, and then I couldn't keep my balance anymore. I sat down in a little heap on the perfect, tiled floor. Tired tears rolled down my cheeks. I thought about the lock of hair, and it seemed to me that this macabre collection was an accusatory one, a reproachful one, set here to make me feel guilty.

Guilty for the terrible thing I'd done.

Because I was sure, now, that I *had* done something. Why else was I being punished like this?

I just didn't know what it was.

What had I done?

What had I…

"All exhibits present and correct?"

"All handpicked exhibits present and correct, just as the Psych ordered."

The Boss rubs at her top lip, thoughtfully, once again scribbling in her work pad. "Do we have an inventory?"

"No, only the scripts, but they should all be referenced in there. Why so worried?"

"I just want to be sure. These aren't mere 'things' to her, they're supposed to act as an extension of her body, her consciousness. Objects have meaning and all that."

"I'm confident, we've done our research, spoken to her family. The exhibits are all there. The important ones, anyway. Christ, we had a lot of material to choose from. She took something like sixty-five thousand photographs across a ten-year period. Lot of hard drives to dig through, I felt like an archaeologist."

The older woman snorted. "Everyone's a photographer, these days. Smartphones have a lot to answer for."

"Don't knock it. That kind of collateral makes our artist's lives a million times easier."

The Boss says nothing, but takes her own smartphone out of her jacket pocket and checks it for any messages. The screensaver on her phone shows her family behind the apps and widgets. Two boys, her partner. She considers them, then puts the phone away, unhappily.

Beyond the giant window, the patient in the cradle twitches, lets out a tiny moan. She is crying again, openly. One of her tears drops onto the vinyl floor beneath, leaving a dark brown, mud-coloured spot behind, a spot that spreads, slowly, like an ink blot, across the ground, moving as if it has a mind of its own.

The techs in the room next door do not notice this.

"Why are you so upset?" My new friend asked, not unkindly. "Talk to me."

I sat there, sniffling and feeling sorry for myself, trying to get a grip on my emotions so that I could speak. Eventually, I said: "Because, well, *look* at all this stuff." I waved a despairing hand at the Gallery. "Why else is it all here, if not to make me feel guilty?"

"Now, wait a minute," my friend replied, kneeling down. "Guilty for what?"

"I can't fucking remember!" I shouted back, instantly regretting it as soon as the words left my mouth. It was true, though. Things came and went but never seemed to stay.

"Sorry," I finished, subdued. "I'm sorry."

He offered me a tissue with which to wipe the tears from my face. I stared at it. He kept holding it out, and I took it, mopping my cheeks. Once it was sodden, I stupidly tried to give it back. The tissue was no longer white as I held it out, but a strange, brownish colour that didn't look very healthy. My new friend shook his head minutely, and we both laughed.

"I wouldn't want it either," I said. I found the grief went out of me almost as quickly as it had arrived.

Once he was satisfied that my face was clean, my friend continued.

"This might not be what you think it is. You *could* see all of this as a… reproach. For some mysterious misdemeanour." He gave me a piercing look, but I kept my head down.

"Or," he continued, gesturing to the columns, the plinths, the display cases, the beams of light hurtling down from the high-up windows, "Or, you could see it as… as a detective would. What we're doing here… it's like trying to solve a case, isn't it?"

I nodded, sniffing. "The Mysterious Case of the Idiot Woman Who Threw Herself into the River," I said, feeling very sorry for myself.

"Stop that. Think. You're a detective now. We have a case to solve. So what are these?" he prompted, placing a single finger underneath my chin, stopping my trembling mouth with his thumb. I balked at his over-familiarity, and he seemed just as surprised by it, snatching his hand back and clearing his throat with embarrassment. Heat flooded my face. His touch had been nice; unexpected, but nice.

Something he said resonated. I looked at the alcoves, the pedestals, the glass domes, at the twin ranks of gleaming displays, and thought: *exhibits.*

Like…

Exhibit A, Your Honour.

"Clues," I said eventually. "They're clues."

"Bingo," he said, and I knew suddenly what I was supposed to do.

Begin at the beginning, he had said, *and end at the end.* Which made sense, it really did, but I was a contrary creature, and so I did the exact opposite of what he said. Instead of being logical about it, I stood up, being careful to avoid the alcove with the hair in it, just in case, walked to the middle of the gallery, spun around with my eyes closed, held out a hand and pointed.

When I stopped, and the grand columns also stopped spinning around my head, I opened my eyes to see where my finger pointed, and moved towards the corresponding case.

"Very creative," my new friend said, dryly, but I didn't reply. Instead, I placed both my hands upon the smooth glass dome and looked at what lay within, hoping against hope that whatever it was, it would not be kissed with blood.

It wasn't.

And slowly, by way of a trickle at first, and then in a rush, as if a dam had been breached, more memories came back to me.

In the Observation Room, the woman hanging from the ceiling spins in the air like a ballerina joltingly pirouetting inside a jewellery box, pointing at something not present. The tracks above her head spin too, ensuring her wires don't tangle.

In the room behind the mirror, two techs jointly let out a breath they didn't realise they'd been holding.

"And… We're off!" The Boss says, satisfied at last. "Close the front door and get rid of it. I think we'll be here for a while."

"Yes, Boss."

Back in the programme, the only visible door in the Gallery, the door that had once been the subject's own front door, a door which now shows blackness and tiny, twinkling stars instead of a street double-parked with family vehicles, disappears.

In the split nano-second before it winks out of existence, a thin, sketchy shadow interrupts the clean lines of the door frame, almost as if something twiggy and insectile has taken a hold of the jambs. The impression lasts not even as long as the blink of a human eye, and the door is gone.

In its place, grey, solid stone materialises.

And on the floor of the OR, beneath the hanging woman, a brown stain spreads.

6

FOOL'S GOLD

Here lay gold.

It sat importantly upon a little cushion upon the pedestal. Gingerly, I lifted the glass dome that encased it, picked it up, held it in my hand. Weighed it. Touched it to my lips, breathing in the metallic tang.

It wasn't real gold. It was a mineral, iron pyrite, a small nugget the size of a conker, not precious to anyone except me. Little cubic crystals jutted out from the main cluster, catching the light. It looked like the exact opposite of something nature could create. Its shape was too distinct, engineered, the proportions artificial. It glittered dully against my skin, and I felt something stirring within, something pleasurable.

As a child *(I had a child once I had a child once I had–)* I collected these things the same way I collected words I liked the sound of. Minerals, gemstones, crystals, fossils. Things of the earth. I was fascinated by all the different names: Azurite, Dolomite, Witherite, Aragonite, Howlite, Agate, Aquamarine, Tourmaline, Malachite (a favourite, for both the colour and the deliciously evil name), Opal, Obsidian. They were exotic, and each stone or geode or crystal cluster had its own, distinct character. I'd had a glass cabinet I meticulously arranged everything within. I remembered that case so vividly, standing there in the Gallery mere hours after my death. Cheap mahogany-effect, curved legs, a little brass keyhole so you could lock your valuables securely away inside. When we are young, we love the idea of locks and keys that fit. We want to protect our things, our precious things. I would hide the key so no-one else could control the environment within. It was sacred, shrine-like. It was mine. I was not lonely when I was occupied by my pretty things.

And occupied I was. I spent hours in museums, poring over displays, leafing through catalogues, marvelling at the shapes and the colours, the beautiful greens and blues and yellows and browns and reds, golds, colours I'd never even imagined. I would stare at opals and get lost. Black opals, when polished, looked as if they held tiny, brilliant galaxies within. I'd gaze at the fractured fire under the glossy surface and my heart would skip a beat. I only ever saw one black opal in real life. I envied the woman who would one day own that opal. If I had owned it, I would never have left the house. I would have sat in a closed room fondling it, staring, lost in the tiny universe at the heart.

My pocket money never stretched to the luxuries of opal, diamond, ruby, but that was fine. I was content with my agates, my quartzes, and my Fool's Gold. This brassy sulfide, this little lump, had been my first. When I had picked it out of a bowl of junk in a small antiques shop in Norfolk, my imagination had exploded. It was hard, physical evidence of creation and life and of the very earth moving and shifting and morphing and rising up beneath my feet. Millions of years of craft, there in my little hand. I felt comforted yet humbled.

It was proof of life, because even the earth had been alive once, and it had given birth to this golden, glittering child.

(*Golden child. Falling asleep together in his bed after I'd read him his bedtime story, my arm slung across his shoulder, his hair tickling my chin. The smaller version of me slotted in place, like a warm jigsaw puzzle piece. The rise and fall of soft breath, of easy sleep. Children sleep so deeply. He smelled incredible. He smelled like love, vulnerable and sweet and earthy, I wish I had a bottle of him, I wish–*)

Where was he now?

(He is gone)
What was his name?
I could not remember.

"She's doing it again."

"Doing what, exactly?" The Boss is intent on reading her emails, catching up on various company bulletins she's been ignoring thus far.

Evans gestures in annoyance.

"Boss, she's been staring at that lump of rock for twenty solid minutes. It's driving me mad."

In the Observation Room the patient stands, straight-backed. She holds her hand up before her visor, fingers pinched as if holding something, even though there is nothing there.

"I fail to see how this is helpful, you know. She's supposed to engage with the Psych before launching into guided reflection. How is she going to even begin to start coming to terms with things if there is no talking therapy first?"

The older woman slurps the cold dregs of her coffee and grimaces, swallowing grits by mistake. "Well, we don't pay you for your clinical expertise or opinion, thank goodness. She's not ready for any in-depth session with the Psych, not yet. She has groundwork to do first. Besides, she's a highly sensory, visually driven person. If this helps memory repair, then let her work through it. Give her time."

"There's time, and then there's me trying not to chew my own fists off with boredom."

"Do stop being quite so dramatic, Evans."

Evans sulkily taps his pen against the side of his face, blowing his cheeks out in boredom. Then, he starts to doodle on a piece of paper by his keyboard. His scribble turns into a crude portrait of a sleeping woman with wires coming out of her scalp. The woman is naked, and Evans garnishes the doodle with an expertly rendered pair of large, perky breasts.

His Boss sees what he is doing and raises an eyebrow, but allows it.

She has a feeling they will be stuck in this room together for quite some time.

"You were a collector, then? A magpie. I like that as a name for you. Magpie."

My new friend broke into my reverie. I jumped, glared at him. Had I been speaking out loud? I didn't think so. How could he have known what I was thinking? How could he have known this rock was part of a collection?

An educated guess?

I shook my head. "I hate that name," I said. The man raised his hands, stepped back discreetly.

Whatever thought process I'd been going through dissipated like steam. It had been something important. A sweet smell lingered. A name scratched at the door of my brain. Scratched, then gave up.

My new friend was right, though. I *was* a collector. It felt good to be able to remember that, at least. It came to me like a soft song on a nearby radio. I had been through several phases. Rocks. Books. Letters. Photographs. Music. Coloured glass. Words. Later on, men. Well, at least I *thought* I was collecting men. Really, I was collecting sexual anecdotes. Some good, some bitter, some painful, *(remember when he held you down by your throat? Remember how he pulled your hair and you wriggled with excitement? Remember he said he would always–)* some downright absurd. Episodes of outlandish promiscuity, kept under lock and key in a glass cabinet. *The diminutive chain of habit*, I had read somewhere. We do not feel the weight of them, our bad habits, until the chain has become too strong to break. And even now, in this most inconvenient of places and times, with my emotions swinging wildly from one extreme to another, even now, the chain tugged.

I looked at the man standing next to me and realised I found him handsome. Fuckable.

I had an instant flash of desire, appraising him anew. He watched different expressions dance across my face and smiled.

I found I had to restrain myself.

"Interesting," The Boss says, leaning forward. "Heart rate has changed. Blood pressure has dropped. Her oxytocin levels are elevated."

Evans stops doodling. "Wait... she's horny? Over a rock!?"

"I doubt it's the rock. I suspect the rock has triggered a thought process that has led to... hmm. We'll see."

"I thought it was a mistake to make the Psych a male. Woman to woman made much more sense to me."

"I thought you said you hadn't read her file."

"I browsed the juicy bits. She likes to sleep around, and I'm a middle-aged married man with no sex life to speak of. I live vicariously through others."

The Boss shakes her head, pressing her fingertips into her eye sockets in exasperation.

Evans shrugs. "What?" he says.

"Well, maybe you're right," the older woman replies. "It might end up being too distracting for her. If we need to, we can think about changing the gender as we proceed."

"Have we ever done that before? Changed the Psych's avatar mid-programme?"

"Once. Only once, before you joined us. It has to be done subtly, incrementally, so it's barely noticeable, but we've definitely done it."

"Huh. Every day is a school day in this job."

"Indeed. And while we're on the subject of horny, can you please stop doodling whatever filth it is that you're inscribing on our department-branded stationary, and at least try to focus on the task at hand, please?"

Evans reluctantly scribbles over the lewd sketch, grumbling under his breath as he does so.

I shook myself, blushing, my feelings still veering about as wildly as a weathervane in a storm. The Gallery that stood where my house should have been was bright, artificial. I thought again how everything was so clean, so symmetrical. The plinths, the perfectly tiled floor, the gracefully arched ceiling, the high windows, the fluted columns. The alcoves, the glass display cases. An assembly case of my life's worth. All my most important memories, arranged carefully within.

What was I doing here? I was dead. How could I be here, too? And where was my house? My real house? My husband?

My son?

Did I even have a son, or did I make that part up?

Of course I hadn't made it up. There was a lock of blonde hair sitting on a cushion beneath a dome of glass somewhere behind me: proof of life. But for some reason, getting a handle on what he looked like, how old he was, what his name was… glimpses of him came and went, but never stayed for long. I felt like I no sooner remembered something, some tiny detail, than I forgot it again, almost immediately. The same with my husband. I knew I had one, I knew I was married, but the details… the details were smeared like sleeve-smudged chalk on a blackboard.

I thought of my husband, the faceless concept. Did we even like each other? Were we still in love? I thought of him alone in our house, my real house, not this one, with all my things around him. I was dead, did he know that yet? I wondered how long it would take him to start boxing my things away. Perhaps he would keep some of it, for memory's sake. Or perhaps he would make a bonfire in our back garden and burn the lot. Perhaps. I'd never know, so it was useless to speculate.

I thought of a blank-faced version of him sitting on the floor of our bedroom, reading through my childhood diaries (I collected diaries too, filled them with nonsense and bundled them into shoe boxes), searching for clues, for things that he could have done better, ideas as to why I'd chosen to end my own life. I thought of him crying. I couldn't remember his features, so the crying man had a smooth orb for a face out of which tears leaked like sweat. I thought of myself as a child, on the same bedroom floor, sorting and labelling and polishing and arranging the precious minerals and gems that made up my peace of mind.

I felt a sudden, great injustice at the way things had turned out.

The weathervane swivelled.

"It's not fair," I said out loud. My brief flash of desire was replaced with shame, more guilt and anger.

I was dead, and I was pissed about it.

"I'm sorry, I don't understand," my friend said, carefully.

"I said, it's not fair. I deserved better than… this," I spat.

"Life can be unfair, Magpie," the man replied, his face taking on a gentle aspect.

Irritated, I turned away from him. I was supposed to be uncovering an epiphany, I was supposed to be figuring out why I had died, but so far, all I had uncovered was a piece of aptly named Fool's Gold. I looked at it, unsure of what it meant and how to read this particular clue. I placed it back in its display case, back on the little black velvet cushion.

When I went to cover it again with the glass housing, I realised it had disappeared. In its place, rotating about an inch above the velvet cushion, was a shiny golden coin. I frowned, trying to make the pattern out on either side of the coin. When I did, it didn't make much sense to me: both sides were decorated with embossed checkmarks, the type you use when ticking something off on a list. Actually, that did make sense, I supposed, after a moment. Whatever purpose the rock had been designed for, had presumably been served, which is why it had vanished.

Check.

I was just clueless as to what that purpose was.

I looked at my new companion.

"That's it?" I said disbelievingly. "That's the lesson here? Life is unfair, and that's that?"

"Radical acceptance," the man said, then.

(This too shall pass this too shall–)

And I had no idea what he meant by it, but it annoyed the shit out of me.

"Rapport is not great, is it? So much for Mr. Anonymous."

"Rapport is *not* great, I must admit. It was definitely a mistake to make the avatar male."

Evans snorts. "Especially this 'tough love' approach he's got. Doesn't seem to be resonating, does it? She clearly either wants to fuck him or spank his bottom. Hardly someone she might relax around enough to confide in."

"Quite." The Boss runs her hands through her hair, ruminating. "I'll have a think. Changing his avatar at this point would be inconvenient, I need her in a more… tranquil mood before I start adjusting any of the parameters."

"So, we make him cuddlier, demeanour-wise. Shall we patch him into the panel, start the guidance process? There are four other Psychs on call today we can bring in. Maybe they can help him moderate his approach."

"Christ, no, not yet." The Boss shakes her head vehemently. "No, I don't have the energy for the paperwork that requires, thank you. From experience, you start bringing in extra Psychs, and it's like putting too many chefs into one small kitchen, it descends into farce. Everyone with their own take, their own diagnosis. Besides, it's early days. I have faith. He has a good track record when it comes to Breakthroughs – I read up on him. He might take his time building the connection, but he usually cracks it. I suspect he is in full observation mode at the moment."

"If you say so. Time is something we have a lot of, at the very least. I feel like there's no longer a world outside this stinking hot room."

"Your love for your work is nourishment to my soul, Evans."

"I had high hopes for my career, you know."

"Didn't we all, Evans. Didn't we all."

"Are you okay? Perhaps you can tell me how you feel."

I moved on, angrily stalking towards the next alcove.

"I'm dead, how do you think I fucking feel?"

"Angry, confused, frustrated. But we don't necessarily have to walk away from those feelings, or be ashamed of them."

"Who says I am ashamed?"

"Sometimes it is enough to simply own those feelings, and live in the truth of them."

I stopped mid-step and stared at him.

"What?" I said, and I could feel the exasperation rolling off of me in hot little waves. "You sound like shit motivational artwork. I should frame you and hang you in an open-plan office."

He gentled his tone. "I'm simply saying it's okay to feel bad. You've been through a lot."

"How do you know what I've been through?" Why did I feel so hostile towards him, all of a sudden? He was only trying to help.

"I helped you drag your own corpse out of the river today," he replied. "I think that's grounds enough for empathy."

I sighed. He wasn't going to give up his gentle bullshit, and he was right, anyway. I was ashamed, and angry.

"Sorry," I said. "I'm being a twat again, aren't I?"

The man folded his arms, a small smile playing at his lips,

which I wanted to kiss, very much. "There is no possible way I can answer that without getting into trouble."

I laughed reluctantly, but it was there. Humour. A tiny spark of lightness.

"Fair enough," I said.

"So, how are you feeling now?"

"Well, right now I don't have very High Hopes that we'll solve this case, you know," I admitted, my voice heavy and resigned. For some reason, I heard myself place emphasis on the consonants of "high hopes", as if repeating someone else's pronunciation.

"One step at a time, Magpie," the man replied, unphased, and I didn't hate the name quite so much this time. "Let's just follow the clues, shall we?"

I made a rude face, but chose not to argue.

"Wait. Wait... was that an echo?"

"The mics are all off, right?"

"Of course they are. That was, wasn't it? That was a sodding echo!"

"Relax, it was just a coincidence, more like."

"Boss, she used the same exact words that I just did. "High hopes", you just heard it! She literally mimicked the exact same way I speak. I'm calling an echo."

"And I'm calling a coincidence, Evans, alright? I have enough to worry about in this scenario without worrying about the impossible. If our mics are off, there is no way she could have heard you. Her eyes are fixed on the visor, she's sedated, and she can't see through the glass, so we can rule out lip-reading. This room is soundproofed to boot. There are more than a million words in the English language, Evans. It is entirely possible that two people might just use the same words in the same sequence at different points in time without it signifying some terrifying mind-meld with our immersion software."

Evans scowls at his ruined notepad.

"I don't like this one, Boss. It makes me… itchy."

"Your concerns are noted, Evans. Now how about less chat, and more watching, okay? Are our transcriptions running?"

"Running fine, Boss."

"Good. I have a feeling that when this is over, a lot of people are going to want to read them."

7

THE BRIEFCASE

The next alcove was bigger, the pedestal and glass dome wider, built to accommodate a larger object. It sat encased within, solid, unapologetic. It took me a moment for the memory it triggered to surface, coalesce. When I finally recognised it, I frowned, displeased. Why were these memories so difficult, so painful? Why not good memories? The sensation of being punished intensified. I felt more anger.

The lines and solid shapes of the gallery shimmered, shifted for an instant, like a blip on a television screen. I thought I saw a shape hovering in the air just in my peripheral vision. A vague, juddery sort of shape that was not recognisably anything, but was most discernibly there. I batted at it, as if batting away a mosquito. Things settled down. The shape vanished.

A deep sense of unease spread further in my mind.

"What was that?" The Boss sits up straight, frowning.

"I don't know, Boss. Another glitch? I need to… let me just run a diagnostic…" Evans begins tapping at his keyboard, and a beige window pops up on one of the screens. He scans through the performance log, but cannot see anything noticeably wrong.

"Not a glitch, at least, not on our end, Boss."

"Our end is the only end, Evans," the older woman says,

shaking her head in annoyance. "Run it again. We've had too many glitches already today. It's giving me a headache."

"You and me both, Boss," Evans says.

He runs the diagnostic again.

In the room beyond the mirror, the woman's body stiffens, then relaxes.

Nobody notices.

"So what is it?" my new companion asked me.

"This?" I said, turning to the item under the dome. "It's a briefcase."

And, as if the simple act of giving the thing a name somehow acted as permission, more memories began trickling in.

I always knew my stepfather was home when I saw the briefcase in the hall. He was handsome and tall, with coal black hair and, as a child, I remember always trying to touch it. He would smooth wax over his tight clipped curls so they glistened. His teeth were very straight. He had a neat black moustache and wore nice, tailored suits. He was well put together, polished like my gemstones. Other people used the word "different", because different was not something you were allowed to be where I grew up. But different he was, and so different our small family became. I adored every striking inch of him.

He liked to carry a briefcase around. It was a giant, black, cracked leather case with brass clasps that stood proudly in our hall at night when he came home from the office. Sometimes he would pop the locks open and heave it onto his lap, scrabble about inside and pull out great wedges of paper, none of which made any sense to me, or held any particular interest to him. It was simply work, work to be done and disposed of.

My mother hated the briefcase. I saw her savagely kick it over once, when she thought no-one was looking. It was not an object she could rely on. Sometimes, it was in the hallway where she thought it belonged. Other times, it was noticeable in its absence and, at those times, she was miserable, tense, lonely. She would cry in secret and pretend she had a headache. At other times she would rage, seemingly at nothing. The rage would fly outwards, catching all in its path. The unpredictable nature of the briefcase, and of its master, held us both under a terrible spell.

Sometimes, things were good. I remember walking with my stepfather one evening in *(stickman stickman stickman)* December, when the Christmas lights had popped up in our neighbour's windows and made luminous blobs of colour against the fogged glass. It was so cold he was shivering, even in his huge woollen jacket. Growing up in Uganda, he was always cold now. He looked down at my hand, which was curled up inside his long brown fingers, and smiled a smile so great I thought he would swallow the world whole. "Your hands are like little radiators," he said, and the moment crystallised in my mind, as these tender moments you are supposed to have with your father figures do.

In the summer he wore shorts. He had long legs, just like his long fingers, and played football, semi-pro when he wasn't at the office. He had three huge scars that wrapped around his knees and down his calves like worms. He told me that when he was a boy, he would play hide and seek on the land behind his back yard. The grass there, he said, was taller than a house, fantastic for hiding in. One day, when he was waiting for his brother to find him, the grass towering high above his head, he knelt on a discarded knife. There was blood, and mess, and for the boy, battle scars. He didn't seem to mind them much, as an adult. My stepfather's scars were shiny and hairless, lighter in colour than the skin around them, and my mother would sometimes run a fingernail along one of them affectionately.

Whenever I thought of him, which I rarely did now that I was grown, quite deliberately, I always thought of the scars, the ones he owned and the ones he bequeathed. He left nothing behind him elsewise, just a legacy of things torn, things that slowly healed and fused back together: our lives.

"Nope. I can't find a single thing wrong, although I'll let the diagnostic run a little longer. Also, I'm getting hungry."

"Me too."

"Want me to place an order with the canteen?"

"Are you kidding? I'd rather eat raw donkey dick than their pigswill, thank you very much."

Evans chokes on the mouthful of water he is swigging, eyes wide.

"That's not a combination of words I ever expected to hear from you," he says carefully, once he has recovered. It is not often that his Boss's professionalism slips, but he knows better than to make a big deal out of it.

"Sorry. I'm a bear when I'm hungry. Let's order something in. Pizza work for you?"

"Pizza works just fine for me. No pineapple, though."

"Of course no pineapple. I'm not a psychopath."

Evans chuckles, picks up a phone and starts dialling the pizza company he is far too well acquainted with. While his attention is elsewhere, an image pops up in the top left-hand corner of his laptop, which now rests in a rare clear spot on the surface behind his main computer monitor and is partially obscured from him as a result. The image is there so fleetingly it would have been hard for him to make out anyway, however, if he had been lucky enough to catch it, he might have seen that the image was one of a stick man, crudely depicted with a smudged outline, as if drawn onto the screen by a crabbed hand with a marker pen.

In the harness in the next room, the woman shifts, and her arms roll outwards slightly, exposing the insides of her wrists.

Tattooed onto her right inner wrist is the simple outline of a stick man.

* * *

"I don't see how this is a clue," I said suddenly, breaking the memory's hold and turning to my friend. He had been waiting patiently as I examined the briefcase. "It's no secret. My stepfather left when I was eleven years old. I came to terms with it quickly, it doesn't bother me on a day-to-day basis. I wouldn't have... killed myself because of this."

The man looked at me, thinking. "These objects are clues, but not necessarily related to the actual act of you ending your life," he said, carefully. "Sometimes, a single clue by itself is not enough to solve a case. But taken as a whole... it's like pieces of a jigsaw, I suppose."

(Jigsaw. Soft hair in my nostrils and–)

"*You* suppose. And who are *you*, exactly?" I knew he wouldn't answer, but thought I would try my luck anyway.

"A friend," he said, simply. "Now, what is it about this object specifically that makes it so important, do you think? Important enough to be here."

I thought about that, and my mind slipped back to the past.

One day, a happy day for me at the time, my mother, my stepfather, myself and a few close relatives found ourselves in the garden of a registry office, standing around, politely making conversation, the adults hiding their trepidation behind hopeful, strained smiles. A wedding had just taken place, and we were making the most of the warm sun, outside.

I slipped my hand into my stepfather's, full of happiness. I was wearing a cornflower blue dress with little purple flowers printed all across it, and matching shoes. I had a cream turtleneck on beneath, and a straw *(STICKMANSTICKMANSTICKMANSTI–)* hat. I was content, sure that things would always be this way now that everything was *official*. It was in writing, now. Written words were meant to be binding.

I looked up at him, and said: "Does this mean I can call you Dad now?"

"Yes," he said, but he couldn't have meant it, because he was gone a few weeks later. My mother carried his name for a complete month, and then changed it back to my father's. He was gone too, and at that point, a little niggling voice of doubt started to grow inside my head. Why did all these father figures keep vanishing like smoke?

Was there something wrong with me?

I realised with a bolt of clarity, as I looked at the briefcase, that he'd taken my heart away with him in that boxy black leather thing. He was the first man to ever do that. The very first, but he certainly wouldn't be the last.

I stared at the case for a long, long time. I said nothing to my friend, lost in thought as I was, but he seemed okay with that arrangement. He appeared to be letting me work through my emotions, and I appreciated that.

Eventually, I looked down at my right hand and with a jolt, realised that I was holding a hammer. My friend had placed it there, evidently. Or had he? I couldn't decide. But, regardless, it was there, in my hand, heavy and resolute. My friend patted me on the back, kindly.

"Go on," he said, and I raised my arm, automatically understanding what I was supposed to do.

"Are you sure?" I hesitated briefly, the hammer high up above my head.

My friend nodded. I brought the hammer down on the glass dome, and it exploded.

In a far corner of the Control Room, behind the backs of the techs who sit, thinking about their impending pizza delivery, a tiny, hairline crack suddenly appears in the wall. A little shower of plaster and dust rains to the floor. The crack widens, ever so slightly, and begins to creep, like a vine crawling along a tree branch, an encroaching movement imperceptible to the human eye, and had the control team been paying attention, they might have noticed it coming, might have noticed it working its way along the wall towards the exact spot where they sat, staring into the glowing screens of another woman's consciousness.

The case exploded. There was a short, sharp burst of pure white light. When I no longer felt any resistance under the hammer, I opened my eyes. The case, the dome, its fragments and shards of glass, the marble plinth, all were gone.

My new friend reached over and gently took the hammer back from me. I watched as he tucked it up his left jacket sleeve, where it vanished, never to be seen again.

"Did that feel good?" he asked me, and I let out a huge sigh.

"That felt very good," I said, and I meant it. "But no coin this time?" I was almost disappointed. I felt like a video gamer who had been denied reward for completing a particularly difficult level.

My friend smiled, and a spinning, golden coin suddenly popped into view, the golden embossed checkmarks on both sides winking at me as the coin spun.

"Much better," I said, and moved determinedly onto the next alcove.

Evans yawns and stretches.

"Looks like we got away with it," he said, his mouth a dark, wet cavern. The Boss stifles her own yawn by way of response.

"Got away with what?"

"She didn't notice that it wasn't based on the actual briefcase."

The Boss shoots him a look. "Well of course not. How was she going to remember that? No one has a photographic memory that accurate, despite what you see in the movies. A briefcase is a briefcase. Her brain fills in the rest."

"I guess so."

"I wish the pizza would hurry up. I can feel my gut eating itself." The Boss struggles to function when she is hungry, and her breakfast is now a long distant memory.

"Poor Bernard."

"Who is Bernard?"

"The new intern. He spent five solid weeks on that briefcase. I think he spent six days alone just working on the clasp mechanism. All for a few minutes of glory."

The older woman waves a hand somewhat dismissively. "Background animators always get too attached to their art. The attention to detail is admirable, nonetheless."

"Yeah, but you know how it is in this industry, everything you create is a masterpiece. Plus he probably spent another solid month working out the lighting parameters. Did you see the detail in those brass clasps?"

"Ah, the energy of youth."

"I miss my energy. I lost it somewhere on the day of my wedding."

"I'm not sure your wife would be happy to hear you say that."

"You leave my wife alone, Boss."

"Too late for that, Evans," the Boss replies, then checks herself, blushing. Where on earth had that come from? Since when has she ever engaged in Evans's smutty, bawdy banter? She clears her throat strenuously, pulling out her phone to give herself something to hide behind.

"Wow," is all Evans can think to say.

Silence rises like thick wet dough in the Control Room.

Unobserved, Evan's laptop screen blinks out of sleep mode and back into life. A moment later, something moves once again in the corner of the screen, not a static image this time, but a moving object. It takes a moment to fully form. When it does, it is in the shape of a stick man. It appears against the bright desktop background, which is currently set to display a green rolling meadow punctuated with bright white daisies. The stick man drifts down from the corner of the screen so it hovers mid-field. Then, as if animated, it appears to flex first its arms, then its legs. It drops, its feet touching the grass of the desktop, and then stands upright, wobbling as it figures out how to balance. Once it has gained confidence, it strides out across the meadow, crushing daisies underfoot as it goes. It moves in an erratic yet determined manner until it reaches a folder sitting on the desktop, one of several nesting files that represent Evans's messy filing system.

This particular folder is called *01_ProjectFiles_Magpie*.

The small stick-figure bends at the waist, examines the file, and then disappears behind the folder image, or rather, *inside* the folder, putting first one leg in, and then the other, as if stepping into a warm bath.

Minutes later, a tiny trickle of something muddy and brown oozes slowly from the laptop's microphone port and makes a small sticky pool on the surface of the desk.

8

THREE WOMEN IN A PHOTOGRAPH

The next exhibit was a photograph. Looking around at all the other cases, I was surprised there weren't more in my Gallery. I liked photographs. Small, frozen pieces of time. Carefully doctored time, of course. All of the good bits, with none of the bad.

This photograph was of my university graduation ceremony. I was twenty years old, and bookended by my mother and my grandmother, both of whom wore their best jackets, best smiles. We were freezing; it was pouring and an icy wind blew directly into our faces, as it always does on an important occasion in Britain, so our smiles were stretched, holding on for dear life. Still, it was a nice picture. Well, apart from an odd smudge in one corner. I bent forward, peered at it. For a second, the smudge looked less like a smudge, and more like an ink blot, or a doodle, with a thin central strand that ended in a round blob. I leaned in closer, thinking how like a stick man the blot looked. Had someone defaced this photograph? Doodled on it? I blinked, my eyes suddenly sore and dry. I rubbed them, and the blot was gone. I tried not to read too much into that. Life in this strange place was a fluid, unpredictable thing.

I supposed at least it wasn't boring.

I realised I wasn't really ready for this picture. It felt too soon. I glanced at the plaque under the glass case, at the roman numerals I'd ignored thus far. It hit me that I had gone about this all wrong, attacking the alcoves at random, instead of in sequence, as dictated by the numerals. The numbers were there to help build a chronology, a narrative around my memories. Like that TV show, *This Is Your Life*. Ugh. The very thought of it wearied me, but I could see the underlying logic in it. Logic I'd chosen to ignore.

I was aware, as I looked at the image, of a feeling of injustice growing again. None of what was happening felt very fair. I was beginning to contemplate the devastating effect of what I'd probably done to them, these women. I had let them down in spectacular fashion. My family had loved me. What was their reward? A bloated corpse on a mud bank. I'd failed at the very basics of everyday living: get up, eat, drink, exercise, work, marry, procreate, sleep.

Live.

There was a song about that, wasn't there? By a band I'd once liked. Not really a song, more of a monologue with a score. Sombre. Something about being fitter and more productive, a recital by a computerised voice, about duality and how exhausting it was, this thing we did every day. Fitter... happier... *(It's Microsoft Sam from Windows 95, scored in 4/4, but I'd–)* the rest of the lyrics were lost in my swampy, soupy brain.

I felt compelled to recite it out loud anyway, using nonsense words in place of the actual lyrics I couldn't recall. What was the term for something that got stuck in your head to the point where you couldn't shake it out? An earworm. I performed my version of the earworm, finding the practice soothing. A lump grew in my throat as I did. Words *(fitter, happier, no longer uncomfortable, no murder, never washing blood down the sinkhole, baby smiling, why is the baby fucking smiling, paranoia at manageable levels, eating shit, sleeping badly, no chance of ever escaping, terrible memories, terrible melodies, terrible–)* and melodies flooded my system. Was I speaking for real, or simply in my head? I couldn't tell.

I hated how I could no longer determine fact from fiction, reality from fancy.

"Huh. Radiohead." Evans nods along in recognition.

"Is that what this is?"

In the room next door the patient is talking to herself, softly. She has a nice voice, but it quickly morphs to imitate a monotone, computerised speech that sets the tech's teeth on edge. The sight of her hanging there, wide-eyed, sorrowfully working through the lyrics to something she has clearly misremembered with that processed, fragmented voice gives Evans pause for a moment. He rubs gooseflesh that has popped up on his arms.

"And you mock *me* for being culturally unaware," he says, half-heartedly.

"Those aren't the lyrics, surely?'

Evans listens, frowning.

"Certainly not. Figures, though. Maybe she needs a slightly cheerier soundtrack to her life in general, Radiohead might not be the best choice for her brain."

"Eat your pizza, Evans. There is absolutely nothing wrong with Radiohead."

"Hey, you didn't even know it *was* Radiohead until I pointed it out! And I'm not saying there is. I love them! Not so keen on *OK Computer*, though. Personally speaking." He blows himself up, unaware of how pompous he sounds.

"What?"

"*OK Computer*. The album. This song is from it."

"I see."

"*Moon Shaped Pool* was their best, in my opinion."

The Boss tongues a piece of mozzarella that refuses to detach from her slice. Around a mouthful of greasy cheese, she tries to remain balanced.

"Well, taste is subjective, isn't it? We can't all like the same things. And if Radiohead actually gave two shits what anyone, let alone some random man in a lanyard sitting in a basement in Bristol that smells like Pepperoni Passion pizza, thought of their music, they'd never have made it, would they?"

"But it's..."

"Evans, I don't mean to be rude, but just eat your pizza, okay? I'm tired."

Evans does as he is told, shaking his head at her newly abrupt manner. The Boss is definitely not herself today, and he is finding her mood shifts unsettling.

The silver-haired woman checks her wristwatch, and then the time on a clock on the wall next to her.

Long ways to go yet, she thinks.

Noise swelled around me. The strains of a piano. Strings. Other sounds.

My words faltered, and I listened. My new friend cocked his head to one side, doing the same.

Interestingly, the monologue was no longer just playing in my memory, but out loud in the Gallery, for real. I looked up at the ceiling, eyes darting from place to place, and eventually spotted some cleverly disguised speakers set high into the vaulted, arched roof. Had they been there before? I couldn't remember.

"Are you responsible for that?" I asked my new friend, but he shrugged.

"Not me. I'm more of a classical music fan."

"Huh. Figures." I went back to reciting the song, keeping time with the real-world version on the speakers. With the backing track, I found I remembered the actual lyrics. The Gallery filled up with wondrous sound, and I closed my eyes, leaned into it.

It was good to hear music, real music. I felt like it had been a long, long time.

* * *

"Er, Boss… That wasn't you, was it?" Evans scoots around the control deck on his swivel chair, pizza juice smothered all over his chin, checking various monitors. He is worried.

The Boss shakes her head. "Don't look at me, this is your remit."

"I'm serious. Was it?"

"The Psych must have done his due diligence on what music she likes, that's all. He probably had a curated playlist cued up. He has access to all her apps and download history."

"If there was a playlist, I would know about it. And there isn't. Ambient sound, FX, all that jazz… but no mention of Radiohead, trust me. He can only play from the library of sounds we give him access to."

"Well maybe he filed a last-minute request. Check the logs."

"Fine, but even so. He's gone off script if he's decided to start playing disk-jockey. Is he allowed to do that yet?"

"I don't understand, what are you asking me?"

"Go off-script, I mean. I thought we were supposed to maintain–"

The woman interjects. "The Psych must have decided the timing was right."

"But I don't see a confirmation alert. Usually they tell us, right? When they're about to change something? So we can prepare, report. Compensate."

The Boss wipes her fingers fastidiously on a paper napkin.

"Usually. But this isn't a 'usual' scenario. There are degrees of interaction. He must have done it to put her at ease. The script isn't working as well as we thought it might."

"I don't doubt that the script needs tweaking, but I'm just not sure it's a good idea, not yet. Especially with the glitches we've been having…"

"Look, the way I see it, it's all programmed in and waiting for him to play with anyway. Music, ambience, different scenes and settings, props… it's a toolbox, right? I don't see a problem in allowing a trained professional to activate certain variables based on the patient's natural triggers. It all helps with–"

"The immersion process, yeah, yeah, I know. But she's a bit different to most of our patients, isn't she?"

"What do you mean?"

"You don't think it's weird? She's scarily comfortable moving around in this environment. Are you sure this is her first time in a VR setting like this?"

"With VR sickness that extreme? Come on. Some people are just made for this treatment, that's all. We should be happy if she is responding well."

"Taking us off script has consequences if it happens too often and too fast. It doesn't only damage her. It damages us. We'll get a reputation for being irresponsible."

"You're being alarmist, Evans. It's just a song."

"It always starts with something small. And it's not a song that's part of our soundtrack!"

"Evans." The Boss folds her arms and glares at her report sternly. "When in the entire history of this programme have you ever known a Psych to put a foot wrong? We have the best of the best working with us for a reason. And the paperwork we make the family sign at the induction meeting takes care of all that. We can't be found liable for something the Psych initiates; our legalese is watertight. As far as the law is concerned, both the patient and her Psych knew the risks and willingly volunteered to take part."

"But what if it wasn't the Psych? What if… somehow, the music was… her?"

The Boss laughs out loud. "Impossible. She's in a medically induced state of hypnagogia. Pretty hard to manipulate anything backend from the land of fragmented consciousness."

"Yeah, but legalities aside… shouldn't we be doing, you know, the best thing for her brain?"

"Who is to say that this isn't the best thing? So she likes

listening to Radiohead, so what? Whatever makes her more comfortable, I say. Have you seen her levels? She's zoning, which is good."

"Fine. But I still want to see a confirmation alert from the Psych. Because if it *was* him, he should be following due process, and if it *wasn't* him, and music is randomly triggering from an accidental voice-search or because we've been hacked or something nefarious like that, then we have a problem."

"So speak to the Psych, but don't make a meal out of it, Evans, alright?"

"You mean, if he actually deigns to talk to us or listen to our messages."

The Boss sighs. Evans tries, and fails, to swallow his annoyance at not being taken seriously. "Fine," he says, his mouth red with tomato sauce. "All I am saying is, five minutes ago, you were freaking out over glitches. Now you're being cavalier about background changes we didn't authorise. I'm just saying. Something is off here."

The Boss says nothing, because it is the simplest and most effective way to end the conversation.

Evans picks up a now cold half-eaten triangle of pizza, folds it in half, and angrily stuffs it in his mouth with one hand. With his other, he unmutes his mic and between mouthfuls of stodgy, cold carbs, he brusquely asks the Psych for confirmation that he changed the music settings in the construct.

The Psych, predictably, doesn't respond.

Behind the two techs, the crack creeps further along the wall.

The women in the photo continued to smile at me as the music spread through the Gallery.

Had they failed me, or had I failed them?

Did it matter? Blame was a useless vessel, a cup that held no water for the dead.

And I had to keep reminding myself that that was what I was.

Dead.

Covered in mud.

Slowly decomposing.

But I couldn't make it work in my head, for some reason. Not anymore. Because despite all evidence to the contrary, it somehow suddenly didn't seem possible.

I didn't *feel* dead.

I felt... halfway between states, as if I were neither one thing nor the other.

And as I thought about this, the Gallery glitched again, and this time I *saw* it glitch. Clearly, not just an imagined tic, but a definite shimmer. It gave me the same sensation you get when you catch someone looking at you, and raise your eyes to theirs, only to see their gaze flit, lightning fast, away. A sense of catching someone out.

I sucked in a breath. The Gallery settled, re-solidified. I held that breath, but all remained calm.

There were layers to what was happening to me, I theorised.

First, a surface layer: I was dead, my house was no longer my house but a halfway place, a giant repository for my past. Then, a second layer: I was here to solve a riddle, and I had a companion along for the ride, one I wasn't entirely sure about, not just yet. A third layer: somehow, I was able to affect my surroundings, although I hadn't yet worked out how, exactly. It just seemed to happen. Music. Glitches. I knew it was tied to my thought processes. And when these things happened, I became aware that there might be something sitting *behind* all this, behind the Gallery, as if my present environment was only an illusion, and underneath lay something... something more... real. Like scratching off the silver layer on a lottery ticket, to reveal the solid bold numbers underneath.

And that was the fourth layer.

"Are you alright?" My new friend interrupted me. He was becoming a pest for how often he strode in and cut off my thought processes. He had a habit of doing this the longer I dwelt on things, and I had an impression that he didn't *want* me to dwell on things too much, or at least, he wanted me to dwell on the *right sorts* of things. Friend-approved things. He was like a pickpocket, or a magician, distracting me from a secret trick. This reminded me of the hammer up his sleeve. Was it still there? Had it ever been there?

"I was until you interrupted me," I replied, rather coldly, and his smile wavered. I decided to push it, just to see what would happen.

"Or is personal space not a thing in purgatory?" I continued.

The man bowed his head, his face turning wry. Then he spread his hands out by way of a silent apology and stepped back a few paces.

Message received, I thought.

I closed my eyes and tried to enjoy the music before the song ended.

"Ouch."

"I wouldn't worry. He's got the measure of her. I think it takes a lot to phase this guy."

"No, it's not that. It's the glitching, Boss. I'm trying to source this sodding song track, but I can't keep up. All my diagnostics are coming back normal. But something is clearly up with the system, and if it gets much worse..."

"I'm not quitting the scenario, not as it stands."

"Well, either we've got a gremlin, or... well. I don't know what. I still think... I mean, it could be... her."

"You know that isn't possible, Evans. We've been over this. She's a passenger on the plane, not the pilot. I think you've had too much coffee." The Boss narrows her eyes, seeing Evans clearly as if for the first time. "Can I ask you something?"

"Sure." Evan's tone contradicts the word.

"Is everything okay at home?"

Evans flinches.

"Since you ask, no, it is not. Moira is asking for a divorce."

"Oh, Evans." The Boss reaches out a hand, lays it on her colleague's shoulder. "I had no idea. Is it really that bad? You can't try counselling?"

Evans stares into the Observation Room, a muscle working in his jaw.

"I don't really want to talk about it," he replies, staring fixedly at the woman behind the glass.

The Boss silently gets up to fetch him a glass of water from a nearby cooler.

Evans studies the patient, who tries to close her eyes but is unable to because of the clamps. Instead, her irides roll upwards violently, exposing the whites of her eyeballs, an involuntary movement simulating what should be happening if her eyelids were allowed to close. It makes the patient look wild, pained. She still mouths the words to the song, correctly now, wrapped in her own little reverie. Like a cartoon villain, reciting a mantra.

A strange feeling comes over the watching tech.

It is a mixture of pity and fear, he realises.

Unseen, the cracks in the wall nearby get a little longer, and a little wider, and a little deeper.

The song ended, then began to play again, stuck on a loop.

"Oh shut up," I said, flapping my hand in the general direction of the speakers. I loved the song, but it was no longer the time for it. The music snapped off. I barely noticed. I opened my eyes and found the three women still smiled out at me from the confines of the glossy photograph.

Life is full of Good People and Bad People, I thought. This is what we are taught from a young age. I knew it was dangerous to define myself by the Bad People, instead of the Good, and perhaps that was my lesson for this exhibit.

Still didn't help me figure out why, or indeed if, I was dead.

I took the framed photograph down from its plinth, wandering along the harlequin floor until I found a spot where the sunlight hit the tiles. I sat down, cross-legged, wanting to think, reminisce, without purpose, just enjoy the act of remembering.

A memory duly came to me, gently this time, not in a rush like the others. It was like someone slowly turning up the volume on a television; first I saw the characters and the setting, and then I heard the voices.

And found myself sitting in my grandmother's bright and pleasant living room.

9

DAFFODIL YELLOW WALLS

I looked around, startled.

This wasn't just a memory.

The Gallery had gone.

So had my friend.

In his place, my mother and grandmother sat side by side on a couch in front of me. Seeing them up close made the breath stick in my throat. Oh god, I had missed them. I resisted the urge to spring across the room and bury myself in their embrace. It was difficult, but I needed to get the lie of the land, first. I couldn't decide if this was still a memory I had just sunk really deep into, or a scenario, like finding my own body under the bridge. I thought about saying something (*I love you, thank you for everything*) but couldn't, so I just sat there trying to get a grip on things, looking around at the room I'd spent many hours in as a child. It felt incredible to be back. This was a good place, a home, for home is where the heart is, they say, but really, I knew that home was where a person felt safe, above all other things.

The walls, painted daffodil yellow, were hung with pictures of various family members, but perhaps more reverently with large colour photos of dogs, who had always enjoyed exalted positions within our family, especially after they were gone. There were vases full of silk flowers, tastefully arranged. A large mahogany desk with a green banker's lamp. Porcelain birds.

An old wooden banjo barometer. Side tables with colourful drink coasters. Sun crystals hanging in the windows, catching light, breaking it to pieces, scattering it across the walls like rainbow confetti.

It was all so very pleasant and comfortable.

A thought interrupted: would there be a corner for me on the photo wall now? Would I get the same treatment as the dogs?

I tuned into the low, familiar chatter in the room: a routine, slightly laboured back-and-forth between my mother and her mother. I usually sat aloof from these exchanges, clutching a magazine to my face as a shield. I found the familiarity sometimes alienating, having long ago decided that I didn't really fit in with my family as well as I would have liked. Occasionally, when I was younger, I tried to assert my own conversational needs upon them in that demanding, angry way younger people have. *Foreign affairs! Politics! Travel! Literature!* All that did was highlight the differences between us, or provoke arguments, arguments I always won very competently, which only served to worsen the divide. I grew out of it eventually, that need to plaster my identity across every mundane exchange. I kept my conversation appropriate to the audience, and it made life easier, if a little compartmentalised.

The conversation went on, except every now and then, one of the women would realise I wasn't participating in the chat, and would become self-conscious, a little irritated.

"Are you with us?" my mother said.

"Yes," my Nan said, in a softer way. "Tell us about your day."

I apologised and made a token effort at conversation, whilst secretly still reading the magazine from the corner of my eye. It didn't feel right to have a voice, not in that moment. I was worried that speaking out might break the spell, dispel the scenario somehow. Whether memory, dream or construct, I wanted to stay here for a bit. Absorb the intimacy of this experience. All that was really expected of me was to repeat what had already been said anyway, to indicate my support. I was there as an authenticator, never as a disruptor.

The subject matter usually fell into one or several of the following allowable categories: the weather, what the plans for the day were, what the correct route to drive to wherever those plans were located was, what had happened on the most recent episode of the television show they were watching (*what if he just stopped crying one day what if you hurt him by mistake what if they take him away from you*), when the low and high tides were, who they had seen in town and whether or not either one of them had finished with the local paper yet. As mother and daughter they were very different people, with a lot in common. My grandmother was gentle, an open field. My mother, on the other hand, surrounded herself with great, high walls. Behind the walls, a hurt creature longed for love *(he's better off without me)* and laughed at silly, frivolous things when she felt safe enough to do so. We did not see each other as much as she wished, and it always took us a while to settle back into each other when we did. We all spoke every week on the phone, until we didn't. When my grandmother grew sick, that was the thing I missed the most: our weekly phone calls. The end of our discourse felt like a cord that someone had cruelly snipped in two. I mourned the loss of her, and felt orphaned, often.

Despite this, *(better off)* despite feeling displaced and looking in at my family from the outside, I loved them fiercely. I wished they knew me better, but I loved them.

They had known nothing of the darkness stalking through my head. I glanced down at my wrist. I had a tattoo there, on the inside. It was simple, a wobbly outline of a stick man. Sometimes it burned, like now.

(Better off without you better off better off without you better–)

I grimaced at it and covered it with a hand so I didn't have to look at it.

* * *

"Did you see that?"

"See what?"

"She turned the music off, no intervention needed."

"I did see that, yes. I assume the Psych is on point."

"That's just it, Boss. He's still not responding to any of our messages. I don't get it. Why not just shoot me a quick text, confirm? It doesn't take five seconds. She's fully preoccupied with that photograph, she won't notice."

The Boss chews her lip. She is reluctantly starting to agree with Evans. Something does feel off about this assignment. The growing sensation of unease wars with her reluctance to interfere until strictly necessary. She feels as if, despite all the glitches and unexpected occurrences, the scenario is slowly starting to help the patient. It feels good to be able to say that, because her personal feelings towards the other woman are complex. Not that she would ever admit this, out loud.

Complexity of feeling is not acceptable at her pay grade.

"I think it's more than preoccupation," she says, speculating. "I think, from the way she's so intent on things... I think she's anchoring." The Boss has not long finished a paper on this subject or, more specifically, the Von Restorff effect, or "mnemonic object method". In it, she used a lot of fancy language about how isolated items sometimes stay more firmly rooted in memory, perform better. When presented with a particular object or item that stands out, people remember that thing more than other objects around them at the time. Like a yellow balloon in a cluster of red balloons. Often, those things are linked to happy memories, or sad ones. The mundane, day to day stuff slips through the cracks.

The Boss thinks about how the patient has a whole Gallery of objects to choose from, about how she could have started looking at them chronologically, as indicated by the numbers. But she didn't. The patient subconsciously returned to items that stood out the most to her. Her brain is sorting through the strongest or most significant memories as a matter of priority.

Which means they are starting to make headway. The patient is anchoring herself in some sort of past. Her suicidal ideation also being rooted in her past, in a memory, in something that happened to her, it makes sense.

Slowly, carefully, the patient is panning for gold in her brain whilst simultaneously strengthening her sense of belonging to something.

The Boss suspects that secretly, the patient, above all other things, wants to live.

Evans leans in closer to one of the monitors. "Does she look... a bit... transparent, to you? Like she's not really there?"

His Boss also frowns, and squints at the screen. "I don't know. I don't think so. Maybe?" She taps the side of the monitor to see if this makes a difference to the image. It doesn't.

"We definitely need to check her hook-up. And you still haven't answered me about the music."

The Boss knows Evans will not let this go, so she gives in. He is, after all, only trying to do his job.

"Can you replay the clip?" the Boss asks wearily, and Evans obliges.

The techs watch on a secondary screen as the patient in the Gallery flaps a hand, by all appearances shutting off the music by doing so. Evans loops the clip, and they re-watch it several times.

"But this doesn't make any sense," the Boss grudgingly acknowledges.

Evans nods. "I know I keep banging on about this, but she should only be able to interact with and manipulate the parameters she's been assigned. Anything else not designated to the Psych is backend, our remit. And look." Evans pulls up a task management list. "This is his list." Evans scrolls, checking. "There is no playlist or soundtrack assigned to him for this construct. All sound has been designated to us, to Control. Right here..." A few more hurried mouse clicks. "A list of fifty of her favourite songs. That the Psych has no access to. That neither of us triggered. Not a sniff of any Radiohead, either."

"Has to be another glitch. You're right. We should try and get a handle on this, Evans."

"A glitch is the entire system freezing or something not working as it should. This is different. This is deliberate. She meant to shut the music off. And the programme...well, it did as she told it to."

"No, Evans. She doesn't and cannot have that level of control. All I can think is that it's the Psych, and your list is inaccurate, or we have an error in the system that keeps throwing us a curve ball."

"Technology doesn't really work like that, Boss. Random errors don't present like, well. Whatever is going on here." Evans searches for something concrete to attach his mounting anxiety to. "I'm going to check her visor one last time whilst this latest diagnostic runs. It'll make me feel better."

"The Nurse is not due back for twenty minutes; do you feel comfortable going in there by yourself?" his Boss replies.

"Yes," he says, disentangling himself from his desk.

"Alright," the older woman says. "Just make sure you wash your hands, is all."

Evans leaves the room. There is a pause, during which his Boss imagines him washing his hands, sanitising them, pulling on fresh latex gloves kept in a box on the wall near the door of the OR. A few minutes later, the OR door opens, and Evans pushes in, approaching the patient cautiously.

She is hanging in a seated position, the cradle supporting her tailbone like an armchair. Her arms are held up in front of her, as if she is turning the invisible pages of a magazine that isn't there. Her rig is facing the door, for she has turned full circle without realising it. Evans cannot see her face from the angle he approaches; it is obscured by the large curving visor. He is grateful for this.

He presses a button on a small remote-control pad he picks up on entering the OR. There is a whirring sound, and the cradle gently lowers, just enough for Evans to comfortably reach the patient's head, not enough to disturb her significantly.

He steps close, aware of his increased heart rate. There is something so eerie about this woman, so deeply different to other patients he has worked with. She is whispering to herself, something the mics couldn't pick up clearly. The feeling of being in the room with a large, sentient marionette has him on edge, even though he knows that she can't possibly do anything untoward, not trussed up as she is.

He moves so that he is able to examine her visor, at the foam inserts and elasticated headbands holding it in place. It looks a little like a medical safety visor, modified to fully surround the head, so all peripheral vision is taken care of. On the inside curved surface, stereoscopic images, one for the left eye and one for the right. The patient absorbs the images as intended, and although the visor looks a bit low down, it is not enough of a displacement to have any real effect. Still, Evans tentatively jiggles the head straps, tightening things just enough to hoist the visor up a centimetre or so. He has to be careful not to displace any of the sensors stuck to the patient's lightly stubbled scalp while he does so.

The whispers continue throughout, although Evans cannot make out any distinct, individual words.

He moves so that he can peer in around the visor's edge, enough see some of what the patient is seeing through her clamped-open eyes. This puts his face so close to hers than he can smell her breath, feel the heat radiating from her. As he does so, she shivers, and then a sudden, burgeoning desire to sneeze grips hold of him. Panicked, he jerks backward, frantically searching in his pocket for something to stem the outburst. He finds a greasy pizza napkin, and just in time, saves himself from showering the woman's head and visor in mucus.

"Jesus, Evans!" His Boss's voice hisses out into the OR via her desk mic. But Evans pays no heed. He is instead staring at the patient with watery eyes, frozen in the act of wiping his nose.

The patient has stopped turning the pages of her invisible magazine.

Her eyes have flicked to the extreme right, away from the VR display, and she side-stares directly, if uncomfortably, at Evans.

"Stick Man say everyone is better off without me," she declares, loudly.

Evans makes a surprised sound in the base of his throat. He is convinced she is still hypnagogic; he knows she cannot really *see* him and cannot remotely be aware of his presence, but his pulse betrays his fear nonetheless. The unwelcome eye contact is akin to that feeling you get with an antique oil painting, convinced the eyes are following you as you move around the room.

"Sorry," he whispers, without knowing why.

The patient's gaze rolls slowly back to the front. Evans notices worry lines around her mouth. She is beautiful, up close, which is something he's never appreciated until now. The patient reminds him a little of his wife, and he thinks that makes it worse, somehow.

He leaves, feeling guilty about things he cannot articulate.

He does not see the brown stain on the vinyl floor expanding further, spreading, eagerly reaching, now almost the size of a small dinner plate.

As I sat and listened to my mother and grandmother talk, I felt suddenly as if someone were standing behind me, breathing over my shoulder. I shivered. The presence moved to one side. Something tugged, on my brain, but also... on my skin, somehow, on my scalp. I focused on the sensation at the roots of my hair and it subsided, then strengthened.

I stopped reading, let my eyes whip to the right. Maybe if I moved fast enough, I would catch it in the act.

There! A faint shadow, a blurred patch of light, moving at

the edges of my vision. The lingering aroma of… pizza? After a second, it was gone. I went back to the magazine, shuddering as if a cold draft had gone down my spine. Would it come back? Perhaps if I pretended nonchalance, it might.

Whatever *it* was.

Unable to concentrate on my reading material, I looked around my grandmother's living room again. I searched for my strange new friend, who usually stood behind me or off to one side patiently, hands clasped behind his back as if he were waiting for a bus, but he was nowhere to be found. I felt upset by this, because the backup had been nice. Now I was alone again, even surrounded by things and people I knew and *(always alone, love)* loved.

The chill continued to travel down my body. The edges of my vision felt blurred, warped, as if… my world was expanding sideways, somehow.

What was this, exactly? If I analysed my situation?

This wasn't really my grandmother's house. I recalled that it couldn't be. Her house had been demolished four years ago; the land sold off for development.

But also… I understood suddenly that this wasn't a memory, either. It was too clear, too real, and the women in the room were interacting directly with me, like they would in a dream.

What *was* this whole fucking thing?

If I got up and went to the women, hugged them in the way I desperately wanted to, would I feel anything?

I started to feel deeply, deeply afraid.

"Her adrenaline levels are climbing up, Evans. I'm not sure how helpful that was." The Boss feels annoyed at herself for letting him go into the OR without the Nurse, even if the pretext was valid. She has an uncomfortable, growing awareness of not being entirely in control of this project, and she knows she needs to up her game, do better by the patient.

On the other hand, fluctuating hormones are part and parcel of the day job, and she's seen worse escalations during her time in this room.

"I know, I know. But the visor was a little low, for what it's worth."

"She spoke to you."

"I don't think she was speaking to me, Boss. I think she was just chuntering on, as they do."

"I'm writing it up anyway," the Boss replies, bending her head to the task.

While she is distracted, Evans subtly and covertly re-administers a small dose of sedatives to the patient via a tiny slider on the med panel. He shouldn't have access to the med panel at all, only The Boss can authorise and administer medication, but Evans knows his way around security protocols and has an obsessive need for control. It is, after all, his programme. His work. His neck on the line.

And her adrenaline levels do look dangerous, he tells himself.

His Boss, caught up in her note writing, does not notice Evans's thumb on the slider.

Evans completes the dose, then watches and waits.

The patient's levels continue to climb, then take a sharp, steep upwards jump. A warning beep sounds out into the quiet.

"Er…what?" The Boss says, confused.

Evans quietly shits himself, convinced the patient is having an adverse reaction to the sedative. In the room next door, the woman's chest now rises and falls rapidly.

"Might be time for some happy hormones," The Boss muses, sounding faintly worried.

Her colleague makes hasty attempts to stay her hand. "Give it a moment or two, Boss. She might settle." He chooses not to tell her that he has been playing doctor behind her back. He hopes against hope that he has done the right thing, for on top of everything else going on in his life, he does not want a negligence report slapped on him.

"I can ready some beta blockers, what do you think?" she says, instead.

"Why are you asking me, what the hell do I know about it?" Evan's subterfuge makes him panicky, defensive. "And where on earth did the Psych go? To take a shit?"

"Evans. I'm not keen on being spoken to like that. Try to calm down a little."

"I'm sorry. It's like… her rising panic is infectious, you know?"

The Boss swallows. She does know, and she doesn't like it.

She doesn't like it one little bit.

The women in the room chatted, but it was no longer the comforting sound it had been. Instead, it felt like a cover.

Because I found I could hear more voices, talking underneath them.

I frowned, straining my ears.

Yes, I could definitely hear two voices, a woman and a man, going back and forth. I couldn't make out the words, exactly, but I knew they were speaking in English. I tried to cut through the voices of my family to access the hidden conversation, but couldn't quite seem to grasp it, no matter how hard I tried. This secondary conversation was slippery as an eel, although I thought I could make out the word "infectious". Maybe.

Again, I had a sense of a secret, different world, sitting beneath me. It didn't take long for me to piece this together with the other things I'd learned during my time here.

The voices were coming from the fourth layer, of course.

My fear spiked further.

The voices of my mother and grandmother disappeared.

A second later, so did they.

"No!" I cried, for I had not had a chance to tell them I loved them, or say goodbye.

The hidden voices went quiet.

I was left alone in my armchair, a sudden, huge sense of

loss threatening to flatten me like a pancake. In my hands, a photograph, three women in a row. We were all smiling, and that was the saddest thing of all.

"Oh, wow. Her cortisol is sky high. Fuck!"

"How bad?"

"There's no history of hypersecretion that you haven't told me about, right? No Cushing's or anything?"

"Nope. Just standard panic disorder, although her last saliva swab hasn't come back yet, and I... wait a minute. Who told you to start playing doctor of the house?"

"Sorry, it was just a thought." A small beeping noise continues to make its presence known in the Control Room.

"Heart rate climbing," Evans says.

"Yes, I can hear, thanks."

"Maybe hormones now," Evans whispers, tired.

"I'm going to give it another minute or so. She might ride this out. And you're right. Where the fuck *is* the Psych?"

The tech team cannot see the daffodil yellow living room on their monitors, they never could. They only see the Gallery, and the patient sitting on the floor, grappling with the beginning stages of a panic attack, the photograph in a frame held loosely in her lap.

The Psych is nowhere to be seen.

It dawned on me that I was fighting a losing battle.

Whatever it was that I was doing here, was pointless. It wouldn't change the fact that every day of whatever future I had left to me, I would wake up, and every day I would find out that I was just another day older. The same person, only with more time behind me, and less time in front. Moving through life slowly, inevitably, like parts of a doll on an assembly line conveyor belt. Churning inexorably on; arms, legs, heads, all the words for those parts of your body, plug them all together, just like the doll before and the doll behind you.

The towering pointlessness of it all took my breath away.

My heart raced, and my head started to pound.

I realised I was crying. I tried to stop it, swallow it down, smother it (*smother him, smother him, stop crying, won't you stop?! Oh god I am so bad at this, you are so much better off without me–*) But I could feel myself hollowing out, my innards turning to powder, heart first, then lungs, then my bones, my muscles, my veins, words, words for my poor decaying body.

In the dark room lit by glowing appliances, the control team scramble furiously to shut off a new panic alarm that has just begun to shrill.

"Okay, this is really, really not good!" Evans cries, over the noise.

"Let's not overreact!" The Boss holds up a hand, ignoring the alarm and intently watching as the woman on the screen and the woman in the OR starts to cry, then hyperventilate.

"Boss, I..." Evans is on the verge of admitting his transgression, knowing the implications, no longer caring. His Boss cuts him off, firmly.

"We have an override protocol in place. I'd rather not touch it until *absolutely* necessary, but I have the synthetic hormones on standby. I think she'll level out, though. She's working something through."

"What, though? Christ, it's hot in here!" Evans is sweating uncontrollably. His pizza lunch no longer feels as safe in his belly as it did ten minutes ago.

"Something big. Something... significant."

"She makes me nervous, Boss. I feel... I don't feel right..."

"I know. Me either. But let's... let's just wait."

* * *

"Friend?" I cried out; voice strangled. I clutched at my throat as my breath came faster, and shallower.

"I'm here." He was by my side in an instant, kneeling next to the armchair to comfort me whilst still managing to maintain a respectable distance.

"I think... I think I know what this is," I gasped. Tears *(stickmansaysstickmansays)* flooded down my face.

"Tell me," he said, taking the photograph away from me, and making it disappear. I had an irrational flash of disappointment, despite everything, that I wasn't going to get my shiny gold coin.

"This is the moment," I said, trying to stay focused, struggling.

"The moment?"

"This is the precise moment I realised I didn't want to live anymore."

10

BINGO

"And... Bingo!" The Boss pumps the air with her fist triumphantly.

The patient's levels start to drop. The alarm cuts out, as abruptly as it began.

Evans swallows a huge ball of stress that has jammed itself in his throat somewhere behind his Adam's apple.

Thank fuck, he thinks, over and over.

When he has a handle on himself, he says out loud:

"So what... that was her Event Horizon? Did I miss something?!"

"If that is another pop culture reference, Evans, I am going to throttle you. No, it's not ground zero, not yet, but it is a *big* help. Because it gives us a timeline to work with."

"I'm lost."

"You've had a lot on your plate, but try and focus, can you?"

"I *am* trying to focus, Boss, but I presume you want me to keep her alive too, right? Her heartrate is currently two *hundred* beats per minute!"

"And falling. She'll be fine, but I take your point. For clarity, I know it sounded innocuous, but she just identified the moment she first realised she wanted to die. It doesn't explain why, or constitute a reason. But it does mean we can timestamp the suicidal ideation."

"Boss, her levels are dangerously low, now. She's like a see-saw, I can't keep up!"

A voice comes in on the Nursecom. "Everything okay in there?" A concerned voice asks.

The Boss rushes to minimise the situation. "Just a panic attack, is all. We've got it under control, now. No need to intervene."

The com rattles a little static. Then: "Are you sure? Usually when an alarm goes off we–"

"We're fine. I promise. Thank you for checking in."

"Alright. Just let us know if you need anything. We're changing shifts soon, but someone will be around, regardless." The com cuts out, and the Boss rubs her temples, stressed, as Evans looks on.

"Just a little more time, trust me, Evans. Eureka moments like this usually bring levels back up to equilibrium eventually. Anyway, our Psych has got it under control now, by the looks of it."

"He should never have abandoned her in the first fucking place. Where the hell was he? I couldn't see him anywhere in the Gallery."

"Good question," the Boss replies, a steely glint appearing in her eyes. "Good question."

The voices in the fourth layer came back, sounded elated, relieved about something. Good for them.

I myself felt as if I was perched on the edge of a dark, endless, terrifying pit. I could feel things stirring inside my head, like my brain was flipping over, a sizzling egg in a pan of fat. I began to shake, shiver. Sweat popped out on my brow. My hands and feet no longer felt like they belonged to me.

And a slow and heavy rumble began, starting from right underneath me.

My grandmother's living room had dissolved. I was back in

the Gallery, and the whole place was shaking, wracked with violent tremors. The plinths lined up on either side of the Gallery began to wobble. I heard a tiny, distinct cracking noise, looked down, and saw one of the tiles on the ground fissure, separate into two pieces.

"What's happening?!" I cried as another tile cracked in two.

My new friend hesitated briefly, then said, over the noise of the disturbance:

"What would you say to them now, if you could?"

"What?"

"What would you say to them. Your mother. Your grandmother. If you could speak to them now. If they were here in front of you, instead of me."

But they were, I thought. *They were, and I wasted it.*

The shaking and rumbling suddenly died down.

The Gallery stilled.

"Why don't I know who you are?" I answered, distrustfully. My breathing slowed. The storm in my mind was passing, slowly.

"It seems very strange that I would just let you in here, into this place. This personal place. That I would have these… intimate conversations with you." I gestured to the Gallery, *my* Gallery. The tremors had done damage, and large cracks snaked up most of the columns like ivy. The floor tiles were all cracked in half.

The plinths and their exhibits seemed fine, by contrast.

"What is all this, really? Who are you?"

My friend smiled amiably, although I could tell I had him rattled. I sensed that underpinning this whole experience, some sort of plan existed. I also sensed that events, as they unfolded, were fucking with that plan, quite decidedly.

"You're the Detective, Magpie," he said, making a good show of disguising his unease. I could tell, though. Sometimes you just can.

I was tired of games, of layers, of deceptions. The tattoo on my wrist burned. My anger rippled outwards, lashing like a whip, and I saw it go, a living thing, travelling across the short distance between us as a surge of energy, a furious gust of wind. It battered against my friend, ruffling his hair, buffeting his body, and he stepped back, an involuntary movement. And quickly, so quickly that I almost missed it, I saw his right hand move to cover his left. His right thumb pressed down on the pad of his left thumb, and for an instant, a second, I thought I saw a small, red, raised dot stuck to the pad, although it vanished when I blinked. I *had* seen it though. There was a tiny red button on this man's left hand, and he had just pressed it, as if in response to something.

Me, I thought.

He held my gaze, and I understood. He was still doing a good job of hiding it, but I knew.

He was afraid of me.

Why?

I looked at the shaken Gallery, the damage I'd wrought.

The silence stretched out between us. I decided that enough was enough.

It was time for some answers.

In the control room, an alarm is sounding again. A different timbre, but no less insistent. It is the Psych's panic alarm, although it already seems to be redundant, for the patient has calmed considerably, as if her angry outburst has reset things.

"For fuck's *sake!*" Evans cries, struggling to get the alarm to turn off. The Psych is still not answering his messages, and Evans cannot override and disengage the alarm without the Psych's input.

His Boss, meanwhile, gazes at the screen, confused. It is as if the alarm does not exist, for her. The only things that exist are the monitors, and what is visible upon them.

The construct is full of cracks, fractures, piles of dust and masonry.

Her gaze travels to the patient in the OR. She is standing now, back straight, head up. She should be swaying on the end of her cables, because her body is, after all, subject to the same laws of physics as the rest of us: momentum, force, velocity, but she is not. She is completely, totally still, motionless, frozen in time like a woman in a photograph.

"Impossible," the Boss breathes.

A second later, the woman in the OR starts to sway, gently, a human pendulum hanging from a fixed point once again.

11

MY NEW FRIEND

I stood up. "Where did you go, before?"

The man looked confused. "Go? What do you mean?"

"You went somewhere. While I was in the photograph. Where do you go when I'm, you know... examining the exhibits?"

He looked uncomfortable that I'd caught him in the act, but he had to know that leaving me was a trigger. He had come and gone, like my stepfather, like the tide, only reappearing when I was desperate. It was disconcerting but also, it felt stage-managed. Like he was following...

"A script," I murmured. Either a script, or a set of instructions. My friend definitely had more to him than he was willing to let on. He had layers too, it seemed.

My new friend pressed his thumb-button again, and I made no secret of the fact that I'd spotted him doing it this time. We locked eyes, and I could have sworn he was almost *listening* for something. He was silent a moment longer, then reached an internal decision of some sort, nodding to himself.

"I have a place that I go, to wait for you. Would you like to see it?"

"In here?" I had not explored every inch of the Gallery, but I didn't need to. Somehow I knew that the only things in here were the walls, the alcoves, the ceiling, the high windows I could not reach, the shafts of sunlight, the swirling, glittering fragments of dust and debris, and my artefacts, my belongings. There was nowhere to go, no way to get away from me. No doors or corners or nooks to hide in. Just the Gallery, stretching as far as my eyes could see.

I said as much.

"But there *is* no place here."

He cleared his throat. Something about the way he did it niggled at the back of my mind, like it was a familiar tic, a behavioural peculiarity that struck a chord with me somehow.

"This place..." he began, and then tailed off, searching for appropriate words.

I was not slow to pick up on what he was trying to do. I could tell from his posture and from the clearing of his throat that he was about to explain something he considered complex.

Which meant he had knowledge.

That moment, that pivotal moment when I had discovered my own dead body. He had not just been a stranger passing by, a friendly soul in my time of need.

His help *was* a pre-planned thing.

We *were* following a script.

I was here by design.

His? Mine? Whatever. I felt equal parts fascinated, and fearful. *Why* was the big question. Why, and what plan?

And then it hit me. If he knew this place, he knew what it really was, then presumably, he knew how to get out of it.

"Tell me," I said, and I leaned into him as threateningly as I knew how.

"First off," he said, putting his hands up as a barrier, "you are here through your own volition. This was *your* idea, although I am not surprised you don't remember. You asked us to help you, and that's why I am here. But, this place... well. You have to understand. It is not just yours," he continued, carefully.

"What do you mean?"

"This place. This construct. It isn't just yours to play with.

I mean, to a certain extent, it is. But you and I sort of... share it, equally."

"Okay," I said, slowly, trying to swallow another mounting surge of anger. "But what does any of that *mean?*" He might as well have been speaking to me in Greek.

He sighed. "It's okay, it's a complicated thing to get a grip on. What I mean, in very simple and not entirely accurate terms, is that this is a reality we both share, at this precise moment in time."

I stared at him. "A reality," I said, flatly. "But it's not real. An unreal reality."

He tipped his head to one side. "If you like."

"And that's supposed to make sense?" I said.

"It means–"

I held up a hand of my own. "Do you think you can manage to tell me whatever you are about to tell me in plain English, please? Without being patronising, for a change?"

He chooses his words more carefully.

"The Gallery is real, for both of us. It's real in the sense that we can see, and smell, and touch, and hear everything that's going on around us. By this I mean to say, you can't actually see, or smell, or hear, or touch these things, because they aren't real in a tangible sense, but your brain makes assumptions and thinks they are, which is good enough. So far so good?"

I grunted. He continued.

"But my reality is different to yours, in subtle ways. So I'm here, seeing what you see, except there are... differences for me."

"I still don't understand," I said, because I didn't.

"When you go to a library, it's for a purpose, isn't it? To read, to learn. Study. The building has a function, a point to it. So does this place."

"And what is that purpose?"

"That's for you to determine."

I lowered my head, let out a small laugh. "I thought this was some sort of... purgatory." Although as soon as the words left my mouth, they sounded ridiculous.

"Because you're dead." His voice was droll.

"Well, yes!" But again, the doubt. I had seen my own corpse, but I still didn't *feel* it. Dead.

He raised an eyebrow, glanced around. "Seems a bit... ornate... for purgatory, don't you think?"

"I don't know, I haven't got a bloody clue what purgatory is supposed to fucking look like!" I was defensive, now. Being scared always made me feel defensive.

"But you don't believe in God, do you?"

"I guess not." I laughed, suddenly, not knowing what else to think. "So you're telling me..." I thought hard, my brain trying to put it all together like little mosaic pieces. Then, I raised pleading eyes to my friend.

"Please, *please* tell me this is not some fucking mind palace, or whatever you call it. Please, no. I can't be any more of a giant cliché than I already am."

"Well..." My friend folded his arms and looked at me quizzically. "Not a mind palace, not as such. But it *is* a virtual construct you can manipulate and interact with, taken from a mixture of your memories and our real-world research. If that makes sense."

It didn't.

"Not yet."

He rolled his head around, loosening tension from his shoulders.

"This is... what you see, here. It's a tapestry, if you like. It weaves together your memories, as recounted to family, friends, in your diaries, your photos, your internet history, your social media profiles, and real things, real data, to create this..." He waved a hand, searching for the word. "Environment."

"Does this mean I'm *not* dead?"

"I can't answer that. There are rules."

"What rules? You literally just told me this is a fabricated reality. There can't be any rules, except arbitrary ones."

"Even arbitrary rules need to be followed."

"I don't like that."

"You don't have to. All you have to do is understand that I am trying to help you, and that's what all this is about." He waves his arms to encompass the shaken Gallery. "Although you've made a right mess of the place, somehow."

"I knew it! I knew I couldn't be dead. Tell me I'm not dead!"

"I can't, so please don't ask me again."

I let it go for the moment. *Not dead.* I knew I was right, and was genuinely happy to discover it, amazed, taken aback, brain grinding through the implications.

"And what are we doing here, exactly?" A tiny nugget of hope glinted in a stream.

"Again. Only you can tell me that," he said.

"Well." I breathed out, long and heavy. "Whatever the purpose, we have to get out of here, right now, straight away, before I disappear entirely up my own arse." I looked at him beseechingly. "Didn't you see me back there? Gazing long and deep into the abyss? This place is... I know it's been built to help, but it's bad for me. Surrounded by all these things. I feel like a failure, looking at them."

"You might feel that way, but they are helping you, Magpie."

"I want to leave."

He was reluctant. "Now? Don't you feel like you are getting somewhere?"

"I don't know where it is I am supposed to be getting!"

"Ah." My new friend sighed. "Well, it's quite simple, really. The real-world version of you thinks there are hidden triggers in your past, in your memories, that might explain why..."

"Why what?" Then it clicked. "Ohhh! Why I keep..." I mimicked the act of diving off of something high and vertiginous. It was a grotesque little display, but it got the point across.

My friend shook his head ruefully. "Well, quite. The other version of you asked for help in trying to uncover this potential trigger. Event. Catalyst, if you like."

"And this… construct is supposed to be helping with that?"

"That's the idea. It's an experimental programme, but there has been some success with other patients. Do you think it's not working for you?"

"A moment ago I was ready to give up, all over again."

"Give up? Or 'give up'?" He attached a weight to the second repetition so we both understood how serious those words were.

"The latter. I think. I don't know. I can't even remember my own fucking name. All I can think of now is the name "Magpie". I felt exasperated. "I don't think this is helping at all, not one bit."

He sighed. "That's natural. Progress is never linear, with this sort of thing. Look, I should reiterate. All of this – it is voluntary. You agreed to the process. And you put a lot of work into this place, as did I. And the team."

"You mean… *I* came up with all this?"

"A large part of it, yeah."

Knowing I had a hand in it made me more kindly disposed towards the Gallery.

"Huh." I grunted, in begrudging appreciation. "Not too shabby, in that case."

"Typical, take all the bloody credit, woman, why don't you?" Evans grumbles. His hair is in a state of disarray, and giant sweat puddles soak through the fabric of his shirt beneath his armpits, across his back and chest. The alarms in the room have silenced, finally, and both Evans and his Boss are feeling exhausted after the cacophony.

"She said 'in the photograph'," The Boss says, a little shakily. "What do you think she meant by that?"

"I have no idea, and honestly, at this moment in time, we have bigger fish to fry, we really do." Evans uses his damp, snotty pizza napkin to mop his wet brow.

"Are we fully back online?" The Boss asks, worriedly. "How's she doing?"

"She's levelled out completely. I wish I could say the same for me."

"I know what you mean."

"Why do you think he triggered it? His panic button, I mean?"

"The Psych? I imagine he sensed some... threat from her. Something we couldn't see, maybe. Either way, he seems more comfortable now."

"Is she?"

"Is she what?"

Evans looks at his Boss, and his face is pale, deadly serious. "A threat."

The older woman looks back at him, her confidence fading.

"Have you seen the Gallery?" she says, by way of reply.

Evans takes in the damage properly for the first time, and his mouth drops open.

"I don't understand," he says, weakly.

"Nor do I," his Boss replies. "She's just an ordinary woman. She isn't supposed to be able to... whatever this is."

Evans nibbles his lower lip, peeling a shred of skin away and leaving it raw, bleeding.

The crack in the wall, still unnoticed, has begun to make its path across the ceiling. It is just wide enough that a small insect might be able to crawl out of it or through it, were it so inclined, like an earwig or a spider or a woodlouse. Just wide enough that a thin trickle of sticky brown matter might ooze its way lazily out of the crack, and after a second or two, detach from the ceiling altogether, and drip onto the workspace of the two techs below.

Just one drip, at first.

And then, another. A steady trickle. A slow, and creeping succession.

* * *

"Yes," my new friend said. "Scene-setting, shall we call it that? Yes. You came up with this place. You are very good at this, as it turns out. It must be the writer in you."

"I want to leave!" I screamed at him suddenly, and the scream echoed around the alcoves, lingering in the air long after my mouth had closed.

It shocked us both, for I had thought I was calm.

"I'm sorry," I said, then, my whole body trembling. "I don't know where that came from."

"It's alright, Magpie." My friend thought for a second, and then reached out his hand. "Let's have a break."

I began to cry. "Please," I said, and he bowed his head a little.

"We… I'm just trying to help you," he reminded me and, by that, I knew he meant that he was trying to save my life.

He led me by the hand to the left-hand wall of the Gallery. We stared at the fractured marble surface in front of us for a few moments, and, gradually, a door materialised. It was a red door, painted in fresh, gloss paint, and it had a huge brass doorknob in the centre of it, so big it needed both my friend's hands to turn. I could see our faces in the polished brass, distorted, golden, as if we were trapped inside a Christmas ornament.

I gasped, and dug my heels in. "I'm not going in there," I said faintly.

"Why?" He frowned. "After everything you've seen?"

"It's the colour." I licked my lips. "The door is red. I'll… I'll explain later. Can we change the colour of the door, please?"

He shrugged. "It doesn't really work like that; you see this is all pre-pro…"

I pointed at the door. "Blue" I said, more firmly than I felt.

Slowly, the door shifted, rippled, and turned from red, to purple, to blue.

* * *

"Close your mouth, Evans," the Boss says faintly, after closing her own.

"Can someone explain to me what just happened?!"

"No, no, I really can't."

"She just... she just live-edited the fucking code!"

"I can't explain it, Evans." The older woman swallows and loosens her collar. Her eyes are round with a growing awareness that hadn't been there before. "I can't. This is unprecedented. But isn't it..."

"Isn't it what?!"

"Isn't she marvellous?" The Boss's face shines with a sudden, visceral excitement.

My friend's right hand twitched, almost pressing the invisible button on his left thumb-pad, stopping short by a millimetre.

Then, he turned the handle of the now blue door, and it swung open.

And there, in all its glory, lay the sailboat.

We stepped through the door.

12

THE BOAT

"What the fuck?"

"Where did they go, Evans?"

"Where did they go?! Good fucking question!"

"I–"

"WHERE THE FUCK DID THEY GO?"

The boat was more of a yacht really, a sixty-foot vessel of polished wood and chrome with a glossy white gelcoat. We opened the door directly onto the boat's deck, which was a thing of sheer craftsmanship and beauty. On the deck, which gleamed under a bright blue sky and a powerfully warm sun, a large cobalt and white striped towel was laid out, with a stack of cushions at one end, a jug of fresh lemonade and a pile of books sitting neatly at the other.

"Wait a minute," I said, squinting into the sunlight, delighted momentarily despite myself. "While I'm putting all that hard work into piecing together the fragments of my life for your general gratification, you're here, sunbathing?"

He smiled. "Can one get a virtual tan?" He dismissed the idea with a flapping hand. "You like to go over things in some detail, you know. What else should I do while I wait? The sea is my favourite place to be."

"Mine too," I breathed, and closed my eyes, tilting back my

head, letting the smell of what was no doubt artificial salt creep into my nostrils. I could feel waves moving beneath us, a slow and predictable heartbeat. A lonely tern squealed somewhere in the distance. I remained perfectly still and silent, feeling every muscle in my body let go, and eventually, for the first time in so long I could barely remember, I relaxed.

"So I can leave the Gallery whenever I want to?" I said, suddenly thinking that this whole experience would be much more tolerable if that was the case.

"It isn't a prison; it's supposed to be a tool." We lowered ourselves onto the towel, and I kept my face raised to the sun.

"You can leave whenever you like, of course you can. But I wouldn't recommend it too often," he continued, reaching for the jug of lemonade. "It's one thing to rest, another thing to keep running away."

"Are you a construct too? An avatar? Or are you really here with me?"

He chose not to answer, although I hadn't really expected him to. "Fine," I said, and then, after a beat, I added: "Thank you."

"You're welcome," he replied.

I laughed. "So big headed."

He frowned and stopped in the act of pouring. "I don't follow."

"You asked me what I would say to my mother and grandmother if I could see them now. Well, I did see them just now, and I was so preoccupied with how real the memory felt and where the hell you'd gone and all manner of other things, that I didn't say anything at all. But if I had been on form, I'd have said "Thank you".

"Oh." He looked mildly embarrassed. "Well, that's understandable."

I snorted. "Are you always this noncommittal?"

"Comes with the job."

"Aha!" I seized upon the clue. "Part of the job. I knew it!"

I snapped my fingers in victory. He set down the lemonade jug, and gave me a look, a long-suffering parent indulging an insistent child. I forged on nonetheless. I was, after all, the Detective.

"You said you were just trying to help me. It didn't make sense at the time, but then I wasn't really paying attention. You're a therapist, aren't you? Or a psychiatrist. The way you talk, conduct yourself... you've got 'shrink' written all over you."

He looked at me, again, trying to decide how much to tell me. "Of sorts. I suppose you could say that."

"You suppose?"

A realisation that I wasn't about to let it go. "Yes, okay, if it makes things easier."

I breathed my own huge sigh of relief. "Thank fuck for that," I said, and sat back. "I thought you were an angel, or ghost or some shit. I watch too many movies."

"You do," he agreed, and elegantly rearranged his legs underneath him, to better face me.

"In exchange," he said, "I want you to tell me something. I want you to tell me what it feels like when you have your thoughts."

"Thoughts?"

"Thoughts," he repeated, and I got his drift. Suicidal ideation, they called it. Intrusive thoughts.

Dark, rotten, insistent little thoughts that came out of nowhere, with no warning. I tried not to focus on them too much, but it was like trying to ignore an irritating noise once you became aware of it: impossible. They had become a constant, like the twin pulses on my wrists.

(He's better off without me, his Dad can look after him better, I–)

How could he possibly know about those?

I realised I wasn't ready for that yet, not with him. I deflected.

"Is this part of the treatment? The script? Establishing rapport, building a close working relationship?"

"You sound like you've done some homework."

I tried to remember if I had, but couldn't. A magazine cover flashed into my mind and was gone before I could get a decent grip on it. Something intellectual, sciencey. I decided it wasn't worth chasing memories like that, nor was it worth giving him a hard time. He was, after all, still only "trying to help". I relented.

"The thoughts."

"Yes. Can you describe how they feel to me?"

I bit my lip, thinking. "It's not that easy, Doc."

The man balked visibly. "I'd prefer you not to call me that."

"Well, what can I call you?"

"Anything you like... just not that."

"Fine. I'll think of something. And, if I were being truly honest, I should say that I don't *know* what it feels like. When I have those thoughts. It's not really something I actively engage in as a thought process, more of a... compulsion, a knee-jerk series of sentences and ideas that sometimes require me to react, respond. Like machine gun fire, sometimes. I don't seem to be able to control them, not really. Is that helpful? I was never very good at explaining that sort of thing to anyone else, out loud."

"That must be frustrating, for a writer?"

"It is," I agreed, sadly. "But words are tricky. Words and thoughts are essentially the same thing, for me. Both are unreliable. And writing is not really verbalising, is it? Hiding behind a cleverly written sentence. There's written truth, and then there's the truth that comes out of your mouth into the air, the real words you don't plan. The "honest" words. I was never good at those types of words."

"Did you ever–"

I shook my head, pre-empting him. "The diary thing never worked that well for me either. I kept them, but...I wonder how often I lied to myself, even as a kid. And letters... I do write letters, and yes, it's easier, but I'm not writing *you* a letter. Forget that."

He shrugged. He was always so amicable, and calm. "You already did," he said.

"Did what?"

"Write me a letter. Or rather, my employer."

"Oh," I replied. "Is that why I'm here?"

"In part," the man said.

We sat in silence for a bit longer, and then an idea came to me. "All of this..." I indicated the yacht on which we sat, the vast, sun-speckled ocean around us, and the blue door behind us, through which I could still see the Gallery. "This is all in my mind, in your mind? It's something we can manipulate?"

"Not quite. This construct lives in a separate space, on a massive server housed in a basement in one of the university's department buildings in central Bristol. But it's like a corridor I guess, a safe space where we can meet, away from the stresses and strains and unreliability of the real world. This particular part of it belongs to me, is my own private plot of the virtual real estate."

"But I can change things. Like the colour of the door."

"It seems that way," he said, although I got the impression he felt on shaky ground now. He waited for me to continue, a small smile trying to create the falsehood that he knew where I was going with this, which of course he didn't, and he knew that I knew that he didn't, and there was a wary shadow in his eyes that gave all of that away.

I knew him, I knew his facial tics, his expressions. I knew what he was thinking before he did, seemingly.

I fought the urge to reach out and run my finger through his hair, along his nose. Touching was not appropriate, it felt like a violation of both sides of this relationship, thing, whatever it was, but I wanted to. How I wanted to.

I stood up instead. I closed my eyes. I breathed deeply through my nose. I listened to the noises around me, and reached out my hand, indicating that he should stand up beside me. He did so, reluctantly, and I was aroused by his proximity. I hadn't been close to another person for a while, a long while. Not like this. Not with intimacy.

"It's easier to show you than to explain," I murmured.

"Show me what?" my friend said.

"The room behind *my* door," I replied, and suddenly, I could no longer hear the sea.

"This is absurd. Can't you track them?"

"Do you think I'd be this upset if I could?"

Before the Control team, an empty Gallery sits, dust occasionally falling from new cracks in the ceiling that shouldn't be there.

"She's not awake."

"No, she isn't."

"She can't just leave the programme, I can see her hooked up, right in front of us!"

"It's not the programme or the equipment, Boss. I'm ninety-percent sure. They are simply not there anymore. They've somehow gone off grid, or gone sideways to a different space, one not linked to our servers, and I didn't even think that was possible. Fuck! We must have been hacked somehow, that's the only thing that makes sense, Boss."

"Hacked? By who? Who would even care?"

"I don't know!" Evans lets his frustration out. "Saboteurs, students with too much time on their hands, someone looking to steal our shit, who knows?"

"I thought we were like Fort Knox in that respect?"

Evans rests his head in his hands. "Evidently not," he says, through his fingers. Then: "I'm going to get fired for this, aren't I. Fuck, my wife is going to be so fucking vindicated."

The Boss paces the small space beside the desk, thinking.

"She can't be off grid, it's just not possible, it's not how any of this works. I think she's in there somewhere."

"We should cut the cord, Boss. This has never happened

to us before. We need time to figure it out, before we do real damage."

"If we abort now, we could do real damage. Maybe even kill her, worst case scenario. Completely fuck her brain over, best. I say she's in there somewhere."

"What do you mean, somewhere? It's software! A server! Not the fucking multiverse!"

"I stand by my theory." The Boss refuses to elaborate further.

"So what, you're suggesting we just sit here, and wait for her to come back? Hope for the best? Are you nuts? We should at least log it, or call management, surely?"

"So they can close us down? No thank you, this is too important, what we have built here is too important. *She* is too important. I don't see what else we can do, for the moment. I think we just have to wait, and hope that she comes back."

"And hope that she brings our guy back with her, too!"

His Boss pulls out her phone, furiously dialling the Psych's personal mobile number, which she has in her emails. She holds the phone to her ear and lets it ring out, hanging up and dialling again, staring into first one monitor screen, then the next, then the next, in a vain attempt to catch a glimpse of their now invisible virtual patient.

Evans sits back in his swivel chair and stares blankly upwards as he processes the potential implications of what has just taken place.

"Not so fucking marvellous to behold now, is she?" he says, bitterly, but his heart isn't in it.

And then, for the first time, he notices the crack in the ceiling.

13

The Room Behind the Red Door

We were engulfed in a familiar blackness. After the brightness of the sailboat, the darkness was instantly disorienting, although I had been expecting it.

"Where are we?" my friend's voice said, into the dark.

"You asked me to describe how it feels, when I have bad thoughts. I've visualised it instead. This is the Room. My Room."

Slowly, a little light came to us, a thin glowing rectangular outline right in front of our faces that was only just strong enough to see our surroundings by. "Room" was perhaps the wrong word. We were in a tiny cubby hole, with a closed door in front of us, a door that was painted red.

"You visualise it?"

"I have to. In my head, if I can give it an aesthetic, definable dimensions, angles, real physical descriptors... I don't know, I suppose it's a trick I learned somewhere. Sometimes it helps. I wasn't sure I'd be able to recreate it here, though."

"You shouldn't be able to – never mind. This is a cupboard," he replied, and there was an undercurrent of something in his voice that again told me he was not on familiar turf anymore, that he was adapting his behaviour on the fly, rather than sticking to the script. He was uncomfortable, trying to mask it. I could smell his sweat. My ability to manipulate our surroundings was not something he had anticipated, was not part of the regularly scheduled programme.

I couldn't really think about this in any great detail, however. I had bigger *(stick man stick man)* problems. A familiar black dread had begun to crawl along my skin, wriggle into my body, soak in through my pores, squeeze under my fingernails, tunnel into my brain from underneath my eyelids: I was being invaded.

The tattoo on my wrist began to burn.

"This is what it feels like," I said, trembling, and I felt, rather than saw my friend nod in the blackness. He did something he shouldn't have, then.

He reached out and took my clammy hand in his.

His hold was firm, and did not break. He was silent. Then, he said:

"So walk me through it."

"Well." I struggled to not caress the back of his hand with my thumb. "This is the room behind the red door. It's where I find myself when things are really bad, I suppose. In here. Waiting."

"For what?"

"You'll see."

He was silent for a moment. Then: "It's a bit squashed in here, Magpie."

"It's precisely six feet by three feet."

"You don't say." His voice was dry. So were his hands. "And here I was thinking you had a problem with personal space."

"I don't usually have to share the room with anyone else. Contemplating your own mortality is a singular activity, some would say."

"What's that noise? I can hear noise, outside. Is that more music?"

My heart skipped a beat, but he didn't mean the noise I feared. He meant the background hum that seeped in through the room's door, just like usual.

"Oh, that's just the world outside. I like to know it's still there, but I prefer to be separate from it, walled off. Listening, but at..." I searched around for the words. "A reduced capacity.

When it's muted like this, it's more bearable. There is *so* much noise out in the world, haven't you noticed that? Everything is always so fucking noisy, everywhere you go."

"I see. And what is that you do when you are here?"

"I wait," I repeated.

"What do you think about while you wait?"

Words failed me. Surely, it was obvious. I stood with my head bowed, my insides full, and burning. After a while, he squeezed my hand.

"Are you sure you're a real psychiatrist?" I asked. "Are you sure you don't just live inside my head?"

"I can't tell you that," he said.

"Am I really not dead?"

"I can't tell you that, either, I already told you, and I would appreciate it if you could stop asking."

"Why? Why not just tell me? When we first met you seemed happy enough to confirm I was nothing more than a corpse. Why all this cloak and dagger stuff now? It's making it very hard to trust you, if that's your objective."

"It won't help you to know, either way. Answering my question might help you though. If you can. What do you think about, when you find yourself in here?"

I struggled, and eventually, I said:

"Imagine the most profound, desperate sense of loss." As I spoke the words, a rash of gooseflesh swept up and down my arms, despite the warmth of the cupboard. Anticipation, for I knew what was coming.

My friend didn't.

"Okay," he said.

"Then… Imagine a numbness spreading through your body. You can't move, and you can't really think. All you can do is *feel*, and the feelings are terrible."

He waited, and I struggled on, my ears trained on the door. *Any minute now*, I thought. Out loud, I said:

"And time is not a real thing anymore, because the future

doesn't exist. There is a past, and a now, but nothing ahead."

Still, he kept quiet, waiting as I dragged the words out like deep-rooted weeds from gravel. My heart was pounding in my chest so loud my friend must have been able to hear it.

Because it was close. My burning wrist could feel it.

I swallowed. "And… There are no other feelings, like pain, or hunger, or tiredness, because there is only room in this place for one thing: sadness."

"We can stop now, if you want to."

"It feels like… *grief*, you see."

"You are a very brave woman."

"It feels like grief."

And then, it came.

Three simple sounds:

Rap, Rap, Rap!

Against the door.

(Will you stop banging?! You're always so noisy, please stop, please, Mummy can't–)

My friend grew still beside me. "What's that?" he whispered.

I drew in a huge, shaky breath.

Rap, Rap, Rap!

"Magpie?"

I freed my hand from his, covered my ears.

"It's the Silhouette," I said, my wrist now red-hot with pain, as if someone had branded me with a scorching iron, and the door shook another three times.

Because Silhouette always knocked in threes.

"Who?"

Rap, Rap, Rap!

"Magpie? Who is he? Who is the Silhouette?"

"I don't know," I whispered, "But he… he tells me things. Horrible, horrible things."

And I could bear it no longer, being in there, with him, and the pain I'd voiced, and the Silhouette banging on the door like he always did: insistent, relentless. Trying to get in.

I kicked out hard with my left leg.

The red door crashed open, and there was light, a blinding cavalry, here to chase away the death-bringer, and I had a second where I saw him, the Silhouette, his rough, trembling, oversized stick man outline and his oddly arranged arms and legs and his horrifying, featureless, blank face, I saw him, and then he dissolved into the light, and we both tumbled out of the room, and found ourselves back in the Gallery.

"Oh thank God, I nearly had a heart attack!"

"I told you, like Little Bo Peep's sheep, there they are." The Boss is triumphant, even as she is desperately aware that things could have gone very differently indeed. She puts her phone down, all attempts at having contacted the Psych fallen flat. She knows he is ignoring them, but she starts tapping out a furious email to him anyway. The Psych's job is to facilitate communication between the construct, the patient, and Control, without them having to be directly involved. So far, he has failed at this part of his job to a breath-taking degree.

"Unharmed?" she goes onto enquire, feeling silly for asking after the virtual wellbeing of two avatars whilst debating whether or not she should be filling out an incident form as she stabs her fingers at the draft email.

"Seemingly. Christ, I've never felt relief like this in my life before, I tell you. I've aged a hundred years in the last ten minutes."

The older woman shakes her head, chuckling in sympathy. The tension in the room thins out, a little. Both techs swig from plastic cups of filter water, and silence reigns for a while, until Evans breaks it.

"Boss?"

"Yes?"

"Two things."

"Shoot."

"Did you see something, when they came back through? I thought I saw something."

"What sort of something?"

"I don't know, exactly. It looked like a shadow, maybe, only that's not quite right. It was right behind them when they reappeared, only there for a split second but... I'm sure it was something. Moving."

The Boss shakes her head. "I didn't see a thing, Evans. I don't like the fact that *you're* seeing things, though. Stress will do that. This one is getting to you, isn't she?"

"She can literally alter the code of our construct, live, in real time, using only her brain. I think I need a colossal pay rise, Boss."

"So you saw something moving. Perhaps something she came up with. Maybe we should give her a job, instead, hey? Then I wouldn't have to give you a raise." The Boss giggles at her own joke, then sobers, rubs her face. "What's the second thing?"

Evans points to the crack in the ceiling. Silently, the pair of them follow it across and back down to the wall, where it disappears behind one of the whiteboards, which now looks like it is hanging off-kilter. They make note of a brown, sticky substance dribbling out of the crack above their workstations. The Boss shakes her head.

"This is what happens when you try and hide us away in a crappy old Victorian basement like Mulder and Scully. Well, we'll change that, you mark my words, Evans. If we're not in a shiny new office by the end of the year, I'll eat my shirt."

Evans stares at his Boss as if she has gone mad. She doesn't seem phased by any of this, he realises. Her eyes are bright, fixed on the patient in the OR.

He understands that things are about to change, for both of them, for the patient too.

"Piss break," he mutters, needing to leave the room for a while.

* * *

We lay on the floor, a tangled pile of sweating arms and legs, and, despite my fear, despite my pounding heart, despite the Silhouette beating his terrifying tattoo upon my wrist and my soul, I realised how silly we must have looked, like two actors in a grainy, black and white slapstick movie. I began to giggle, then to roar with laughter.

"It's all so absurd, isn't it?" I said, in between great gulps of mirth, and, after he had extricated himself from me, my friend let out a single dry chuckle too. "It is that," he affirmed, and we lay there side by side on the monochrome floor, cracked tiles beneath us like winter fractals on an icy lake.

The laughter subsided quickly, and I grew still, staring up at a vaulted ceiling, wondering if I had the strength to carry on with this sideshow.

"Magpie?" my friend said, also staring up at the ceiling. "Who is Silhouette?"

"Not now," I breathed, feeling a huge wave of tiredness roll over me. "I can't go into it, not now."

"Silhouette? What is he talking about?" Evans catches the conversation as he leaves for his toilet break. He pauses, hand on the Control Room door.

"Something obviously happened to them while they were off screen."

"Does he mean the shadow? I told you there was a shadow."

"I don't know, Evans. Make a note of it when you get back."

"I shouldn't have to. The Psych should be communicating these things to us, but he's not. There's so much we don't understand. Where did they go? What were they doing? How is that even possible? How can she change things the way she does? It shouldn't be conceivable! She does things with her mind that it takes a team of my staff weeks to do. And that's leaving aside the actual, physical impossibility of it all!"

"I have no idea, Evans. Not one single clue."

Frustrated, Evans yanks the door wide, and barrels through, hoping it will slam behind him, remembering too late that it is spring-hinged, and only closes with a soft, anti-climactic *whoosh*, a sound that fills him with impotent ire.

I rolled my head to one side, wondering which of the many plinths I would have to confront next. As I scanned the Gallery, a cloud passed over whichever sun shone outside the too-high windows. It passed, and then a concentrated shaft of light spear-headed down into the corridor, picking out one single alcove. I rolled my eyes. If this was a construct, and if we were still following a script, then whoever was responsible for writing that script had all the narrative subtlety of a bull in a china shop.

Either way, it seemed the best chance I had of getting through this was to go along with it, and do as I was told. For now.

It was also the quickest way to forget about Silhouette, who eventually, I'd found, through years of bitter research, disappeared if you just ignored him. Distraction was a powerful weapon – not only for therapists. Perhaps that was why I was so adept at spotting it as a technique.

"Oh come on, then," I moaned, scrambling to my feet.

I shuffled across to the next alcove.

And came face to face with a notebook.

14

A Notebook

The notebook belonged to my grandfather. It was an old-fashioned, lined, hard-backed exercise book, the sort they used to give to children in schools *(Mummy I don't want to go to school, I'm tired, can I stay home with you today? No darling, Mummy has to work, you know that, we need money, and–)* for their homework and lessons. It had a spine bound in light blue linen and a shiny, navy-blue cover.

The notebook was my single, most prized possession. I was surprised I hadn't spotted it earlier, for this reason, although I had fully expected to see it here. I lifted off the glass dome and took the book back into my own, careful embrace.

"Do you think that just for a little while, you could leave me alone?" I asked my friend, who had been about to lean in over my shoulder and talk to me about the notebook, ask me what the significance of it was. I hugged the object to my chest protectively, shielding it from him, and he looked momentarily hurt, but managed to smooth his features before the expression took hold.

"Whatever you are comfortable with," he said. "Although I should point out that I am not the enemy, I am here to help. Treat this like a thought experiment, if you want. I'm just here to guide you through it all."

I stood my ground. "Please," I said. "I don't want to share this with you, not yet. If you could just leave me alone. For now. Please."

He tilted his head in assent, spun slowly on his heel and wandered off towards the other end of the Gallery, presumably headed back to his boat. I realised I hadn't asked him the name of the boat, and regretted that. Knowing what he called his virtual, ocean-bound waiting room would have given me some insight into his brain, insight I desperately needed. Because I was still unsure as to whether or not he was a figment of my imagination, another version of me, an alter-ego, or a computerised avatar, following me around. What did they call that, in the gaming world- NPC? Non-player character, except that didn't suit him at all. There was clearly a player behind the pixels, if that was indeed what he was made of, instead of carbon, atoms, nitrogen...I wasn't a scientist.

Or maybe, like he said, this was all a simple thought experiment. Maybe he was a guileless parameter, and I was really alone.

Or maybe he was real, and he was real *outside* of this reality, too, and he was, as he had said multiple times now, merely trying to help. It hurt my brain to think about it for too long, so I was relieved when he left, which I knew was contrary, because the last time he had left me I had resented it. But I was growing fonder of him by the hour, and that made me vulnerable, which I didn't like.

He knew I was watching him leave. He did a comedy hop and skip for my benefit as he went, flicking a look at me over his shoulder as he did so.

I smiled after him. He had a nice arse.

He was far too attractive to be a real therapist, I thought.

I looked back down at the notebook, sighing heavily. I was tired, I realised. I sat cross-legged on the floor, then stood up again. It was cold down there, the splintered tiles hard and sharp and unwelcoming. I chewed on my lip, thinking. My head itched a little, not physically, but internally, like it was gearing up for something. Flexing. Reacting automatically to some stimulus I hadn't consciously recognised. I stayed with the sensation for a little while, and then found myself able to identify it. It was anticipation, anticipation associated with change. My brain was preparing to modify something, and I realised I had felt this way before, only I had been so distracted by other things I hadn't paid much attention to it. But earlier, I had been able to transform the colour of the door from red to blue. This feeling had been a precursor to me doing that, a prelude to being able to adapt my surroundings.

Could I do it again? Change my environment?

The door I had recoloured had already been there, had already been put in place by someone else.

Surely that shouldn't make a difference, though? I reasoned, thinking back to the room behind the red door, which I had been able to recreate in entirety, with remarkable accuracy. And what about my grandmother's living room? That had felt like me, too. I had no idea how I had done it, but I had. I had taken a visualisation, a theoretical interpretation of something in my head, and made it real, somehow.

How about you stop overthinking it and just try, I told myself. I concentrated hard, focussing on the itchy, anticipatory sensation in my brain, and all of sudden, easy as one, two three, *(A, B, C, see, Mummy, I can write my name now, can you see? Oh darling, that's wonderf–)*, a beautiful burnished leather Chesterfield materialised in front of me, complete with a plump tapestry cushion propped up invitingly upon the seat, and next to it, a matching chestnut-coloured footstool that offered itself up like a squat, shiny little spaniel waiting to be petted.

I smiled, and the sunlight that streamed in through the high, open windows of the Gallery intensified.

"That's better," I said, and I sat down, sighing in comfort as the chair moulded perfectly to my contours.

Then, I tentatively lifted the front cover of the book.

* * *

The control team sit side by side, their mouths open. The Boss thinks she will never get used to the sight of this woman simply materialising life-like objects in a virtual space whilst not fully conscious. She drags her eyes away from the screens to the patient in the OR, who is now back in a seated position amongst her wires, feet up before her as if resting on a footstool, her ankles supported in their foam loops, the cable tension automatically adjusting to compensate for the changes in her posture. She holds her arms up again, interacting with an invisible notebook. A small smile on her face betrays a certain awareness of what her virtual self is doing, but otherwise she is inert, insensate.

"So let's get this straight, shall we?" Evans eventually says, dry-swallowing nervously as he tries to make sense of what is happening. Something drips and splats on to the table by his mouse hand, and he absentmindedly wipes it away without looking at it.

"Not only can she manipulate the existing environmental parameters of our construct with a frightening ease, not only can she edit our code in real-time – which, by the way, should be impossible, because nothing we do is open-source, everything is encrypted, and our code editor is not set up for collaborative input – oh, and also, SHE'S IN A SEMI-COMA, not only can she disappear off the fucking grid altogether, despite being in a virtual environment that I and a team of talented professionals fucking designed that has no "off grid", not only can she do all this, but now… now she can add new details to our existing construct using a programming language I've never seen before in my whole, entire life as a technician and programmer. Using only, somehow, her brain. The power of thought. Like she's a fucking…wizard, or something." He gulps for breath, a large bead of sweat dripping from the tip of his nose as he gets more and more worked up.

His Boss says nothing, for she is thinking hard, her own brain racing to try and catch up with the constantly changing state of play that this patient has brought about.

"I mean, look at this." Evans brings up a rolling display in one of his monitors, and a string of strange symbols and glyphs march down the screen. "It's like that fucking movie, the Matrix, in here. I don't recognise any of this, it's a totally alien language to me. It's not written following any of the usual protocols or in any actual semantic that makes sense. Yet it's clearly code, right? And the worst thing is, I don't even think she knows that she is doing it, at least, not completely. I mean it's obviously intentional, but... she's learning as she goes, intuitively, without any need to practice, or really understand what she's creating. It's just pouring out of her like... like..." He throws up his hands, unable to articulate himself. "I'm so out of my depth right now it's absurd, Boss. She is changing things, controlling this construct in a way that is totally beyond her remit as a patient. We are supposed to guide this, right? We are supposed to be the experts! She is supposed to be the patient. They don't call us Control for nothing, you know what I'm saying?"

"But she isn't a patient, anymore, don't you see that, Evans?" The older woman murmurs.

"What? What are you talking about?"

"She is, as you say, taking control. She is... evolving, for want of a better word."

"But, A, that's fucking *insane*, and B, if it weren't... we can't sanction that, can we?"

"What else is therapy for, Evans? Move away from the technical side of things, just for a moment. This isn't just a computer programme, is it? It's not a game. It's therapy. And the purpose of therapy is growth. Emotional growth, and the absolution of severe emotional disturbances."

"I'm becoming severely fucking emotionally disturbed Boss, never mind her!"

"She is simply taking the tools we have put at her disposal, and using them. She is becoming more. She is becoming an architect, in her own right."

"I don't like it. I don't understand it. And I think we are

leaving ourselves open to massive risk. I think we should call someone in. I think we should stop before she buggers up almost fifteen years' worth of your hard work!"

"What if we see this as an opportunity, instead of a threat?" The Boss's eyes are wide with excitement. "Think of what we could learn from her. Think of what we could do with her abilities, if she was on our side, Evans. Think of the possibilities! She is connected to this fake reality in a way I never even imagined possible. Something about her brain is special. She is really, truly using our work as it has always intended to be used – as a tool, as an exploratory device to help her investigate her own consciousness. This is..." She wipes away an errant tear that escapes from the inner corner of her left eye while her colleague looks on, astonished.

"This is the most remarkable thing I've ever seen."

"I think we should call someone." Evans's hand hovers over his desk phone anxiously.

The Boss's gaze sharpens, as does her voice. "If you touch that phone again, Evans, I will not only fire you on the spot, but eviscerate you thoroughly with this pen. I mean it. I am not about to interrupt the biggest moment of my career, or risk the progress she's made, not until I've seen more of what she can do. Now sit down, and shut up, for goodness sake. You should be taking notes. What we're seeing here..." The grey-haired woman's face is radiant in the harsh light of a dozen monitors.

"Well. It's unprecedented, isn't it?"

Evans silently picks up his notepad, but the corners of his mouth droop sourly as he does so.

Inside the notebook, a small, precious collection of poems lay scrawled in my grandfather's slanted hand across the pages. There were not many: five pages at the most. The pages were only marked on one side, the paper being so thin that the ink showed through on the reverse. It gave the notebook an air of fragility that only added to the preciousness of it.

The poems were about nature, flowers, the sea, the country, animals, love, old age, and sex. There were a few rough doodles and sketches, too, of plants, an ammonite, a bird's head, and a strange jerkily scrawled stick figure, the outline of which had been drawn over several times so that the edges were fuzzy and thatched. I stared at that sketch for a while. It looked a lot like Silhouette, and I didn't like that. I also didn't remember it being there before.

As I thought this, the sketch faded from the page. I nodded in satisfaction.

Stay away, Silhouette, I thought. *There is only good here.*

The last entry was a passage taken from a book written by a man called Miguel de Unamuno, a book called *The Tragic Sense of Life*, and God only knows where my grandfather came across it. I was not aware that this sort of writing had ever been his thing. He spent most of his life covered in oil, grease and metal shavings, and the only thing I ever saw him read religiously was the weekly television guide, which he pored over, bright pink highlighter in hand with which to circle things of interest.

The entry was titled *"Love, Suffering, Pity"*, and was about life, and orgasm, and renewing ourselves in others. It was about resurrection, in perpetuity. It was romantic, and I'd been wholly unprepared to discover that side of him. My grandfather was not a man of words. Or at least, so I'd thought.

And yet here was evidence to the contrary. Like me, he had collected words too, stashed them away for later. This was significant: he was careful and selective about what he said, and to whom. Reading and writing did not come easily to him. He had grown up poor, rural, dropped out of school at a young age. He made his way through the world with his hands, by making things, from wood, from metal, from stone, from anything he could bend to his will. He built houses, welded steel, turned, planed, sanded, dug, hammered, screwed, nailed, sawed, glued, screwed, joined and split. He never professed any affection for, or great interest in, poetry, literature. He left the reading to me.

I thought about this as I flipped through the notebook, and a warm sensation of love and nostalgia grew steadily in my heart. It came with a fresh appreciation of my grandfather as a man in his own right. Because as a child you never see your parents for who they really are. You see the family-friendly versions of your forebears, the versions that take you for walks along the beach, climb trees, watch films, collect pebbles, make things together. You see them for the picnics, the silly games, the swimming lessons, the forbidden ice-cream treats. You see the frustrations and the punishments and the exasperation when you misbehave. You see how they hold your hand when you are sad, and how they defend you when you are being treated unfairly, how they laugh when you laugh, how they check to see if you are enjoying something they like as much as they enjoy it. You never think about the things they loved *before* you came along, the values and desires and hopes they had before you were ever born. He was my grandfather, and I was confident in what I knew about him, confident that I knew what or who exactly I was grieving when he betrayed me by dying. A practical man, a man of actions and not words.

But I hadn't been able to see the entire picture, the picture that lay here, within these hard covers. When he died, and I found this notebook, and I opened it, wondering what would be inside, I was startled by the sentimentality. "*Where the bee sucks, there suck I*", I read, wondering who this man was, and how to reconcile it with the oil-stained fingers, the overalls, the flat-caps, the faded peacock tattoo on his forearm, a stamp from his army days.

And to me, a young woman grieving for a man who had left her fatherless for the third time, finding the notebook was a revelatory thing. We had always been kindred spirits, troublemakers, partners in crime, he and I, and here he was, still speaking to me, even after his death, in a language I understood and cherished.

I stood up, clutching the notebook. "I'm not quite sure what to do with this," I said, to no-one in particular.

Like a cat at feeding time, my friend reappeared in my peripheral vision, and sauntered over.

"That one can go back, I think," he said as he reached me, and he lifted up the notebook's glass dome in readiness.

I placed the book back inside the case, relieved.

Destroying it wasn't in my power.

It sat there for a moment, as if contemplating something, then gently dissolved out of view, being replaced by the spinning, check-marked coin I had grown used to so quickly. Whatever purpose it had been intended to serve, the notebook had clearly fulfilled, and I had another useless shiny trophy to show for it. I put this coin in my pocket, but had a feeling it wouldn't remain in there.

I would have rather had the notebook.

15

A Little Bag of Powder

"When was the last time we checked her vitals? Properly checked them, I mean."

"A while. Although she seemed okay when I went in earlier." Evans is sulking. He always sulks when he is overwhelmed.

The Boss, on the other hand, is beginning to hit her stride.

"It has to be time for a nurse check, surely. Long overdue, in fact. She needs moving, her circulation stimulated, her med tubes could use some scrutiny, too. Don't want to risk any infection. Can you do the honours?"

Evans does so, a queer, almost mutinous expression upon his face. He does not like the adoration with which his superior has started to talk about the patient behind the glass, as if she is a great discovery, or a religious coming – especially as the Boss has always, always preached the importance of impartiality in their work. He keeps his mouth shut, however, while his confidence in his own role wavers. The woman behind the glass represents something that Evans has never liked that much: change. And not that it is an immediate priority for him right now, but there have been too many jokes for him to ignore. The patient – once she comes out the other side of her treatment – potentially threatens his own position within the department, which thus far has been unchallenged. His relationship with his Boss has always been healthy, Evans is loyal if somewhat bad-tempered about it, but he doubts whether that loyalty is a two-way street. And the Boss is right: what need would there be for a technician such as him, or any of his team for that matter, if a person could somehow generate code, build entire worlds, subconsciously? She could write a whole new programme in a day, just by strapping herself into the harness. This terrifies Evans, for multiple reasons.

He presses the button anyway, because this is his job.

After two minutes, a different nurse in green scrubs, male this time, enters the room where the patient sleeps and begins fiddling with the equipment, checking the patient's pulse, checking her breathing, administering more eye-drops. He lifts the woman's limbs in their soft stirrups, working them gently one by one, rotating ankle and knee joints in small circles to stimulate circulation. He swabs under the patient's armpits and buttocks with a hot, clean cloth, replacing the paper pyjamas with another set and rearranging the patient's body so that strap sores do not develop.

Briefly, Evans catches a glimpse of a small tattoo on the patient's wrist, a tattoo in the shape of a stick man, crudely drawn, the lines wobbly around the edges. Evans tries to remember if he knew that tattoo was there before, and can't recall.

The routine continues, and a cannula taped to the back of the patient's hand gets careful scrutiny. The nurse frowns as he checks it. Then, he waves at Control. Evans enables two-way comms.

"I'll need to change this," the nurse says, looking almost directly at the techs even though the mirrored glass obscures them. "There seems to be something stuck in here. I don't want to risk infection."

"Proceed." The Boss grants permission and the nurse slowly untapes the cannula, wincing in concentration, and pulls it out of the patient's hand. Blood spatters. The nurse tuts, deftly pressing a wad of cotton wool across the patient's hand and taping it down before examining the equipment more closely.

"That's funny," he murmurs, holding it up to the light. "Whatever is in here… it's, huh. It's liquid, but dark brown, kind of viscous looking. Like tar, almost."

The Boss frowns, concern heavy on her face. "How did it get in there? Everything we use is supposed to be sterile."

"It is, and I have no clue," the nurse replies. "None of us would have put it in her like this, so it must have happened after she was hooked up. A secretion of some sort? Maybe someone tampered with it."

"Impossible," Evans says, feeling that if he says this word enough times it will lose all meaning. "We've been watching her every second. No one has been in that room apart from you and the other nurse. Well, and me, but *I* certainly didn't tamper with anything."

At this, the Boss looks at him, and Evans shrugs innocently.

"What?" he says, resenting the silent implications of her stare.

The nurse bags the faulty cannula and tucks the bag under his arm. "Well, this stuff is unlikely to have come out of the patient, unless her blood is made of crude oil. God knows what it is, but it's a good job I checked. We'll do another blood test, check that nothing nefarious is working its way around her system as we speak." He quickly draws a syringe full of blood, frowns as he taps it with his fingernail. "Seems okay, but I'll make a note of the… discrepancy in her records, get her samples sent off for testing. In the meantime, keep a close eye on her vitals and I'll be back for another check-up in half an hour." The nurse gives the mirror a disapproving look, then busies himself preparing a new cannula.

The techs behind the mirror lean forward, peering at the patient for any signs of disturbance. They are concerned about her for two wholly different reasons.

The patient hangs serenely, her breathing undisturbed.

"I wish we *could* hear her thoughts," the Boss says, fingering her lip absent-mindedly as she watches the woman sleep. On the monitors surrounding Control, the virtual version of the woman has moved along the Gallery to the next alcove. Sitting inside the glass dome that waits for her is a small clear plastic bag, at the bottom of which, a thin measure of white powder sits.

"I don't," Evans says, darkly.

Another alcove. Another pedestal, another glass case.

I knew what the purpose of all this was. I knew a little about anthropomorphism. I understood, within the context of my conversation on the boat, that the objects placed here were supposed to be emotional touchstones, psychological focal points upon which I could hang ascribed feelings as I sorted through the confusing tangle of memories in my exhausted mind, looking for the thing, the trigger, the *event*. I was, as my new friend has said, simply following the clues, trying to solve the mystery of my own end, but while that was still true, and while I knew this to be the case, I nevertheless found myself getting restless. I *knew* the story behind each object, even if it was taking some work to bring each memory back. The problem was, this knowledge interfered with my ability to enjoy the process. It was part of the reason I struggled with things like meditation. Being aware of myself trying to relax, like trying to switch my brain off when falling asleep, only made me feel *less* relaxed, more awake. Contrary, maybe? Or simply the makeup of my brain. Or both, it didn't matter.

What mattered was that I knew this Gallery scenario was part of a script, and I was beginning to find the script too restrictive.

"Can we change this up at all?" I asked out loud, staring at the item in the glass dome. Even though I knew the little bag filled with powder that sat there wasn't "real" in the traditional sense, I violently itched for it.

"How?" my new friend said, and I could hear caution in his voice.

I thought carefully, trying to phrase what I wanted to say in the right way.

"So this… construct. Thought experiment. Therapy setting, whatever. I understand what it's for, and I get it. Sort through a series of 'significant' personal objects, try and think about important moments in my life, try and figure out what it is that is eating me up and making me behave in certain ways out there in the real world. Try and solve the mystery… wait." My words trailed off.

From somewhere in the distance, I heard a child crying. It made the flesh on my arms prickle.

"What is it, Magpie?"

"Did you… do you hear that?"

"No, I don't hear anything. What do you think you heard?"

I stood stock still, waiting for the sound to come again, but it *(Mummy, I love you. I'm sorry I made such a big mess I'M SO FUCKING TIRED OF PICKING UP AFTER YOU, I feel like a drudge, do you know that? People used to respect me, they–)* didn't.

I shook my head, rattled. "Never mind," I said. Then, in a stronger voice: "This setting is a series of life points I can anchor to, a device to help me remember and discover things about myself, right?"

My friend waited for me to continue. I was glad. Confirmations were rare from him, which was a nice trait, one I realised I appreciated. He preferred to let me reach conclusions on my own, without influence. I'd found it annoying to begin with, but was now starting to think, begrudgingly, that he was actually quite good at his job, whatever that was.

"So I get that," I continued, bringing myself back on track with a quick mental shake. "And I can understand how it might work… for someone else. But it's like… I don't know. As a writer, I don't plan any of my stories. Not in any detail. Because if I do, and I know exactly what's going to happen *before* I've written it, I struggle. I suddenly can't write anymore."

"Are you struggling now?"

I pulled a face. "Yes. Yes, I think I am."

"Struggling with... your own future?"

I spread my hands out, apologetic. "No, it's not that. I know, I'm being a brat. But... I just... I wonder if we can get a little creative. Stick to the script, mostly, but... improvise, every now and then. Just a little. Make it more interesting for me, you know? The Gallery... what can I say? I'm getting bored, is all."

He looked at me, his face inscrutable as ever, and I smiled, and tried to make it a persuasive one.

"Honestly, what more does she want?" Evans shakes his head at the screen, his mouth a disapproving, thin line.

"That's certainly a first." The Boss smiles indulgently, as if talking about a favourite child. The change in her demeanour, from perturbed and slightly standoffish to parental and rather starry-eyed continues to irk Evans, even though he knows he should be above such things.

"Anyway, it's out of the question," he continues. "A bad, bad idea."

"But what if...?" The Boss says, quietly.

"You can't be serious. Think of how dangerous it could be!"

The older woman rubs her hands together, working through something. "I *am* thinking. I am thinking long and hard. What if she is right? Our approach is restrictive, by nature. It was bound to come up against resistance at some point, especially with the small number of patients we've had thus far. I think she is old enough to decide where she wants her own therapy to take her, on reflection."

Evans blinks. "I thought that was against everything we always purported to be," he continues, stubbornly. "Guided therapy. Controlled environments. Structure versus spontaneity. Not to mention the fact we can measure everything, report on it. Provide demonstrable evidence that our approach works."

"Perhaps it is time we considered a more client focused approach too? Something more... free-form."

Incredulous, Evans wonders if his Boss is drunk.

"Is that really our call to make? Doesn't this all have to be approved by Upstairs?"

"Let's ask the Psych what he thinks."

"The Psych is sitting comfortably somewhere miles away from here on the other side of the city, Boss! He isn't sat here sweating dead centre in the middle of it all, is he? Think about it, there is almost no risk to him. I imagine that's why he is ignoring us."

"No physical, bodily risk, perhaps, but then the same applies to us, Evans. All of this..." The older woman waves at the equipment, at the patient who hangs from her electrical vines. "This is just wires, engineering. We control it. This is our realm, and there is no threat here, you can see that. Everything else, well. It's all in her head. Or in the programme. Or both. I haven't figured out where the lines are exactly, just yet." She chuckles, aware of how crazy that last statement sounds. "Either way, it's not *real*. It can't manifest physically out here, whatever it is that you're afraid of."

"I'm afraid that she'll damage herself. More than she already has."

The Boss gives him an odd look, and he feels shocked to realise it is one that borders on dislike.

"Do you know," she says, coldly, "back in the old days, they would have diagnosed her with 'hysteria', most likely. Doctors, the overwhelming majority of whom were male at the time I might add, often prescribed something called a "rest cure" by way of treatment. This cure involved removing the woman from all physical and intellectual stimulation, cutting her off from friends and family, and forcing her to rest, alone, in bed for months and months on end. Effectively imprisoning her inside her own body in the hope that her brain would mend itself. I've never thought about it before, but seeing her, how

she can change things as soon as the restraints are taken off...
I wonder. We think ourselves so progressive. Are we really any
better than those Doctors of old?"

Evans holds his ground. "I know this is important to you, I
can see that, and I know you want to test her potential, but I
just think it's a bad idea! We're techs, Boss. We're not Psychs,
we're not Professors. We're not even middle management.
We're Tech. And besides. She'll go off-grid again, you know
she will."

"All I am proposing is that we let her tap into the power of
her own imagination, her own psyche. She isn't a god. She
can't create new, physical entities out of thin air. The worst
that can happen is that she takes her therapy too far, imagines
a scenario that isn't perhaps the most helpful, and gets too
heavily invested in it."

"Or she short-circuits, somehow. Becomes emotionally
traumatised. More than she already is, I mean."

"But this is what we pay the Psych for. He should be able to
guide her through safely enough."

Evans realises she has made up her mind. He tries to appeal
to her common sense one last time.

"It's irresponsible, Boss. We have no idea where this might
lead. I just want you to know I'm not comfortable with this,
and I'm glad we record the shit out of everything, because my
opinion is now officially on file."

The Boss nods to show that the message has been received,
then starts tapping out a series of directives to the Psych.

"He won't answer, you know."

"He will if I send him the same message, in capitals, fifty
times over," the Boss replies, smiling wolfishly. "I will not be
ignored."

On screen, the Psych winces and touches his ear as the first
of the barrage of messages hits his inbox. It is the first visible
sign Control have seen that he is absent-mindedly listening,
and they both take it as a small triumph.

Unobserved while all this is unfolding, a tiny dark blip pops up in the corner of the small blue glowing window on one of the room's printers. The LED display there flickers for a moment, then seems to bulge outwards, as if the plastic screen is blistering under a great heat, or as if something is pushing up from underneath the display. Suddenly, a thick glob of a sticky brown tar-like substance wells up out of the screen, slopping down the smooth sides of the printer and flopping to the floor with a gentle SPLAT. The globule sits for a moment, flattened by the impact of its fall. Then, it starts to recoup. It swells, and gathers itself into a small, gelatinous ball, which rolls carefully and slowly across the floor, disappearing underneath Evan's desk.

My friend touched his ear, wincing as if an insect had crawled into his ear canal, and it reminded me so strongly of the time he pressed the button on his thumb pad that I suddenly realised what he was doing. He was wired up, via a series of transmitters or sensors or microphones or God knew what, plugged in and communicating with someone outside of the construct. Not physically, of course, nothing in this environment was physical in the true sense, but the virtual equivalent of a communication system that enabled him to listen or speak with whomever it was.

Fourth layer, I thought.

I considered this. I considered how he needed an actual comms device to enable conversation with whomever he was reporting in to. Or was someone reporting into him? Point was, he *needed* an earpiece or whatever it was to facilitate a connection.

But I didn't, I realised.

I smiled. *Knowledge really is power,* I thought, feeling a surge of energy race through me.

"Ask them," I said out loud, remembering the voices I'd heard before. Whatever it was that we were doing here was being monitored, I was sure of it. The script, the environment, the performance of my new friend. They were watching everything, keeping an eye, taking notes, and this made me feel... well, actually I wasn't entirely sure how it made me feel. More in control, perhaps. Perversely. I was beginning to comprehend more and more about my situation, and with that comprehension, a feeling of certainty grew.

Knowledge is power.

Running with the feeling, I decided to experiment. I concentrated and an old-fashioned cordless microphone appeared in my hand. I tapped the bronze cap, and feedback echoed around the Gallery. My friend winced, clapping his hand more obviously to his ear. His tech was clearly not compatible with mine.

"Hello?" I spoke into the microphone, in a low, enquiring voice. "Is this thing on?"

"That hardly seems necessary," my friend replied, a strained expression on his face. "They can hear you without that."

"They can hear what I'm saying out *loud*, sure," I replied, enjoying this little diversion from all the seriousness. "But can they hear what I am *thinking?*"

The microphone vanished, and in its place, a small white pill materialised. I examined it, and up close I could see it was stamped with a tiny symbol – that of a microphone.

I swallowed it, felt it go down, tasted something briefly, a metallic, almost cinnamon flavour.

I waited a moment or two, and then felt something, somewhere, *connect.*

Hello, I thought then. I felt the word resonate. My feelings of being in control intensified.

And I knew the message would be heard loud, and clear.

In the Control Room, the techs gawp as a dialogue window pops up in the right hand corner of every single screen. A printer- not the one now dripping with brownish goo- bursts into life, spitting out a sheet of paper with one word printed in bold, red capitals:

HELLO.

And then another, and another, until it is snowing words.

The same greeting appears in multiple dialogue boxes that start tiling random monitors in complex patterns. It also chugs out of the built-in printer on the health monitor, the thin red heart rate lines converging to make the letters instead of their usual mountains and valleys.

Vital signs, Evans thinks, aware that he is feeling a little strange. He sinks his head into his hands.

"You said you wanted to hear what she was thinking," he groaned, voice muffled by his fingers.

"I did," his Boss whispers, collecting a sheet of paper spilling from the printer and holding it out in front of her like it was a new-born child, and Evans can hear nothing but awe in her voice. Her phone buzzes in her pocket, a text, an IM, whatever – she knows what it'll say.

"You haven't thought this through properly, have you?" Evans retorts, bracing himself for what he knows will follow.

"What do you mean?"

"That was just one, singular thought, right?"

The Boss looks at him, trying to catch up.

"Right."

"Since when do you only ever have one, singular thought at a time? And have you considered…that mentally, she isn't, well…" he trails off, not needing to finish the sentence.

The Boss stares at him, trying to connect the dots, but before she can do so, the Control Room erupts.

The patient's brain unloads.

In the OR, the hanging woman smiles wide.

"What did you just do?" my new friend asked curiously.

I shrugged. "I gave them what they wanted," I replied. "The

people sitting behind all this, I mean. There's two of them, am I right?" He opened his mouth but I pre-empted his reply. "It's okay, you don't have to answer, I know there are. And I don't know which one it was, but I heard them talking. They said they wanted to know what I was thinking, so I obliged."

"But... how?"

I shook my head. "If I knew how to explain it, I would. But I feel... comfortable here, now. Like... like I'm learning my way around the place."

My friend nodded. "You feel better when you can control things, don't you?"

I nodded back. "I do. Is that surprising?"

"Not really. Control, or the illusion of it, can be important. To a degree. Although it's also important to recognise there are lots of things in life that we cannot control, ultimately. Still. If you think this is useful, let's go with it. I have to admit, this is..." He blew out his cheeks in one of those rare displays of emotion. "This is new ground for me."

Finally, I thought. In exchange for his long-waited for honesty, I offered an olive branch.

"So..." I said, thinking out loud. "How about this. How about you let me have a little more... control over this construct, but I do it with an eye to what you've already designed. Prescribed. For want of a better word."

"Elaborate," he said.

I looked at the bag of powder in the glass dome. "We can still use these objects. I don't take too much issue with that, although the choice of artefacts is... egh. But I assume it's because you went through my diaries and socials and shit, highlighted things you thought were significant."

"You assume correctly."

"But I didn't record *everything* in my diary, see. I didn't photograph everything significant. I kept secrets, even from myself." Saying this made me ache, although I could not have said why.

"This does not surprise me. Would you rather–"

I interrupted, trying to maintain my sense of control at all costs. "It's fine. We can use the objects here. I'm not touching that one, for reasons." I pointed at the offending bag of powder. Virtual or otherwise, I didn't trust myself with it. "But I want to do it my own way."

He folded his arms, keeping his face expressionless. "Show me," he said.

So I did. I used my hands, because I didn't know how else yet to do it, and I began to…

Weave.

"Glorious," The Boss breathes as the Control Room – and Evans – continues to meltdown around her. Things onscreen, behind the million frenzied notifications of half-formed thoughts and feelings, begin to change. In the OR, the patient starts to weave her hands in front of her visor as if she is dancing, or practising tai-chi. In the construct, the Gallery morphs, tiny details dissolving into new imagery. The ceiling space lowers, dims. The windows sprout curtains. A carpet grows upon the floor like grass filmed via time-lapse. Sometimes little square patches of white pepper the scene like snowflakes: stuck pixels. The patient fixes those quickly, like a painter fixing a smudge upon the canvas as she works.

"She's an artist." The Boss cannot believe she'll ever tire of watching this.

Evans, who is now in hell, watches helplessly as alien code, random words and half-finished sentences (ARE YOU THERE ARE YOU HAPPY NOW HOW DOES IT FEEL LOOKING INTO THE MIND OF A TRULY AWFUL PIECE OF HOPELESS–) flashing images, sound clips and other unidentifiable things flood his workspace. He watches the reliable, familiar shapes of the Gallery, which he designed, he and his team, designed, conceptualised, slaved over for months, he watches it change, and transform.

He rests his chin heavily on his fist, feeling hugely depressed.

Another splash of brown gunk lands, unseen, upon the desktop. It dribbles across some paperwork, finds a desk grommet covering a cable hole, and uses the cables to shimmy down to the ground, where it joins the larger quivering mass hiding not far from Evan's tired, rather swollen feet.

"Is there a word for this?" I asked as I spun a new reality around us. Spinning was the best way I could describe it, really, spinning, or weaving a tapestry. Or hand-painting, perhaps. Shaping something new. I didn't have to use my hands, I knew, but for now it helped me to focus. Like magicians in novels. Like my friend, with his thumb pad and his ear-mic.

"A word for what?" my friend said, in a small, preoccupied voice. He stared at the Gallery as it began to change, and I could see tiny beads of sweat on his upper lip again.

"Taking things from your imagination, and making them… appear, like this. There must be a word."

"Manifestation," my friend replied, without hesitation. "Creative visualisation underpinned by innate self-belief."

"Oh," I said, simply, and a table materialised in front of me. It was covered in an old cloth, tie-dyed and stamped with elephants and the yin and yang symbol. On top of the table, a large set of decks appeared, and on the floor next to the table, an assortment of huge speakers.

My friend looked at them, and said:

"I'm only endorsing this because I think a little confidence goes a long way, especially if you want to think about the future."

"And I appreciate it, I do," I said, pondering how powerful a thing it was that we could work together on this, that there was a commitment to solving this whole riddle side by side. It was like climbing up a mountain, hooked to a line with a trekking partner. I liked that idea. It felt good to not be alone as I climbed.

"Now," I continued, and a bright, honest smile broke out on my face. "I'd cover my ears, if I were you. This is about to get..."

"Noisy?" he said, eyeing the deck and speakers again. There was a hint of an answering smile on his own lips.

"Fuck yeah," I said, and the speakers burst into life.

The team behind the mirror rip off their headsets as drum and bass music crashes violently into their ears and fills every corner *(FUCK YEAH FUCKKK)* of the Control Room.

"I can't... I can't turn it down!" Evans says, jabbing away at different control keys feverishly.

His Boss doesn't answer. She simply helps herself to more water with trembling hands and a racing heart, and settles in to watch the show.

Instead of the Gallery, we now stood in a dark, crowded, high-ceilinged room in a Victorian townhouse that had once belonged to a friend of mine. Around us, a throng of people danced, laughed, hugged, drank, and snorted coke off of the back of each other's hands or from small mug-coasters balanced precariously on their knees. I could faintly hear a couple shagging loudly in the toilet in the hallway, moaning and giggling in alternating bouts of pleasure. The front door of the house (*Look Mummy, I painted us! That's me and Daddy in the house, and you're outside. It's cold outside*), I could see from where I stood, was open a little, to signal its welcome-all status. Through it I could see the moon partially shining from behind a cloud. The tinkle of laughing gas canisters hitting the pavement outside like little shiny joy-bullets also came to me beneath the music, which meant I had not gotten the sound levels completely right, because in real life, nothing else could have made its way through the jaw-breaking *womp womp* of the speakers.

Practice makes perfect, I thought, still proud of my work. The house was warm, smelly, a sweat box, and full of sound, full of fun, full of life.

All in all, it was a hell of a party.

"Is this a memory, or a fantasy?" My friend moved closer and shouted, struggling to be heard above the thumping beats. I liked having him near to me, and spent a long moment staring at his mouth before dragging my eyes away and back to the room.

"A memory," I said, but already I could see issues with recreating scenarios from memory, because my memory was patchy, and that was putting it politely. For example, we *were* at a party, a party I had actually been to a long time ago, and I could remember the house, and the layout, and the accessories and some of the little details like the stacks of booze, like the decks, like some of the people, but... large parts of this particular night had also dissolved into obscurity for me. There were certain clues that gave this away: paintings on the wall that were smudgy and devoid of form and detail, because I could remember that there was art, but not what that art *was*, exactly. Labels on alcohol bottles where the words were nonsense because my brain had forgotten the actual contents of the bottle. Parts of the room that lacked any detail whatsoever, where a skirting board ended in a large, indistinct splotch, where a door merged into the background because I couldn't recall which way it had opened, inwards, or outwards, and my brain had compensated by making it dissolve conveniently into a wall instead, creating an effect like that of something melting. Lamps jumped around, their exact positions long lost, and other items of furniture zipped in and out of view, or changed dimension and form before us. Once, a double fridge-freezer flickered to life against a far wall, covered in fridge-magnets, but was gone again a moment later. The carpet changed colour and texture like an octopus shifting into different camouflage shades, and the worst, most unsettling things were the faces of the people dancing all around us, some of which were close friends, and thus well remembered, and some of whom I had no lasting memory, and thus were curiously devoid of features, blank, and smudgy, like the face of my husband in my earlier memory, like the face of the Silhouette.

Don't think about him! I warned myself. Thinking about him only invited him in.

My friend shivered as he saw the smeared people dancing, and I rushed to reassure him. "It's okay," I said, slipping a hand through his arm. He was warm, and I could smell sweat. "I know they look a bit like him, but… Silhouette isn't here. This is a good memory. A really good one."

He relaxed only a little.

I looked down at myself. My clothes had changed to a tight top, a pair of baggy jeans, and a worn-out pair of converses. I shivered. Despite the crowded space, a cool breeze suddenly cut into the room from the open front door, which was often the way with these parties, the door would open and people drawn in from the streets like moths to a naked bulb would flutter in and out as they pleased. If you weren't careful, your coat and handbag or purse would disappear back through that front door and out into the night, carried away by an enterprising chancer who had sampled the party for just long enough to harvest its unguarded goods.

My friend spotted something, nudged me. "Look," he said, pointing to a low, shifting couch crowded with too many bodies. "That's you, isn't it?"

I looked at the younger version of me sitting on the couch. She had fuller cheeks, short hair and eager hands, which opened to take delivery of a small bag of something white: MDMA, Mum and Dad, Molly, etcetera, etcetera. I saw my hands shake a little with uncertainty: up until this point in my life, I'd never taken hard drugs before.

"Are you going to snort that?" my friend asked me, his mouth turned down in a curve of disapproval as I nodded.

"I just followed what everyone else did, to be honest," I replied. "Sometimes we would wrap it up in a Rizla, bomb it down."

My friend shuddered briefly. "No thanks," he said.

I shrugged, feeling defensive. "I was young," I replied. "And looking for escape."

The young version of me juddered and shifted noticeably, her face changing to become my face, and then slipping back to the younger version of me again as I struggled to hold onto the mental image of what I had actually looked like back then. Fewer lines, thicker hair, the mole growing under my eye smaller, less pronounced. I was slimmer but a different shape, this was pre-motherhood me (*I'm so fucking sick of feeling like my body isn't my own! Of watching it change all the fucking time, of having to learn to fall in love with it again! It's alright for you, you have none of this to deal with, none of the blood or bloating or scars or pain or–*), before my proportions had softened.

I watched as she bent her head, inexpertly snorted a small amount of the drug from the back of a pocket mirror with a tightly rolled up five pound note.

"Please take care of me," she then whispered to the complete stranger sitting beside her, a stranger who would later become a friend. I smiled indulgently, knowing what would come next: "the hairy half hour". I would feel cold, I would feel my stomach sinking, I would feel my vision turning in on itself, my breathing get shallow, my heart thump in time with the music. Standing there watching myself go through this for the first time made my skin crawl, for some reason. Half of me wanted to rip the bag out of her hands and throw it down my gullet. The other half wanted to slap it away from her and throw it in the bin.

"Why are we here?" my friend said, and I could tell I had finally pierced the armour of his profession with this scenario: he was not in any way tolerant of drugs, which reminded me of someone, but I couldn't recall who, exactly, and I filed away that information for later, a little relieved that he had finally begun to display something approaching a genuine emotional response.

"There is a good reason," I said. "And it's not as if I chose the object anyway, you did. I did warn you."

"I choose it as a discussion point, yes. I am not entirely sure reliving your own intoxication in quite such minute detail is a particularly constructive use of our time."

"Relax," I said, squeezing his arm tight. "I feel okay. I know what I am doing."

He shook his head minutely, but said nothing.

The hairy half hour passed, and then the words began to flow. Younger me woke up, started to talk to the people around her, slowly at first, and then with an unstoppable torrent of words that came out at high velocity, landing in the ears of strangers who quickly became the very best of lifelong friends, and I saw her chew on the tender flesh of the inside of her mouth and then stand up, joining the people who danced to the music, throwing her arms around in time to a bass loud enough to bring the ceiling plaster down, and I saw that she felt completely, utterly, totally at ease. Her brain was finally still, despite the flow of words that came from it, and this stillness allowed her to experience the pure, unadulterated freedom of an ataraxic state. Her body, let loose from the constraints of the brain, did whatever it felt like. It was an enhanced state of bliss that was so forgotten to me it hurt like a knife wound. I realised I had long been denied something that I was perfectly entitled to: euphoria. All young people should feel like that. Older people should feel like that too, but we don't. Not often.

I turned to my friend. I could see his foot tapping in time, despite himself.

"Do you want to dance?" I asked, smiling.

He looked directly into my eyes, his nose only an inch from mine. I could feel him, and yet I couldn't. His presence was odd, fluctuating. Sometimes I thought I could smell him, feel his body heat. Other times, he felt no more substantial and alive than a piece of paper.

"I'm afraid I can't," he said softly, although his eyes never left mine.

I could tell he wanted to, though. He wanted to, but he was behaving himself. He was a professional, after all. A professional what, I still didn't know, but it wouldn't have made a difference if I did. No meant no, I understood that.

"Mind if I dance?"

"Go for your life."

So I did. I danced, while my other self danced. I felt self-conscious at first, but then I remembered that none of these people, my friend aside, were really there. I was alone, and didn't they say music was therapy, that dancing was good for you?

Myself and I moved together, and it was strange, but rather wonderful, too.

In the OR, the patient is dancing. Music rattles the two-way glass between her and Control. She bounces on the end of her wires, head bobbing, arms and legs matching each other. She has rhythm. The overhead tracks struggle to keep up with her limbs as she moves them around, testing out the full extent of their range.

For the watchers, and for Evans in particular, the image of a puppet on strings, dancing upon command, is impossible to shake.

He gives up on the notion of controlling the music's volume, of stemming the tide of thoughts battering his system and hardware. Her thick streams of consciousness have slowed down a bit anyway, as she relaxes into the party, loses grip of the flow of information from her to them. Better to let her work through it, and hope for peace.

Evans watches the patient dance. He feels ill.

Time passed. Younger me didn't show signs of *(Mummy please stop! Sto–)* stopping.

I did.

Panting, I came back to my friend. My feet hurt, but in a good way. I had a stitch in my side, and my face felt hot, flushed.

"I had forgotten how it felt to have energy like that," I said as the music wound down to something more relaxed. My friend remained silent, his eyes drifting around the room. I could tell he didn't quite believe me when I said we were safe here. He was looking for Silhouette, in a state of high alert.

By dawn, the house was still busy, but the crowds had thinned to close friends and neighbours. They lay in companionable heaps on bed, couches, beanbags, propped themselves up against each other by a wall, or sat on the front doorstep, smoking. I looked for the younger version of myself and realised I had disappeared.

"Where did you go?" my friend asked, and I was glad I wasn't the only one who had taken the eye off the ball.

"Upstairs," I said, and we made our way to the top of the party house, which was three floors high, plus an attic space. In that space, which had been turned into the topmost bedroom, we found the younger me, climbing through a skylight in the ceiling, friends hauling her up so that she could sit on the flat junction between roofs and watch the night clouds melt away.

I tilted my head to one side as the soles of my converse disappeared through the skylight. Somehow I knew my new friend wouldn't be too keen on dragging himself up there through the small square in the ceiling. I licked my lips, and a wide trap door opened up next to the skylight, from which a deep-stepped ladder dropped down.

"You didn't use your hands," my friend remarked. It was true, I hadn't. My confidence was growing the whole time.

I grinned. "Shall we?" I said, and he looked at the ladder dubiously, but obliged, reluctantly setting his foot on the bottom rung with a rather grim expression of determination. I could see he was tired, and I experienced a pang of sympathy for him, but then I remembered that this was his job, that he wouldn't be here unless he was paid for his trouble, and the regret faded a little.

We climbed out onto the roof and settled down near the small group already sitting there, watched as a joint was rolled and passed around. Blankets were retrieved from the room downstairs, dragged over pimpled arms. The sun rose slowly over the skyline of the city, which spread out below us like a patterned quilt, and in particular, we admired the ornate, square, stepped tower of St. Paul's church in nearby Portland Square. Younger me looked around at her friends and smiled. In the light of this new day, she was pale and wan, and her exhausted face was smudged with makeup, her hair slick with sweat, but also, she looked peaceful. Happy. Nothing else really mattered to her except the act of allowing herself to feel and experience new things, and one of those new things was contentment. She was giddy with wonder at so much: drugs, friends, sensations, alcohol, music. The moment itself, the distinct pinprick in the thin membrane of her life, a tiny hole through which light shone. She could appreciate and enjoy the simple act of just *being*.

"I love seeing her so happy," I murmured, and a profound sadness suddenly grabbed at my heart, for I mourned the loss of her, that woman-child, and her unlined skin, her unscarred belly, her starry eyes.

(Where did I go? I was so young.)

My friend made a small noise in the back of his throat, and I felt him go rigid.

"What's wrong?" I asked, but his eyes were fixed on something beyond me – the church spire.

"It found us," he said, his face pale. He pointed, and I looked.

Crawling up the side of St. Paul's spire was the Silhouette.

My stomach lurched. "No," I whispered, shaking my head. "No. This is supposed to be a good memory. I was happy. Look at me, you can see I am happy!" As I said this, a bird that had been flying past plummeted suddenly to the ground, landing hard on the road below in a small explosion of feathers and blood. I swallowed, feeling sick. Had I just done that?

The bird wasn't real, I told myself. None of this was real. Silhouette wasn't real. The younger version of me wasn't real. This rooftop wasn't *(you never deserved to be happy. Never deserved love, you knew that, didn't you? It didn't matter how many parties you went to, how much shit you crammed in your nose, you were always still you by the light of dawn)* real.

"Magpie?"

"What," I said, trying to get a handle on my breath, which was now coming in shallow, strained bursts.

"Whatever you're thinking, you need to stop. Look at the roof," my friend said, and I dragged my eyes away from Silhouette, and down to the tiled rooftop beneath us.

I saw what he meant. The roof tiles had begun to melt around us, slipping downwards and off the slopes of the surrounding gables like ice cream sliding off of a warm spoon. I lifted my hand up, and it came away sticky, covered in a blackish brown, melted roof-tile goo that clung to my skin like tar.

The construct was slipping.

"Oh," I said, and my newfound confidence burst like a cyst. Clearly, I still had a lot to learn about manifestation. And de-manifestation, too, it seemed, because the more I tried to remind myself that none of this was really real, the more ephemeral the scene became.

"What do I do?" I asked my friend, wiping my hand frantically against my trousers to rid myself of the roof-goo.

He looked at his own feet, similarly glued in place by the melting residue of my memory.

"When do you first remember seeing it?" My friend kept his voice low, but his eyes locked on the Silhouette, which crawled its way slowly and steadily to the top of the church tower like a beastly four-limbed spider, clinging to the weathervane that capped the spire like the Hunchback of Notre Dame. It started scanning the city, craning its neck forward, its smudgy, weird face tilted to the breeze as if scenting the air.

"I don't..." I trailed off, confused, more than a little afraid. I had thought myself safe here. Younger me took a large drag of the spliff as it made its way back to her, and I could see she was slowly sinking into the roof of the house, her feet disappearing first, eaten up to her ankles as if she had stepped into a swamp, or sinking sand. Oblivious, she languorously blew out a cloud of smoke and watched it drift away on an early morning breeze.

I wasn't safe anywhere.

"I don't remember the first time I saw it," I said, struggling to think straight. "It just started to be in my life. I suppose..." I thought about it and swallowed. "Maybe it's always been there, maybe I just couldn't... fuck. Maybe I just didn't..."

"See it before." My friend finished my sentence for me.

"I don't like that." I swallowed a lump in my throat. "I just want to be left alone to enjoy a good memory. Why is it here? I don't understand! This was a good thing!" Panic edged closer to me.

(You don't deserve good things)

Silhouette gripped the church tower and continued to scan around itself, the scribbled outline of its stick-body in a constant state of flux. Looking at the framework of him for too long hurt my head.

My friend was very still and calm beside me.

"I don't know why it's here, Magpie, but I think... I think we should move."

I took in a sharp breath as he said this.

Because the Silhouette had frozen in the act of sniffing, and was now motionless, its head fixed and pointing in our direction.

"It's seen you," my friend whispered, and he was right, for the Silhouette spasmed in recognition, tensed its peculiar, sketchy frame, and with a burst of terrible, neurotic energy, leapt from the tower, sailing through the sky, landing on a nearby rooftop with a loud crash. It galloped across the tiles of that space and leapt again, soaring through the air, a nasty jumping thing intent on tracking me down, and I could feel my control on the construct slipping further as I began to panic properly. The sky, tinted with soft pinks and oranges, crackled suddenly with static, and the colours strobed to a garish red striped with jagged lines of black – the colours of fear.

"We should go back to the Gallery, *now!*" my friend cried, but I could not recall it, I could not get us back there. I knew there were columns, and a rough approximation of a forest of tall, white pillars flickered into view again, but I could not hold onto the image, I could not manifest. I hadn't created the Gallery in the first place, and I realised too late how dangerous it had been to leave it without at least a reference picture to help me find my way back. We were stuck. I was unable to let go entirely of the existing memory construct, and equally unable to drag us back to the safety of the therapy construct.

What the fuck was I going to do?

I had to do something. If I let Silhouette catch up to me, well...

I did not want to let it catch me ever again.

I squeezed my eyes shut, blotting out the awful dark stick man shadow as it leapt from roof to roof, scrambling over chimney stacks and ducking under television aerials, getting closer and closer with every jump.

If I couldn't send us to the Gallery, I would have to try somewhere else, I reasoned. It was frantic logic, but it would have to do.

I began to think, and think hard. My brain skittered madly across a dozen scenes, images, locations before settling on one. Pine needles. Greens. Flowers. Wind, gentle. Snow. A mountainside.

"Hurry, hurry, *hurry!*" My friend grabbed my arm, breaking my concentration. My eyes flew open in just enough time to see Silhouette up close, and terrifying. The memory version of me, the younger, carefree version, cowered beneath its shadow, and I watched, half-mesmerised, half-paralysed, still trying to build an escape in a green and pleasant place, as the vast, sketchy abomination reached down with two arms, grabbed the other version of me tight around the waist with hands that would not stay still, wrung her out like a wet towel, and ripped her beautiful *(you're so beautiful Mummy)* body cleanly in two.

Entrails and blood scattered wide in the air around me.

I screamed, and clenched my eyelids shut again – why did that hurt so much? What was that resistance? Desperately trying to manifest somewhere safe to send us to. Behind my lids, Silhouette shrieked back, a high-pitched, excoriating sound that drew little trickles of liquid from my ear drums, and I heard it throw the parts of me down, I felt it move closer, filling the space near us with its livid, poisoned presence, and–

"Magpie!" my friend shouted. *"Now!"*

And when I opened my eyes again, we were in a forest.

Tall trees, maybe pines, maybe redwoods, I didn't know, or much care, towered above us. I rubbed my face, and the tree trunks turned white, their bark brilliant and bleached as if they had been carved out of marble, but moments later they were brown again. A dank carpet of mouldering, wet leaves and needles lay underfoot, and I could smell peat, and rot, and earth, and dead things.

I swayed on the spot, looking about me frantically for the Silhouette.

"Magpie?" my friend asked, panting with fear and relief as we both realised the monster was no longer with us.

I wanted to answer, I wanted to tell him I was okay, that we were safe *(shhh, shhh baby, did you have a bad dream? It's okay, you're safe, Mummy's here n–)*, that Silhouette hadn't followed us, wherever we were, but I felt heavy, suddenly, too heavy, and woozy, and my eyes wanted so badly to close, and my tongue felt too thick in my mouth, and I tried to say something, tried to speak, but I couldn't do it, all I could do was rest my heavy eyelids, and before I knew it, I was sinking, and my friend was shouting at me, shouting something about not falling asleep, not leaving him stranded, but it was too late, it was all too late, and then...

There was bla–

16

CHOICES

In the OR, the patient suddenly convulses, as if an electric current has jolted through her body. She stills. A sliver of time passes.

Then, she convulses again.

Evans frowns, leaning forward. "What the fuck?"

The patient's entire body begins to quake. Her arms and legs contort with rolling spasms. Her spine arches, and her fingers go stiff, splaying out like tree branches. Veins stand proud on her neck.

Evans and his Boss watch this unfold with wide, confused eyes. On the other side of the mirror the patient's body twists tightly, locked in the throes of a rolling succession of spasms. She no longer reminds Evans of a puppet, but of a maggot caught on a hook, thrashing about in a vain effort to save itself.

"But... her readings are fine!" Evans says stupidly, looking back to the stats monitor in confusion. "Look – BPM, blood pressure, vitals – everything is fine! There hasn't been a single warning!"

His Boss rears up, genuine concern for the patient having now turned into a quiet, livid panic.

"Well, she doesn't *look* fine, does she?!"

The patient's face beneath her visor turns from pale white to a dark, dangerous puce. Her bloodshot eyes, already held open, now bulge alarmingly.

"She's… is she choking?! Fuck!" Evans jabs at the nurse call button repeatedly. "I told you, I *told* you this was a bad idea!"

The Boss doesn't have time to make conversation with her report. She scrambles across to the nearest wall, tripping over wires and pizza boxes, to where a large red alarm button is mounted. At some point in the past, Evans jokingly graffitied the wall beneath it with the words "FUBAR BUTTON", back before there ever was a true Fubar situation. Now it doesn't feel like a particularly funny joke. The alarm, like all the others, is usually triggered by the software, not manually, but nothing is working as it should in Control. The Boss slaps the emergency button hard with her palm, and it prompts a red flashing light bulb over the main door to blink into life, and a horrible, whooping warning sound, not unlike an old air-raid siren, to start blaring.

Evans gulps as he watches the patient jerk about at the end of her wires. Then he realises his Boss is not going to wait for the nurse, who should have been here by now.

"Don't!" Evans cries, in sudden, irrational fear. "You can't go in there! She isn't safe!"

The Boss ignores him, starts to push her way out of Control, not knowing what else to do, but before she can leave, both nurses – the man who took the cannula and the nurse who was first on duty – burst into the OR and rush to attend to the patient. The first to reach her is the morning nurse, who runs point-blank into the patient's kicking, flailing foot, and falls back, clutching her nose, which now spurts red. Swearing, the other nurse struggles to grab hold of the patient and keep her still while she sways about in her harness. He shouts at his colleague, who collects herself, quickly stuffs gauze up her nostrils to stem the flow, runs over, yanks off the visor clumsily and opens the patient's airway by roughly grabbing then tilting her head back and peering down her throat.

"There's something in there!" She inserts her curled index finger into the patient's mouth, pushes it to the back of her throat and deftly hooks out a large, gelatinous mass of what looks like sticky brown chewing-gum. Disgusted, she throws the nasty clump into a sample bag, checks her airways again, closes her eyes momentarily in relief, and then jabs the patient, who is still convulsing, with anti-seizure medication.

It takes a second or two to work, but the violent contortions finally calm to a series of gentle, rolling tremulations.

Evans and his Boss sag in relief as the patient's seizures eventually grind to a halt and her face returns to a normal shade of pale. Spent, she hangs limply in her cradle, arms and legs dangling where before they had been in a state of hyper-animation. Her chest rises and falls in small shallow breaths, but that is the only real sign of life. There is drool on her chin. The Boss feels an urge to clean it up for her. The nurses are too busy to attend to it.

The medical staff talk quietly to each other as they work on the patient, switching over tubes and medication, checking the patient's cannula, repeatedly looking in her airway, monitoring her temperature, palpating her stomach, checking her nails and skin, testing her reflexes, looking into her eyes, even examining her private parts and taking a quick vaginal swab, something the female nurse does while the male nurse obstructs Control Room's view with a large sheet of blue roll. Evans averts his eyes anyway, feeling a sudden flash of pity for the patient's lack of privacy, and ashamed of himself for looking at her the first time she was naked

After all the checks have been completed, the patient is once again redressed, rather tenderly, in fresh paper pyjamas. The cradle is positioned so the patient can lie back and rest with her head supported. The cables holding her limbs are shortened to arrange them by her sides, for all the world as if she is lying flat on an invisible bed, mid-air.

"It might be time to schedule her in for some real sleep," the male nurse says, checking his timings. "It's been a while. She could use some proper rest."

The Boss nods, no hesitation. "Fine. Sure. Whatever she needs. Give her an hour? Several?"

The nurses confer. "At least an hour. Then you need to think about wrapping this up."

"Up?" The Boss knows what he is saying.

"Seizures are never a sign of anything good. She needs a scan, and a proper bed before we start to damage her circulation. The fitting aside, and the discharge, or whatever it is... being suspended for this long, no matter how comfortably, no matter how mobile... none of it is good for her. I'm going to recommend a cease to the treatment. I'm sorry."

Evans is immensely relieved. He desperately needs a break.

The Boss sinks her head into her hands, devastated.

"Alright," she says, eventually.

"You'll monitor her through the next hour, obviously. So shall we. We'll need to get things in motion, arrange transport, find space for her somewhere else. We will also need to file a report, you know that right?"

The Boss nods. "I understand. File whatever you need."

Evans wants to know something. "The stuff in her throat... is it the same as the stuff in the cannula?"

The male nurse studies the sample bag, squeezes it experimentally between his fingers. "Could be. Same colour and texture, but much denser. More like a mucusy plug than a liquid. We're going to draw some more blood, get more tests scheduled. Curiously, all her other vitals seem..."

"Perfectly fine," the female nurse concurs. "No temperature, no abnormalities in heart rate, all vitals seem perfectly stable. Now that the obstruction is gone, her breathing is fine. Lungs sound clear. No abnormalities in her abdomen or anything like that. Her blood pressure is a touch low, but then it was before."

"Do we really need to cease, if that's the case?"

The male nurse shoots a stern look at the mirrored glass. "I'm afraid so," he says, in a tone that brooks no refusal.

The Boss admits defeat.

"Put her to sleep, then, and thank you. Evans, dip the lights?"

The patient's eye-restraints are removed. With her eyelids closed, she starts to look more human, less like a puppet. Evans finds that this small thing changes how afraid of her he feels, if only marginally.

"Do you think she'll dream?" he asks his Boss, once the nurses have left. The OR is dim, now, dusky shades of blue leaking from coloured strip lights bordering the room.

The Boss nods. "I do," she says, not wanting to talk any more.

I don't know how I knew I was asleep, but I did. It was a very different sensation to how it felt to navigate the Gallery, or my memories. It felt deeper, and I was less aware of myself, of how my body felt. There were no smells or sensations, no sense of being able to physically touch anything, but that was okay. I realised how tired I had been of all that. It was sort of nice to exist in a sensory vacuum, if only for a little while.

In my dream, I was pulling hairs from my arms, plucking them out with my fingernails, one by one. As soon as they were free from my skin, they turned into leaves, and I stuck them to the bare branches of trees nearby. Once my arms were clear and smooth, I moved to my eyelashes, denuding each lid with remarkable skill and dexterity. I used to pull my eyelashes out before, I remembered dimly, on my worst days. There was a word for it, tricho-something-something, but words didn't have much significance here in the dream.

Below me, a voice drifted up.

"Mummy, what are you doing up there?"

I looked down. My son stood beneath me, which made me realise I was floating. His face, which I could finally, suddenly, gloriously remember, did to me what it always did when I looked upon it. It filled me up with a terrifying mix of emotions: love, guilt, the weight of responsibility, pride, sadness, affection, joy. It had always been that way, since the day he was born. Colossal joy, unimaginable fear, indelibly intertwined. A thorny vine upon which roses grew.

"Making leaves, baby," I said.

"Why?"

"I don't know. I think it's just what people do in dreams."

"I miss you," he said, eyes solemn.

I floated down to him, wrapped him in an embrace. I could not really feel him, or smell him, or bask in his warmth, but for the moment that we held each other, none of that mattered.

"I miss you too," I replied, and then I just stayed like that, thinking: *Why didn't I do this more?*

Evan's primary screen bursts into life as he is taking a short nap, his head resting on his arm. The Boss alerts him to this new activity by whacking the back of his head unceremoniously with a paper folder of patient notes.

"Wake up," she hisses. "Something is happening."

The screen relays a single sentence (*WHY DIDN'T I DO THIS MORE*). Then, it does what Control are all too quickly getting used to: displays a rolling parade of more alien code, code which morphs from a series of what could almost have been instructional words rendered in conversational algorithm, to more specific words, words spelled in English, words that are essentially medical jargon like "generalized tonic-clonic seizure" and "postictal phase", interspersed with random half-sentences and exclamations like "can't breathe", and "SCARED". Sprinkled in amongst those words are more strings of symbols that Evans can't decipher, but nevertheless recognises the origin of: this is the patient's own personal coding language. It isn't a numerical code, or binary, and it isn't alphabetised. It could be pictorial, but Evans doesn't understand whether or not this is what he is looking at, because there are images, perhaps, symbols, maybe glyphs? But they seem to constantly morph and change state, like clouds of gnats skittering across the surface of a lake. Every time he thinks he has a grasp on a particular form, it shifts into something else, as if it knows he is looking at it and is evading detection, doing so by turning into something equally as alien and unrecognisable.

And then, he spots something he *does* recognise. He spots code, snippets from some consequence script he remembers working on for the Gallery. As he watches, the patient's own language starts to infiltrate the script, and he is reminded of a picture he once saw of toxins invading cells under an electron microscope.

Evans, who now has a pounding headache, scans through this scrolling litany of mixed languages with an increasing sense of frustration and reluctant wonder, and then he turns to his Boss, his face somewhat sickly in the light of his computer monitors, as if he has literally turned green about the gills.

"Boss," he says, huskily. "Look at this."

"I *am* looking at it. Buggered if I know what any of it means, though."

"I think..." Evans tests the words out in his mind first, and realises his shirt collar feels tight, too tight, so he loosens his tie, then takes it off altogether in an abstracted gesture of discomfort. "I know it sounds... well. We know she can code via thought, right? Well, bear with me, this is all new territory, but... this looks like the same sort of activity to me. Only now she is sleeping. And if she is sleeping, there should be some cognitive decline, right? The brain is still doing important shit, but her thoughts aren't organised like they are when we're awake. Not focused. That's why we schedule naps, take them out of hypnagogia. So our brain cells can heal, rest?"

"Right. A lot of biological stuff happens in the brain when a person is sleeping. Processing information, the glymphatic system getting rid of toxic waste, nerve cells doing their thing... cell repair, hormone regulation and–"

"Yes, well. Anyway." Evans cuts her off, worried he'll lose his train of thought. "She's sleeping, so she's not *consciously* thinking, or is that too simplistic?"

"Too simplistic. She's dreaming, we can see that. And when you dream, you are having a conscious experience. Of sorts. There are studies that say sleep, and dreams, are simply an extension of waking consciousness." They look to the dimly lit OR, where the patient twitches and mutters faintly. Beneath her eyelids, her eyes are rolling, a sure sign of dreaming. "If she's in REM sleep, then her cognitive agency should be decreased, yes, but..." The Boss searches for words. "She's probably still piecing together her thoughts and processing events and consolidating some sort of new memory. So yeah. She's still thinking, in answer to your question."

"Except I think it's more than that." Evans taps the code on screen. "She's still projecting her thoughts into code, somehow, if this stuff is saying what I think it is." He waves at the other screens, upon which no virtual scenarios are displayed, only screensavers, then back to the main screen.

"It's all muddled up with what she's obviously heard while hypnagogic, the nurses talking as they worked on her – us – God knows *how*, what with the earbuds in place and everything else going on – but, here's the thing. Even though she is, well..." He gestures to the woman who still twitches at the end of her strings. "Somehow, she is still coding, Boss. Fluently. Despite everything. She is fast asleep, in that construct and also in this reality. But somehow she is still aware of her own thinking."

"Metacognition. Thinking about thinking. Or lucid dreaming?"

"I don't know, whatever. Point is, she is still coding. Where and what, I don't know, I can't see anything, I can't access her brain. But she is creating. Something. Somewhere. Like... putting down roots, you know? And if I look at the construct back-end..." He clicks around, pulling up a grey window with a large chunk of code in it. "It's changed, Boss. In real-time, she is still editing our work. Our engine runs a very specific type of script, dialect, whatever, and not only is she fluent in it, but she's... well I don't know what the fuck she's doing to it, actually."

"But it seems deliberate, is that what you're saying?"

"Yes, it's deliberate. But if she's asleep, then... I don't know. It's like... like the program and she have this co-joined, sentient identity of their own, now, like she is *blending* with it somehow, like a creeper wrapped around a tree, but they share the same root structure or something... fuck, this is so hard to articulate. I don't really know what the fuck I'm looking at."

His Boss pulls on her lower lip. "But our infrastructure isn't hosted in a way that..." She trails off.

"We're not being hacked by her. It's beyond that. It's... she's thinking in our language and hers at the same time, and blending them together to write something new. It's Immersion, Boss," Evans concludes, and his hands are trembling visibly as they point to the offending screen. "I think she's approaching Full Immersion."

"Full Immersion is a myth, Evans. It's not a real thing, it's just something we talk about at cons to..."

"I don't think it's a myth anymore, Boss."

And just like that, the display on the monitors shifts, so Control can now see the patient lying flat on her back beneath the virtual canopy of a large, green forest. She appears to be unconscious, but about to wake, what they call hypnopompia, although Evans can never pronounce it properly. As her eyelids tremble, as her mouth twitches, the tree trunks around her dissolve, to be replaced by clouds. The scene transforms again, resolves into that of a mountain, the very summit of which is crowned by a thick, velvety blanket of cloud. Above this cloud line, the patient now lies on a bed of rock.

She groans, and stirs.

"Shit, we're not ready, we need the visor, and..." Evans

scrambles to hammer the Nursecom, but the Boss grabs his hand in hers.

"Wait, don't do that. They want us to cease, remember? If they know we've hooked her back up despite their cease order…"

"So what do you want me to do? They'll be in to check on her soon, anyway."

The Boss knows she has to make a decision, and it is not an easy one. She has to choose between the patient's safety, and the biggest discovery of the century.

"The nurse said her vitals were okay, didn't she?" It sounds like a defence she can rely on in court, later, and she knows it.

"Yeah, but…"

"And they'll send an ambulance for her as soon as they find a bed somewhere else, probably the Royal Infirmary, but that'll take at least another thirty minutes…"

"Boss, she's almost fully awake!"

The Boss straightens her spine. She has made her choice.

"Put her back to hypnagogic. I'll do the rest."

"Are you sure? Are we… fuck! Are we doing the right thing?"

"Only time will tell, Evans." The Boss strides across the room, yanks open the door. "And Evans?"

"Yeah?"

"Lock the door to the OR behind me, okay?"

Evans swallows, a hollow feeling forming in the pit of his stomach as he watches his Boss rush into the OR and hastily reattach the VR visor to the patient's head.

On screen, in the new scenario that the patient has built, the Psych is nowhere to be seen.

17

COMMAND PROMPT

I decided I was done with the dream. As hard as it was to let go, I knew I had to.

I had work left to do, after all.

I kissed the top of my son's head. His scalp smelled of nothing, dreams don't work like that, but a new-growth memory that sprang up like a dandelion out of nowhere reminded me that his hair had smelled of mint, usually, because of the shampoo we always used.

It felt good to remember something positive.

It did not feel good to let him go. Dream versions of him were all that were left to me, now. Choosing to wake from him felt like more failure, no matter how necessary.

I did it anyway.

I woke up slowly, feeling as if I'd been kicked in the ribs by a horse several times over, and then trampled on for good measure. My chest was tight, my eyes were sore, and my head ached. I tried not to think about whether I was actually awake, or a version of awake that suited my surroundings. Going down that path would send me mad, I knew it.

I sat up, looked around for my friend. I was no longer beneath the trees, the last things I remembered seeing before passing out. I was sitting instead on a cold finger of rock, high, high up in the atmosphere. Around me were thick white clouds, so thick they looked solid, they looked as if you could walk across them in spongy, pillowy little leaps. Like clouds look when you see them from a plane: solid, deceptive.

I stood, did a complete three-sixty and made the conclusion that this was the summit of a mountain. It was hard to be completely sure, because my surroundings were peculiar, in that they were inexpertly rendered, like the graphics in an early video game. Things looked blocky and flat, and had strange, cuboid angles to them. But yes, I was on top of a mountain. This finger of rock was the peak, the part that rises above the cloud line, the snow zone, the nival level. The level at which nothing could grow except mosses and lichens, some of which I saw clinging to the rock with soft, green little hands. I tried to recall, was this a mountain I had climbed, once? Was this a memory, or a scenario I had imagined? Or was it something else? The surroundings weren't familiar to me, which suggested... I wasn't sure what it suggested. Had I somehow transported myself to a different part of... whatever this was? A different construct, a new therapeutic room? Was I here by design, or accident?

It was scary, being on the mountain top alone with no real idea of where I was, or how I'd gotten there. I wanted to believe the strange new environment was part of whatever my new friend had in store for me, part of the prescribed treatment, but that didn't feel right. My throat hurt, was sore when I swallowed. I had a headache, almost like a hangover, and my limbs ached, my left foot in particular, as if I'd stubbed it against something. My friend was nowhere to be seen. This worried me, a lot. Had I left him behind, stranded in another scenario? There had been trees, hadn't there? A carpet of wet leaves... I felt so groggy. Why hadn't he followed me here? He'd had no problems following me into different visualisations before now. In fact, he had told me that we shared the virtual space that was the Gallery, so I assumed he was able to control himself and navigate the environment with confidence, but... had I changed all of that with my... improvisations? I was able to do things he was not, that much was obvious. Was he lost in a world of my making? Or had he simply had enough, taken himself off to his boat, too scared by Silhouette? Too scared by *me*? I shook my head. That didn't feel right. He wasn't scared of me, quite the opposite. He felt sorry for me, I was sure of it. Sorry for me, and there was something more. He was invested. I knew that the same way that I knew the earth, the real one, orbited around the sun. He was unlikely to leave me when I was in danger, or compromised. He was a friend, a therapist, a person trained to deal with trauma. It didn't fit that he would abandon me just as we were starting to make progress.

So, if he had been left back there in the forest, was he safe? It mattered to me that he was. Despite my earlier resistance to him, I had begun to feel as if we were, for want of a better phrase, a team. I was invested in him, too. We were in this together, whatever "this" was. Whether he had removed himself from me, or I had lost him in between realities, neither scenario made me feel terribly comfortable. I felt alone, without him, and it wasn't a good feeling.

But then a thought occurred to me. I wasn't alone, was I?

What about the watchers?

The ones up there, somewhere, beyond the layers, beneath the layers, between the layers, wherever the hell they were and however it worked, looking in? Did they know where my friend was? Did they know where *I* was?

Could they still see me? Hear what I was thinking?

Only one way to find out.

I thought hard, forming one word in my mind, knowing that a rush of undirected thoughts did not constitute a conversation. I made the word as loud as I could, to be extra sure they could hear me above any errant background mental noise:

HELLO.

Then, I listened.

Only the sound of wind came back to me.

* * *

"Argh!"

Evans rears back as the word "HELLO" roars out into the Control Room.

"Fuck sake!" He fiddles with the system volume, trying and failing to mitigate further damage. "The entire system is now stuck in some sort of vocal rut, I can't…" He hammers at some keys, yet the word remains, lingers in his ears, as if it has been spoken out loud in a cave, and the reverb is endless.

"I think we gave up all illusion of control a while back, Evans, don't you?" The Boss is back by his side, nervously monitoring her emails for an incoming transportation confirmation. "So much for her being fluent in your programming language. Beginner level, maybe."

"Why is she shouting at us?" Evans replies, rubbing his ears.

Files begin to pop up randomly on Evan's various desktop monitors. They are all named the same thing, numbered sequentially from 1: "HELLO1.wav". Evans, with horror, realises that the patient is suddenly, inexplicably exporting her own thoughts into sound files, and saving them to his location. Within moments, the desktop is overrun with file icons: she is overloading his computer with her unique brand of mental diarrhoea. He begins frantically selecting and deleting these new files, only to find dozens more replace the ones he deletes. Knowing it is futile, he keeps jabbing away at the delete key, hoping against hope that she'll stop trying to communicate with them in such an oddly specific way and find some other route, one that doesn't fuck up every bit of equipment they own.

"She's not shouting," the Boss says, raising her voice to be heard above the patient's, which still rumbles around the room. She rubs her own ears and winces. "She's just thinking in capital letters, for some reason."

"Five years of my life, I've been here," Evans grumbles, barely holding it together. "And this is how it ends, not with a whimper, but with a… fuck, what is that expression?" Words fail him, and he gives up on trying to delete the sound files, instead throwing a cup across the room in frustration and massaging his earlobes. A loud tinnitus buzz fills his head.

"Calm down, Evans," his Boss says, wearily. "There's a bigger issue, here. She can hear us, although not all the time, it seems. So we need to be a little more careful about what we say, out loud, at least. More importantly, now that she can communicate with us natively, do we communicate back?" The last word blares into a suddenly quiet Control Room, for the echo has finally died. Sound files continue to flood Evan's desktop.

"And risk fucking things up even more? No thanks," he says, angrily jabbing his delete key once again. "Anyway, what value would I add to any of this? She's the golden one. I'm sure you two will get on like a house on fire."

His Boss narrows his eyes. "Are you jealous, Evans?"

Evans cannot reply. A lump rises in his throat. The answer to that question is yes, he is jealous. Acutely jealous, and he hates himself for it.

"Not so much jealous as worried about my finances. I've got a divorce to pay for, remember?" he mutters.

The Boss lets something steely flash in her eyes.

"At some point, we need to have a little chat about empathy."

"I have empathy. Can I put myself completely in her shoes? Of course not. Her experiences are too specific. What do I know about kids, birth, all that stuff? But I know about depression, anxiety. I know she's been failed. They don't tend to end up here unless they've completely slipped through the cracks, do they? We are usually a last resort."

"You know," the Boss says, her eyes on her phone screensaver, where her family smile up at her. "When both mine were born, and Jocelyn was in the hospital, lying in bed, all bloody and sore and beaten up, a sales rep came around the ward, from a parenting club. Tried to give out packs of promotional stuff, vouchers for formula, a nappy, cute baby clothes, that sort of thing. That rep just opened the curtains, unannounced, and walked right up to my wife with no warning, no introduction, while she was feeding – or trying to – our babies. I was furious."

"Jesus," Evans mutters, wondering where this is going.

"Worse? Not one person offered her any information on mental healthcare or aftercare. Her entire body had been opened up, changed beyond recognition, she had two babies to handle after a horrific experience, she was the dictionary definition of vulnerable. The hospital thought it was more important to let a saleswoman near her than a registered mental healthcare professional. There was no dignity in it. There never is. And that's just one example. Every day, some dismissal of our pain, our struggles. There's a pain bias, you know. For women. We're still gas-lighting half the population, regularly. Apparently."

Evans stays quiet. Anything he says now will likely not be well received.

"When we say 'post-natal depression', there's this idea of a wailing degenerate running about tearing her own hair out, refusing to be near her child, being an awful human because she can't parent properly. Stigma. A weakness. A character flaw. Times have moved on, but people still find it hard to ask for help. Sometimes, they don't even know what to ask for help *for*."

Evans can't stop himself. He is having an adverse reaction to being lectured.

"If you care about her so much, why have you just plugged her back in?" He realises his anger comes from a different place than just jealousy. It comes from a place of concern, too.

He is worried about the patient.

The Boss stares at him, shocked.

"Or is that too empathetic? Sorry." Evans resorts to passive aggression, because he does not like this new dynamic between himself and his superior.

The Boss swallows. Little red spots of temper colour her cheeks.

"Because she's brave, Evans. I can see it."

"You don't know her. You *do* know her medical history though, which isn't great. We're gambling with her health. Her life. I hope you realise that."

"Well, it's a gamble I'm willing to take!" The Boss finds she is shouting, and barely, just barely, gets a grip on herself. Calming her tone, she continues.

"And maybe, with what we're doing here… maybe we can help others. Maybe we can be a lifeline. Undo some of the damage done. I think she can show us amazing things. Things that could change everything, change the face of mental healthcare, everything."

"Sacrificial lamb, is it? Exploit her mental illnesses for the greater good?"

The Boss sighs. "You had a chance to stop me, earlier. You had a chance, and you didn't."

"That isn't fair."

"Life isn't fair, Evans. If it were, we wouldn't all be here, in this cursed basement, would we?"

Evans finds he is too tired to continue the conversation. He thinks about taking a bathroom break, and simply not returning, but that would leave the patient in the sole care of his Boss, who he no longer entirely trusts.

He weighs up his options. Stay, and take part in what has essentially become an unethical experiment with a vulnerable patient, or leave, and lose any opportunity to mitigate his Boss's increasingly zealous behaviour.

"Where even is she?" Evans says, eventually, not knowing how else to reply. Instinct tells him that they are sliding down a slippery slope towards a precipice. Instinct also tells him that communicating directly with the patient is a very, very bad idea, so he tries to distract his Boss, and chooses to focus on the issue of her location within the programme.

The Boss lets out a breath she didn't know she had been holding, and places her hands on her hips.

"Your guess is as good as mine. This doesn't look like anything from her memory bank, and it certainly isn't any environment of ours. It's too… well, look at it. It's crude.

"Yeah. Like a five year-old painted it, or something."

The older woman leans forward, staring intently at something that has caught her attention. "I don't know where we are now," she murmurs, squinting. "But there's something floating in the sky above her head. Look."

Evans looks, and what he sees confuses him even more.

Something caught my attention as I waited.

A black, vertical line hovered in the air about three feet above my head. It was roughly the length of my forearm, and it blinked in and out, like…

Like a cursor.

Had it been there before? I couldn't be sure. It popped up in response to my earlier greeting.

I tried again, clearing my mind of all other distractions, and thinking the word as forcefully and concisely as I could:

HELLO.

For a second, a split second, after the word was spoken, I thought I heard the sound of someone crying out in pain. Was that one of the watchers? What was wrong? I frowned, then it dawned on me.

Of course, I thought to myself, amused. *I'm shouting.*

Well, at least I know I'm not alone out here. I consciously dialled down the level of my internal dialogue so that it wouldn't hurt the ears of the watchers anymore.

The cursor continued to blink in the sky, as if thinking. I waited. Then, letters began to appear behind the cursor, capitalised, just as my thoughts had been, popping into existence in rapid succession as if typed in real-time.

They said:

TYPE IN COMMAND.

I shook my head, flummoxed. "I don't know what that means," I said, out loud. "What command? What is this place? Where is my friend?"

The cursor blinked, spat out more text.

COMMAND PROMPT: ENTER COMMAND.

I spread my hands wide. "I don't know what that means," I repeated.

But that wasn't strictly true. My sleep had done me some good, it turned out. I'd made a few connections, while dreaming. Sorted some shit out that hadn't made sense before.

Despite my protestations, I was beginning to get a fairly rounded idea of what was going on.

I was stuck. That was first on the list. Stuck, in some sort of rudimentary scenario, a scenario constructed from things pulled out of my brain and assembled in a cursory fashion. Like the cupboard, and the party, only this mountaintop was not based on anything I could actively remember, even as I thought about it. Which is probably why it looked like it did, because there were no real reference points to work from. The scenarios prior to this had been built meticulously by others around real-life scenes and locations. Like the bridge where I had found my own corpse. Other things had been built from my memories. Things I was familiar with, significant items from my past, like the briefcase, like the lump of pyrite, like my grandfather's notebook. Those items had been strategically placed in front of me in an easily digestible format: the Gallery. Walking me through everything: my absent friend. He'd told me to view my surroundings as a "thought experiment". A construct. A series of clues, for I had a mystery to solve – the mystery of my own apparent death.

And I had taken that all on board, I had acknowledged, without questioning anything too much, that what I was experiencing was a fake environment, built for a purpose. I had accepted I was in the Gallery because I had a task to carry out, and that, while I was there, I was able to navigate around, alter, interact with and influence the Gallery, but I hadn't ever stopped to think of *how*, or what exactly the construct *was*. It was a melting pot of ideas and memories and objects and sensations and feelings, but what *was* it, exactly? A lucid dream? A hallucination? A thought experiment, like my friend had said? Was I hypnotised? In a coma?

What?

This pixelated mountain was me trying to figure that all out. And that was also why it looked as half-baked as it did. Because I could control it, whatever it was, but control of something without fully understanding the nature of it wasn't really control, was it?

And why had it taken me this long to start properly thinking about all this? Even when I'd begun to explore the environments outside of the Gallery, even when I'd begun to visualise the layers of reality I was sandwiched between, flex my manifestation muscles, I'd been so swept along by everything I hadn't even given a moment's thought to the practicalities of my situation. Which was typical of me. Accept, rather than question, settle for the easiest option. Go along with it all. *I always was a pleaser*, I thought.

But standing on that mountain top, looking at the blinking dark line in the sky, it hit me. It wasn't magic, all this. It wasn't all a product of my imagination. Not entirely. I wasn't under the influence of anything, I wasn't dreaming, or drugged (although sometimes I wondered), or hallucinating.

I wasn't dead, or in a coma, and I wasn't insane – which was a relief.

I was simply interacting with a computer programme.

A simulation, or a role-play, or a peculiar sort of game, or a virtual walkthrough. I was in no way technically minded, so lacked the vocabulary to fully define it, but I knew I was in a programme, some sort of therapeutic, experimental virtual reality bullshit that had been built, personalised, and programmed just for me. That much the Psych had confirmed.

Or at least, the Gallery had been programmed just for me. Other areas, like the boat, this mountain, I wasn't so sure about. But that didn't matter, not right now. I was in treatment, and just ascribing something I could understand to all of this made me feel much safer, much less alone.

The cursor spat out more text, nagging me.

COMMAND PROMPT: ENTER COMMAND.

"Shhh," I said, softly. "I'm thinking."

What I was thinking was simple: I did not have a shiny, freshly-shat clue how a simulation actually worked. I didn't understand programming. I was nigh-on allergic to computers, in real life. The cursor above my head wasn't a real depiction of how a construct like this actually operated.

I was projecting what I thought it *should* look like, how it *should* interact with me, like a human trying to initiate conversation.

COMMAND PROMPT: ENTER COMMAND.

COMMAND PROMPT: ENTER COMMAND.

I was, essentially, talking to myself, using a weird, imagined coded language.

Were the voices in the fourth layer part of that, or were they as I'd thought: remote watchers, real people I could speak to?

And there was another question. Now that I'd figured out all this stuff as computer generated... what now? Instinct told me I wasn't supposed to have figured it out, not really. The same instinct told me that conscious awareness of the manufactured nature of my condition would, in theory, make it harder to fully engage with my "treatment". Complete acceptance of the things I was being shown, at a conscious and subconscious level, meant I was more likely to adopt any therapeutic recommendations pushed in my direction. I could see the logic and sense in that.

But having an awareness of the Gallery, the boat, the

bridge, and my own dead body as nothing more than digital fabrications created a barrier between myself and suggestion, or "guidance", as my new friend would probably prefer to describe it.

In short, what was required from me in order to make this all worthwhile, was a complete suspension of disbelief. Once that had been achieved, the programme could proceed in its structured, pre-programmed, heavily monitored way. It made sense.

It made sense, but I didn't agree with it.

Quite the opposite, in fact. It was less frightening to understand what was going on. I was armed with insight. I had an explanatory framework to lean upon. This made a difference. This made me hopeful. Because I was having treatment, which meant someone had, at some point, believed in me enough to take me on *(I believe in you, Mummy)*.

To make me better.

A door opened somewhere inside of me as I looked at the blinking cursor in the sky. A memory of a letter swum to the forefront of my mind, a letter I had written whilst broken and drunk and high, to a small, niche university department I'd read about online. A select team of programmers, psychologists, practicing therapists and a Professor of Virtual Environments. They had advertised a bursary, allowing those who were financially strapped access to the programme on a semi-funded basis.

I had applied for this bursary, because I'd been desperate.

I'd been on the brink of... the brink of...

Well, that wasn't important, not in this moment.

I'd written the letter, blacked out. Now I was... where? Lying in the bowels of a department building over on Cathedral Square, hooked up to computers and monitors by a thick tangle of cables?

The air around me shook, and for a second, I thought I could see something through the clouds: a large mirror. Reflected in it, the still form of a woman, sleeping in a cradle that was supported by a complex system of wires.

Was that me?

Was that real?

Or was I imagining this to fit the logic of my present thought process?

Fuck, it was all so *much*. So, so much.

Another thought occurred to me. If this was all a simulation, a programme, then what was Silhouette? He'd existed in my head before all this, he'd been the result of some art therapy, I think, some clumsy attempt at processing...

What exactly?

I had a tattoo on my wrist. It gave me no answers.

The cursor grew impatient. Two large words blinked angrily at me in the sky.

ENTER COMMAND.

I shrugged. "Okay, okay," I said, scratching my neck in irritation. "Fine. Er... Command: *FIND FRIEND*".

The cursor blinked.

COMMAND NOT RECOGNISED.

I sighed, rolled my eyes. "Well, what *is* the command, then?"

Blink, blink, blink.

ENTER COMMAND.

I spread my hands, pleading. "I told you. Command: *FIND FRIEND.*"

COMMAND NOT RECOGNISED.

"For fuck's sake. Um... try this instead. Command: *FIND BOAT.*"

COMMAND NOT RECOGNISED.

I threw back my head in exasperation.

"Well what do you expect? I'm not a programmer, I don't code! I have no idea what I'm doing here!"

I had always hated computers.

ENTER COMMAND.

"Command: *GO FUCK YOURSELF!*" I shouted, feeling as if

I was never going to get anywhere. I just wanted to talk to someone, have a real conversation. I missed my friend. I did not want to do this alone, not a bit of it.

The cursor blinked, and I fancied it did so in a disapproving way, although I knew that was just projection on my part.

ENTER COMMAND.

"Command: *LOCATE MY CHILD,*" I blurted suddenly. Then I sucked in a pained breath.

Why had I asked that?

Wishful thinking, maybe. He lived on only in my memory, in my dreams, and no amount of talking to myself was going to change that.

But why was that? Why exactly was he not here, with me?

I couldn't remember.

Tears welled up in my eyes.

COMMAND NOT RECOGNISED.

Then, I recalled something. Something about the boat that my friend had taken me to. It hadn't just been a place for him to hide while I was exploring my past. It was more than that. It was neutral ground, a safe zone. A calm place, but an expectant one, if that made sense. I had been places like that before, rooms rather than boats. They had contained a similar atmosphere of quiet tension, of anticipation. A place to gather thoughts before an important meeting, or an in-depth session.

I cleared my throat.

"Command: *LOCATE WAITING ROOM,*" I said.

The cursor blinked and then transformed into a small, dark wheel, a wheel that turned as the command was read and, eventually, interpreted in the sky.

LOOKING FOR BVETWAITINGROOM_ANONYMOUS FILES IN C:/USERS/EVANS/HELLOBETMAGPIECONSTRUCT... RUNNING FACE RECOGNITION SEARCH...

I stomped my foot, impatient. "Hurry up," I said. "I haven't got all day."

/?

/?

/?

/?

/?

"Yes!" I said, desperate. "Help! Help me find my friend!"

The wheel stopped turning and began to grow in size. The text dissolved into thin air underneath it. Within moments, the wheel had become a large, pixelated arrow, an arrow that pointed down the mountain. I looked, the clouds cleared away to reveal a distinct path that led downwards, and I could see the tops of trees. I frowned.

"Are you sure?" I said.

The arrow morphed, became a thumbs-up emoji. I shook my head.

"Very droll," I said, and without waiting any further, I plunged down the path, away from the mountaintop.

18

POTENTIAL

Control are watching the patient trip down the mountainside. Neither of them are any the wiser as to what's happening.

"Who was she talking to? In the sky?"

Evans lifts his hands up, a gesture of surrender.

"Fucked if I know." He wonders how much longer he can stay in this room without snapping. "It reminded me of Moses with the ten bloody commandments on the mountain top."

"So we have no idea who is communicating with her outside of this room, or where that path she's now trotting merrily along leads to."

Evans rubs his face. "Are we forgetting this isn't a real place? There is no path, only code. Servers. Hardware. One would hope she isn't going anywhere; she's strolling along in that cradle not ten feet away." Evans gestures at the room next door, where the patient is once again upright, hopping along from foot to foot like a mountain goat.

"It's funny," The Boss says, thoughtfully. "We have seen what she can do, and it's nothing like… like this. Her actualisations were far more sophisticated, organic. This… this is, well. I don't know. It just feels different."

Evans slouches forward over his desk, wondering if it would be too much to suggest ordering more pizza. Evans always wants to eat shit when he is anxious. He stretches his legs out, worried about his circulation. As he does so, his foot nudges against something soft, spongy, resistant. He retracts his foot, grimacing and reminding himself that he must stop throwing pizza boxes under his desk like a slob.

"Maybe coding in one's sleep is harder than I gave her credit for," he says, unaware that a brown, sticky residue is now coating the tip of his right shoe, and slowly exploring the length of his foot.

"I mean, it would make sense. She would have had a hard time directing those skills whilst in REM. Like trying to draw a portrait of someone without knowing who, exactly."

"All I know is less than an hour ago, we almost lost her to seizures. That in itself means... I don't care what it means. I don't care if she has somehow stumbled into virtual nirvana, or a higher plane, or the fucking underworld itself."

Evans raises his head and pushes back his wheeled office chair, sharply. He gathers himself, unplugs, and makes to leave.

His boss blocks his path.

"You can't quit, Evans. I won't let you."

"I can do what I like," Evans retorts, with an uncharacteristic display of single-mindedness. "I'm going home. I don't feel very well."

"A minute ago, you were all noble concern. Now you want to quit?"

"A man can change his mind. Besides. I *really* don't feel well. I'm not lying." His eyes linger on the crack in the ceiling, a crack he has forgotten about, until now.

It looks larger. It is also still leaking, and Evan's mouth turns upside down.

"This place is a fucking dump, you know that?" he says, miserably.

"I don't care. I need you. You can't quit on me. Not if you want a decent reference and any chance at a career outside of this department, at any rate."

Evans laughs, incredulous. "Are you blackmailing me? Wow." Disappointment floods his heart.

The Boss waits a beat for his feelings to settle.

"No," she says, more kindly. "I am just being very persuasive. We're in this together, now. You, me, her."

"I don't want to live with it for the rest of my life, you know? Her brain damage. Her psychological issues, exacerbated. Her death? We're risking it all."

"The virtual version of her seems happy enough, for now."

"For now. But that's beside the point!" Evans scratches his head, floundering in his attempts to better explain himself. "You don't need me for this. I'm a fucking computer nerd. There are thousands of other computer nerds out there, desperate for a job that pays like this one. Go find one of them. That's what I'm saying." He realises he means it. He has spent all this time and energy feeling defensive over his position in the programme, and suddenly, he couldn't care less. A person can only be pushed so far, and arguing over what's best for the patient appears to be his limit.

"Imagine," the Boss says, ignoring Evans completely. She has found this an effective tactic for handling protests before, like starving a fire of oxygen. "Imagine being part of the team that discovers the full potential of the human brain."

Evans grips his Boss hard on the wrist.

"Look me in the eyes," he says, "and tell me you're not using her. Tell me you want to help *her*, not just the brain that can somehow project itself digitally across liquid crystal displays and polarised glass. You want to help the physical, real form of her, the flesh, the blood, the breath, the sweat, the tears, the skin, the hair. Not the virtual embodiment of her. Tell me you don't only care about her potential. That it's not about feeling vindicated. An acknowledgment that you haven't wasted the last ten years of your career chasing shadows."

The Boss moves in so close Evans can smell her, a sensation he is not used to, or comfortable with.

"Imagine being the person who can say he was there when a human subject was able to fully project her consciousness into a computer programme, onto a screen for us all to see. Imagine being able to say you were part of the team that figured out how to see inside someone's brain, a living, thinking brain, properly. Like a movie, like we're at the fucking cinema. Imagine the money, the funding that this department could secure, for that kind of discovery. Imagine seeing Full Immersion play out, in front of us, like a man walking on the moon, or inventing the wheel, or discovering fire. *Imagine.* Think of the implications." She starts to tick them off using her fingers. "Police work, investigating crime, working with trauma patients, child psychology, every therapy setting imaginable, the entertainment industry, politics, porn, advertising... think of it!"

Evans swallows, shakes his head. "I don't care," he says, but the fight is going out of him again.

"You do, I know you do."

Evans puts some distance between them. "And what about that fucking... stick monster? Thing? Whatever the fuck it is. What about that? The brown stuff? The glitches? The fucking... crack in the fucking ceiling?!" He points to it, but the Boss is in no mood for further obstacles.

"I'll authorise that pay rise and promotion you've been after for so long," she says.

Evans shakes his head. "I don't want it. Not now."

"Two hundred thousand, per year. Plus holidays. Performance bonus. Free membership to the gym. We can afford it, now."

Evans licks his lips. There is silence as he juggles his ethics with his current financial situation, which is dire. "Two hundred and fifty," he says, eventually, his voice hoarse. "And I already have free fucking membership to the gym. We all do."

His Boss smiles and picks up a pen, ripping a sheet of paper from a nearby printer. He realises she is formalising the offer, in writing.

"Sit down, would you?" she says to her report as she scribbles something energetically on the page. "Be an idea to save your energy, I think."

Evans, defeated, sinks wearily back into his chair. He hates himself for needing money as much as he does. He hates himself, but he sits down, despite that, and carefully dons his headset. In doing so, he feels something in his hair, something chalky and sticky. He runs his hands over it, pulls his fingers to his face and examines them closely, frowning. It is ceiling plaster, mixed with a nasty brownish goo. He looks up, curses. Decides he can do nothing about it, not now. The quickest way out of this room is for him to sit tight and try and do his job, pushing things forward until the end, as quickly as possible.

"If she dies," he mutters, knowing his Boss isn't listening, "I was never here. I was never fucking here."

19

THE MEADOW

I wandered down the small, stony and steep path, and a song ran through my mind unbidden as I did so.

"Tie a yellow ribbon round the old oak tree..."

I shook my head to try and dislodge the song, but it got to the end of the chorus and looped back jauntily to the beginning. Where had it come from? I hated how my brain did that: threw up random snippets from some past experience and fixated upon them, replaying them on loop until they drove me near mad with frustration. Because now the song was in there, I wouldn't be able to get it out until something else came along and dislodged it. It would play on endless repeat in the background, a low-level soundtrack that would eat away at me, even if I wasn't fully aware of it all the time.

"Tie a yellow ribbon..." I caught myself humming the first few bars out loud and shook my head hard to jolt myself out of it. I wondered then if there were speakers here, speakers that would pop up and start blaring out the song like before, in the Gallery. I scanned the environment, but saw and heard nothing. I thought about this. Perhaps the speakers were no longer necessary. Like waving my hands around was no longer necessary. I used more... back door techniques now. Subterranean. Hidden mechanics. I had a sense of being behind the scenes, somehow, and this sense only solidified the further I walked.

The path wound down the side of the mountain, meandering through patches of snow and ice and scree, until small scrubby bushes with tiny yellow flowers on them started to poke their heads out of the stone. These grew in size and density the lower I descended, until finally I came to a treeline, a thick band of larches and pines, not enough in number to constitute a forest, but enough to signal a distinct change in elevation. The trees on the outer layer of the treeline were heavily deformed by wind and cold, and were stunted, bent into awkward, crooked shapes like old ladies hunched over and facing into bad weather. Further in, they straightened out a little, as if the ladies were working the kinks out of their backs. A few minutes more of walking, and the trees grew taller still, were able to pull more moisture up through their roots. The needles grew more abundantly, and the side of the mountain became a cool and green space. I enjoyed walking there, allowing myself to relax a little and absorb some of the details of the environment I was in.

From a distance, at least.

Unlike the Gallery, this place didn't hold up to close scrutiny.

If I got too close to a particular boulder or bent to examine one of the short scrubby bushes still littering the floor beneath the trees, I found that the finer detail disappeared under examination, smoothing out into a blocky cloud of colour and suggestive shapes and blank planes. I realised I needed to adjust my thinking: there probably hadn't been any detail on these objects in the first place. My brain had been making assumptions as to what this flower or that rock *should* look like, and filled in the blanks for me. Under close study, the modelling was just as amateurish, child-like as the mountaintop. As if these details were not really an essential part of the construct, and whoever had thought them up had gotten bored halfway through dressing up the place, decided to skimp on the wrapping. I got an impression of hastiness, a lack of commitment. Like a half-abandoned sketch, or a neglected manuscript. Something to return to at a later date, maybe.

The tree trunks were better, more carefully described, but even though I could make out the swirls and knots and ridges and natural scars that made up the bark of a tree, I could tell that somehow, the pattern was multi-purpose, a generic, cloned texture of some sort. Because the trunk of one tree was exactly identical to the trunk of the next, and the next, and the next, and so on until my eyes grew sore from looking. It also felt flat, lacking in the tiny complexities of depth and texture that real bark was.

I shook my head, tutting.

Lazy, I thought.

The word LAZY echoes around control, where two techs sweat, side by side in an uneasy truce. Both of them feel rather old, and tired, and sore, as if they've run a marathon. The speakers have been turned down to minimum volume, after much fiddling from Evans. It's the only way to cope now that the patient's every waking thought is carried, in intermittent bursts, into their domain. Every now and then, a single loud thought makes it through the volume restrictions, when the patient puts particular emphasis on it, but otherwise, it's a low background chatter, like the ambient noise in a restaurant. Evans is not sure how exactly he's gotten around the patient's aggressive sound system override, but he has, and he takes that as another tiny yet important victory.

"She's not wrong," he mutters, furiously clicking his mouse at a dozen red crosses to try and abolish a fresh torrent of reproachful dialogue windows that keep reappearing in his peripheral. Thankfully, no sound files this time: he has only just deleted the last batch. "It *is* lazy. Tree prototypes were never our strong suit, but this... Her trees don't even blow in the wind, look."

The older woman sees that Evans is right. Not a single needle or leaf moves, or a single branch. Everything is static, statue-still.

"It's improving though, the further downhill she walks. Curious." The Boss speaks carefully, her voice low. She keeps forgetting that the new audio link the patient has forged with them is two-way: she can hear them, too. The Boss is reluctant to give too much of their ignorance away now that she knows she can damn herself with her own words.

"The light is all wrong, too. In fact, *everything* is all wrong. LOD transition, billboarding, no natural wind animation…"

The Boss *hmmm-hmms*, pretending to listen, preoccupied with something else.

"Did you get a location on the Psych yet?" Evans asks, figuring it out.

His Boss shakes her head, sighing. "No, but at this point, he sure would be useful, no matter how dubious his qualifications. We need to hurry her through this. It won't be long until the nursing team log their report and then…"

"What have you tried?"

"Calls, IM, texts, email… he's either ignoring us or he's just not there. Or he's had a heart attack and is lying dead somewhere. I can't say I'm thrilled with any of those eventualities."

"Why don't we just talk to him directly?"

"His ear peace is off too."

"No, no, I mean…"

"Talk to him out loud? In front of her?"

"Yeah. I mean, I know he's not there, here, but he's got to be somewhere. He'll hear us if he's plugged in."

"You don't have kids, do you. Arguing in front of them never ends well. They play you off of each other, you know. Not to mention the psychological damage it does. If we project an impression that we've lost control in front of her, openly, we're done. Who knows what she can do with that information."

"But she can hear us anyway, right?"

The Boss shakes her head. "I don't know. We can certainly hear her, but I wonder. I wonder how much of what we say here makes it back through to her."

"I just think it would be a lot easier if we–"

"We have to maintain some discreet sense of still being in charge, Evans. Even if the Psych is not playing by the books."

"He's not been playing by the books since we started this. I'm not even sure he *is* a Psych, but you're the one that does the background checks, not me."

The older woman chews her lip. "I did my due diligence. There is no concrete reason not to trust him. His background checks were all clear. But you would think... you would think that he would reach out to us if he was in trouble. If he was stuck, somewhere."

"But Boss... you're doing it again," Evans says, exasperated. "It's physically impossible for him to be 'stuck' anywhere. None of this is real, right? All he has to do is remove his headset if things get a little intense. It's not the same set-up as a patient link, not like it is with her. All he has to do to exit the programme is take his gear off."

"Precisely. So he is either present, and keeping silent, and hidden, or he is busy with something else. Seems unlikely he would just... wander off, mid-session, doesn't it?"

"This is the problem with having them log-in remotely."

"They wouldn't be Anonymous if they were here on site, would they."

The pair pause for a second, working through their individual concerns. Evans, who is fed up with trying to navigate a maze with no clear exits, looks to his Boss for guidance.

"What are you thinking, Boss?"

"Maybe... maybe there is something else going on here." The Boss speculates aloud, now, her brain working on a new and somewhat uncomfortable possibility.

"Like what?"

"Like, maybe the Psych is not as impartial as we would like to believe."

"You mean he is hiding on purpose? To what agenda?"

"I hardly like to say."

"You're thinking… he has a connection to her somehow? Outside a standard patient-Psych relationship?"

"Maybe."

"Like… he knows her? In real life?" Evans's voice climbs an octave, and the Boss shushes him, hurriedly.

"Maybe I'll email Human Resources, run those checks again," she murmurs, wondering how much of their exchange the patient just heard. "The last thing we need is a conflict of interest at that level. Not now."

Something else occurs to Evans.

"Boss, the Silhouette thing… it's a manifestation of her mental illness, right? Something out of her brain."

"That's my guess. It's the only one that makes sense, and the only guess stopping me from soiling myself at the moment."

"Well, about that… it can't… like… you don't think it can get *out*, at all, do you? Like… out of the programme." He giggles suddenly. "It can't hurt us, right?" The cracks in the wall and ceiling continue to play at the edges of his reason. He imagines Silhouette sliding through, one flat limb at a time.

The Boss stares at him in horror. "What on earth are you talking about, Evans?"

"You heard me."

"Don't be ridiculous. Her manipulation of a virtual environment with the power of her mind is one thing. But monsters? Crawling out of the computer screen to eat us? Don't be daft."

"I was only asking, Boss."

"Well don't."

"I mean, the media would love it. We could sell the movie rights." His clumsy attempt at humour disguises his deep unease. Sweat pours down his back and the sides of his face.

He is amazed that there is any sweat left in him to leak out. What he can't see is that his sweat is tinged with brown, but that is a good thing. Seeing that might send him over the edge, and he is close enough already.

The Boss clears her throat again. She feels like lying face-down on a bed in a darkened room, sleeping for a week.

Instead, she starts drafting an email to HR.

I came to a sudden break in the trees, a break which revealed a wide, open clearing. It was an alpine meadow, richly carpeted in green, and in the middle of this meadow, which was dotted with bright yellow buttercups and small purple flowers I didn't recognise and long, feathery grasses, there was a single plinth.

Around the trunk of the plinth, a frayed yellow ribbon was tied.

On top of the plinth, a glass dome, just like the ones in my Gallery.

Standing next to the plinth, my new friend, waiting for me.

I breathed a huge, happy sigh of relief.

"Well, well, well… speak of the devil."

"Is that – well fuck me, so it is! Waltzing back in like nothing fucking happened! Do you think he heard us?"

"Don't know."

"Seems like a bit of a coincidence, doesn't it?"

"There are no coincidences here, Evans. Ignore what I said earlier."

Tech falls silent. In their fascination with what's happening on-screen, they forget to check on the patient who is off-screen, skipping across an invisible meadow while still anchored to her strings in the OR. They will forget to check on her for some time, because, despite The Boss's prior protestations, she has, for the moment, become secondary to the proceedings. And out of sight is out of mind, as both techs well know, but it is hard to keep an eye on a sleeping woman when such a vibrant, intriguing version of her exists elsewhere. Thus, their attention is diverted.

This is a mistake.

I crossed the meadow on light feet, feeling genuine joy at discovering my companion again. As I approached, the environment around me changed, subtly. Became richer, more detailed. My eyes struggled to adapt to the shift, as if everything had been dialled up, colour, contrast, highlights, exposure. It was like walking from one painting into another, like stepping over from the impressionist to the romantic, from pointillism into realism. The meadow felt familiar, but I was too preoccupied with my reunion to try and figure out where it was.

I just wanted to see my friend again, up close.

I came to a rush-stop in front of him, just shy of barrelling him over, and smiled.

He answered me with his own smile.

"I thought I'd lost you," he said, and I couldn't help it: I drew him into a hug and felt him stiffen, then return the affection, reluctantly at first, then with increasing vigour. I had breached our formal, appropriate arrangement, and I didn't plan on doing it again, but in that moment, at that precise point in time, I was just happy to find a friend, a real friend, not a memory, or a shadow, or a dream, or a distant voice, or a blinking cursor in the sky.

Again, as I pulled away, I had to fight back a wave of something powerful, something purely physical, because even though I knew it wasn't possible, he felt warm, and solid, and safe, and his smell was... he smelled...

How could he smell, in this environment?

It didn't matter, maybe the smell wasn't real, maybe I just

recalled it because something else about him triggered a flash of memory, but either way... it was familiar.

The pedestal caught my attention as I pulled back.

"I thought I was done with the Gallery," I teased. "You don't take no for an answer, do you?"

"Don't look at me," my friend said. "None of this is my doing. I don't even fully know how I got back here. Lucky for you, I do at least know where I am now, though. Your brain has decided to go back to the structure, for a little bit."

I drank in the welcome sight of the meadow. "I must admit, this is better than where I was before. Maybe improvising isn't such a good idea."

"Actually, I was about to say that maybe the Gallery was a little too... constricting," my friend countered. "Luckily for us, or I should say, for *you*, we have a wealth of locations we can use instead. Recognise this one?"

I knew I did, but it took me a few moments more to place it. Then, I snapped my fingers.

"China," I said.

"China," my new friend confirmed.

"You've been through all my travel photos, haven't you?"

"To be fair, you gave us permission."

"I don't remember that."

"I know. There's a reason for why."

I shook my head, taking his word for it. He was the professional, after all.

The meadow was a completely self-contained space bordered by green woodland and the steep rise of the mountainside, down which rivulets of meltwater ran. There hadn't been snow and ice at the top, as far as I could remember, but now I could see small white cracks in the peak, if I looked carefully: tiny, isolated ridges of snow thawing out, feeding the lush green grass and thick carpet of blue wildflowers below. Beams of sunlight streaked down from behind the summit, spreading out like splayed fingers on a giant hand, making bright spots in the green grasses. It was a meadow in the clouds, this place, which is what I had loved about it the first time I had ever seen it: halfway up a peak, a flat, iridescent plateau sitting in a natural crevice that felt like a floating garden, because when you looked out from the meadow, all you could see was rich blue sky: the rest of the world lay below, out of reach. It was like looking up at the clouds from ground level only to see vapour, when in reality, what sat on top of the fluffy masses that moved through the blue was a verdant green oasis, hidden from those beneath. From then on in, I only ever imagined clouds like that: secret gardens, scudding across the sky.

Running around the edges of the meadow, a slatted wooden walkway with a rustic, wobbly wooden railing. In the far distance, a whirring sound. It took me a minute, but then I remembered. Access to the meadow had been via cable car only.

"Why did you choose this place?" I asked, breathing in a type of air you only get when up high: thinner, but cleaner.

"I told you. I didn't. *You* did. Anyway. We could always use more time outdoors," my friend said, but I could tell he was evading the truth. I decided not to push it. I was happy with our new location.

Or I would be as long as I could enjoy it without Silhouette marching in.

"What's on the menu, then, sunshine?" I asked, approaching the plinth with a resigned sigh.

"That's for you to find out," he said, but I was already blotting him out.

Because inside the glass dome lay another strip of yellow ribbon. I blinked, for the ribbon looked like the dreaded lock of hair, and I flinched, but on second examination it returned to just being a ribbon, and I sighed.

I was not sure this was much better.

20

SALIENCY

The ribbon was pale yellow, more of a thick strip of cloth really. I knew exactly where it was from, and where it's real-life counterpart currently resided, outside of this glass container.

And I wasn't sure I wanted to confront it.

I sighed, knowing that this wasn't how we played the game. The only way forward was by accepting the process, trusting the process, even though the process was painful.

So painful.

The real version of this ribbon was tied around a tree in a forest somewhere in Korea, where my husband had attached it. Memories moved less sluggishly to the front of things than they had before. Slowly, my brain was repairing some of the holes it was riddled with, like flesh knitting over a wound.

He hadn't been my husband at the time. In fact, I remembered I had just broken up with him, moved out of our apartment of seven years, shacked up with a friend. I had hurt him in the process, and he had taken himself off to a far corner of the globe, as was his habit, to lick lacerations, think about things. I had gone somewhere else: Nepal. Trying to discover ourselves through separation. We ran from each other like frightened mice skittering away from a cat.

"Can I ask you something?" I said to my companion, eyes fixed on the strip of yellow beneath the glass.

"Of course."

"Why… objects? Clues. Why not just sit me down, ask me about my life? Wouldn't it be easier than all… all this?"

He nodded, as if approving of my question. "You're right to ask."

"I am?"

"Believe it or not, this is not your first rodeo, when it comes to therapy. The more conventional techniques, unfortunately, didn't ever seem to land." He snapped a finger, and two red armchairs sprouted from the ground like strange velvety mushrooms.

"You can do that too?"

He winked. "I've been learning from you," he said, sitting down in one of the chairs and sighing in comfort.

"You have?"

"You inspire me," he said, winking.

I followed suit by sitting, and laughed. "Now I *know* you're a shrink," I said, because that is exactly how it felt, as if I were sitting in session at his private practice, even though the room was decorated with my personal memory, a wallpaper unique to my own experiences. The chairs were the exact sort you would expect to find in a therapist's study: comfortable and attractive without being overly ornate. In place of potted plants artfully arranged on white shelves or in tall pots, thin pines and spruces filled the background. Instead of large, framed prints of neutral landscapes photographed in black and white upon the walls, a verdant, beautiful backdrop served instead, a soothing, soft vista to put me at ease. The meadow, I realised, was perfect territory for this sort of thing. It was a place in which to relax. It wasn't neutral territory, not exactly, but it was familiar ground. There was space to breathe, here. Places to direct my vision and attention when facing him became too much.

And I had been happy here, in the real, live version of this place, wandering amongst the wildflowers.

"You're missing the coffee table with the box of tissues," I pointed out, and he gave a single snort of acknowledgement. I made a sort of flexing motion with my right index finger, more as a courtesy than anything else, for I didn't need the motion, but he might need the warning. A large, polished wooden table popped into view; two steaming mugs of fresh coffee placed neatly on drinks coasters that would protect the wooden surface. I flicked my finger again, feeling a little like the witch in a technicolour TV show, and a large box of tissues materialised, one lily-white piece of paper poking up out of the box in readiness for me.

Then, my friend steepled his fingers, and began to talk.

"Saliency," he said.

I had absolutely no idea what he was on about.

"How long do you think we've got, Boss?"

As Evans asks this, the medical report pings into the Boss's inbox, with a single word in the subject line: CEASE.

She shows it to her colleague, mutely.

"Ah. Not long at all, then."

"I can hold them off for a little bit – no one can do anything without my acknowledgement of this report. Besides, they haven't found a room for her at the infirmary, not yet. And our locks are all wired to the system, and technically…"

"You're battening down the hatches for a siege, Boss?"

"I suppose I am." The Boss gets up, walks around, stretches, drinks more water.

"At least the Psych is back to doing his job. Which is something, I suppose. How are her vitals?"

"Fine. She seems just fine. Not that I am sure we can trust any of this equipment anymore, mind you."

"I will take fine. She must be feeling safer again. Good. We've all seen what happens when she doesn't feel safe." Both techs think back to the Silhouette that leapt from rooftop to rooftop in the patient's ad-libbed memory construct, and shudder.

* * *

"What now?"

"Saliency."

"Am I supposed to know what that means?" I said, running the word over in my mind. *Saliency.*

"No. Saliency is two things, two things that are relevant to you here, at this moment in time."

"Enlighten me."

"First, it's a quality. It means something that is particularly noticeable."

I frowned. "Like a blue marble in a jar full of white marbles?"

He nodded his head, pleased. "Yes! Exactly like that."

"But I thought that was…" I frowned. What was I trying to recall? Something I had seen somewhere in a fancy magazine: *mnemonic object method.* It didn't matter.

"Try and stay focused, Magpie."

"Sorry. Saliency. Like a yellow ribbon tied around a single tree in a forest."

"Precisely. Imagine walking into that forest for the first time. Out of all the tree trunks before you, which one are you going to focus on, or notice, the most?"

"The one with the yellow ribbon tied to it."

"Of course. Because that object stands out. Its contrasts with those around it. Saliency, in this sense, is an attentional mechanism, it helps us to learn and survive. It means we focus on the most important things first. Put all the resources in the right place. Our ancestors probably found themselves better able to hunt and survive and avoid threats because of it."

"What does that have to do with me?"

"Well, what we have done here, in this construct, is gather together those objects that your brain has, over the years, deemed salient. We spent time in your world, talking to your family, looking at your diaries, sifting through your photographs, looking at the things in your house. Choosing items that stood out for you, more than others. Like the briefcase, like the rock. Like the photograph of your mother and your grandmother.

Like your grandfather's notebook, or this yellow ribbon. Granted, there will be things we have missed. Secrets you kept, as you told me. Things not photographed or recorded. But we feel we curated a fairly representative collection. Salient stimuli come in a number of forms: objects, sounds, images, certain words. They can be reactive, or memory-dependent."

"And you think by focusing on these objects, I'll solve the mystery?"

He rubbed a hand carefully across his bearded chin. "It's important to remember that there may be *no* mystery, Magpie. Your depression… your suicidal ideations… could be hormonal, or chemical. It wouldn't be right for me to pass professional judgment. But we are on a mission of sorts, aren't we? To see if we can figure it out. You do have a recurring… issue."

"I keep trying to die." Although funnily enough, I hadn't felt the urge lately. Everything was so powerfully surreal and unpredictable, I had been so preoccupied there had been no room for anything else.

"But like I said, we don't really know *why* that is, beyond hormones, or brain chemistry. You wrote a letter that strongly indicated you thought there was some hidden trauma in your past, trauma that might explain why you keep having these urges."

"So why not just hypnotise me, get to it that way?"

"Hypnosis works better when we have a stronger idea of *what* it is we are trying to find, exactly, or who it is that we are trying to talk to. Do we need three-year-old Magpie? Do we need eleven-year-old Magpie? Teenage Magpie? New mother Magpie?"

"No! Not her!" I spat this violently at him.

"Okay." He noted the response, moved on without making a big deal of it. I swallowed and tried to slow my suddenly racing heartbeat.

"Look. It's entirely possible there are purely biological reasons for your ideation. A hormonal sensitivity, for example.

But we can't rule out the idea of a triggering event, and that is the point of all… this." My friend waved his hands at the meadow, and then pointed to the plinth, which still stood proud in the centre of the green and blue field.

"Focusing on objects of emotional importance… there are several terms for it, but salience bias is a pretty good label, if we have to use one."

"Salience bias."

"Yeah. Preference over one item. Items you've mentioned, anecdotally, or kept around your house, or written about in your diaries."

"Am I to take it you've read *all* my diaries, then?" I should have been more annoyed about it, but I wasn't. It felt like he knew me pretty well, diary or no.

He moved past this, too. "We can combine the idea of salience bias quite nicely with the idea of salience in computing. It's called visual saliency detection."

"Meaning…"

"Imagine this is all a giant computer programme, right?" The way he said imagine, and then half-winked… he was essentially confirming what I had just figured out, on top of the mountain. That I was plugged into a virtual construct. He knew that *I knew*. How, I had no idea, but that wasn't what was important in this particular moment.

"Not a big stretch, if I'm honest," I said, drily.

"Smart," he replied, sitting up straighter in his chair. "Visual saliency detection is like, um… a model. Or a technique, in computing, to mimic human behaviour. A simulation of the human visual system, something that helps whoever is engaging with the environment to perceive something in the most useful way possible."

I took a deep breath. "So, this is a giant virtual video game. Classic quest format. Classic travelling companion set-up." I pointed at my friend, who bowed from his seated position. "Along the way, I encounter different environments, and different objects present themselves, significant objects. And how I choose to interact with them sets my mind on a path. And along that path, we uncover things that might be hidden. Secrets. Events. Traumas. And we make decisions based on those objects, until we reach the... conclusion."

A slow and creeping succession of traumas, I thought, suddenly, and I remembered it then, the letter I had written. *A diminutive chain of...*

My friend chewed on a longer strand of beard that sprouted from beneath his bottom lip. His eyes were very blue, in that moment. "Sort of," he conceded. "Sort of, but not quite."

I got up, went back over to the yellow ribbon. I could see what he meant, about saliency, because despite everything in the meadow that was of note and arguably far more deserving of my attention, it was the yellow fabric that my eyes were continually drawn back to.

So, I let myself get drawn in. I lifted the dome, picked up the ribbon, wrapped it around my wrist, went back to the chair, and sat down again.

"Ready?" My friend asked.

"As ever," I sighed, and the ribbon filled my vision.

21

YELLOW RIBBON

In life, I did not have a physical yellow ribbon hidden in a memory box. Instead, I had a glossy print-out of a photograph of the ribbon, tied around the aforementioned tree in Korea. The tree trunk it adorned was scaly, like the thick, dry skin of a lizard. The ribbon stood out in the forest, a bright yellow statement in a wall of green and *(green is my favourite colour, Mummy, what's yours?)* brown.

Salient.

My husband had printed the photo and given it to me one day over dinner.

When he gave it to me, I looked at him quizzically. We were in a fancy restaurant. We always were on the night before Valentine's. That was the night he had proposed to me, the night where I had finally said "yes". Every year after, we lived it up like royalty on February the 13th, and we thought ourselves better for it.

My husband was not one for what I called "day-to-day" romance. But he was one for grand occasional statements, and gestures. He was good at them. Thoughtful. He used to call it "drawing a line in the sand". Doing something physical, and imbuing it with real meaning, resolve, promise. "You can either be black or white, in life," he'd say. "Not grey."

Later on, someone else would tell me to stop being quite so black and white, and embrace the murky in-between, live more in the grey, because that way led to greater possibilities. Differing ideologies, same outcome: my life, moving in different directions.

"So what's this?" I'd said, slugging back a huge mouthful of red wine. We always got so drunk at these dinners that the long-awaited sex-festival that was supposed to happen afterwards never did. We'd fall asleep instead, full, drunk, happy nonetheless, in a way, in a specialised way that was unique to us, wake up hungover and aggravated, horny yet ever so slightly resigned.

He'd looked at me with his green eyes, and I'd known that this was important.

"It was when I was in Korea. You'd left me to live with someone else."

When I met my husband I was very young. We were both still finding our way as people. We found our way together, but it had consequences. I didn't know how to grow outside of him. I wasn't really capable of looking after myself. And, seven years in, I experienced the itch: except the itch wasn't another man, but myself. I'd grown so dependent on this other human that I realised one day I had absolutely no idea who I was. So I left. I got a loan from the bank, moved in with a girlfriend, went trekking in Nepal. Partied. Felt sad. Felt happy, too. It was all very strange. He didn't cope with it well. He parked his car on streets he knew I would walk down, waited for me to pass by, in case I'd left him for someone else. He bought a huge television, almost as big as a fridge. He learned how to make jam. Pots and pots of jam. Why, I don't think even he remembers.

He travelled to Korea for the same reasons, I suppose, as I'd gone to Nepal. To think, to reflect. To get away. To take himself out of the life we'd trapped ourselves inside of, gain some perspective.

When he got back, we'd gone for dinner. I'd waved my wine glass at him, slopping some over the side so that it stained the white tablecloth. "Go on," I'd prompted.

He was serious, the sting of our breakup still raw. "I went for a walk around the burial site of one dynasty of Korean kings and queens. There were these large... lumps everywhere in the ground. It was a long walk along the road between sites, and I decided to do a proper walk, in a loop. I was thinking about you, and how wonderful you were."

(But you're a piece of shit, aren't you? Really. A worthless piece of shit. Can't hold down a job. Can't contribute. Can't parent properly. You make a terrible wife. You make people unhappy. You're a piece of shit, shit, shit, shit...)

I'd grimaced, embarrassed. I hated hyperbole, and compliments, but craved romance, in that contrary way that people who think they are one thing, but are secretly another, do.

"I really wanted you to be there with me, but I knew that if you were, I'd have made excuses, not done the thinking I needed to do. I walked and walked through a forest. There was a yellow ribbon lying on the ground. It seemed out of place, and I picked it up. I kept going, and it was very quiet, and I decided to marry you, then, and I decided not to go back on my decision, so I tied the ribbon onto the tree as a promise to myself, and to us, that I would go through with it, that we would get back together. I tied it up, took this photo, and kept walking. Saw some tombs, went for a lonely dinner."

This was how we made decisions for each other: not by asking for the other's permission or participation, because talk, we would find, was cheap and in ample supply, but by determining that things were going to be a certain way and then acting on that decision. Incredibly, it seemed to work, most of the time. For a while. Perhaps we could sense when the other person had run out of energy, or strength, and needed to abdicate responsibility. Perhaps we both just needed to feel like we were in control. Relationships were always like that, for me: a ceaseless swing of the balancing scales, sometimes tipped this way, sometimes tipped that way.

Back in the moment, looking at an object upon a plinth, I knew what this photograph meant. When my husband had tied that ribbon around that tree, he had made a decision to give our lives together a chance. It was a declaration of life.

I had not repaid him in kind.

I wondered if the ribbon was still knotted around that tree trunk in Korea, surrounded by sleeping kings and queens. I hoped it was. But also, the thought of it fluttering in a thin breeze, ends tattered and ragged from the elements, made me sad.

I stood up, unwrapped the other yellow ribbon from my wrist. Slid it into my back jean pocket, instead. Out of sight, yet not quite out of mind.

Declarations. Gestures, drawing a line in the sand. Was I supposed to make a similar proclamation of intent? Is that what all this was about? How was that going to help me?

"I don't know what I am supposed to do with this," I said, looking at my new friend.

He gazed back up at me from his position in the chair. Was that disappointment I had seen flare in his eyes? A brief flash of pain, or was I projecting again? It was so hard to know what to do. I needed guidance.

He understood. Nodding, he said, calmly, "Why don't we leave things there for a bit, explore something else for a while?"

"What do you mean?"

He twisted his hand, a sharp, definitive movement from the wrist, like turning a doorknob on a heavy oak door. I saw a dial that hadn't been visible before.

"I thought you said we didn't need hand gestures."

"I said that *you* don't need them. And I was right. I am nowhere near as skilled with all this as you are."

It showed. The dial felt crude. "Does that bother you?"

He chuckled. "Why should it? All I care about is helping you. Life is not a competition, Magpie. We can all be good at different things."

"What are you good at?" Was I flirting with him? Trying to.

He smiled. It was suggestive.

He was flirting with me too.

A large, glowing rectangle popped up in the air between us, breaking the moment. On it, a slowly scrolling sequence of images drifted past.

"What's this?" I said, not fully understanding.

"Well, you said it yourself. We don't need the Gallery anymore. We have a whole world of places open to us, after all – we went through all your photographs. There were a *lot*."

"I've been lucky." I admitted, somewhat embarrassed. "But can't I just do what I did before? Imagine it up myself? Why do I need a menu of choices? I thought we were going to be a little more creative than that."

"I think, on reflection..." He meant after Silhouette, and I knew it. "We perhaps need to slow down a bit," my friend admitted. "You'll exhaust yourself if you aren't careful. We can still embrace variety whilst also giving your brain a bit of a rest."

"I suppose so," I said, reluctantly.

"See anywhere that takes your fancy?" A parade of exotic locations drifted between us. I screwed up my face, thinking. The menu scrolled too slowly, so I raised my own hand and flicked through the options at a speed I was more comfortable with, so fast the images shot by in a blur of colour. Something caught my attention, and I reversed the hand motion, bringing a picture sharply back into focus.

A huge smile spread across my face as I looked at it and realised what I was staring at.

"Here," I said, and as I spoke, the image grew in size, breaking out of the scrolling menu window, filling up my horizons, deep azure blues and contrasting yellowy greens rapidly overwriting the meadow with the plinth and the trees and the boardwalk and the tiny sweet wildflowers and the incongruously red chairs arranged neatly opposite each other upon the long, thick grass.

In its place, grew...

* * *

"Well," Evans says, blinking. "I did not expect that."

The Boss says nothing. She chews on the end of a pen, oblivious to the red ink leaking out of the plastic tube and staining the corners of her mouth. She is thinking about her email to HR, which has thus far gone unanswered, and the nurse report, calling for a cease. She absentmindedly refreshes her inbox every few minutes, impatient for an answer from HR and an idea of when the ambulance is coming. The hospital will call her when transport has been dispatched, but The Boss has diverted all calls to a voicemail-to-email service.

HR's silence irritates her, as time stretches out. The HR Director and she do not always get along, and it wouldn't surprise The Boss if she went to the bottom of the priority pile until the end of the day, despite her email having been tagged as "urgent". Office politics. If she doesn't hear back in another five minutes, she will take a risk, make a long and unwelcome hike up five flights of stairs to the HR office, knock the damn door down if she has to. The more she thinks about the Psych's behaviour, his strange push-pull rapport with the patient, his disappearing acts, his inconsistent communication and lack of reports back, and the clearly palpable sexual tension that flares between both people on the screen every now and then, the more alarm bells start ringing in her mind. Not enough to pull the Psych's plug, not quite, not when things are so vulnerable, but enough that she wants to be better armed with information. She has already cued up a replacement Psych who waits on standby for the call to join whenever she deems necessary. That is new territory, however. Never in the history of the programme have they had to replace one Psych with another, mid-treatment.

But then never in the history of the programme have they had a patient like Magpie.

While The Boss wrestles with all this, beneath Evans's desk, the dark, sticky blob that emerged from the printer shudders, shaking like a jelly on a plate, and stretches outwards, seeming to double in size. A tiny, questing, wriggling little growth emerges from the central body mass, poking up and feeling around itself like a long, prehensile tongue, or the tail of a monkey, or the tentacle of an octopus. It scrabbles about, past dust bunnies and discarded paper clips, around scrunched up note paper filled with Evan's crude doodles, across old, greasy pizza boxes and dropped pepperoni slices, underneath the tangled web of cables and wires, until it finds purchase on the rim of a USB port set into one of the desktop computers not far from Evans's feet. It braces itself, drags its mass closer to the whirring black box, which sounds as if it is working overtime, sucking in as much cool air from behind the unit as possible with a fan that has developed a tiny, high-pitched squeak, making it sound as if it is in a state of constant distress.

The blob cautiously explores the depth of the USB port with its tactile proboscis, and then slowly, painstakingly contracts in on itself, shuddering. It feeds its mass into the computer base unit through the port, distorting its shape and pushing its brown, tacky flesh into the rectangular slot with laborious care, crawling back into the network whence it came, an exercise of exploration, like a fledgling bird leaving the nest for the first time, figuring out its exits and entrances, testing its own boundaries, and limits, flexing its theoretical muscles, and neither Evans, nor his boss, nor the woman in the cradle from where the infectious little blob once came, nor the Psych, who has his own secrets, have any idea what's in store for them.

22

EASTER ISLAND

"I did not expect this," my new/old friend said, blinking and squinting in the fierce light of a South Pacific sun.

I grinned, feeling happy. "I like to keep you on your toes," I replied, and I meant it. There was something rather empowering about keeping him guessing like this. Partly because he was so enigmatic himself. Where had he been, before the meadow? Where had he gone? To his boat? Somewhere else? His prolonged absence had felt deliberate, rather than accidental. Wherever he had gone, he hadn't wanted to talk about it. He had seemed relieved to see me, but he was still holding back. So yes, it was enjoyable to fuck with that, to choose the most unlikely destination on a menu of pre-programmed treats. On a more personal level, there was something fun about showing him these places too, something nice about opening up slowly and letting him into more and more of my memories, even if he already knew where I'd travelled, even if he had already seen the photographs. For some reason, that didn't seem to matter. What mattered was that I was once again in a place where I'd been happy, and that was nice. It had been so long since I'd allowed myself to have fun, to experience joy, contentment.

And content I was, because we were standing in one of my favourite places on earth.

Arranged before us in a solemn rank upon a raised plinth, their faces angled upward, noses proudly tilted, mouths faintly pursed, eyes blank and arms held close by their sides, stood fifteen giant men carved from rock. They loomed with their backs to a blue, deep sea that stretched out far beyond. The second to last statue on the far right wore a jaunty red hat made from volcanic rock. Moai statues, these were. The Easter Island heads. Except these weren't the picture-postcard stone heads resting upon a green hillside, lying on their backs or buried up to their chins and beyond. These were proud ancestral statues arranged in a standing ceremony. They had rounded shoulders and pot bellies and wide, broad chests. Long, curled earlobes bracketed their faces. A crust of sea salt and lichen had grown around their mouths and eyes. At the foot of the plinth, wild ponies grazed the scrubby grass, nipping it to the roots with blunt, busy teeth. Rising out of the grass nearby were the remains of ancient structures built with more of the same porous volcanic rock, structures that had long since worn down to brown little nubs. Some of these nubs had suggestions of carvings in them: fish, a bird-headed man, swirls and scrolls and patterns that were almost indistinguishable unless you knew what to look for, which I did, but only because I'd been here before.

I pivoted on my heel, taking in the whole landscape. In the distance, a hill smoked: a controlled fire was turning the grass there to charcoal, the yellowy-green crisping to a rich black as the fire crept inexorably across the hillside. Thick smoke spiralled up into the sky. More horses dotted the rolling hillsides closer to us. Beyond them, the island sprouted as many as eight now dormant volcanic peaks, unmistakable, their flat tops and lopsided cone-structures jutting up like pimples in flesh. At the foot of these volcanoes, small white houses nestled into the earth. There was only one town on the island that I could remember, Hanga Roa, but a few other residences had been built not far from it: holiday bungalows for tourists, probably.

The level of detail that had gone into recreating this environment, memory, whatever you wanted to call it, was incredible: for all intents and purposes it was like being back on the island again for real. Whoever was responsible for designing it, for putting it all together just for me, had not only been through all of my travel photos and diaries with a very fine-toothed comb, but scoured other resources and reference points diligently, too. I was suddenly not sure how I felt about that. I was aware now, more than ever, that this was a reconstruction not of my making, and that left me feeling a bit confused. How could I engage fully with memories turned by a different hand? Is a rose still a rose by any other name? Is a memory still your memory if someone else paints it?

Thinking this way caused something to happen in the air around me. There was another ripple, another blast of what felt like static energy, as if the very consistency of reality changed momentarily. Behind that reality, other bodies, other worlds. My body? My real form, flesh and blood?

(Blood)

(So, so much blood)

(Oh, God, it's everywhere)

(His favourite shirt, ruined)

(What did you do?? WHAT DID YOU DO??)

I snapped out of it, remembering what had happened the last time I'd lost grip like this.

Silhouette.

I didn't have the time or energy to start questioning the very nature of my own existence. If nothing else, overthinking on that level was exhausting and a colossal waste of my limited energy reserves.

"I didn't realise it was so hot here," my friend said, fanning his face with a hand. He was growing very adept at pulling me out of myself at exactly the right point in time.

"All this in front of you, and that's all you can think to say?" I shook my head. "I'm disappointed in you."

"Be gentle with me," my friend replied, smiling. "It's not every day your job takes you to Easter Island."

* * *

"Easter Island," Evans says, rolling his eyes. "Fucking Easter Island."

"Your team built these environments; you must have known it was on the menu."

"No, it's just… talk about privileged. Anyway, I don't keep tabs on every single scene. That's what we have spreadsheets for. And besides, with her, there is just… so much. She's been *everywhere*, Boss. Even to Antarctica. I'm surprised she didn't pick that, that's one environment I do remember. Vividly. Took Alf weeks to figure out realistic iceberg texturing. And have you any idea how complicated it is to accurately simulate an albatross in flight? I'm not kidding. Weeks. I thought he was going to have a heart attack."

"Apparently, icebergs are good for chronic pain," The Boss muses out loud, trying to distract herself from her mounting anxiety. She is feeling pressured to act from all sides, and yet at the same time, nothing is happening. No emails. No ambulance alert. It is shredding her nerves, waiting for the guillotine to drop like this.

"What?"

"In a VR setting, I mean," is how she replies.

Evans still doesn't get it. "What?"

"Imperial College did a study. Immersive, three-sixty videos of the arctic were proven to help fight sensitivity to pain when they were experiencing it. Something to do with perceived cold temperatures."

"You're taking the piss."

"No, I'm really not. They ran a trial, rubbed chilli paste onto people's skin and sat them down with VR headsets, did the whole National Geographic thing, and saw… surprising results. VR influences pathological processing. Ice and snow, versus burning chili paste… makes sense, I guess."

"So what, because they were *looking* at something cold, their skin didn't burn as much?"

"The theory is that they didn't feel the pain as keenly, yes.

And you know it isn't as simple as just looking. VR is more than that."

"Their brains overrode the physical symptoms of pain? I mean, it's not like I don't believe you, but…"

The older woman sighs, brings up a browser window on her phone, and types something into a search engine. "Not that I need to prove anything to you, but here we go: *Attenuation of capsaicin-induced ongoing pain and secondary hyperalgesia during exposure to an immersive virtual reality environment.*"

Evans scoffs. "'Immersive environment'. Three sixty videos aren't 'immersive environments'," they're like fucking zoetropes in comparison to what we do here. Imperial would have a field day if we let them loose in our little basement."

"All the more reason to keep working on our Magpie, Evans. All the more reason. I told you, think of the applications. *Think.* Surgery, without anaesthesia? Long term pain relief for burns victims? So many applications."

"I'm tired of thinking all the time, Boss. No offence. And as for this… display," he waves his hands at the row of monoliths, the giant men on a plinth, the classic Easter Island optics, "Well, we don't really have time for this, do we?"

"No, no, you're right. We don't. I'll try and hurry things along again with the Psych." She is tapping out a message to him as she speaks.

"You know he won't answer."

"He will if I tell him I have his replacement queued up and ready to go."

"Do you really think he cares about being fired, Boss? He's got his own agenda, you said that much before."

The older woman sighs, undeterred. She can only keep trying, at this point. She finishes her message, hits send. *HURRY THINGS ALONG,* she says.

Evans checks the patient's vitals again, for want of something better to do. He takes only a cursory glance at the woman in the OR, finding it easier to interact with her data than the real-life person. Behind the glass, she seems relaxed enough, chatting to herself and smiling for all the world as if she is not trussed in a harness, rigged up to a server, about to change the face of modern medicine and psychology. Her happiness is at odds with what is happening out in the real world: a dangerous slide into unknown territory, the probable end of Evans's career, considerable damage to the reputation of the department, not to mention the University, if they continue the treatment despite the cease order… the tech is not excited by the potential hiding in the patient's brain, not like his Boss is. He is scared of it, and the implications of something so profound.

Evans looks back at the med monitor, frowns. He could swear… something blips near the corner of the window, a tiny moment of unexpected movement, as if something amorphous is wriggling around behind the colour display, although he knows this is absurd. It feels akin to catching sight of the floating, glassy things that swim past his vision at unexpected moments: wigglers.

He wipes his eyes and looks at the screen again. The blip has gone, but he saw it.

Great, he thinks. Something else fucking up.

The wireless health nodes going haywire? The body sensors were always the first to go, for some reason, perhaps because, pound for pound, they were one of the most expensive components of the entire system. They had to endure a lot; sweat, other bodily fluids, temperature fluctuations, violent motion… Wearables took time to build, and theirs were all manufactured by hand by a small, local company, rather than fabricated in a factory.

He keeps his gaze firmly fixed on the med monitor, but no further blips occur. He decides not to tell his Boss about it, there would be no point. She isn't going to stop, no matter what. He knows that.

He lets his frustration leak out.

"When does the Psych, like, do therapy shit?" he asks,

impatient. "Or is he just going to wander about in there with her forever like he's on a fucking world tour or something. Nice for some, maybe I'll dive in too, I could use a holiday right now."

"I think your blood sugars are getting low again Evans. More coffee?"

Evans grimaces, the thought of caffeine or sugar making him feel sick.

Off to his left, a computer screen starts to blink, on and off, on and off.

Evans scowls, thumps the side of the monitor.

"Fuck *off!* Nothing else, for the love of God!"

He thumps it again, cold-powers it off, then back on. The screen's image settles, remains steady.

Evans shakes his fist at it. "That's better. Do as you're fucking told."

"You're talking to the equipment, Evans," his Boss remarks.

"Leave me alone," he replies.

She obliges.

"I have a question," I said.

"Uh-oh," my friend replied.

"So this... this was made by *your* people. This is not... *me* right now. Not like earlier." I waved at the island, the heads, the volcanos. Keeping track of *who* was responsible for each part of the construct I found myself in, as I moved through it, was proving a little tricky. Because it felt like I was a threaded needle, working my way through a large patchwork quilt. Different patches embroidered by different artists. Sometimes, I stitched on something of my own design, like the cupboard behind the red door, the party, the room with my mother and grandmother. The mountain. Sometimes, the patches on the quilt were embroidered by my friend, like his boat. His waiting room. Something he had created for himself, as a bolthole or a neutral space. The rest of the construct, the rest of the quilt, like the Gallery, the meadow, and now this place, was a pre-programmed walkthrough, a templated pattern, a virtual framework of standardised layout patches and environments.

One space, one quilt, several different artists.

But the patches that were the brightest were the ones I'd made for myself. It was exciting to think about, and scary: being able to create things to such an immersive degree. It felt I was projecting a picture from my mind onto a four-dimensional canvas. My friend seemed keen on me doing this, too. He pushed me, encouraged me to explore my surroundings and my own innate potential with a level of gentle reassurance I had not felt for a long time. When I thought about that, I felt a small burst of real pride on his part for what I had managed to achieve so far. I realised how important and powerful a sentiment pride could be. His quiet sense of happiness at my achievements was a rare and wonderful thing to experience. It kept me powering on through this, even though I

(But what is the point? What's the point? Who cares about any of this? You don't deserve praise, encouragement. You don't deserve any of it. You're–)

"This one?" My friend cleared his throat, bringing me back into the moment again. "This environment is theirs…" He self-corrected: "*Ours,* I mean, yes. And they're not my people. I work for them. In theory. I prefer to think I work for you, though. Makes the stakes higher." He winked at me, then looked up admiringly at the Moai while I pondered this. I had gotten the impression up until now that he was a company man. Part of the team who lived in the final layer. But he seemed to want to distance himself from them. Why? Again, I had a feeling of a secret agenda being stealthily laid before me.

He went on. "Impressive, though, isn't it? They get better all the time. You can almost *smell* the sea salt in the air, can't you?"

I lifted my nose, like the Moai did, and breathed in. He was right.

A faint echo of scent, where there shouldn't be any.

Evans lifts his head without realising he is doing so, sniffs the musty air in the observation room. Only, it isn't musty anymore. It smells... salty. Tangy.

Like sea air.

"Can you smell that?" he asks his Boss, wondering if he has finally lost his shit. "Salt?"

His Boss, preoccupied, slips her arms into a crumpled blazer that hangs from the back of her chair. She doesn't answer Evans, because an email has come in, finally, summoning her to HR. She has a sinking feeling in her stomach that she has been played, somehow, but the full extent of how is yet to be revealed.

"I'm just nipping out for a moment, Evans," she says, in a far-away voice.

He stares. "What? But you can't leave me here to face the music alone! What if they come for her? Am I supposed to do what, fight them off or something?"

"I know, and you're right, but I don't have a choice. There's something else going on here, something I don't understand, and... well. It's... an emergency."

"Tell me the truth," Evans asks, his face cold. "Are you doing a bunk? Going on the run? Leaving me here to take all the blame when it all goes tits up?"

She shakes her head. "No. I would never do that. HR have something to tell me about the Psych, and I don't think it's going to be good. Sit tight, I'll be as quick as I can. And you'll be fine. I'll have my phone on me. Oh. And keep a close eye on him, would you?" She points to the Psych. "If he does anything else... unorthodox, boot him from the programme, okay? Just cut the link."

"What's going on, Boss?"

"I'm not sure yet, Evans," the silver-haired woman says, and she grabs the door handle. A bright crack of light appears around the edges of the door as she pulls it open. "Just... sit tight."

With that, she is through the door before Evans can say another word.

"Sit tight," he mutters, shaking his head. "The fuck else am I going to do?"

The younger man turns silently back to his bank of screens, feeling hugely alone, overwhelmed, and distinctly sick. Before him, a row of stone men stares out at him in blank-eyed judgement.

He hates them.

Overhead, a striplight that hangs directly above becomes host to a small patch of brown, viscous, tar-like substance that seeps in, flooding the light-casing, slowly creeping across the fluorescent tube, intent on complete coverage.

Evans is too exhausted and over-wrought to notice the light slowly dimming around him.

"Can I ask you a question?"

My friend shaded his reddening face with one hand, looking about for cover, for shelter, but there was little to be had on Easter Island, the small lump of volcanic rock having been almost entirely denuded of trees over time. I remembered this sun, or that sun, the *real* sun, remembered how easily it had burned my skin. I had peeled for days after, shedding little papery shavings of myself all over the place. They had floated off on a pacific breeze, particles on a journey. In that way, I supposed, I had left pieces of myself all over the world, become part of a wider geography than I'd ever realised. I liked that idea. Well-travelled dust.

What I did *not* like was the nagging feeling of suspicion that was building up about my new travel partner.

He moved closer to the plinth, standing in the broad, solid shadow of the tallest Moai.

"What is it?" he replied, fanning himself with his hands again.

"Can I trust you?" I asked, bluntly.

He thought about that.

"Well, the simple fact that you're asking me implies that you don't," he said. "Which is not ideal, obviously. For this to work, you need to feel comfortable with me. You need to trust me. You need a safe space."

I nodded. "You're right." I came clean. "But you're starting to… bother me."

"Okay," he said, calmly. "So talk to me."

"Why do I feel like sometimes I know you? From before… this."

"Maybe I remind you of somebody you once knew. That happens."

I frowned. "No. It's more than that. Sometimes I feel this… *pull* towards you. And sometimes I feel as if I know exactly what you're about to say. Not déjà vu exactly, but… It's hard to describe… I feel like…" I shrugged. "I know you."

"Magpie, there are large parts of your personal history we haven't covered yet. Large parts of your memory still missing, your past. We haven't gotten to it all, we interrupted the Gallery sequencing before we could finish every artefact. It has to be that I remind you of someone you knew once, someone you're having a hard time recalling."

I could tell he was lying because he was bad at it.

"Sometimes people just fit well together, I suppose," he continued. "Like–"

"Puzzle pieces," I murmured.

(*We used to fit, we used to be a team, now I don't recognise you anymore. I miss you. I miss my wife, I miss–*)

(*Why do we have to have the same argument over time and time again?*)

(I regret this, you know. I regret all of this)
(I've been so selfish)
(We're done here, I–)

He snapped his mouth shut, unable to hide that he had been about to say the same thing.

And a feeling came over me then, a feeling so rich and complex and intense that it clean took my breath away: a feeling of longing. As my friend looked up, our eyes met, and it was in him, too, this feeling, I knew it. And the longer we stood like that, the more I felt like maybe I knew his name, felt like it was on the tip of my tongue, familiar as a prayer, sweet as a song, I just couldn't quite get to it, and it was infuriating, it was absolutely fucking *infuriating*, and my longing turned to anger, swift as the weathervane that changes direction on a stormy day. I balled up my fists.

"I know you," I said, in a low, threatening voice.

My friend held out a hand in a placatory gesture. "Whatever you're feeling, Magpie, it isn't… you aren't… not yet, okay? Just trust me."

I narrowed my eyes. I realised my hair was suddenly whirling up around my face: a stiff, cool wind had blown in where before the air had been still and warm and fragrant.

"Where did you go, earlier?" I asked. "When Silhouette came for us? Did you get scared? It's not very supportive to leave me… stranded like that. Alone. Are therapists allowed to run out on their patients? Isn't there like, a code or something?"

"Are you afraid of being alone, Magpie?"

"I'm afraid of not getting a straight fucking answer from you every time I ask a simple fucking question!"

He nodded his head. "Okay, that's fair. I'm… not sure the best way to explain this, but let me try."

"Yes. That would be a good idea." The angry wind still blew, and my hair whipped about like the nest of snakes upon Medusa's head.

"So, this programme is designed around you, around your

life, and your unique needs, personality traits, influences, memories, right? It's a space for you to explore and grow within. I am not as firmly attached to this construct as you are, for that reason. It is not my... it is not my life, my experience of living. For me it is just a tool. I have a headset, some gloves, a microphone... and a script, although we deviated from that a long time ago." He chuckled ruefully. "I'm not 'wired in' quite as completely as you are. So when unexpected things happen, like Silhouette... it means I don't always know how to respond. The arrival of that... *thing*... it interfered with my equipment, booted me offline somehow. Cut the connection to the programme. I came back as quickly as I could. Does that make sense?"

The wind died down as I mulled it over. I imagined a woman lying on her back, a woman who looked like me, with multi-coloured wires sprouting out all over her body.

"I'm not even going to begin to try and understand how it works," I said, making a concession to his honesty, "But you mean, I guess, that because I'm more 'plugged in', I'm more fully... immersed than you are."

"Exactly," he confirmed, his eyes sparking up with something. "And, up until recently, you were not aware that this was all a fabrication, either. You thought this was reality. The bridge, the Gallery. I, however, never lost sight of my real situation. I know that this is all a virtual setting. Right now, my *real* self is sitting in a darkened room in the small apartment I rent over three miles away in Clifton. If you must know, I'm currently sitting cross-legged in my joggers on the floor, surrounded by cushions and various unhealthy snacks and dozens of bottles of water. I am wearing a headset and gloves and various sensors and things are attached to my body, although nowhere near as many as are attached to you. For that reason, even though I'm dying for a piss, I haven't had a bathroom break for three hours. Beyond that, I know, deep down, as I move around and interact with both you and these environments, that all I have to do to leave this place is remove my headset, or signal that I want out."

"Signal to who?"

"The others. There are moderators, trained technicians who monitor all this from a control centre in a basement building at the university, right next to where your sleeping self lies. They can control my input into the construct, too. To a certain extent."

"The Watchers," I mumbled, thinking about the voices that existed in a different layer.

"You can talk to them, if you like, but I don't think you'd get much out of it." He smirked as he said this, aware they could hear him.

"So you can leave at any time, but I'm supposed to wait to be physically unhooked?"

He nodded. "There is also a panic button if things get too intense, and I want a fast exit." He held up his hand, and I saw the small button at the base of his thumb again.

"I don't have a panic button?" I asked, not liking that idea very much.

"Magpie," my friend said. "I think we are way past the point where you need things like that to control this place, aren't we? *Way* past."

"What do you mean?"

He became uncomfortable, although not because of me, I sensed, but rather because we were being watched. He had things he wanted to tell me, or show me, but in secret.

"Fine," I said, staring up at the row of Moai. "That'll do, for now. Thanks for being honest."

"It's why I'm here," he said, smiling. "I just want you to be happy."

I didn't believe him, not entirely, but it was a good opportunity to segue. "And that's why I chose here," I said.

"Easter Island?"

"Yeah. I chose this place because... well. I was just very happy here."

"You can't be happy at home? Instead of eight thousand miles away on a tiny rock in the middle of the ocean?"

I didn't like how he phrased that so I ignored it.

"I was... very... free."

That word sparked excitement in my friend. "And what does it mean to you, to be free?" he asked.

I felt like a lot was riding on my response.

"It means everything," I said, so fiercely I surprised myself.

(Free! I wish I was free of this pain, free of this stress, free of myself, wouldn't everyone just be better off without me? Isn't it better for everyone, in the long run? Freedom, no more pain, no more worry, freedom in flight, no gravity, arms and legs supported by the air, flying downwards, you always liked the water, how would that feel? Weightlessness, no more–)

"Can we explore that a little?"

"In what sense?"

My friend grinned, a genuine, restraint-free show of pleasure. It was completely unprofessional, and utterly captivating.

I found myself smiling back.

"How about we try something a little... unconventional," he said, his enthusiasm infectious.

"Unconventional?"

"All in good time, Magpie. All in good time. Let's walk, shall we?"

"No!" Evans throws another pen at the Psych. It bounces off the part of the screen where his head is. "Nothing else unconventional, not now!"

But the Psych isn't listening, and hasn't been for a long time. Evans tries several times to message him, but these go unanswered. He knows the Psych is about to lead Magpie down some experimental path none of them are prepared for, he can sense it from here: intent. The Psych's behaviour reeks of malpractice.

Evans continues failing to make contact with the Psych while his mood descends into a low-lying type of fury that gives him a fierce headache, a real front-and-backer, as his wife used to say before she decided she didn't like him anymore. He feels abandoned by his Boss, who has fucked off precisely when Evans needs her the most: to pull rank. To advise. To take responsibility.

He considers what he has been told, that if the Psych were to try anything shady, he should pull the connection. Despite having been given permission to do so, Evans is still hesitant. Any abrupt loss of contact with the Psych could trigger a response in the patient: a subconscious panic attack, a fit of anger, or, more specifically, the return of Silhouette.

Beyond this, Evans does not feel comfortable pulling the plug because he still has a feeling his Boss is trying to set him up as a scapegoat for anything that goes wrong as a result of cutting the cord. He understands that his Boss is not his friend, no matter how chummy she appeared on the surface in the past. At the first opportunity, Evans will be thrown to the wolves so that the Boss can keep her job, and Evans does not wish to chuck years of his life down the toilet with the single press of a button unless he has absolutely no choice whatsoever.

So he dithers, trying without success to reach the Psych by any of the usual means and failing to get any response from the mysterious man who, unbeknownst to Evans, is currently giving his Boss a headache of her own as she sits in HR and stares in surprise at a photograph: a photograph of Magpie and the Psych, sitting next to each other in a restaurant, smiling into the camera. They look happy to be in each other's company and are close enough that their legs could be touching under the table, out of sight of the camera's eye.

They look good together.

He started to lead me towards the sea, and as we walked, side by side, I resisted the urge, a very real, very primal urge, to slip my hand into his, weave our fingers into a lattice. Instead, I just stayed close to him, letting my arm touch his occasionally, and then I came up short, shocked.

"Hang on a moment," I said, confused. "If I'm not really here, and you are not really here, then how come I can feel you? Touch you?"

"Because of how our brains work in tandem with our bodies. They call it proprioception, awareness of our bodies and how they move. Ever heard of phantom limb syndrome?"

This wasn't good enough. "But I can *feel* things. Interact with them. Pick them up. Touch them, touch you!"

"Your brain is simply telling your body you can feel things because it is assuming that what you're interacting with here is real. It's processing false data, in a way. Drawing assumptions based on the visual and auditory evidence in front of it. Like... trying to guess a hidden word, filling in the blanks for you on a game of hangman."

I flinched as the image of a stick man hanging from a noose hit my brain.

"That's a terrible analogy, sorry. But does that make sense?"

"So... there's nothing really here if I touch you?" I couldn't help myself. I snatched up his hand, held it in both of mine.

He extricated it gently.

"You can't feel that?" I pleaded, needing him to.

"I'm not really in front of you, no."

"That's not an answer."

He looked at his hand, then deep into my eyes.

"Alright," he admitted, softly. "Yes. I can feel you. I always could."

I felt my heart grow two sizes up.

In the construct, the pair start to walk slowly towards the sea, away from the statues on the plinth. This in itself is no reason to be alarmed: walk and talk therapy is a common fixture in this programme, or at least, it should have been.

What bothers Evans is the subject matter. Evans can see the physical and emotional tension between the patient and the Psych. He knows boundaries are being crossed, and that no good can come of it.

A nauseating feeling of premonition spreads throughout his body, because he has an idea that he knows what the Psych is up to. The patient, after all, is full of potential, latent, undefinable potential, and a strange ability to influence and affect things she should not be able to influence or affect. He wonders what that would look like if someone close to her, someone of a persuasive bent, could direct that ability in a targeted fashion. Could she use it to affect things outside of the construct? Evans recalls system glitches that shouldn't have been possible. Tremors, shaking the walls of the basement. Music playing when it shouldn't have. Words, spoken directly into the Control Room.

Silhouette, leaping across the rooftops of Bristol.

He is not sure, he feels as if he is going fucking insane even thinking along these lines, but his instinct tells him...

His instinct tells him he is right.

Something is about to go really fucking wrong.

He swears again, finger hovering over the abort button, but before he can make any further decisions or actions, the fluorescent strip bulb hanging directly over him detaches suddenly from its bracket, the entire unit pulling away from a ceiling that has been weakened by the giant crack running across it. Dragged downwards by the weight of something brown, sticky and viscous like molasses that has attached itself to the strip bulb in the same way a limpet attaches to a rock at high tide, it plummets heavily, its weight doubled. The bracket follows moments later. Both bulb and bracket smash onto the back of Evans's head with a loud bang and a popping noise like a gunshot, slicing open his scalp and rendering him instantly, effectively, completely unconscious.

And as the unfortunate man slumps forward onto his desk, dead to the world, a thin line of blood snaking down the side of his face and spreading out under him, a thick, gelatinous organism unfolds itself from the shattered remains of the strip bulb, stretches out a bulbous growth that quickly sharpens into a questing tentacle, and starts to haul itself up and onto Evans's head, completely obscuring his features from view.

23

FREEDOM

"So when you say freedom, what do you mean, exactly?" My friend walked me slowly away from the row of Moai and down towards the rocky coastline. True to type, I was gravitating towards the sea, a thing I had always done since childhood. There was something about the enormity of it, the ocean, that vast, constantly moving body of blue that had always captivated me. I wondered briefly if the team behind the virtual construct had gotten to my collection of sea-glass yet. As I thought this, a small globule of bright green glass, worn smooth by the ceaseless caress of waves over time, materialised in the air by my shoulder. I grimaced and dismissed it.

I thought about my friend's question. "I think I mean... freedom to be myself. Freedom to act, without worrying about the consequences of those actions on others."

"You're talking about guilt," my friend said.

"I suppose I am." I shuddered involuntarily.

"And being a wife, being a mother... those things didn't make you feel free?" There was a slight edge to my friend's voice that I chose to ignore, largely because the word "mother" had its usual effect on me. I felt a jolt, like a jump cable had been clamped to my heart. An ugly, hot sensation twisted in my gut.

(Golden hair, caught by the sun)

(A lock of golden hair, red atop the gold)

"Magpie?"

"No," I said, eventually, hating myself even as I said it. "No, they didn't. Not always. Maybe sometimes... I don't know. It's hard to feel free when you are responsible for so much, I suppose. Why are you asking me this? I can't really remember."

And I realised I couldn't. I couldn't remember anything about my life as a mother, as a parent. Not really. Small things, small moments, fragmented sensations, dreams... I knew I *was* a mother, just as I knew I had been or was still married, but that was a headline. The details were still lost in the fog. Perhaps it had been a mistake to leave the regulated safety of the Gallery. The objects on their pedestals *had* been helping me to remember, slowly.

My friend persisted.

"Can't remember? But starting a family... raising a child... those moments are arguably the most memorable moments of our lives."

"I suppose they are," I replied, flatly. Why was he so intent on this? What was that tone, creeping in? Was he... upset with me?

Yes, yes he was. He was upset with me, and finding it increasingly difficult to hide the fact. His therapy persona was slipping further the more time that passed.

Worse, his words made me feel... shame. I had been a mother, a wife, and yet I had blanked all of that from my memory. Edited out the most important highlights of my life to date.

(Because you didn't deserve any of it, everyone knew you were going to fuck it up, and you did, didn't you? You didn't deserve any o–)

I swallowed, feeling awful. "How is this helpful?"

"As a species, biologically, we're designed to achieve one thing and one thing only: the procreation of the next generation of our kind. As a woman, your entire body has been adapted for that one, singular purpose: childbirth. Wouldn't you say that having a child, engaging in the ultimate act of creation... wouldn't you say that was a type of freedom?"

"No, I wouldn't." I was unwilling to debate this further.

"The highest form of freedom. Creation. It makes you almost... almost. *God*-like."

I stared at him, seething inwardly.

"No. Not God-like."

"Then what?"

(He giveth life and he taketh away. Just like you took–)

"I don't know," I struggled to find a way to articulate everything I needed to. It felt like too much was riding on my response again.

"You don't know? What don't you know, Magpie?"

My guts boiled, and I gazed upon the sea, letting the big blue fill my mind, and its gentle movement was so hypnotic I found it lulled me back into a more agreeable mood despite the subject matter. The hot feeling in my gut calmed.

We kept on walking, and I tried to explain myself.

"It's like... ever since I found my dead body, I've been rebuilding my life, right? In a manner of speaking. In here, with you, piecing together my memories, object by object. But that part, the part of me that was a mother... it's still... missing."

"A hole in your mind?"

From somewhere far behind us, a heavy noise rang out into the air. It made the earth under my foot tremble ever so slightly. I had an absurd flashback to a movie I had once seen: a glass of water on the dashboard of a brightly painted jeep, rippling with concentric warning circles.

We both stopped, and turned, looking for the source of the noise, but neither of us could see anything immediately wrong.

Nothing moved on the vista behind us except for seabirds wheeling in the sky and ponies moving about as they grazed peacefully.

I shook my head. "No, more like... a fog."

(red mist, anger takes over, don't think, just react, stop the noise, stop the stress, stop everything, he will be better off, stopstopstopstopredredredred–)

We started up again, reached the shoreline, which was actually less of a shore and more of a sharp drop-off into deep water as a low, rough volcanic rock ledge careened straight into the blue without warning. The sea beyond the ledge was wonderfully clear, a greenish colour closer in, and a vivid sapphire hue further out. These were good waters for diving. Crystal clear, visibility for miles. It had been a long time since I had dived. I missed it.

As we stood there, I spotted a disturbance in the water not far from the ledge. A swelling, or rather a rising motion within the waves. I squinted at it. "Is this something to do with you?" I asked, pointing as a tall and slim column rose abruptly from the ocean.

My friend said nothing. I took his silence to mean that yes, this was his doing.

A now familiar marble plinth with its glass exhibition case mounted atop emerged from the sea, water pouring off of it as if it were an ornamental fountain in a garden. I wondered what treats it had in store for me, this time. I shook my head and started to laugh.

"What is it?"

"Oh, nothing."

My friend stared at the new plinth and made a very obvious decision to change the subject, unable to reconcile my honesty with whatever it was that he was chewing over in his own head.

His silence stretched out.

"Are you okay?" Wasn't that his job, to ask me?

He didn't answer.

"How do I even get over there, anyway?" I said, trying to prompt him out of his funk. I judged the distance between the plinth and where I was standing to be about twenty feet. I could swim, if I wanted to, but it felt like an awkward process, and a step too far even for my friend.

My friend wiped a hand across a suddenly sweaty brow.

"You know, it's an odd word, isn't it: 'freedom'."

"Oh, we're back on that again, are we? Is this your... unconventional thing?"

He ignored me. "It's uniquely personal to each and every one of us. The way we define the word, that is. Your idea of freedom is to move through the world in a way that means you are less restricted by the needs of others. To live a life where you do not feel guilt for desiring that freedom." He swallowed. "Want to know my definition of freedom?"

This felt all wrong to me. It was too suggestive, too leading. Too instructive. I was entitled to my own descriptors of how I wanted to live. What was his goal, here?

Why was he trying to carve his own space in my psyche?

Out loud, I said: "Okay."

"My definition," he said, his face a swirling mix of emotions, "my definition of freedom is different. When I think of freedom, do you know what comes to mind?"

I said nothing, not wanting to be shamed anymore about the joys of motherhood and childbirth and the beauty of creation, and he took this as an invitation to proceed.

"I think of my fundamental human right, the right to express myself, in any way I choose."

"What are we talking about here... poetry? Art? Interpretive dance?" I didn't have a clue what he was driving at. I kept looking at the plinth, squinting as I tried to see what the glass case held this time, but it was too far away to make out.

"I mean liberty, perhaps in the American sense of the word. Freedom of thought, and action. Independence. Autonomy. And you know what makes me think of that?"

"What?" I sighed.

"This place. This... this *playground* for the brain. Sure, it has boundaries, or at least, the people who built it, designed it, programmed it, they *think* it has boundaries. But a construct is merely the design laid out by another person's mind, right?"

"I don't understand."

"This, what we are experiencing right now. It's a blueprint. A series of virtual spaces within which you can explore and play... up to a certain point. Within the parameters of the software, of the design laid out by the programmers and artists who built it. Like... a colouring book. You keep the colour inside the lines."

I shook my head. "I wish you'd get to the fucking point."

He moved closer, grabbed me by both my wrists.

"Hey!" I protested, trying to wriggle out of his grip. Perceived or real, it hurt. "Get off me!"

"What if you were free to colour *outside* of the lines?" he asked.

I stared at him. "I'm not a clever sort of person," I said, flatly. "I have no fucking idea what you're trying to get to, but like I said: I wish you'd spell it out for me in plain English."

"Okay. So... freedom, in one sense of the word, is the ability to do whatever you want, right? Say whatever you want, do whatever you want, and create whatever you want. And what better place to create than... here? In this playground. You've already gotten to grips with the potential of it so easily. Think of what that mind of yours could do, if it were *really* free. Think of what it could *create*."

"For what purpose?" Again, that hidden agenda. Again, that secret plan.

"For the purpose of healing, of organising your thoughts, of... throwing a beam of light into the fog."

"How? By making shit appear?" I gestured with my hand, and a large, bright yellow submarine appeared in the sky, cartoonish and half-realised, but there, nonetheless. "Like that?"

He laughed, but he was getting desperate, I could see. "Clearly you've never had art therapy. I'm surprised that you, as a writer, are having trouble with the idea of creation as a source of comfort."

"You're obsessed with creation!" I snapped, trying again to free myself. I made the submarine disappear. Then, blinking, I realised that the volcanic ledge upon which we stood was no longer a ledge, but a thin, arched stone bridge, leading straight to the plinth. I had created it without really knowing I was doing so, as if my friend's conversational tactics had suddenly ignited a part of my mind I didn't know existed.

"Freedom of expression, Magpie," he said, a weird, intense light in his eyes.

I was suddenly driving a car on autopilot: creating the bridge had been an automatic process, rather than a considered one.

"Can we... can we do this later?" I asked, for my friend was beginning to make me feel nervous.

"We can do anything you want, whenever you want. That's the whole point." He said this with a straight face, but I no longer believed him. He still wouldn't let go of my wrists.

"I want to see what's on the plinth. It's... bothering me."

"Magpie," he said, leaning his head suddenly on mine. "Come back to me. I need you back. I need you better. Come back, please. I miss you so much."

I pushed him off, violently. It didn't work: he kept his grip.

"Who the fuck are you?" I asked, feeling betrayed. His own eyes were swimming, and it tormented me.

Instead of answering, he stared into me. It was too much: I looked away.

"As you wish," he said, bitterly. "But you're not going to like it much."

He frogmarched me across the stone arch, dragging me by my wrists as I fought against him. On approaching the plinth, he freed up one hand, reached out for the domed case, lifted the sea-splattered glass, and I saw...

"No!" I shrieked.

(Thereitisthereitisthereitisthere–)

"I'm not doing this. What the fuck is this? No. No!"

"It's time, Magpie," my friend said, from behind me. His voice was choked with emotion. "It's time."

The plinth had a little brass plaque embedded into it, the Roman numeral "I" engraved onto the metal with a grim finality. I had seen this plinth before, back in the Gallery, it was the first one I had approached upon arrival. I had seen the object resting inside the case before, too.

Now it was here.

Waiting for me.

"No," I said, shaking my head. "Not now. I'm not ready. I'm not... fuck!"

And before me, the single lock of golden hair shone in the sunlight, each strand an accusation.

I felt the bridge beneath my feet begin to tremble. The hair, the soft, beautiful, bright lock of hair, was spattered with red, a dark, dried red, like spots of rust upon a gold bracelet, and as this swirled around inside my head with all of my friend's talk of freedom and creation, I heard the sound we had heard earlier, the heavy impact of something large and predatory stalking across the island towards us, and I closed my eyes, feeling as if my entire being were about to burst into a thousand tiny disorganised pieces.

A memory came to me from the fog, looming suddenly, a horrifying thing rising from the mist in my mind.

A memory of a child, screaming.

(stopstopstopstopstopstopstopstop–)

I had done something terrible. Something my mind had blotted, something the real world version of me had not been able to handle, and this was the root of my problems, the centre of the black hole, the well-spring beneath the soil, and I was so afraid then, so afraid, so very, *very* afraid *(Mummystop!Stop!)* of those memories returning, because I did not want to know what I had done, I did not *want* to solve the mystery of my own death any longer. My own dead body could go fuck itself, I deserved to be dead, I didn't want to know anything else, I wanted to live in ignorance, blissful, easy ignorance...

I...

I...

From behind me, my new friend said:

"You never really talk about our son much; do you know that?"

The bridge shook again. Chunks of rock splashed into the sea below. With my trembling free hand, I reached out, and ran a finger over the golden, blood-splattered curl, and it was soft, so soft, nothing had ever felt so soft, and I tenderly grasped it with my index finger and thumb, and then curled my hand around it, and felt a vast emptiness open up within.

"Such a huge part of your life, and yet you barely mention him," my friend continued, doggedly, and I turned to him, tears mixing with the sea spray on my cheeks, and he stood, his face resolute, and I could see that this was his agenda all along, forcing me to confront the thing I was not ready to confront, ripping off the sticking plaster and exposing the raw, festering wound beneath, thinking that it was good for me, thinking that he knew best, thinking that breaking down my defences, bringing me to my knees, would what? Reset everything in my brain? Magically solve the riddle of my own failures?

I looked at him with anguish open upon my face, and then I saw it.

Behind him.

Crawling along the stone bridge like a vast, humanoid spider, edges blurred and juddery and indistinct.

The massive, inevitable shape of Silhouette.

"FUCK YOU!" I screamed, as the bridge disintegrated suddenly beneath my feet, and the three of us, my friend, the Silhouette and I, plunged into the ocean, and even though it was not real, it was cold, and wet, and it closed over me completely, and I prayed then, even though I was not religious, I prayed for it to take me away, or at the very least, for it to

wash away my sin, but no ocean would ever be wide enough, ever be deep enough, and I knew that.

I knew it, and so did the sea.

24

WET

In the observation room, Evans is jolted rudely awake. At first, his head pounding, he cannot figure out what, or who has woken him, but he can tell he is injured, and that he is wet, and cold. His clothes are soaked through, and not with sweat. He feels like he has taken a shower fully clothed. With a trembling hand, he feels the back of his head, which throbs, and touches a large mass of something sticky, clumped at the roots of his hair. It feels like egg yolk, or frogspawn. It is warm, like flesh. He pulls his hand away sharply, and studies it, expecting to find blood on his fingers, and instead finds a dark brown gloopy substance that gives under pressure as he squeezes it between his thumb and index finger.

Revolted, he yanks the mass from his head and hurls it at one of the whiteboards. It splats hard against the shiny surface and slowly rolls to the ground, where it lies, unmoving.

Evans stares at it, then tries frantically to wipe the remaining residue off of his hands and onto his now sodden trousers. He scans his workspace, wondering what the fuck just happened, what the fuck knocked him out. The brown goop refuses to detach itself from his skin, but he can't think about that right now, for he has concluded two things simultaneously: that the fluorescent strip light hanging overhead has come away from the ceiling and is responsible for knocking him out, a fact which he only knows because thin, lethal shards of glass now lie all around him, as if his control centre were suddenly booby-trapped, but more than this, more frightening than his dance with the shattered bulb, is that all the screens in the room are now filled with the unmistakable image of the ocean, specifically the ocean from the perspective of a person swimming beneath the surface of the waves, an ocean swirling with tiny particles and swimming things and bubbles of air and fragments of coral and shells and sea sand, and he thinks he remembers a term for this, something he heard once on a documentary, marine snow, it is, and with a crushing sense of dread and disbelief, he licks his cracked lips with a timid tongue, and realises that all he can taste…

All he can taste is salt.

Then the image on the computer screen changes to a scene in an operating theatre, in a hospital.

The patient is lying on her back in a position not unlike the one she occupies in the next room over from Evans, her legs suspended in stirrups in both realities, and Evans can see this is a memory, a memory that the patient shouldn't be re-creating because it is too traumatic, and his previous hesitation about hitting the abort button evaporates. Evans may not be the most empathetic person in the world, but he draws the line at forcing the patient to relive her worst memories like this. Especially when he doesn't know what doing so will unleash upon the world.

He scrabbles across the room, keeping his eyes on the brown blob in case it moves again. His sticky hand slams hard upon the large red abort button on the wall, the FUBAR button, the one he has never needed until now, slipping off without having effect. Almost choking on his frustration, he hammers it again, and again, sagging in relief as the button finally depresses.

It is done. The programme is over, at least for this patient.

He hopes they haven't fucked her up too badly.

He hopes she doesn't sue, although he fucking would, if it were him. Sue them for everything they had.

Then, with a sinking sense of horror, he realises the screens have not shifted to the standard exit protocol display. The scene on every monitor is still of the hospital, the operating theatre, the woman on her back.

He presses the button again, and again.

"Come *on!*" he roars, blood now welling out of the wound on his head.

Nothing happens.

The programme refuses to abort.

25

SURGERY/BIRTH

I was no longer in the sea.

Where I was, however, was no less terrifying.

It was a room in a hospital. An operating theatre, in fact. It was crowded with people in surgical masks and caps and gloves and aprons and glasses, or goggles. Sterile people, people walled off from me, people wearing spacesuits made of plastic and blue scrubs, people on a mission, and that mission had something to do with why I was lying on my back with my legs in the air, suspended from stirrups. I couldn't see much of what lay beyond my chest, because I was ripe with a baby, my belly poking up high and taught on the horizon of my tired, sore body.

"No," I whispered, for I was not ready for this, I would never be ready for this.

"It's okay," a familiar voice said from beside me, and I turned my head to find my friend sitting next to me, also trussed in a mask and gown and cap. The only part of him I could see properly were his eyes, those blue eyes, or were they green? He squeezed my hand, and I could tell he was trying to smile. "This is just a process," he said, then, but I knew he was afraid.

"Am I doing this?" I asked, for I could not believe that this memory was of my making, but it must have been, for who else would be able to recreate this in such sickening, realistic detail? Although I hadn't exactly been taking pictures, the first time around. And this was one experience I had never written into any diary. There were medical notes, probably, a yellow book full of maternity notes, but... but...

My friend laid a cool hand across my sweat-soaked brow. "This is you, Magpie. I helped with some prompting, and you can forgive me later, but this is all you. It's time. Trust the process."

"Get me out of here," I whispered, terrified, unable to accept what my friend was telling me, but before I could say anything else, my body convulsed, my belly tightened, and a wave of white-hot pain seized me, squeezed me, unmade me. I screamed, and the pain passed, only to return seconds later.

"I can see the head!" One of the blue astronauts at my lower end cried. "Get ready!"

And then I felt it, a nudging, pushing sensation against my thighs, only barely felt because of all the drugs coursing through me, the epidural, the antibiotics, the... whatever they had given me made me shake, almost uncontrollably, my legs jerking around as if I were having a seizure, but I could still feel it, *it*, the reason, the centre of the black hole, the... something... down there, between my legs, where a man in scrubs was busy doing god knows what.

And as I looked down in horror, my belly rippled again, the pain squeezed, and I roared aloud. Was that my blood all over the surgeon's hands? Was it? I had never seen my own blood in such vast quantities. It didn't look... normal. It was dark, glutinous, treacly, a strange, clotted brown in colour and texture. It smelled strange, too, I could smell it from here. It smelled sulphurous, eggy. It frightened me.

There was another nudge, and my belly rolled once more.

"I see it! I've... I've got him!" a voice shouted in excitement.

And then, he was born.

My baby, my baby boy, mine.

"Well done, Magpie," my friend says, over and over, his voice breaking. "Well done, you have done so well, so well, so..."

He fades into a faint buzz, because here was my baby, covered in white slime and my blood, his blood, *our* blood. He was placed into my arms for what felt like a microsecond, a tiny, fleeting moment of glory, of magic, of... of...

"Where are you taking him?" I cried, as his tiny body was reclaimed and whisked away. I could see, then, that my baby was blue. I could see that he was not breathing.

The world became a very loud place.

And my belly tightened again.

The surgeon working on me with a needle and surgical thread reared back, swearing.

"There is something still inside her!" he shouted, scrambling back.

"I don't want to do this!" I screamed, but my friend continued to babble on about how brave I was, how well I had done, how I must keep going, how this was only part of the process, that we all have to face the worst of our fears before we can come to terms with them, but all I could think is what the surgeon said:

There is something still inside me.

And he was right.

There was something still alive inside of me.

Something large, something alive.

My body convulsed.

In the OR, the patient, who is now lying on her back, legs akimbo and up in their soft foam cuffs, almost the mirror image of the woman on the screen in the Control Room, screams. Her belly, although it shouldn't have been, is distended, and swollen. She throws back her head in agony, as Evans looks on, no longer feeling protected by the mirrored, reinforced glass between them.

She is giving birth, he realises. Right there in the room next door.

But to what?

To what?!

Transfixed, he watches as something emerges from between her legs. It rips through her paper pyjamas, and as it hits the light of the OR, Evans can't help himself.

He screams too.

And, out it came.

From between my legs, a hand thrust its way into the room. A rough approximation of a hand, at least. It was sketchy, the lines of it indistinct and difficult to focus upon, but I could still tell that it was a hand, because it took a firm hold of my left knee, using it as an anchor. A second hand slid out and gripped onto my right knee. I knew that there was no physical way I could naturally harbour an entity of such a huge size and shape inside of me, but it hauled itself out of my body nevertheless, covered in a sludgy brown ichor. Its edges were sharp, abrasive, like barbed wire, and it made new cuts, new furrows in my ruined flesh as it dragged itself into the light. Hands, arms, elbows, head, body, legs, feet. It slithered between my loins and flopped onto the floor beneath me as I screamed and screamed and screamed, and I couldn't get a proper look at it, see it clearly, because I was still immobile, I was still in a bed with my legs akimbo, tied up in stirrups, I was still unable to stop shaking or regain complete motor control, and, in the background, my baby was still not crying, and a nurse rubbed his blue body vigorously with a bloodied towel, and my friend spent his time looking at the baby first, and then me, worry and concern pouring out of his eyes, and I kept trying to ask him:

"Where did it go?"

"Where did the fucking thing *go*?!"

And then it stood up, shakily, wobbling on its legs like a newborn calf. It sloughed off the slimy brown cowl it had been born with, shaking itself like a wet dog as filthy, clotted fluid spattered all across the room, covering the people standing around like sprayed mud, and my eyes stayed fixed on my baby, who was still not crying, why was he not crying? What was wrong with him?

And the beast that crawled out of me rolled its head around on its body, and went still, as if waiting for something, and I finally understood what it was, this scenario.

This was the day I gave birth to Silhouette.

I felt something snap, loudly and cleanly, in the back of my mind.

I fainted.

In the OR, a bomb explodes. A bomb of brown, coagulated matter that covers every visible surface with thick, awful slime. Slime that moves as if it has a mind of its own. The patient stops quivering and goes slack at the end of her wires.

But this is not what keeps Evans screaming. No, what pulls the terror from his throat in an endless screech of fear is the fact that, moments before erupting in a shower of foulness, the thing between the patient's legs looks like a man, a crudely drawn, horrific approximation of a man, shaped, without doubt, like a stick man.

26

LIGHTBOX

I came to slowly, found myself sitting on the floor of what looked like a giant, clear plastic box suspended, or floating, beneath the surface of the ocean. The vertices of the box glowed a luminescent green. As I sat there adjusting, the green shifted slowly to a vivid orange, then to red, then to green again. It cycled through all the colours twice more as I fought back vivid echoes of the operating theatre, feeling the bulk of Silhouette creeping out from between my thighs. I looked around for him frantically, and then my baby, but it was just me and my friend, and the deep, wide ocean.

The lock of hair still rested in my cupped palm.

Trembling from head to toe, I realised I was splayed out upon the floor, facing my friend, who was seated close by in his customary cross-legged fashion. The box was not hard beneath us and seemed to sag a little to accommodate our weight, like soft, transparent neoprene, which was a relief, for the residual pain from my memory of giving birth lingered: my pelvis ached, as did my belly, my back, and my thighs. My groin burned with remembered trauma, and I sucked in my breath, shifting around gingerly on my bottom to get more comfortable.

"Are you okay?" my friend asked me, gently. "That was… intense."

"Fuck you." I spat.

"Magpie…"

"Seriously. Fuck you." I meant it.

"Magpie…"

"Is that what you meant by 'freedom'?" I asked, bitterly. I was furious with him, but too drained to express it properly. But what he had done… my trust was well and truly broken. I felt like a dog that had been kicked in the ribs by its master.

I hated how that made me feel.

He shook his head, at least had the grace to look at me with chagrin. "No, but we'll get to that in good time. What you experienced was a good, old-fashioned trauma flashback. It's common to experience those many years after a significant event."

I shook my head. "That wasn't an unprompted flashback, and you know it. You pushed me into that memory. You fucking *pushed* me, with that lock of hair. It triggered me, and you knew it would."

"Do you feel better?"

"Admit it!" I resisted the urge to punch him square in the face, although barely.

My friend spread his hands. "I can't lie to you anymore, Magpie. Yes, I pushed you. In the old days, they used to call it 'confrontation therapy'. Pioneered by a man called Kolb, mostly to help with addictions and addictive behaviours. It's largely frowned upon today."

"Oh, good," I said, feeling as if I'd been hit by a truck.

"Frowned upon, and unconventional, but in your case, I felt you needed a… jolt. Your defence mechanisms are so well-constructed, Magpie. Almost impenetrable. I thought we were progressing too… slowly."

"Too slowly for what? My son is gone! He's… GONE!"

The word shook the cube. I felt empty inside.

(Gone, and you know why, you piece of shi–)

My new friend said nothing. *Wise of him,* I thought.

"Is there a time limit on this thing? An expiry date

for grief?" I hadn't thought about that. It made sense, I supposed – there couldn't be infinite resources made available for my recovery. Time, money, all of these things put pressure on the people around me. I wondered if this was why he was rushing me through things that should not have been rushed.

My friend chose to ignore me. "Your brain has put multiple layers of protection in place to help you cope with certain things that have happened to you, Magpie. Like the birth of your son."

"Things that you clearly already know about."

He nodded. "Yes, but the whole premise of this therapeutic construct is that you have to make certain realisations and discoveries and mental connections for yourself."

"Except when it suits you." I was angry about the plinth, about the lock of hair, about his confrontation bullshit, but I was also finding it difficult to focus on him, because the more awake I became, the more I remembered *(PIECEOFSHITPIECEOFSHITPIECEOFSHITPIEC–)* that I had done something bad, and that something had involved my child, and *not* the birth, *not* the delivery, and I began to shake again, rocking slowly backwards and forwards.

My friend saw my distress. "Hey," he said, trying to place a hand on my knee. I slapped it away.

"*Hey.*"

"Don't pretend to be concerned for me now. What you did back there, it was…"

(Unforgivable. What you did was unforgivable)

"He was all right, you know."

"What?" I could barely hear him beyond the barrage of nasty thoughts swilling around in my skull like sewage.

"After the birth. I know this was a traumatic memory for you, but… you do know he was alright, don't you?"

"He was… what?"

"There is nothing for you to feel guilty about."

"What?" I could only hear enough to know how wrong he was.

About my guilt.

For I had everything in the world to feel guilty about.

My friend leaned forward and rested his index finger lightly on my right kneecap instead of the whole hand. Creeping in, little by little, like a long-buried memory.

"Our son. After an hour or two. He was very, very sick when he was born, and it was a close call. But they put him under a UV lamp, gave him some antibiotics, monitored him closely... he rallied. He was back in your arms before dawn. It took him a while to figure out how to feed, but he got there, in the end. He survived. In case you think... Magpie? He survived. You did a magnificent job."

I frowned and fingered the golden lock of hair which still rested in my hand.

"I remember cutting his hair," I whispered. "Later, when he was older. He wriggled a lot. I tied a ribbon round the end to keep it all intact. I put it in my memory box, in a brown paper envelope. There... there wasn't blood on it, then. I don't think." Hot tears began to roll down my face.

"Blood?"

I showed him the hair in my hand. Showed him the rust spots. He frowned, looking shocked.

A realisation dawned on him.

"Can I ask you something, Magpie?"

"No," I said, miserably.

"Do you think your son is dead, now?"

"I said no!" How many times was he going to violate my boundaries?

He squeezed my knee, hard. "This is important," he said, trying to keep the fire out of his voice and failing.

I looked at him, surprised. "I don't understand the question. Of course he is dead. Didn't that... wasn't that in my notes? I would have thought that was the first thing they would mention. He's been dead…" I scrambled for it, and remembered, eventually. "Seven months, now."

My heart was a chasm filled with shadows.

His face struggled as a dozen emotions warred there. Then, he said, slowly:

"What else do you think you remember, Magpie? About your son?"

"No, I'm not doing this with you now, I'm not, you broke trust with me. I can't do this anymore. I feel… I feel…" I was too ashamed to tell him what I felt.

(Mummy, I love you)

"It's up to you. But I think this is very, *very* important. And don't you feel like we are finally starting to get somewhere?"

"Shut up."

"Your choice, Magpie. But I really, really want you to answer the question."

I tried desperately to change the subject. "Where is Silhouette?" I croaked.

My friend gestured to the wide ocean around us irritably. "Somewhere out there," he replied. "I've seen him swimming around. If you think he's terrifying on land, you should see him under the water. Makes Cthulhu look like a pet squid."

I didn't laugh. "What is this?" I nodded to the box we were sitting inside.

"A Therapy Box."

"Oh," I replied, not really interested.

"Magpie? Talk to me. You've gone very far away."

"I…"

"What? What is it?"

"I did something," I said, miserably.

"You did something?"

"Yes. I have… this… enormous guilt."

"I don't understand. You gave birth, you mean? Are you talking about the guilt of…"

"No. I *did* something. Later on. To… my child. My boy. And

now he is gone." A scream echoed around my mind again, and I swallowed down a mouth of bile.

"The Reason, you mean? You can remember it, now?"

"Yes." It dawned on me. That's what this was. This was the exposition. "I can remember. The Reason. The answer to... to The Question."

He took a moment. Maybe he didn't want to know that answer, after all.

"What are you trying to tell me, Magpie?"

I swallowed. Outside the clear box, an enormous whale swam ponderously past. I watched it go, sadly.

"The birth... it was awful, but... it isn't... it is not the... root. The cause. There is more."

"The reason for the body on the riverbank, you mean. Your death. The Reason."

"Yes. Something else."

"Okay. But before we continue... perhaps it's fair to say that the birth... it was a starting point, for you, I think? A catalyst? It explains Silhouette."

"Silhouette was born the same day as my son, yes."

"That's no coincidence, Magpie."

"It isn't?"

"Know what I think?"

"No." Around me, colours cycled. Did he want me to spit it out or not? He seemed as barely capable of controlling his emotions as I was.

"I think sometimes," he said, his voice a soft spell, "that women get very sick after they have babies. Mentally, I mean, for a number of reasons. Hormonally, a lot changes in their bodies, but also, the act of caring for a child, the reality of such enormous responsibility, the fatigue and sleep deprivation that comes with a new born, the physical trauma and the pain and difficulties of breast-feeding, or not being able to feed... it's a lot for a person to bear. And I wonder... did we ever talk about Postnatal depression?"

I shook my head. "Nope. Never."

"Excuse me for overstepping, but I know we didn't." He sounded angry with himself. "But that's beside the point. I think... I think that Silhouette is... I think it's how you manifested your illness, mentally."

"Manifested?"

"Yeah. You're a writer, so you gave this huge, indefinable thing a name, and a form, and it became a monster in your mind. A metaphorical monster. Writers do that kind of thing all the time, you could say it's a bit of a trope."

"A trope?"

"You always used to say you didn't care about tropes. Tropes were just a sign of an author having a good time on her own dollar, you used to say."

"Did I?" I would have to take his word for it.

He looked feverish as he ploughed on. "But there's a reason we need metaphors, and that reason is: it helps us to explain something complex in a simple, uncomplicated fashion. Psychologically, it's like your brain using a technique to help you understand something you might not have, otherwise. A monster. We all grow up knowing the monster is the bad guy, right? We know to be scared of it. And that monster... you're able to project him, I think."

I stared at him. "I don't know what to say. This is all... it's all... so much."

He took my hands in his, and I wanted to pull away, but lacked the energy. "Tell me what you were going to tell me," he said.

I shook my head.

"No," I whispered.

"Please," he pleaded.

"I miss my son," I replied, mournfully.

"I can help you, Magpie. Tell me what it is you think you did." Why did he keep using that choice of words, "you think"?

"No."

"Why not? How bad can it be?!"

I shook my head, and realised I was crying. "You'll wish you hadn't asked me that in a moment."

"Tell me. Please. *Please.*"

"I can't."

"Magpie, I can't do this alone, I…"

"I'm going to show you, instead."

And with that I stood up carefully, convinced I could still feel the tender parts of my body screaming with the pain of delivery, and I wove a new memory for my friend as my knees trembled, and as we stepped slowly into it, he helping me over the threshold like I was an old lady being led to the commode, I saw Silhouette, swimming fast towards us through the speckled deep, his arms outstretched, and then he, and the box, and the ocean melted away, and all that was left was horror.

27

The Root Cause

Blood on golden hair
Red on flax
Eyelashes rest upon a soft pale cheek
Small, shell-shaped nails, with dirt beneath them
A child's scream cut short
A woman cries into the night
It goes on and on and...

"Magpie?"

And we were back in my house, my *real* house, not the Gallery. Inside my kitchen, a small galley kitchen with cream tiles and a black worktop and red accessories: red kettle, red toaster, red utensils, red cafetiere.

Red floor.

Red everywhere.

And a still, small, breathless form lay upon the slick, wet linoleum, a cold island in the red sea. A tuft of blonde hair sprouting from one end of the island moved gently under a faint breeze. The rest was drenched, sodden with red.

I must have left a window open, I thought, fixing on the single tuft, unable to look at anything else.

"What is this?" my friend breathed, and he began to tremble.

"This is what I did."

"No," he replied, monotone.

"This is my secret. This is The Reason. The Root Cause. I remember it now." I said it quietly, presenting my crime as a fact, hoping he would understand, at last, why there was no hope for me.

"No." He shook his head, took a step back, only this time I had recreated the kitchen in such absolute detail that his escape route away from the awful, awful thing on the floor before us was blocked by a wall he didn't realise was there.

"You still want to help me? This is what I did." I pointed to the red. The scene juddered for a moment, and I thought I saw tiny lines of white code scrolling up and down upon the puddles of blood, but I blinked, and they disappeared, leaving behind only my sin.

"Magpie... this... this is not... what *is* this?" He was trying to keep his voice level, but it rose and rose as he worked through the sentence. "What the fuck *is* this?"

"You went away," I said, simply. "All the time. You went on those business trips. I hated it. And then, that night... I was so sick, and you went away anyway. You waved at me as I lay in bed with a fever. So cheerful, as if I wasn't feeling like death. I remember you pulling that suitcase behind you, the one with wheels on the bottom. I remember the door shutting. I wasn't important enough, not anymore. You didn't care enough. I thought my heart would break."

He knew exactly what I was talking about. His face was a portrait of shock and amazement and sheer, unadulterated panic.

"I asked you if it was okay, Magpie. I *asked* you. You said you were fine."

"I didn't want to be the one making you choose between us, or work. I wanted you to make the choice yourself. I wanted us to be more important. I didn't want to have to ask."

"It was a new job, I wanted to make a good impression, I didn't have much choice, I..." He covered his face with his hands for a moment. "Get rid of that, please," he said, from between his fingers, and I knew he meant the body on the floor.

"I can't. This is what I did. It is time for me to face up to it. I buried it, so deep, so, so deep. It's time."

"Get rid of it!" he shouted, and this time his voice was raw anguish.

"I had a temperature of forty-one degrees. I could barely see. You left me with him. And I was so sick. And he wouldn't stop crying. I tried everything, but he wouldn't stop. He didn't understand that I was sick. He didn't care either. He was just a child, I didn't expect him to understand, but I was so alone, you know? I was so alone. And I was bad, I was a bad parent, I knew it, he knew it, you knew it… And I couldn't call anyone, I didn't have the energy. I tried television, but he got so bored, and…"

"Get rid of it, Magpie. *Now.*" His fists were balled up. I thought he was going to strike me.

(No more than you deserve, sugarpie)

"Don't you understand? I knew I had failed. I knew I was a piece of shit, a bad mother. I knew I had no future, not one I wanted to live inside of, anyway, not after… after…"

"No," he said. "No!" He lashed out, not at me, but punching the wall nearest to him, and it shattered into a million spinning fragments, and behind it there was the blue ocean, and, of course, Silhouette. Always Silhouette, waiting in the wings.

Silhouette roared in triumph, a column of bubbles erupting from its mouth as if he were a volcano underwater, and bunched its arms and legs up before extending them in a burst of power, propelling itself forward like a sickly, angular sort of octopus, but I no longer cared.

Metaphor or not, projection, or not, Silhouette was coming for me, and I was about ready to give in and let it take me.

Except my friend had other ideas.

"Magpie!" he cried, as our death swam towards us, as sea

water poured into the kitchen. He put himself in front of me, back to the monster, gripped my face between his hands, leaned in, and placed a very gentle kiss upon my lips. He tasted familiar, like sorrow, like salt, like...

Home.

"This is not what happened, Magpie," he said. His eyes were enormous, and filled with pity.

"We're going to die, what does it matter?" What he was saying wouldn't sink in. Around us, the water rose.

"None of that happened."

"What do you mean? I remember it, now, as clearly as if it were yesterday."

"False narrative," he said, or at least, that's what I thought he said. It was hard to hear him over the noise of the sea invading my memory.

"But I... did something bad."

"False narrative," he whispered again, and it felt like a command word, because the body of my son, which was rising on the tide, disappeared suddenly, leaving behind a room washed free of blood, or shame, or culpability, and as I looked at him, the thing I had been so certain about only moments before, my conviction of guilt, began to subside, and then slowly, slowly collapse, evaporate like water on a stone lying beneath a hot sun, only the stone was my heart, it was my heart, my heart...

Silhouette slammed into an invisible wall that appeared next to us in the exact same moment that my son's body dissipated. I felt the impact tremor as it collided, heard as it shrieked in fury, banging its weird cartoonish hands against the barrier.

My friend looked at it over his shoulder. The transparent wall began to colour, turn opaque, new wall tiles popping up like flowers in spring, slotting back together, concealing Silhouette from view.

"Not today, fucker," he breathed, and when he turned back to me, I finally knew him for who he was.

28

WRONG PSYCH

Evans cannot take his hands away from his eyes for a long time.

When he does, the scene that greets him is as it was moments before he covered them: brown, dripping gore, splattering to the floor and forming disgusting clumps, writhing along the walls, slithering along the contours of the patient, who is now naked, her paper pyjamas having dissolved and sloughed away like dead skin.

She looks almost dead in her cradle.

"Hey!" he shouts, banging on the glass, knowing that even if she was conscious, she would not be able to see or hear him. "Hey, are you okay? Wake up, Magpie! Hey!"

The slime in the OR responds to his noise by heading in his direction, all of it, at once, en masse. The walls and floor and ceiling, it all moves as if it is alive, as if a sheet of ragged brown silk is being dragged across it. The slime is hunting him, he realises, and it won't take long before it finds its way out of the OR and into Control.

He knows he needs to get out of the room, and fast, but when he reaches the door, he finds the lock is covered with more brown slime. It rears up at him as he touches it, like a cobra readying to strike. He yelps, falls back.

What the fuck is he going to do now?

"Stop the programme," he says to himself. Maybe if he can

cut things dead, she'll wake up, or control this shit somehow, or, or...

Stop the programme, by any means necessary. But he cannot get anything in the control room to work. The phone lines are all dead, the internet severed. None of his kill commands work when typed in. The computer monitors stay on, even after he unplugs them. Same for the base units, the fax machine, everything. The abort button does nothing. He even tries inserting a kill switch into the system via the flash drive, but it does not register once he has hammered it into any number of USB ports.

Evans has been overridden, and he hasn't got a fucking clue what to do about it.

Enraged, imprisoned behind a wall of defunct technology, a tide of hungry filth encroaching upon him – he can hear it sucking at the glass of the OR window – he strides over to the glass wall that no longer overlooks the patient, and only displays brown, and slams his fists into it, hoping against hope that she can hear him, despite everything.

"Stop fucking with my programme!" he screams at the hypnagogic woman who sleeps, unaware.

A small patch in the glass clears as he strikes the window. Through it, he can see the patient twitch, move slightly, settle again, oblivious to his situation. Evans is relieved that she is alive, but beyond caring about her state of consciousness.

"Come on!" he cries, hitting the window again. His knuckles leave bloody smears on the glass. "You have to stop! You're ruining everything! *Please wake up!*"

But the patient continues to sleep, and Evans's anger dissipates as quickly as it appeared, leaving behind only a sick sense of his own uselessness, of the futility of it all. Things have well and truly gotten away from him, and all he can do, he supposes, is accept.

It's at that point that his Boss's voice rings out from behind the control room door.

"Evans! Let me in!" the older woman shouts.

Evans rushes back to the door, which has a small, reinforced glass window in it. "I can't," he explains, loudly, for the glass is thick and his voice is muffled. "She's… done something to the system, there's… stuff everywhere, I'm locked in!"

His Boss rattles the door handle. The door is electronically operated and locked, controlled by the same system that runs the programme entire – a precautionary measure, to ensure potential intruders can't intervene and interrupt a critical moment in the therapy schedule.

"Aren't there override protocols for this?"

"There are, but you don't understand… I can't… I can't access anything!"

The Boss peers through the window again, and starts to realise that something is very wrong.

"Fuck. Fuck! Evans, Evans are you there?"

Evans has spotted a fire extinguisher at the back of the control room and has run over to grab it. He returns to the door, cradling it like a child in his arms, and then begins to hammer at the door handle and then the lock pad with it, to no avail. The slime sucks at the end of the extinguisher, muting its blows. The door remains locked.

"Evans, stop!" his Boss pleads, as Evans runs out of steam.

Evans throws the extinguisher to the floor, and leans against the door, panting. The brown stuff on the handle transfers itself to his right hip, clinging onto his belt, but he no longer cares.

"Evans," his Boss says, from the other side. "I need you to listen really carefully, okay?"

"I'm listening," he replies, dully, but this is only half the truth.

"That's not our Psych in there with her. Do you understand? He isn't one of ours!"

Evans's head snaps up. "The fuck did you say?"

"It's not our Psych." The Boss holds up a photograph to the glass window. Inside, three people smile back at Evans:

the Psych, the patient, and a small, blonde-haired boy who is clearly their child.

"What the–" Evans breathes, trying to figure it out. "We've been compromised?"

"In a manner of speaking."

"By what... her fucking husband? Why?! You said you'd done due diligence! Didn't you fucking recognise him, from the preliminary interviews?"

"I wasn't at the prelims for this one, Evans, mind your tongue!" She is embarrassed and it shows. "Besides, I can't remember what they all look like, do you know how many hours I spend down here staring at god knows what for god knows how long, it's a wonder I'm not blind already!"

"But... how can you not have recognised him? How could..." He is angry. "How could you have fucked up *this* much?!"

"I don't fucking know the whys or hows or the wherefores at the moment, Evans. Who gives a shit? The point is, an unauthorised person is wandering around inside our system without a fucking care in the world or a qualification to his name and we have to get him out before... oh, Jesus." Evans watches, confused, as his Boss takes a sudden step back from the glass, her face suddenly drawn and white.

"What?"

"Evans... turn around!" The Boss yells, eyes the size of golf balls, and Evans does as he is told, just in time to see the huge, sticky, jerky, trembling form of a long-legged stick man peel away from the far wall where it has been hiding, perfectly camouflaged by cables and shadows and the unnatural angles of the room, and it walks slowly towards Evans, arms stretched wide, as if preparing to embrace him, and Evans screams, renewing his attack upon the door handle with the extinguisher, but it's no use, because the lock is one of the best money can buy, and the brown stuff has infected it anyway, just as it has infected everything else, because that's how misery works, and then Silhouette is upon him, and all Evans can do is scream as he dies.

And all his Boss can do is watch as the horrible thing consumes the younger man, pressing its long length into Evans's body, melding, fusing, devouring, tearing, rending, roaring, and the Boss can't help herself, her self-preservation instincts are too fierce.

She turns tail, and runs.

And in the Observation Room beyond the now defunct control centre, the inert body of the patient shifts again, as if rousing from a long sleep, and although nobody is around to see it, the woman's face is lit with a slow, spreading smile.

29

FALSE NARRATIVE

"So… is that what you think?" my friend asked, still gripping my face between his hands. Things were quieter, dry. I was thankful for that.

"You're not a real psychiatrist at all," I whispered, in wonder.

"You think you did… *that* to our son?"

I crumpled. "I did, I did, I did," I sobbed. "I remember, I remember everything. I did that terrible thing, and now he's… he's… oh, god. How could anyone ever forgive me?"

His eyes filled with tears, yet he smiled through them.

"No, darling," he said. "Oh my darling, no."

"No?" That word didn't make sense.

"No. No, no, no."

"But. But… I was so tired, and so defeated, and I just wanted the crying to stop, and… And…"

"No, Magpie," and my friend started to chuckle, a low, soft sound that started deep inside his chest and rolled around the rest of him like thunder.

"Why are you laughing?" I went to strike him, on the verge of a complete breakdown. Here I was, at my most vulnerable, my lowest point, and he was *laughing* at me.

He caught my wrist, easily, laid a kiss upon the inside of my arm, right where the stick man tattoo was. It didn't burn anymore. I was so overcome I didn't know how to react.

"I *do* know you," I said as his lips touched my skin. I worried that I was in another dream but then he smiled, then, and oh, I knew that smile.

I knew those blue-green eyes.

"Of course you do," he said. "You've always known it was me."

I tried to stay standing on my feet. "I'm drowning in this, you know."

He shook his head. "No you're not." Then, from his pocket, he pulled out a slim cracked leather wallet. He flipped the top and slid something out of a thin plastic sleeve inside the wallet: a tiny photograph, the size of a passport headshot. He handed it to me.

"There," he said, gently. "That's our son. He is seven years old, Magpie. And disgustingly healthy. He misses his Mum, and this has all been very hard on him, but... otherwise, there's nothing wrong with him."

I looked at the image and felt as if my skin were sliding clean off my bones.

"Are you... is this real?"

"Yes, my love."

"You're telling the truth?"

"Yes."

"He's... not..."

"Dead? No. See for yourself." And the photograph was brought gently up to my face.

Staring up at me from the confines of a two-by-two inch photograph was a smiling, happy threesome – a woman, a man, and a blonde-haired child with impish eyes and a gap-toothed smile. The adults, clearly his parents, encircled the boy with their arms, and they all grinned at the camera with the kind of relaxed happy smiles that only flowered when a family were really having fun together. Only when you looked closely, you could see worry lines around the woman's eyes, a certain tightness in the corner of her mouth that spoke to the fragility of her state. A woman coping, functioning, but inwardly falling, like snow.

"This is us," my friend – my lover, my partner, my husband –
said. "Are you starting to remember properly, yet?"

And as he said this, the final floodgates opened. Memories
came pouring in, but they were *real* memories, this time, I
could tell because they tasted different, they tasted like fruit
that had long ripened in the sun, and they roared and surged
through my head, rushing into every single nook and cranny,
washing away the darkness I had nurtured for so long, blasting
through the fog and sweeping it clean away, soothing the
inflamed walls of my soul, rewriting the truths my damaged
mind had made for myself, and it was like being baptised, I
supposed, it was a whole body experience, it was a humbling
experience, like swimming in music, a religious feeling, only
I was not supplicating myself to any god, but simply declaring
my own worth before an audience of myself, because for some
reason, I had decided that worth had amounted to nothing
before, because of...

Because of a false narrative.

Where in reality, my son was... alive.

Alive.

In a timeframe of mere seconds, I reconstructed my entire
missing history, the timeline of events that had led up to my
discovery of my body under the bridge.

I remembered the difficult birth, and the sleepless nights,
and the struggles to feed.

I remembered the worry, and the heartache, and the fear.

I remembered the sweaty, horrible intrusive thoughts
playing on loop every time I touched my child *(you're a piece of
shit, you know that?)*.

I remembered the dark and vivid fantasies that told me I
was going to do something awful, hurt my baby. The insistent,
unpredictable thoughts that came from nowhere, that made
me think about hurting people I loved. Destroying what was
most precious to me, like it was a viable thing, a viable option.
The thoughts would strike at the most innocuous of moments:

folding shirts. Making coffee. Walking in the park on a sunny day. I never wanted to tell anyone about what the thoughts instructed, because I was scared. Of the thoughts themselves, but also the judgement, of repercussions. They'd have taken him from me, if I'd been honest about it, wouldn't they? Of course, I used to tell myself. On the surface, then, I was smooth, seamless, and I held it together. Beneath the surface, I drowned, sinking by increments, down, down, down, every day, every damn day.

I remembered the good things, too: the quiet sucking sounds he made as he pulled at my breast, the smiles as he lay on his little flannel chair in the bath, the chuckles as he started to crawl, the smell of him, the long walks we would take together, he in his pram looking up at the beautiful trees that rose high near the Suspension Bridge, later on foot, stick in hand, his head up to my chest in height, sunlight on his brow, walking in one of my favourite places to wander with him. I could recall his face, covered with pureed carrot, jam, chocolate, food anywhere but where it should have been. I could remember his hair, so long and unruly, how soft it felt between my fingers as I cut that first lock, tied a ribbon round the stems to keep it all in place.

I remembered the peculiar loneliness of parenting.

I remembered feeling horribly, completely, terrifyingly, alone, and wishing I wasn't.

I remembered my slow decline.

It began with drinking too much, and then partying with the wrong sorts of people. It ended with long, solo walks across the city in the middle of the night. With a leg thrown over a chain-link fence, with hands pulling me back from the edge of a cliff. The Bridge stopped becoming a place of solace and transformed into a beacon, a white light that called to me. A more difficult place from which to fly, but I tried. My wings were clipped for me, but I understood why, now.

When I was no longer allowed out of the house unsupervised,

I tried other things. I tried to swallow things I shouldn't, like pills, household cleaning goods, drugs, alcohol. I tried to cut, hit, thump, hurt my body.

Throughout it all, my family, sticking by me, watching as I ate myself up from the inside out, helpless spectators, roadside at the world's slowest car crash.

I remembered writing a letter to the Department of Virtual and Experimental Therapy. I had read about them somewhere, in a magazine I think. One of my husband's. He bought them in a desperate attempt to understand me better, for I was no longer a woman he knew. I read about this pioneering new therapeutic programme, where the subject was immersed into a virtual environment designed specifically for them, and guided through a simulated personalised therapy programme with the help of a team of specialist psychologists and technicians, trained in the art of utilizing VR for such purposes. In the magazine, a glossy colour photo of a man in a harness of sorts, hooked up to wires, sensors, a large visor. He hung from the ceiling on a system of wires like a puppet, allowing him to navigate his virtual world freely whilst not being fully conscious. It meant his mind could be put in a suggestive, hallucinogenic state, somewhere between asleep and awake, a state that could be manipulated, combined with VR tech to help explore certain psychological practices. It sounded extreme, but I needed that. *You should know that I have tried everything else,* I told them in my letter, and it was part way to the truth. I had tried hormonal therapy and exercise and talking therapy and antidepressants. I wrote the letter, having consumed most of a bottle of whiskey in the process, and I chased that whiskey down with a dozen pills from various packets and bottles I owned, and I had somehow managed to leave my house, dressed still in my pyjamas, and stagger down the road to the post-box, and post the letter, and after that...

The rest, as they say, is history.

Except... for my friend. I couldn't quite figure out how he

slotted into my current situation. He was my husband, and yet somehow also... my therapist? The two things didn't tally. He was an engineer, in the real world. A manager type.

Later, later, I told myself.

Because for now...

"I remember," I breathed. And, as I said that, the most incredible realisation dawned upon me. It broke like morning, like sunlight creeping up from behind a hill.

It was the realisation that I had, in fact, done nothing wrong.

I had hurt nobody.

I had not been bad.

(You did nothing wrong, Magpie)

And as those words dropped and hit the surface of the water in my head, the entire room around us, the house, *everything* dematerialised, right then and there on the spot.

30

INTRUSIVE THOUGHTS

It was replaced with a vast, infinite darkness, defined only by a complete absence of anything definable, no landmarks, no features, no sights or sounds or scents or anything. It was as if we were adrift in space, only a space without stars.

I closed my eyes and floated for a while. It was like floating in a cool bath.

After a moment or two, my friend's hand found mine (he was still my friend, my very best friend, and always would be), and our fingers twined together. We anchored to each other, and drifted in synchrony.

"He's okay," I said, eventually, and my words were almost swallowed by the nothing.

"He's okay," my friend agreed.

"I didn't do anything wrong," I repeated, a little dumbly, but I *really* wanted to be sure, I had never wanted to be more sure of anything in my life as much as I wanted to be sure of this. That I was innocent of the crime I had told myself I had committed.

The hand holding mine squeezed my fingers for a second. "No, Magpie, you did nothing wrong. Our son is fine. Do you hear me? That... That was not a real memory. It was something... something... you created a false narrative, is what it was."

Those words again. Our bodies bumped up against each other, cushioned by the thick, cool black.

"But… why would I do that? Why would I make something up like… that? It's awful, to imagine a crime like… why would I do that to myself?"

"Intrusive thoughts."

"What?"

"Let me… um… I wonder… I'm not sure if I can manipulate anything here."

"Where even are we?"

"I don't know, I assumed this was your doing."

"Maybe."

"Maybe. Maybe this is like the safe space you made before, behind the red door. I doubt we are inside the programme anymore. More like… the black space between lines of code on a screen, perhaps. I don't know, I'm not a computer expert."

"That's comforting."

"The programme was a tool, Magpie. A means to an end. I feel like we are approaching that end, don't you?"

I grimaced, even though he couldn't see me do so. "If we're going to do this, you're going to need to stop talking to me in Therapist, okay?"

"What do you mean?"

"I mean, drop the condescending, yet friendly, yet neutral, yet comforting tone, okay? And the rhetorical, open-ended questions. You know. Shrink Voice. Stop it."

He chuckled. "Fine. Done."

"And I don't think I like things that sound… quite as final as the word 'end'."

I heard the smile continue in his voice. "Well, that is a turn up for the books."

"Behave yourself. You're not a proper psychologist, remember?"

"Resolution, then, if that is less of an intimidating word. So, let me…" He grunted, and nothing happened.

"Magpie?" His voice sounded exasperated.

"Yeah?"

"A little light, maybe?"

I obliged, and suddenly, a large, rotating lightbulb popped into existence a few inches above us, glowing brightly.

"That's better," my friend said, and we righted ourselves, using the lightbulb as a sort of compass point marking north. Before that, it had been impossible to tell which way was *any* way, let alone up.

"Intrusive thoughts?" I nudged, realising how much more relaxed I had become now that I had shrugged off the heavy shawl of tragedy, guilt and shame. The crawling weight of a deed misdone, the sickening feeling of having committed an awful act, now dissipated. I felt inches taller and lighter.

"I'm getting there, just... be patient." He gestured, and again, nothing happened. "This is going to be a problem," he grumbled, indicating with his finger what it was he was trying to materialise. Again, I obliged for him, and a large speech bubble-shaped object appeared in the air before my mouth.

"Crude, but it'll do," my friend said. "Now, this might be difficult, and I understand that not each and every one of your memories will have returned as if by magic, there will still be gaps and things that are perhaps not quite as they were in real life, but I have a good feeling that you've had a... breakthrough, I suppose we must call it, and you're a lot better off in that department than you were before. So."

"You're not about to pull any more of that confrontation therapy shit on me again, are you?" I clenched with the memory of the operating theatre. I didn't want to go back there again for a very, very long time, if ever.

"Definitely not. That was a mistake, and I apologise. Now, answer me this. Have you ever thought of any of the following..." He then reeled off a list of phrases, and every time he spoke, a sentence popped up in the centre of the speech bubble. It reminded me a little of being on top of the mountain, and I remembered the command prompt text that appeared in the sky.

For now, the following litany of thoughts rotated in the centre of the speech bubble. It made for a grim repertoire:

"I am unfit to be a mother"

"I will drop my child"

"I will smother the baby by mistake when I fall asleep"

"My child is better off without me"

"I made a mistake giving birth"

"I will hurt my child"

"I think about blood"

"I am angry, this means I am a bad parent"

"I have failed"

Each sentence felt like a punch to the gut, because I could have ticked every single item on that list off, thought-wise. On the darkest days, back when our son was tiny, I had thought them all in quick succession, or several at once, and they had cycled over and over in my mind just like the colours in the therapy box under the ocean had cycled: endlessly.

"Ouch," was all I could manage to say out loud. I made the bubble disappear, but the white, burning shadow of the word "mistake" still lingered against the black, for some reason.

"Believe it or not, these are all quite common thoughts to have," my friend said, gently. "I know, because I've been... researching."

"I see," I nodded, although I didn't.

He continued. "When a child is born, your whole being becomes preoccupied with the safety of this other person, right? This is not the same way that you worry about the safety of a partner, or a friend, or a sibling, or a parent. This is a tiny helpless creature whose entire wellbeing and safety and survival depends on *you*."

I nodded again.

"So don't you think it's natural that your body and brain would go into a state of high anxiety? Of flight or fight on behalf of another person? It's a maternal instinct, only that instinct is times ten thousand. And when your body is in constant "threat" mode, then it makes it more understandable that these intrusive thoughts would creep in, like they did with you. You're constantly analysing any sources of harm or danger to your child, and that analysis simply turned to yourself. You end up obsessing over things that threaten the most important people in your lives. You've got no real intention of acting on any of the thoughts, but you can't stop them either. If you think about it… it probably makes you quite a good mother, in a way. It's your brain telling you what matters, warning you to protect the things you love from the things you fear."

I floated, digesting all of this. As I did so, a little star winked into existence behind my friend, and then another, and another. The wheels in my mind whirred, and the low, milky light of a birthing galaxy gathered behind the head of my husband, who was not a trained mental health professional, but was doing his damned best. I couldn't tell if I was angry at him for intervening in my own intervention, or happy that he was here and I didn't have to go through all of this alone.

I wondered whether I would have had the same breakthrough with a real psychologist.

"Did you hack into this programme, so you could be here with me?" I asked him, outright.

"Hack is the wrong word. Impersonate… maybe. Perhaps a little identity theft involved too. But we're getting off track."

"But why not talk to me directly?" I asked, aghast. "Why go to such… lengths?"

"I don't think you should underestimate how… sick you have been, Magpie. That's why we sent our boy away, for a while. It was… you were…"

"Beyond reason?"

He shrugged. "You could say that, yes. And besides, since when has simply talking to you ever worked before? You're stubborn, Magpie, you needed a neutral third party to confide in. But I knew you also needed someone who understood you. You aren't a two-page book. Not even close."

A red dot pinged into reality next to his right ear: a planet of some sort. It glowed like a far-off traffic light.

"But instead of confiding in anyone, you sank into yourself more and more. I should have seen it, but I didn't. I failed on that front. I didn't appreciate how…" He sighed. "Anyway. Then we sent our boy away, and I guess this, combined with the intrusive thoughts in your mind… the sickness, the mania… you built a false narrative. Over time, it became a reality for you. A grim fantasy that put down roots, and flowered into a conviction of guilt. That's when it all really started to go wrong with us. That's when you would disappear, for hours on end, at all times of the night, and I tried everything to keep you with me. Even a lock on the bedroom door, like a prison. You climbed out the window, can you believe that? You shimmied down the fucking drainpipe like a cat burglar."

I said nothing. I had a lot of information to work through. The image of me sliding down the drainpipe outside the front of our thirties terraced house was, strangely, not the hardest thing to process.

"By the time you wrote the letter asking for help, you had convinced yourself of the other thing. You thought… well. Even though you spoke to him every day on the phone, your brain partitioned that off, maybe, thought it was a dream. I should have put two and two together, but I didn't. I was barely surviving myself. You went three whole weeks without saying a single word to me, I had no idea what was running through your mind. You evicted me from your head."

"And by the time I wrote the letter…"

"By the time you wrote the letter, I was at my wit's end. But now…"

"We're here together," I smiled, and the sky brightened around us, and the galaxy became a supercluster, and beyond that, a universe of potential waited for me, its breath held.

"Have you ever woken from a bad dream convinced you did something wrong?" I asked him, and he nodded.

"Of course I have," he replied. "But it was only ever a dream, Magpie."

And with that, the stars exploded into a brilliant firework display of hope.

"So what now?" I asked, as I drank in the beauty of everything that had been denied to me for so long. Hope. Relief. Promise. Possibility. A future.

"Let's go back to the Gallery," my friend who was not my friend said. "There is something else I want to show you."

31

INVITATION

It felt strangely good to be back in the Gallery, now that I knew exactly what the score was with the place. It was a peaceful scenario, I realised, as I gazed up at the columns and the high windows that opened directly to an always blue sky. I no longer resented it. Rather, I appreciated the effort that had gone into this particular piece of therapeutic theatre. The details, the craftsmanship. The meticulously recreated objects. The play of light upon the tiles, the grace of the space. I began to think of it as a soothing retreat. One I could return to in my mind, if I needed to.

I supposed that I had reached the "acceptance" phase of my journey with the programme.

"Think we should redecorate when I'm home?" I asked my new friend. "I kind of prefer this to our living room."

He smiled. "I'm not sure we can afford it."

"Sure we can... oh, you mean the programme. It's expensive, right?"

"You applied for a partially funded position. But yes, the part that isn't accounted for is incredibly expensive."

That took the wind out of my sails somewhat. "I'm sorry," I said, dropping my gaze.

"Don't be. There is no price on your life, Magpie. No price."

I lifted my head once again. This was how I always thought relationships should be: lifting, supporting, holding each other up. I liked it. It filled me with a rare and delightful energy, a resolve to make sure I repaid the effort. Like blocks in a roman archway held together by a single keystone and nothing else. Take that away, and the arch collapses. The "physics of statics", I think it was called.

But was he my keystone, or I his?

Then I frowned. "Wait," I said, raising a hand. "Before, when we were talking about something else. You said that the *real*, living and breathing version of you is sitting in an apartment somewhere across town. But we don't own an apartment."

"Yes, but the *real* psychologist who is supposed to be attending you right now does," my friend said, without shame. "Good job he's away in France visiting his mother, isn't it?"

"Jesus Christ," I swore, shaking my head, as the implications of what he was saying sank in.

"Not quite," he replied, "although the beard does bear resemblance." He stroked the hair on his chin and I laughed quietly, marvelling at how good it felt to be able to do so.

"Are you going to get into trouble for this?" I asked, sobering.

He shook his head. "Not if I have my way, I won't."

"But breaking into another man's house, impersonating him, sneaking your way onto an elite academic experimental programme and pretending to be a therapist… these are crimes, you know that, right?"

"I know. But it was worth it."

"I don't want anything to happen to you."

"It won't." He said it so confidently. I should have realised he'd have come up with a contingency plan. He was intelligence unbridled; he always had been way ahead of me in that respect. He was the brains; I was the heart. Between us, we might just make up a halfway decent person.

"Care to share whatever plan it is you're cooking up with me?" I asked, knowing he wouldn't.

He shook his head, predictably. "Not yet," he said.

"Show me what you wanted to show me, then," I sighed, and he led me to a plinth I had not yet visited.

"Do we still need to do this?" I asked, flinching a little at the now familiar glint of sunlight bouncing off a glass dome. "I had the breakthrough; I remember everything now. We found the root cause. We solved the mystery. Don't I get, like... a little holiday now?"

"Get on with it, Magpie," my friend said, ushering me on.

Inside the glass case, sitting on a little carved wooden envelope stand, was a rectangular piece of card. I picked it up, and read the words printed on the front:

We request the pleasure of your company

At our WEDDING on the FIRST OF SEPTEMBER TWO THOUSAND AND TWELVE

PLEASE JOIN US AT TWO O'CLOCK FOR THE WEDDING CEREMONY, BREAKFAST AND RECEPTION TO FOLLOW

"I remember this," I said softly, and I felt him standing at my back.

We had written the details in large, black capitals, rendered in an ornate, vintage font, printed on expensive card to lend the request a formal air, stress the importance of the missive. No wonder people got anxious when they received it. It looked more like a summons to jury service. An invitation that wasn't allowed to be ignored.

Our closest loved ones had seen through the pomp and circumstance to what lay beneath: that getting married was a big deal. An important thing. A thing to be taken seriously, hence the capital letters and ten-gram paper.

And I remembered being amazed at just how seriously people *did* take it. We had been a pair, a two, for as long as anyone could remember and yet suddenly, this wedding, this day of dresses and dancing and cake, speeches, posed pictures, rose petals, drinks that fizzed, all these accoutrements, trappings of commitment, made our pairing a remarkable thing to be suddenly celebrated. It felt as if the wider world were lending our life choice an extra stamp of authenticity, by stint of signing a certificate. I didn't like that idea. In fact, I had struggled with the idea of marriage in general.

The invitation felt heavy, suddenly. "Why did we need to stand up in front of a room full of people we hardly ever see, to be recognised as a legitimate pairing?" I asked, out loud.

"We didn't. Some people just like it, that's all. It was a good party, if nothing else." He winked. "Usually, the woman is the one with the white dress fantasies, not the husband."

I smiled. "Yes, well that's why I chose you."

"And that's why I chose you."

I sighed. "Poor man."

I stared at the invitation, the scrolled font, the black and white outlines, and I remembered trying on dresses. I remembered walking into a room full of huge, white, sail-like things hanging all around, walls and walls of sequins and satin and lace and silk. They were great works of construction, buttressed, galvanised, braced. And they were heavy too, so heavy, I ran my arm underneath one experimentally and was amazed at how solid it was. Women had gathered around me, taken charge of my body. "I like this one," I'd said, weakly, fingering a limp, cream, satin number. I had liked it because it was light. I didn't want to get married already feeling like I carried a huge weight around with me. Surely that was a poor way to start things? A woman with a tape measure hanging around her neck and huge, false nails that tapped and scraped and rasped along everything stepped forward, pursed her lips wisely. "It is beautiful," she agreed, her nails making the silk whisper and sing seductively, "But not for you. You have hips." She pointed at them.

I had looked down at myself, surprised. "Well, yes," I'd said, confused, wondering, were hips a bad thing now?

"You need something with more tailoring," she said, from which I took to mean "something that would cost more money", then I told myself to stop being cynical, enjoy the process. I looked around for champagne, for I had been promised booze. None was forthcoming, just a hot changing room plastered with magazine clippings, impossibly long and angular women draped in satin and silk, women who didn't "have hips", lucky them. My hips were going to cost me, were dresses charged out by the square yard, like land?

The changing room curtain swished aside and the long-nailed woman had strode in clutching great armfuls of lace, tulle, and ribbon. "Is that just one dress?" I remember saying, incredulous. The woman heaved it up onto a padded hanger on the wall, and let it go with an audible groan. It tumbled down like a waterfall, spilling its lacy entrails all over the floor. I'd stared at the enormous thing.

Nevertheless, I had climbed into that dress. The woman with the nails buttoned me in. There was a moment's silence after the last button was tethered into place. I smoothed the lace over my hips repeatedly, nervously trying to plane a layer off of them. I gathered from the noises the other women in the room were making that it was a good dress.

I'd steeled myself, looked in the huge, floor-to-ceiling mirror I was led in front of. I was told to stand on a box, so that the train could be arranged. I did so obediently, and became a giant, lace-sheathed apparition.

"You look beautiful," someone had said, and another person echoed the same sentiment. I'd heard banging on glass; had spun around. Three men were pounding on the window, waving and grinning. They held thumbs up at me when they saw they'd caught my attention, another seal of approval, from people I'd never met.

I remembered smiling, embarrassed, returning to my

reflection. I *did* look beautiful, never an easy thing for me to admit to. But the longer I looked at myself, the more I no longer recognised myself. The dress was casting a spell on me, it bewitched me with its fine boning, its detailed stitching, its tiny, tiny buttons, like eyes, hundreds of eyes, watching me, asking: was I really wife material?

"I think this is the one," I'd said, or rather, the other me had said, while the usual me had just stared incredulously from inside her boned dress.

I sighed.

"You were supposed to enjoy all of that," my friend said, watching my face as I relived those memories.

"I know," I replied, a little sadly.

"Let me ask you something," he replied, undaunted.

"What?"

"Why did you say yes if you didn't want to get married?"

"But I *did* want to get married," I said, although not as convincingly as I could have.

"You wanted to commit. That's different."

Marriage and commitment, two separate things? Yes, I supposed they were.

"What's your point?" I asked, losing the will to explore this item in my Collection rapidly.

He shrugged, looking back at me noncommittally.

"You're a shit therapist," I said, glaring at him.

"Am I? It's not my fault you didn't think marriage was your sort of thing."

"I suppose not," I said, putting the invitation back under its glass case. "But it *was* a lovely day, wasn't it? We had fun. I made that speech, a good speech, about climbing the mountain. People cried. We danced. Children ran amok, everywhere. We fed them sweets and got them high on sugar, the parents got pissed and let them fend for themselves. I remember drinking vodka, and when we got back to the hotel, we ordered every single thing on the breakfast menu. And in the morning, two women arrived with these enormous trays of food, do you remember? Enough to feed ten people. We were so hungover we could barely touch it." I smiled. The memory was a good one. A good start to a marriage. I had been proud of myself for lasting a whole day in the dress. When I took it off that night, I carefully arranged it over a chair. It had looked like another person lying there. That person was the wife, perhaps, not me.

"I wanted to get married."

"If you say so."

"I *did*. But I don't think my version of marriage was quite the same as yours. I am an incurable romantic, but I don't believe in certificates or public declarations. I did when I was young, maybe. And then I learned too much about myself. My dreams were always about us, roaming the world. My dreams were of freedom, not dresses."

"You didn't want to lose your freedom?"

"Of course not."

"And how did the reality live up to the fear?"

I laughed. "Well, then we had a baby."

"Bye-bye freedom?"

I stopped laughing. "You could say that," I said softly, and gently, and insistently, the sadness began to tickle at the edges.

"Why did you bring me here?" I asked, heavily.

"To find out if you still loved me," he said, simply.

"Of course I still love you," I replied, shaking my head. "It's just, with all this... all these feelings... they fill me up, you see. It doesn't leave a lot of room for anything else."

His eyes lit up. "Well, funny you should mention that," he said. "Because I think I have just the thing for a full soul."

And he slipped his hand into mine again, leading me away from the plinth. I let him pull me along. I had come so far, now, that I knew the only way out was through.

Like most things in life.

"Where's my gold coin, by the way?" I asked, a little

petulantly. "I quite liked it when I got a gold coin for my efforts."

"Later, Magpie," my friend said.

32

THE WELL

We walked the length of the gallery and the sunlight strobed through the air before me, lurid spotlights blinding me every ten feet. As I walked I felt a peculiar dissociation from myself, as if the thinking part of me had detached from the breathing, blinking, swallowing part of me. I supposed I had been through an awful lot, in a relatively short space of time, and this was the fallout.

My friend stopped suddenly, and because I was blinking in the glare of another beam of light, I slammed into him, nose to back. He held me steady for a moment while I recovered my balance. Then, he pointed to the ground.

"Take a look," he said, gesturing at a great, round, black hole that had opened up on the tiled floor.

And as I did, the hole widened, and seemed to... rise up, somehow.

"Nice to see your control is back," I murmured, as the large circle swallowed us from the ankles up. It was a little like climbing into a glass elevator and ascending a tall building, only we were descending, or was the building ascending around us? The end result was the same: we were going somewhere, and soon the hole had consumed us, and the Gallery was replaced with something far more minimal in scope and design, but no less impressive in scale.

"So what... you're an architect now?" I said, stepping away

from the dark circle and staring in admiration at our new surroundings, which could only be described as… geometric. By this I mean the floor, the walls and the ceiling were all perfectly… Perfect. Arithmetical. There was no other word for it. We were standing in a cube, a vast, echoey space in which laser-straight, exacting lines met in painfully precise junctions at each corner of the room, junctions so congruous and clean and exact, it looked like… well, like a computer had drawn them. And there was more: every single surface I could see was polished. The room shone like a mirror. Reflections shimmered everywhere I looked, reflections of reflections, reflections of the corners and walls and ceiling and floor, reflections of us. My eyes struggled with it. It felt… dangerous in here. Sharp. It was the kind of room you imagined cutting yourself on, if you leaned up against the wrong thing. I subtly drew my arms into my sides, shivering at the thought.

"This is all your design?" I asked again, impressed but also confused. This was not exactly a warm, comforting space to occupy. It felt distinctly non-therapeutic, uncomfortable by design, and I had to wonder why he had brought me here, especially given the ordeal I had just been through. I also had no idea what was happening regarding the construct anymore. Were the watchers still there, monitoring us? Were we even still inside the programme? We must be, if my friend was able to manipulate it, to design spaces of his own, thread his own patch upon the quilt.

"All my design," he repeated. "Do you like it?"

"I don't know," I said, truthfully. "I think I preferred the boat. Can't we go back there?"

He shook his head. "Not this time, Magpie. Do I take it this means you don't like it?"

"I just… it's so… well, unsettling. It's making me feel…"

"Queasy?"

"Yeah."

"Good," he replied. "That's exactly the point."

"This isn't more confrontational stuff, is it?" I asked nervously. "I think... I think I've had enough for one session. I need a break, really I do. A nice beach, some warm sun, waves crashing on the shore, or maybe a forest... aren't there any more of the fun travel destinations I can choose from? I'd love to go back to the Galapagos..."

"No," he said, pulling on my hand and leading me forward again. Ever forward. "You can rest later, Magpie. For now, we still have work to do. And what you need is a purge. Or perhaps that's the wrong word. What you need... is to draw the poison."

"Riddles," I spat, shaking my head. "So many fucking riddles, with you."

He laughed apologetically. "You'll see."

And I saw that, of course, there was a focal point to this room, other than the optical glory of so much finely polished stone, although it had been lost on me at first glance as I struggled with the multitude of reflections that played with my vision. I let myself be led to the middle of the cube, where, in the dead centre of the space, set into the floor, was a vast, perfectly round and perfectly black recessed hole.

"You've got a thing about shapes," I said, looking at it. The hole made me suddenly very nervous, although I couldn't have said why. Perhaps it was the complete density of the darkness inside the hole that seemed to swallow all surrounding light that unnerved me. It was a shade of black so dark and complete that it absorbed everything in close proximity, sucked it in, somehow, even though when I finally managed to get a purchase on the edges of the hole, I could see it was static.

"Yeah, but you knew that," my friend answered as we came to a stop at the lip. And I wondered, if only for a terrifyingly serious split second, if he was going to push me in, then, and if I would spend eternity falling in the darkness, arms windmilling forever, plummeting down a shaft with no beginning and no end, just an infinite loop in time, and the thought made my stomach cramp. I covered my mouth with my hand, struggling. Then I remembered who I was with. This was a person I trusted. If he *did* push me in, I knew it would be for a damn good reason.

Nevertheless, the hole made me nervous. I held my breath for a second, and a shining crystal guard-rail popped into place, encircling the black hole. I let out the breath, thinking, *that's better.*

"Hey," my friend frowned. "This is my design, hands off." But he allowed the guardrail to stay.

I tried not to let my friend see how white my knuckles were. "What is it?"

"This is a little something I like to call 'The Well'. Think of it like... a metaphorical oubliette. Or maybe that's the wrong word. Hm. A receptacle?"

"For what?"

"I hope I made it deep enough," he murmured, leaning over the rail.

"For what??"

"I should have brought a penny or something to drop in there, test it out..."

"What's at the bottom?"

"Ah." He smiled. "It's not what's at the bottom that counts."

"The cryptic shtick is becoming a little taxing, *friend*." I had to admit, talking to him as an impartial stranger had been easier, in some respects. Familiarity was giving our discourse an edge, now, the kind of edge you only got when two people had known each other a very, very long time. An edge born of intimacy, frustration, understanding, attachment.

He sighed. "I know. I'm just nervous, in case this doesn't work."

"In case *what* doesn't work, for crying out loud?"

"Let me show you." He took my hand. He placed his other hand on my belly. I flinched, but he held fast. His touch did something peculiar to me, something almost miraculous.

It silenced things in my head, noises that had been playing without me really noticing them. As if he had simply reached into my brain and flipped a switch.

And as the quiet took hold, I began to *feel* things.

I had not felt things properly for a very long time.

I began to tremble. He held me fast. And as I stared into The Well, I began to feel myself filling up.

He leaned in and whispered; his breath warm on my neck. "What are you feeling? Right now?"

I could barely speak for the strength of my emotions. I took several deep breaths. I tried to analyse what it was that was swelling in my body. I opened my mouth.

Instead of words, I vomited.

It wasn't food, or bile.

What came out of me in a hot, tingling rush could only be described as... *matter.*

It was brown, and sticky. Like molasses.

And as it exited my body, as my stomach cramped and I doubled over, mouth wide open, birthing this new monstrosity a different way to the way I'd birthed Silhouette, it hung in the air, a foul, dark arc of fetid, stinking, gloopy shit. I tried to close my mouth, stop it from coming, but I could not. I felt like my entire soul was emptying itself out of me. I heaved, and heaved again, and I was dimly aware of my friend holding my hair back, keeping me steady, and even though my eyes watered viciously I could still see little motes of glowing red light that twisted and hung suspended within the sticky matter, and I thought: *what is this? This is coming out of me? What is it? Will it ever stop?* But still it came pouring out, a never-ending stream of... what, I couldn't tell.

My body arched and bowed, wracked with effort. The foul stream just kept coming, on and on until I thought I would turn inside out, collapse, spent, and find that I was only a heap of skin, all my insides liquidated.

I heard my friend say: "Keep going, come on! Get it all out!

All of it! You need this, Magpie, sick it up! Sick up all of it!"

But it was no longer his voice, it was another voice I knew, a voice I was beholden to, or was it? No. It was a different voice to that still, it was the voice of my child, no, it was the voice of my Mother, no, it was... it was...

Silhouette.

The matter made its way slowly and deliberately towards The Well in a steady, unhurried way, like a vast, angry worm intent on escaping down the hole. The viscous, twisted column reared up its head at the very last minute at the mouth of the Well, and then plunged down, down, down into the void.

And I was suddenly empty.

I sagged. And not for the first time, the last thing I remembered were my friend's arms, keeping me safe from harm as my body met the floor.

33

END OF EVANS

Evans watches as Silhouette approaches him and realises two things in quick succession: that he is never going to leave this room alive, and, after looking upon the face of Silhouette, he has no desire to do so anyway. Who wants to live in a world where a nightmare can manifest for real? Who wants to live in a place where the trappings of imagination can rear out of the shadows when you least expect it? Evans knows enough about the vagaries of the human mind to understand that a world in which a person can actualise their deepest darkest fears and turn them into eventualities as complete and terrifying as this is not a world in which he wishes to exist. Where does the buck stop, after this? Where does humanity go when they are governed by the threat of other people's livid traumas stalking the night like the fucking Bogeyman? Where does it all end, if this secret gets out? If this precedent is set? A tiny, defiant part of him that cannot let go of his former self, the version of him that existed before this room, this patient, this shitshow, remembers a line from a movie he once loved, where a chaotician dressed as a rock star says "Your scientists were so preoccupied with whether or not they could, they didn't stop to think if they *should*", and he gets it now, he gets that for all their posterchild good intentions, they have fucked up here. They were so focussed on the technology behind the therapeutic constructs, they were so obsessed with the whys and the hows, that they forgot about the most important aspect of what they were trying to achieve: the person lying in the cradle in the adjoining room.

He watches as Silhouette jerks and fits its way closer to him, its horribly indistinct outline jitterbugging all over the place so that Evans can never get a true fix on it with his eyes, and he thinks: *Fuck, why me? Where the fuck is the Boss? She should be fucking in here, not me!*

And then Evans is no longer thinking anything at all. His feet suddenly dangle an inch or two above the ground, for Silhouette has a firm grip on him by the neck, and he lifts him higher and higher into the air with a single distorted arm. Evans clutches at the iron-hard hands around his throat, he can feel his face turning purple, he can hear his pulse pounding in his ears, and yet he manages, somehow, to force two words out into the room, two words aimed at the only other living person he can see now, through a small clean patch on the filthy window, even though he knows she is unconscious: the patient, lying slack, festooned with wires and sensors. He looks at her as he speaks his last words.

Is she fucking smiling?! His eyes are filled with tears, but he thinks maybe… the fucking bitch is smiling in her sleep!

"Help… me…" he says, in a strangled cry, and then Silhouette brings him back down so that they are face to face, pushes him up against the solid, unopenable door, and presses the entire length of its body into Evans, consuming him, subsuming him, absorbing every single part of his physicality and digesting him slowly, and it is the most excruciating, suffocating, awful, soul-destroying pain Evans has ever experienced in his life. He starts to weep, for he still has a mouth, of sorts, and the part of his brain that is left intact prays that it will end, but it doesn't end, it never ends, and Evans realises he is not dead, nor is he alive, he is somewhere in between, and in that in-between, as his mind flounders to make sense of it all, he can hear another voice, speaking.

It is the voice of a woman.

There is another consciousness down here with him in the swamp of Silhouette's awareness, and he knows who it is, far too late.

It is that of the patient.

She is assimilating him, and in doing so, he is opened up to the sum total of her experiences, her thoughts, her memories, her pain, her torment, her vulnerabilities and deepest, darkest thoughts, and right before the last particles of him dissolve and sink into the bottom of the well that is her beautiful, damaged spirit, he understands, without being able to give voice to it, that she is about to destroy the world entire, just as he understands that he was right to want to die, because life will never be the same again, not for anyone, now that she has uncovered her own latent potential.

Silhouette shudders, having absorbed Evans within a matter of moments, and then stands swaying on long, thin legs as it tries to understand what it should do next.

And in the Observation Room, the woman lying on the bed opens her mouth, wide.

Brown, noxious, sticky shadows erupt out of her, fountaining out of her mouth, eyes, ears, nose, every orifice a gateway to pain, and a fresh swarm of gelatinous shoots burst outwards, once again invading every part of the large mirrored room, covering every single available surface with a wet, dark, fibrous residue, like tar, only different, and the glass of the giant mirrored window, unable to take the pressure anymore, shatters, sharp splinters spearing Silhouette in a thousand places, but the creature cares not, it simply sways, watching as a many-limbed tide of filth surges towards it, and it is assimilated as quickly as Evans was assimilated, without ceremony or struggle, for her mind is a rolling stone hurtling down a mountain, gathering no moss, but instead, gathering fierce momentum.

34

OUT, OUT

Eventually, just as I was beginning to think that all that had gone before was a joke, and that I was in fact not in a virtual construct but actually in hell, and hell was this, forever and ever, lying on the cold polished floor next to the horrendous black of a metaphorical wormhole, panting and dry-heaving, shuddering, the memory of the disgusting mess that was my experience ripping itself out of me assaulting my every waking sense, my face pressed into the glossy mirror-rock of the room, feeling like a heap of skin and bendy bones and nothing more, my stomach slowly began to settle.

My friend knelt beside me, patting my back and stroking my hair gently.

"Leave me alone," I muttered, drooling. The scene juddered and shimmered for a second, settling into focus once more, another glitch, I supposed, but I no longer cared about any of that. All I cared about was the feeling of my body, so bruised and sore and ravaged from expelling whatever it was that I had banished from my core.

"I told you it was experimental," he said, assessing me and smiling. "How do you feel?"

"Fuck off," I muttered, then I closed my eyes, and fell asleep.

He kept gently stroking my back, and as I drifted off, a man's voice crept into my dreams, shattered, raw, crying.

35

FULL IMMERSION

Evans is dead.

The Boss knows this because after she flees the scene of the control room in terror, she pulls herself up short, knowing she cannot leave Evans there, alone in that room with that... thing. She returns ten minutes later with a small team of security guards armed with fire extinguishers and batons and tasers, as if that will do anything against the conceptual nightmare that awaits, but it is better than nothing. How does one defeat a virtual construct that has somehow crossed over into the real world and become a real-life, vicious predator, anyway? With code? A hard reset? Fire? She does not know that Evans has already tried the kill switch to no avail, and would not care if she did. All she cares about is making sure she does not have the blood of a colleague on her hands, but even as she approaches the control room door, she knows that this hope is a futile one, she knows that she is too late, and that ahead of her, horror awaits.

But she pushes this to the back of her mind, renews her grip on the short handled fire-axe she managed to yank out of a glass case mounted to a wall in the corridor nearby. She is afraid, afraid of what the patient has unleashed, afraid for the patient's wellbeing, afraid for what this all means for her definitions of reality and science and afraid of her own role and culpability in these suddenly expanded horizons, but she is also belligerently defensive about it: how the fuck was she supposed to know that a woman could meld her consciousness so completely with their tech that she would forcibly take over the entire programme and create her own fucking Super Brain Computer Interface, even if she had seen it done before, with Tetris, in a pilot trial in Massachusetts General Hospital in Boston, how the fuck was she supposed to know how far it would go?! Sure, she has bandied the term "Full Immersion" around jokingly before, but they all have. No one was ever serious about it. She can't reasonably be blamed for where things stand now, surely? The patient has warped the fabric of reality, for fuck's sake, she has materialised a conceptualised version of her pain and suffering and torment and now it is running around the department like that creature from *The Thing* and there is going to be all hell to pay afterwards for this fuck up, even if the Boss *can* somehow make it out of here alive.

She brings the axe up before her face and advances, her mind a mess of confusion and potential escape routes, for she is simultaneously drawn to help Evans and compelled to save her own skin, but most importantly, she feels ashamed of herself for leaving him alone, unprotected, in that room. She is aware that in doing so, she probably saved her own life, but still. How was she to know? That's what all this boiled down to, at the end of the day.

How could anyone have known?

At least, this is what she tells herself as her heart rises up her throat and threatens to choke her dead.

All is eerily quiet inside the control room as the group come to a stop outside the door. The Boss realises with a sinking stomach that she can no longer see through the small square of reinforced glass into the room, for the portal is covered with a brownish sticky substance that conceals the scene beyond from view.

This does not bode well.

The men she has brought with her dither, waiting for instruction.

"Well," she snaps, doing what she does best. She steps back, hands the axe to the largest man in the group. "Break it down!" The man gives her a look. "Please," she adds, politely.

The Boss subtly retreats to the rear of the group as the security guard obeys. The dull *thunk-thunk-thunk* of the axe against the reinforced steel door-lock accompanies her internal monologue as she simultaneously works on her witness statement and wonders how quickly she can book a flight if it turns out that Evans is indeed dead.

The door eventually gives way, despite the lock being the best that money can buy, it is no match for a fire-axe, apparently. The men clear a path for The Boss as the heavy door swings open. Nobody is stupid enough to be the first inside the room beyond, and the silver-haired woman realises she has no choice. It'll have to be her.

She takes the axe back from the security guard without asking for it, and slowly, carefully inches her way in through the door.

And the scene within is utter chaos.

Brown ichor covers every single available surface of the Control Room, and, as far as she can see, the room beyond that in which the patient used to lie. Is she still there? The Boss can't tell, not from this distance. *Fuck, is she dead?* After everything she's been through? The Boss cannot bear the thought, pushes it away. Something wet and solid splatters onto her forehead from somewhere above, and she flinches and wipes it off, rubbing her fingers together and wondering why the substance coating her skin feels so familiar. As she does this she realises that the space around her is alive with the sound of wet matter sliding down things and off of things, pooling under her feet as she gingerly steps through the doorway. Something has exploded in here, a volcano has erupted and painted everything with a peculiar type of molten lava, and the room is almost pitch dark as a result, the lights from the multitude of monitors blotted out by slime, the fluorescent overhead strip bulbs hanging loose from their brackets or shattered entirely.

She does not want to go any further, but she is duty-bound to look for Evans, who she last saw being mauled by the shadowy form of Silhouette, she is duty bound to check on the patient, who put her life in their hands. The other men she brought with her are all peering into the room now, mouths open. She curses herself silently for having brought a gaggle of witnesses along and, right after that, she curses the part of herself that came here instead of running to the underground car park and jumping into her Prius only to drive off into the night, never to be seen again.

"Anyone bring a torch?" she asks, in a low voice, and one of the men unhooks a large flashlight from his belt and holds it out, refusing to enter. The Boss tuts, backtracks, snatches the torch with a furious look on her face, switches it on, and casts the beam around the room. Now she can see that the large mirror window dividing the two rooms has shattered. The jagged shards of glass that cling stubbornly to the gums of the window frame drip with more of the horrible gooey residue, adding to the chorus of wet little voices already setting the Boss's teeth on edge.

Beyond the shattered window, it is clear the patient is missing. Where she has gone exactly, The Boss cannot tell. She's certainly not lying in an induced coma in her cradle like she should be. Her torchlight wanders around the space beyond the ragged frame, across the now defunct wires and sensor pads that lie strewn about everywhere, across the toppled IV drip stand and burned-out monitors and shredded pyjamas, and comes up with nothing: no patient. The Boss knows the patient should not have been able to escape from the OR without knowing the keypad code for the door, and she also knows it is virtually impossible for the patient to go anywhere this soon after rousing from a hypnagogic state, if indeed that is what has happened. She knows her limbs and muscles will be weak and watery, she knows the woman will be disoriented, she knows there are a million and one reasons as to why the patient should *not* be missing from that room, and yet... Well. Here they were. Two probable deaths on her hands, an entire programme's worth of equipment destroyed, hundreds of people now out of a job, millions of pounds worth of investment lost in the space of a few hours...

She brings the beam of light back to the room she is standing in, trains it on the remains of their equipment, on the walls, the floor, the ceiling. She is fighting back tears, but forces herself to stay, survey the damage. Giant cracks in the plasterwork branch out like roots around the entire length of the room, and fresh, wet brown substance leaks from the cracks, oozing down the walls and onto the carpet.

Not having the faintest idea of what it is she should do next, she starts to giggle, because the alternative is crying, and crying is not in her emotional repertoire, so she laughs instead.

"Er... Boss?" One of the security guards says from the doorway in a slightly strangled voice. The Boss almost doesn't hear him over the sound of her own weird, hysterical chortling.

"Boss?"

"Ha ha... what? Ha ha ha..."

"You might want to... er... head back this way, nice and quick if you can..."

Too late, The Boss hears a pronounced shifting, wet sound as the guard says this, off in a far corner of the Control Room, although it is hard to pinpoint its location exactly with the acoustics so distorted and muffled by residue. She whirls about, the torch held before her like a wizard's staff, laughter still escaping her lips like bubbles of gas leaking out of a partially opened bottle, a wheezing, mirthless exhalation that won't stop, now that she has started.

She whirls and comes face to face with an enormous,

quivering, shifting mound of matter. It glistens under the light of the torch, and The Boss can hear the men in the doorway swearing, then running away, back down the corridor, away from the abomination that encroaches.

The Boss lets out a swear word of her own, then bites her tongue, thinking wildly: *does it know I am here?*

Is its vision based on movement?

Where the fuck is Evans? He would appreciate that cultural joke.

Why am I laughing?

And the patient? Where?

And, for that matter, fucking Silhouette?!

She stares in terror and awe at the disgusting mass as it coalesces, shifts, moves around, redistributing its weight, testing its own dimensions and capabilities until it is no longer an indistinct gelatinous mess but a single, recognisable shape: that of a woman, huge, tall, long in body, arms and legs, long hair, breasts, and instead of a face there is only blankness which occasionally ripples, or shifts, so that the merest impression of a face can be seen, a nose, a tooth, an eyebrow, but it always collapses back into the mess before it can be fixed upon. For a split second, The Boss fancies she can see Evans staring back at her, trying to escape from the nightmarish form, but she dismisses this as a trick of her fear-addled mind, and decides that she has seen enough, anyway.

She could make for the door, but the sight of the giant form before her brings her to her knees.

"Incredible," she whispers, the last words she will say. "You're incredible."

The patient pours herself across the space between them, and before the Boss has taken another breath, she is drowning in a sticky, horrible puddle that firms up around her knees and climbs up her body and pours itself into her now wide open mouth, filling her up from the inside out, and there is a terrible splitting, creaking, popping noise, and then the Boss ruptures, her pale bloated body splitting open, but in the second before it does, she thinks she can hear the sound of Evans crying somewhere from the middle of the terror, and she understands that she, too, has made a terrible mistake, she has underestimated Magpie, underestimated and undervalued her, and her penance for that is annihilation.

36

EMPTY

"How do you feel?" my friend asked me. I lay like a limp rag on the floor, my entire body wracked with aches and pains as if I had the flu, and if I had had the energy, I would have thought murderous things about him, maybe even smacked him if I'd had the ability to lift my arm. It was as if every connection and pathway in my body were broken: I could think an instruction to a particular part of me like a finger or a foot, and it just didn't respond, for the signalmen of my neural pathways had taken a vacation.

And instead of the shiny, polished chamber, I saw code.

Strings of code, scrolling up and up endlessly in my vision. I closed my eyes again, and the code still whizzed past. I reopened them. The code remained.

I was too tired to try and do anything about it.

"Exhausted," I mumbled, instead. "Like I just gave birth again. I hate you."

"You do now. You won't later," he replied, still rubbing my back.

"What… what was that about?" I tried to will myself to sit up, but my body remained limp and lifeless. I decided it was better to admit defeat, stay down until I was ready for myself.

"Well," my friend said, joining me on the floor. "Think of it like an extreme visualisation technique. A means of separating yourself from your bad thoughts, I guess, enabling you to relax.

In theory it activates the same neural networks that get used when you're performing a task, so you're more... connected, body and mind-wise."

"As usual," I mumbled, as drool leaked out of my mouth to the floor beneath my face, "I haven't got the faintest idea what you're banging on about. My head hurts."

"Okay, fine. There's lots of these techniques. Go onto any lifestyle guru's website, and you'll see them talking about 'affirming your desired outcomes – visualise them by activating your creative subconscious, and so on. I think it's safe to say we already did that, didn't we?"

"Did what?"

"Activated your creative subconscious. I mean, just look at where you are."

"I can't see anything but code at the moment, I'm afraid." I meant it. I was still a slave to the crawling jargon, an incessant parade of strings of zeros and brackets and angle brackets and parentheses and words I didn't understand and symbols that didn't make sense all snuggled up inside single quotes and I realised that this was probably a permanent affliction, because it wasn't distressing me as much as it should have been, as if my brain had already decided to acclimatise to a new normal. And actually, if I squinted a little, the code seemed to fade, or maybe space out, so I could begin to see through the digits and letters and glyphs, and what... what was that that I could see beyond? It had a familiar shape, but...

Give yourself time, I told myself, and again, I was reminded of that moment on top of the pixelated mountain, talking to the commandment prompt, and something slowly began to make a sort of sense to me, a feeling of belonging to something new, of opening my horizons, of... of... *joining* something. Fusing. Attaching myself, like moss to a rock.

"Ah. Well, take it from me – it's spectacular," my friend said, and with this, the fingers on my right hand twitched.

My body was slowly returning to me.

"I'm so thrilled you think so," I grumbled, more drool leaking out of the corner of my mouth.

"At least your sense of humour remains intact," he replied. "Anyway. Visualisation techniques. I thought it could... help you place negativity in a box, compartmentalise your feelings so you can focus on other things when you feel overwhelmed. I found lots of these exercises. The double-paned window, for example – you visualise a group of people standing outside a window, talking loudly to each other. And then, you simply close the window, and the noise, the chatter, goes away. Then there is the beach technique, the stop sign, the ball of yarn, the threaded needle, the liquid quiet technique..."

"Stop, please. For the love of all that is unholy." In a moment I'd be shutting a double-paned window on *him*, just to allow myself a little recovery time.

"All of those are what I would call 'light' versions of the technique. But for you? For all the years of toxic crap that's built up in your guts, clogging up your soul and your brain like dirt in a filter, after everything you've been through... I thought you needed something more..."

"Extreme," I said, finally sitting up.

"Exactly," my friend replied, mirroring my action. We faced each other, not for the first time, and certainly not for the last. "So I came up with a new technique, a repository, if you like, for all the awfulness. And I called it The Well."

"So where... where did all that stuff go?" I asked, shuddering as I remembered how it came out of me, but I had a vague feeling that I knew where it had gone, that I was still connected to it, somehow, and that it was out there in the big wild world, fulfilling my potential for me, a terrible thing turned good, turned strong, turned powerful, turned...

What, exactly?

But I forgot about that when I realised the code had integrated so completely into my vision that I no longer saw it, but instead saw the beautiful blue sky, and a patchwork quilt of trees, and a giant, swooping span of iron stretching out to either side of me, and I gasped, because here we were, full circle, at the end and beginning of all things, and I realised we were sitting right in the middle of the Suspension Bridge.

Not far from where I had first discovered my own bloated, drowned body, down below.

"Welcome home, Magpie," my friend said.

37

THE BRIDGE

A light breeze, cool, fresh, suddenly ruffled my hair. Sitting in the midway point of the bridge I loved so much, I remembered the many walks across it, the many times I had traversed the span of it, keeping to the narrow footways to either side of the road, running my fingers against the protective metal grill that is there to stop people like me from learning to fly. I remembered how much I loved this place, and realised how important it was to reclaim it as a good place, and not just a place from which I had leaped when all other options seemed unavailable to me – even if that had only been in my mind, rather than reality. I had tried, several times, and that was what mattered, not whether or not I had achieved my goal.

Beneath us sat the river next to which we had first met, and beyond that, an entire city, humming and throbbing with life. *My* city, my home for so many years. If I thought about it, I could probably point to all the places I'd ever had sex from that single viewpoint. Behind me, by the observatory, on a bench, in the dark. To the west, in amongst the trees, on a grey, flat day. Over there, at the bottom of Cabot's Tower, drunk, after a party. In the doorway of Wills' Memorial tower, with the rain pelting down all around. Over there, in the village, in a restaurant toilet. Way over there, at another party, in another toilet. There, in an alleyway behind a pub as jazz leaked out of the doors and windows all around us. There too, in a bed, a bed that didn't belong to me. That one hurt. I had made a mess, and left myself with a swollen, infected heart.

And over there, somewhere, out of view... my house. A place of little triumphs and successes, memories, bright moments in our shared history, moments that had almost been swept away by the darkness that had clouded our lives for so long. A place where we woke each morning to find a skinny, hot child worming his way underneath the sheets between us, his blonde hair curling across my mouth and tickling my nose, his small hands scratching at our backs, *wake up Mummy and Daddy*, and we would know that it was time to start the day, that this one would be better than the last, because that's simply what people do: they start again, each morning, rise up, conquer, fall back, start again.

And so it goes.

And now I was on the bridge once more, and a man who loved me was staring at me with the kind of eyes a man has when he sees his hope made good, for once.

"How did I not recognise you before?" I said, taking his hands into mine.

He shrugged. "It's been a funny old day, and you had a lot on your mind, didn't you?"

"I really did."

"Ready to tell me what you discovered, Detective lady?"

I broke from his gaze, a little more flustered than I would have liked, and continued my study of the landscape beneath me. A plane flew lazily overhead on the skyline, a small trail of seagulls crossed the sky in the opposite direction.

"It was never about dying, you have to understand," I said, trying to word it in a way he would appreciate. "It was more about... just not living anymore."

"Not good enough. You tried to leave. You've almost ripped us to pieces, if I'm honest. Not to make you feel guilty, or anything."

I stared at him, purse-mouthed, but I supposed I owed him the chance to be angry with me.

"I need more than that." It was a peculiar type of anger, coming out as the parental, understanding type – my least favourite. The *I'm disappointed in you* type. I had become a child again.

Not happening. Not this time.

"Ideation." I said simply, after a moment more of thought. "Somehow, slowly, over time, it just formed. That, *the* idea. To die, except it wasn't to die, it was, like I said, more about simply not having to live anymore. I was so exhausted of living. And I couldn't shake it. That feeling that it just wasn't worth it any longer."

"Why not?"

I shrugged, at a loss. "It just all seemed so pointless. Every day, the same as the one before, and the one after. We had our lives set up in that way, I guess. There was only one certainty, that we could continue going on, and going on, and going on. But I had sort of lost sight of the reason *why*. I suppose that's the nature of the beast. I couldn't bear it, after a while. It was simply too much."

"And now?" There was a lot happening behind his eyes, and for a moment I wondered if we would have to pay out for a therapy VR programme for *him*, and the thought made me chuckle. *I'd like to see anyone try to analyse this one*, I thought.

"Well, I don't know. Biology drives us on, we procreate and die, fertilize the soil for the next lot. Me not being here won't change that. The hard truth of the matter hasn't changed, at all."

"True." He laughed, ran a finger through my hair. "I must say, as existential midlife crises go, this is a textbook example."

"You're hardly helping," I said, wondering why I always fell in love with men who loved to tease me.

"Have you ever thought," he said, serious again, "Have you ever thought, though, that perhaps questioning why we do it, is more important than finding out the answer?"

"No," I said, bluntly. "That's ridiculous."

He tried again. I still could not tell if his eyes were blue, or green. It still didn't matter.

"Some people think that reality doesn't exist until it's measured."

I looked up at him and burst out laughing. "How is it I have known you this long, and I still I don't ever have the faintest fucking idea what that means, you silly bastard!"

"Let me… wait. I'll try and explain in simpler terms." *If I had a penny for every time he had to say that to me,* I thought. He settled himself, ready to impart wisdom. He liked to rearrange his body so that he was comfortable before he gave me his knowledge. It was like a boat setting down anchor before letting off the passengers, waiting for the water to calm and the boat to stop rocking first.

"This isn't going to be another argument about Schrodinger's cat, is it?" I remembered once we had ruined what was meant to have been a romantic picnic in that way. I had refused to accept that the cat could be both alive and dead or neither at the same time. The cat had been poisoned. In my mind, if it wasn't already dead, it would be shortly. First you live, then you die. End of argument.

But then he said this:

"I think of life like this: I have two choices."

I knew all of this already, hadn't I just proved that? I reigned myself in. "Only two?"

"Black, or white. Heads, or tails."

"Jump, or don't jump."

"Shh. Whichever choice I make is immaterial. Simply choosing one of them is like drawing a line in the sand. It wasn't there before, but it is now."

"A line." I thought about it.

"A line. And now it is there, you can measure it. You can make it longer, change the shape, rub it out altogether. The main thing is that you can control it. Manipulate it. And *that's* the point. You can't measure something that doesn't exist. Your reality is only what you choose it to be. So if it seems pointless, then change it so that it *has* a point. Make the point something you can control. Judge yourself by different standards. Move away from the biology and the chemistry and the physics."

"And do what, exactly?"

"Draw a line in the sand, beautiful," he said, and as he did so, a cloud which had passed over the sun moved away, and light spilled across the gorge and across his face, turning the river beneath us into fire, and I reached out and stroked his lips and stared into his eyes and thought again: *Could it really be that easy?*

I felt something suddenly in my pocket. I reached a hand inside and drew out a folded picture. I unfolded it, handed it over. It was a photograph of a yellow ribbon, tied around a tree. Tucked inside of the photograph, was a small lock of soft, blonde hair.

"I wondered where that went," I said.

It was untainted by blood. I saw this, and my heart sang.

Our eyes met.

A silent agreement was reached.

Perhaps it could, if I decided it. Perhaps it could be that easy.

We stood, then, and walked, hand in hand, across the bridge and away from it.

And although I thought about it, many, many times, I never went back.

I made a choice, and drew a line.

And in the distance, as we wandered towards a new and hopeful future, I heard a rumbling sound, a sound like that of a massive stone rolling down the hill, gathering no moss.

38

A Beehive

"Wait, wait, wait."

I opened my eyes.

What?

They had already been open, surely?

But it didn't feel right, and I knew it. I had so many unanswered questions.

"What?" I heard my friend say, but I couldn't place him, not yet.

"That's it?" I heard myself reply. "We just wander off into the sunset, end of story, thanks for the help, everything's fine now, *I don't know what I was so worried about*?"

I was in a room, a white, brightly painted room. Books lined the walls, their coloured spines and assorted titles comforting to me. A sash window let in a thin, grey light, diffused, softening everything.

I was sitting on a chair, a comfortable chair made of leather, a burnished leather Chesterfield, the type of chair you sank into with a good book, a glass of wine, where the leather has a robust shine to it and a tangy smell.

There was a large rug under my feet, red, deeply piled, the sort you want to lie on.

A fire was lit. It crackled and popped next to me.

My friend sat across the room from me, in another deep chair, high-backed, his legs struggling for space as they always did.

"I'm not cured, you know," I said, carefully. "I don't think I ever will be."

"That's not what we're trying to do here," he said. "I don't think you'll ever stop thinking about it. That's natural."

"Probably," I admitted, relaxing in the warmth of the fire. "I think you're right; I have planned it and unplanned it and re-planned it so many times that it will be hard to break the habit."

"I don't want to live with this constant fear, Magpie," he said, a hint of that unanswered anger sliding into his tone, "that you'll do it again." I realised I had aged him considerably since we began this programme. Grey spread liberally through his hair, now, and his eyes had deeper furrows around them than I remembered.

"But you always said I should have a plan," I joked, gently.

"Not funny."

"I know."

The fire crackled, filling the silence with something companionable. I felt as if all my edges had worn away.

"You know," he said to me, searching for a way forward. "There are words for the way you are feeling. Human nature is fragile, you aren't the first person to ever feel this way. You aren't... as alone as you think you are."

"I know."

"It's very... human, as they say in the industry."

"Which you don't belong to."

"Nevertheless."

"I made so many mistakes," I said, sadly.

"You had a beehive in your heart," he replied.

"What?"

"Antonio Machado. Spanish poet. He wrote a poem about failure, and how we rise from it. Basically, your heart was full of holes, but then the bees came along and made honey in it. From it. It's better than how I'm describing it. Jungian stuff."

"Jungian stuff?"

"Jungian stuff. Jung was the founder of analytical psychology, but that's hardly important right now. The point is, you can do this," he said, and his eyes shone with hope, and wonder. "You can do this."

And I thought to myself: *I can, I really can.*

But aloud, I said: "Can you show me how?" Because, from the corner of my eye, I noticed something brown and treacly running down the perfect white smoothness of one of the study walls.

My friend smiled.

"I thought you'd never ask," he said.

More silence, and then I said: "Do you think you can do something for me?"

He looked at me in a way that no-one else knew how to look at me, and I felt two things: a terrible weight of responsibility, and a huge wealth of understanding. Finally, after all these years, I recognised someone with whom I could speak the same language. Two readers on the same page.

Keystones holding up the sacred arch.

"Do you think," I continued, smiling, "that you could help me save my own life again tomorrow?"

He smiled back.

Not cured, never cured, but understood, a little, and redeemed, a little.

I couldn't ask for more than that.

Case closed.

Not solved.

But closed.

"Wait, wait. There is more to do here. You know that right?"

I sighed. "Yeah, I know. I've been avoiding it."

"Of course. Only natural. But you're safe here, for a bit." He does not look so convinced of that. In fact, he looks altogether preoccupied.

"You got somewhere to be?" I asked, archly.

"As a matter of fact, yes I do," he replied, patting my knee. "You'll be alright alone for a little bit, won't you? I won't... I won't be long."

"Sure," I sighed. "This is something I have to do for myself, anyway."

39

A Single Lock of Hair

The lock of hair still fitted perfectly into my cupped palm. It helped me to spin a new memory, the most complete, vivid memory yet. There were no stuck pixels here, no shifting details. There would be no blurred faces. When it came down to it, brass nickels and all, I could remember every detail of this moment.

A white gloss door appeared in front of me, once clean and freshly painted, now with kick-scuff marks decorating the bottom panels. Remnants of stickers further marred the paint job, and scribbles that had been twice glossed over, only the marker pen, stubborn and unbeatable as the artist who held it, still came through. Shadowy, but there.

From behind the closed door, furious voices, a child, and a woman.

"You're shitty! You're a shitty Mummy!" This had hurt because it felt so true, every day. The steady crushing weight of inescapable truth. At this point, Memory Me was no longer a three-dimensional person, so matter how well I remembered her. She only existed on two planes, and even then only barely.

"I just want you to put your pyjamas on." Weary to her bones, it came out in her voice.

"NO! I don't have to do ANYTHING you say anymore! You ruined my day! This is the worst day ever, and it's YOUR FAULT!"

"I know you're angry, and it's been a tough day, but please, I'm begging you, just put your pyjamas on."

"No."

"Please. You need to go to sleep. We've all had a really, really difficult day, haven't we?"

"I won't, and you can't make me."

"Please, I'm asking nicely–"

"Shut up!"

"I'm only going to ask once more, please–"

"SHUT UP!"

"PUT YOUR FUCKING PYJAMAS ON NOW!"

"NO! GET OUT OF MY ROOM!"

An object is thrown with force. It hits the wooden door with a loud crash, making me jump, even though I'd known it was coming.

"I hate you!"

The sound of a scuffle, then a yelp. Then a silence, broken by a pressure gauge going off.

"WELL I HATE YOU TOO!"

A pause. The boy goes to speak, is cut off. Memory Me has lost her grip on any semblance of control she's been desperately clinging to.

"I HATE THIS LIFE! I hate my life, do you understand? I hate everything about it! I hate this house, I hate this life, I hate how we live it! I hate the fights, and the tantrums, and the mess, and the noise, the monotony, the repetition, the stress, and how fucking miserable and *hard* everything is, do you get that? This is not how I thought it would be! None of this is enjoyable! None of this is how people should live! This is not how a family should function, okay? I hate it *all! I just want to die!"*

More silence. Then a small, angry boy, overwhelmed and overburdened with the vast load of an adult's distress, bursts into anguished, confused sobs, quickly followed by his mother. Listening, my ear pressed to the door, I felt my heart, a heavy, sinking stone in my body, settling in my stomach.

This, out of so many low moments, is one of the lowest. A moment of complete and abject failure. A moment that pulled me up short, like a dog straining at a lead, almost choking me.

I push open the door, softly. Oblivious to me, there they stand, facing off, defiance versus defeat, both of them crying on the spot.

Memory Me is the first to break the stasis. She sinks to her knees, trying to wrap her arms around the boy. Furious, he lashes out, strikes her on the side of the head. She blinks and takes the blow, then folds him up.

"Oh god, I'm so sorry," she says. Tears fill my eyes as I watch her. *You idiot,* is all I can think. *Why didn't you ask for help sooner? Why did you let it get to this point? He needed you. He needed you so much. He still does.*

But thinking like that is not helpful.

Memory Me apologises, knowing it is only one out of many such apologies. She feels as if she will be apologising for the rest of her natural life, and even then, it won't be enough.

"I was wrong. Mummy was wrong. She shouldn't have done that. It was unacceptable. It's just... you punched Mummy, and it hurt, and her instincts... I'm so sorry baby."

"Mummy, your face is scary with all that brown stuff on it." He is right. The other me has brown, clogged grime all over her face. It streaks down her cheeks like mud, and makes for a terrifying, almost deranged sight.

"It's just my mascara baby. When I cry, it ruins my makeup."

"Clean it up before cuddles? I don't want it on me."

"I'll do my best."

Memory Me wipes her face with her sleeves, only serving to spread the brown mess further across her cheeks, but the boy seems mollified.

"Mummy?" The boy asked sleepily. "Do you know what it feels like when I'm angry?"

"Tell me."

"No. I'm going to draw it." He sits up, switches on his bedside lamp, pulls his diary from down the side of the bed where he keeps it, starts to draw. Memory Me rests her eyes while he does so. Once he is finished, the boy pokes his mother.

"See?"

She stares at the diary with bleary eyes. I know without having to lean in, what the paper will show.

A rough approximation of a building, with tiny windows and high walls around it, barbed wire coiled clumsily along the wall top.

And in the picture, a wobbly stick man climbs over the wall, long, spiderish arms and legs scaling the wire with ease. Drawn with anger, drawn with sadness, he is angular, unreliable. He looks as if he is about to leap off the page and down my throat any second.

Silhouette.

On my wrist, the corresponding stick man tattoo burns. I had taken that sketch to the tattoo parlour, told the man there to recreate it exactly. He had obliged without asking questions.

"It feels like my head is a prison." My kid points at the building and the walls. "When I'm angry, it's like all the prisoners are escaping. Is that what it feels like to you?"

"No, baby. When I'm angry, it…" Memory Me thinks about it for a moment. Her mascara still drips down her face, drops onto the bedding, soaks into the crisp white sheets. The spots spread, like blood on snow, and keep spreading. Neither of them seem to notice.

"When I'm angry, it feels like nothing. I don't feel anything. I just… no, that's not true. I feel…" She sighs. She is feeling ashamed that her son, thirty years younger than she is, can articulate his feelings with more emotional intelligence than she could ever hope to muster.

"It feels like a monster lives inside of me," she says, eventually. "An ugly, horrible monster that just wants to eat everything. I know it isn't really me. I don't want to let the monster out. But sometimes, like your prisoners... it gets loose."

The boy rolls onto his other side, so that he becomes the little spoon, albeit a spoon swaddled in a brown duvet that was once white. "That makes sense," he says, drowsily.

"Mummy didn't mean it, you know," Memory Me whispers. "I didn't mean it when I said I hated you. You're the most important thing in the whole world to me, you understand that, don't you?"

"I hid a knife in my Lego box, Mummy."

"You did?"

"No, not really."

Brown leaches from the bed, onto the carpet beneath. It creeps. It always creeps.

"If I go and check, will I find it?"

"No, I was only joking."

After he falls asleep, I will check anyway. There will be no knife, at least not this time.

"Thank you for telling me."

"It's okay. It's okay. I love you. Goodnight Mummy. I can't wait to see you when you wake up properly."

"Goodnight, baby. I'll be there soon enough."

The child falls asleep. I crouch next to the bed, where Memory Me is staring into the night with a haunted look on her face. The walls of the bedroom are now turning brown.

"Who are you?" she asks, knowing the answer already.

"I'm you. You're a memory. Of me. I know that doesn't make much sense, but you aren't really real. Also, I made you better looking than I really am." I laughed a little bitterly as I said this, for it was true. Memory Me was slimmer, taller, had no lines on her face, no jowls, no grey hairs or unsightly bags. Memory Me didn't really look like me under the smeared makeup, but close enough.

"Oh," she replies, too tired to question things.

"I'm just here to say... it gets better, you know. It gets a lot,

lot worse beforehand. But then it gets better. I can't explain it, but it does."

Memory Me smiles. "Really?" Brown on the ceiling now. Soon it will fill the whole world.

I smile back, and lay a kiss on her cheek, and then one on the face of my sleeping child, who I will see soon. I don't care how much heart-sludge there is, if I can just see him again.

"Really, really."

40

FINALE

In a part of the city where university buildings cluster together, imposing and ornate and ambitious in both scale and scope, a tremor makes its presence known. It starts deep in the bowels of one of the buildings, the Department of Psychological Studies building, which also houses The Department of Virtual and Experimental Therapy. It gathers in intensity, like a storm radiating upwards from what an outsider could only assume is a basement facility or some other underground space. The tremor becomes a rumble, and the rumble becomes a roar. Masonry crumbles, crashes to the ground. A large graffitied mural of a magpie wearing a crown of cherry blossoms splits in half, right down the middle. Windows rattle in their casements, gutter pipes tremble loose from brackets and potted plants topple over, urns smashing beneath the weight of their descent.

And brown tendrils explode from the heart of the Psych building, thrusting their way out and up from a secretive basement where an experimental programme no longer has tenure, because most of those who were responsible for it are now dead, or dying. The tendrils shoot skyward, like masses of hungry plants desperately seeking sunshine, and they blot out the daylight for those cowering below, before flexing, spreading, exploring the new freedom and space and light they have claimed for themselves, coils and loops and sticky brown feelers multiplying and thickening until soon, the entire university campus is a woven nest of what one woman foolishly thought of as "potential", and amongst it all, wrapped warm and tight and safe in the stronghold of her newfound confidence, a patient laughs, but she is also screaming, for she has become a giant, monstrous thing, a vast and uncontrollable glitch, and although the bulk of her mind is safe inside a new reality that now exists on a remote backup server in a different city, another part of her consciousness is metamorphosing beyond recognition, and she is as powerless to stop it as she is powerful in its stead. For she let it out into the world, she purged, but nobody could have ever prepared for how much there was inside of her she was underestimated right up until the last, even by those who loved her.

The city panics. People and buses and cars flee the scene, all except one car, which drives in the opposite direction. It speeds right up to the edge of the roiling, sprawling phenomenon, screeching to a halt and depositing the frantic figure of a bearded man, in joggers, at its feet.

And without hesitation he dives into the enormous, furious mass, he dives in, and is gone for five minutes, six, seven, ten, fifteen, as the tendrils writhe and reach, tearing things down, tearing it all down, and it seems as if all is destruction now, all is despair, but the mass parts, reluctantly, and out of the chaos, a man walks, a woman limping by his side. She is naked, and streaming foul, noxious plumes of slime, but the further and faster she walks, the more of it she sheds, until she is clean, and safe, and the pair run, then. They run, and keep on running, for they have each other, and in another part of the city, untouched by what has transpired here, a boy waits, and waits, for his mother will be coming home soon, a Mother he loves deeply and unreservedly, a Mother he dreams of, even now.

And as Magpie flees, the residue of her trauma creeps across the skyline, pouring into people's homes, clogging the streets, a joyous infection, a stubborn weed that refuses to die, because it will take work, and hope, and patience, like most things worth fighting for, but in the meantime, she spreads like wildfire, wrapping herself around trees and along cables and clogging up drainpipes and taking over the whole world entire.

She is no longer mere words on a page, unreliable, untrustworthy.

She is free.

RESOURCES

Please note: in a life threatening emergency, the guidance is always to dial 999 (in the UK) first.

The following resources are located in the UK:

THE SAMARITANS
A free suicide prevention hotline and support available 24 hours a day, 365 days a year. Call 116 123, or visit: https://www.samaritans.org/

SUICIDE PREVENTION UK
A volunteer led suicide prevention charity that helps anyone who may be struggling with their mental health and/or thoughts of suicide. Call on 0800 689 5652 or visit: https://www.spuk.org.uk/

SUICIDE PREVENTION UK- BRISTOL TEAM
The same organisation as above, with a Bristol-based team. Call 0800 689 5652 or visit: https://www.spbristol.org/NSPHUK

MIND
Non-urgent support, information and advice for mental health problems. Call 0300 123 3393 or visit: mind.org.uk

PANDAS
A community offering peer-to-peer PND awareness and support. Call 0808 1961 776 or visit: https://pandasfoundation.org.uk/

Apni

The Association for Post Natal Illness offers support to mothers suffering from PNI/PND.

Call 0207 386 0868 from 10 am to 2pm Monday to Friday or visit: https://apni.org/ for more information, including a chat box.

Agenda

Alliance for women and girls at risk, offers a mental health peer support programme for women. Visit: https://weareagenda.org/peer-support-programme/ for more information.

Tommy's

A pregnancy charity working to make the UK a safer place to give birth. Information on postnatal depression can be found here: https://www.tommys.org/pregnancy-information/im-pregnant/mental-health-wellbeing/postnatal-depression-pnd

Wish

A user led women's mental health charity offering support services for under-served women. Call 020 8980 3618 or visit: https://www.womenatwish.org.uk/

Acacia

Pre and postnatal depression support services for parents and families. Acacia dads offers information and support for Dads and partners affected by post and pre natal illnesses. Call 0121 301 5990 or visit:

https://www.acacia.org.uk/dads-partners/acacia-dads/

Young Minds

The UK's leading charity fighting for children and young people's mental wellbeing. The website has a wealth of resources including information on CAMHS support for children and young people struggling with emotional, behavioural or mental health difficulties: https://www.youngminds.org.uk/young-person/your-guide-to-support/guide-to-camhs/. Also various helplines: see website for more information.

ACKNOWLEDGEMENTS

Huge, unending thanks to the following people:

My husband, for never giving up on me.

My son, for just being you. I love you.

My family, for going on this long and convoluted journey with me.

My therapist, who helped me when I was lost.

My doctor, who took me seriously.

B, for climbing the mountain – we're not there yet.

Glen Mazzara, for the fantastic feedback, I owe you.

Eleanor and the Angry Robot Team, for taking a chance on this weird (not so little) book.

Dan Hanks, for cheerleading as ever.

The horror community, for embracing me, supporting my work, and giving me a chance at fulfilling my dreams.

My readers, for reading what I write. You're incredible.

1

There are some things I remember perfectly. I can close my eyes and be there; in school, shaping a stegosaurus with playdough, climbing stone walls and wooden stiles with Mum, or even on the observatory roof, hand-in-hand with Luke, searching through the smog for sparks of life. Even now, I see his face lit green beneath the moon, smiling in absolute awe at the cosmos and proving without doubt that he had eyes only for antiquities. The way things were. The stars were so bright that I could hear them, like glass shattering. They've never shone so brilliantly since.

But the fact I can relive all these things so vividly just convinces me that I've made them all up. Each time I play these memories through, Mum or Luke say something new. It's always something that warms my belly, something that makes me feel better. Only occasionally is it something that hits me hard. But even then, it still strikes a low satisfying note telling me I was right about being wrong, all along. What would you call that?

I wonder if it matters, whether these images are real. It's somewhere to go that's dark and balmy. We all do it, don't we? Where do you go?

A long time ago, Mum told me that in her youth the sky would flock in spring and autumn with migrating starlings, finches, even gulls. Huge grey and white beacons of the sea. I've heard recordings of their calls – somewhere between a lighthouse's horn and a baby's wail. I sometimes close my eyes and imagine how it would sound as hundreds of gulls moved across the blue like shot-spray, all wailing to each other out of sync. Ghosts that swam the sky. I think it would sound like the end of the world.

Over the years, Mum had collected all the fallen feathers she'd found in the garden, on the roof, in the gutter. There was nowhere too low for her to stoop, no mud too deep or sticky for her to squish her knees into and scoop out the treasure. She rinsed the feathers as best she could and balanced them in egg-cups wedged between books on shelves. "Stuff of stories now," she'd murmur as she pointed them out to me one after another, telling me which birds they came from. This one a barn owl. This one a crow. But she might have well been naming dinosaurs – I couldn't picture any of them. All the illustrations in Mum's reference books were completely flat. One time, we were sitting on the garden wall together when a bird landed on a perch above us and made the strangest sound, sort of a low whistle. I'd never seen anything like it, with its fat grey form and striped underbelly, but Mum just laughed at it and clasped my face between her hands. "Are we supposed to think that's a cuckoo? The little patchwork prince. You can almost hear the clockwork." I felt silly then and didn't look back up at the lie, but I kept listening for a telltale ticking that never came. Perhaps Mum could hear something I couldn't.

Still, I continued to stroke Mum's collection of genuine feathers, gliding the silky fronds between my fingers. Something about them always made me want to pull away, but Mum encouraged me to keep going, to know what they felt like. But it was confusing for me. Was the feather still alive, without the body it had been attached to? I wanted to stick their sharp shafts into the skin on the back of my hands and wave them in the wind. "Be gentle, Norah," she'd whisper, "They're fragile, and who knows if we'll find more."

I wished I could see inside her head. I could almost feel them, *her thoughts*, or at least the shape of them. She was my mum.

But the things she said, the things she lifted from mysterious drawers – they were from another world. She looked up to the sky for things I couldn't understand, always through her old binoculars; heavy black things, held into shape by stitched skins. She liked to shock me with little facts, things like, "When I was little, the sky was full of diamonds that you could only see at night," and "Me and your Gran used to lie on our backs and watch fluffy clouds go by. You could see shapes in them, and if you asked the sky a question, it sometimes told you the future." The more stories she told, the less I believed her, and would gently push my hands in to her belly and say, "You're fibbing, tell the truth." But Mum would just shake her head so her red curls bounced over her face and promise that it was real, *she'd seen it with her own eyes*. One night, she even told me that, "the moon used to be as white as a pearl." At the time, I didn't know what a pearl was, which seemed to make her sadder. She pulled me to her side and pressed the binoculars to my face. "Keep looking, Norah. Up there in the dark. The birds – they might come back. They might."

I don't know if I believed that. The birds had just disappeared, it was their choice. The news reported a muddle of reasons for it over the years; climate change, lack of habitats, a faltering ecosystem. The fact that the earth and sky are turning plastic. I remember when I was little, seeing on TV the reports about initiatives to encourage the building of bird boxes and custom annexes on business premises. Children's TV shows had segments where the hosts showed you how to build your own bug-hotel or bird-feeder out of an old pine cone, but I didn't know anyone who managed to actually bring anything to roost. Later, after I'd discovered the joy of watching the world through Mum's binoculars, I did ask her when it'd all started, the fading away of wildlife in the wind and soil. But she just looked out of the window and squinted her eyes against the white-grey sky. "It all happened so gradually," she said. "I don't think any of us noticed until they'd gone."

Mum tried to make me believe the miraculous could happen, that surprises were around every corner. But even then, I only nodded and smiled to be nice, to make her feel better. I've never understood why people need to believe in something we can't see. It's like reality isn't enough – they constantly need wonder, awe. When Art and I were dating, even in the earliest days, he always threw in the unexpected. For our very first date, we arranged to go for a meal at a French restaurant, La Folie. I spent far too long tangling myself up in dozens of outfits before deciding on a pair of rose-gold trousers and a black chiffon shirt, only a bit sheer.

At thirty-one, I wondered if I was a bit too old for clothes that showed so much, or whether I'd come across as desperate. I ran my hands over the shape of me, repeating to myself the mantra, "I do look good, I do look good." Even after I'd committed to an outfit, I couldn't stop faffing. I tried the shirt my usual way of leaving it loose and flowing, but it just didn't seem right. I then tried tucking it in but I couldn't stand feeling constrained. In the end I undid the last three buttons and tied the open panels in a bow. Already the chiffon was sticking to my skin. My hair – a fluffy brown nightmare at the best of times – was unusually coy and submitted to being clipped to the side with a gold triangle pin. I painted my skin in bronze and peach, finishing myself as I would a precious gift. When I caught my reflection in the mirror I hardly recognised myself, and fought the instinct to wipe it all away. Maybe it was good that I felt like a stranger. This was the new me – a new beginning. Perhaps a costume was what I needed.

I took a taxi straight to the restaurant, my cheeks burning at how late I was. At one point I lowered the window to cool myself down and the caustic air stung my nostrils. It was so much worse in this area of the city. How could I forget to wear perfume? *Stupid.* All I could hope was that the restaurant had plenty of scented candles and a top-notch purifier. I rolled the window back up and tried fanning my face with my handbag, but a quick glance at my watch and I was distracted again. *First impressions are so important.* Though in the end, my lateness probably wasn't a bad thing – my desperation to get there quickly proved to be the perfect distraction from my beating heart, the mounting sense of panic rising up my throat.

I flew into the restaurant not at all thinking about how I looked or whether the other diners would guess why I was there. I spotted Art straight away, sitting at a table in the far corner of the restaurant, a leather portfolio resting between the cutlery in front of him as if he was ready to eat it. The bronze ankh and "E.G." stamped on the cover shone in the candlelight.

I weaved my way between tables crushed with friends and lovers all leaning towards each other, all baring their teeth and spilling wine, and finally reached our table. Art stood when he saw me coming, the fingers of his right hand twitching a little, his right arm pinned down by his left.

"I'm so sorry, Arthur–"

He stopped me short by pulling me into an embrace.

"Don't worry about it, you look beautiful."

My arms wrapped around his shoulders, bending on wooden hinges and dangling on strings. I was conscious that I stood a little taller than him, and my elbows awkwardly sought out the place they would have sat before, which now was empty space. I finally let my arms rest on his shoulder blades, acutely aware of how the expanse of my hands fanned across his back.

We sat, and I saw there was already a glass of red wine waiting for me. I picked up the glass by the stem and took a sip, my tongue shrinking away from its dry and mossy texture. Art picked up his glass and took a long, romantic draft, his eyes on my eyes on his eyes. His hair was cropped much shorter than when I'd watched him in the waiting room. Then, he'd had an early hint of a beard too, but now his skin was shaved so close that his cheeks and chin looked like porcelain. I wondered whether he would break if I touched him. Would everything break? As soon as I sat down, he grabbed my hand and gave it a squeeze. His palm was dry and rubbery, not like china at all.

No, it wouldn't break. I'd make sure of it.

But then the worst happened. Within minutes of me getting there, I didn't have anything to say. My tongue rolled in my empty mouth searching for something, *anything* to fill in this enormous chasm before it got even wider. I'd stalled, utterly and completely. Art's eyes were huge and exposing, and all I could think about was how his skin was even paler than mine, how his hair might feel between my fingers. Bristly, maybe. Not soft. It could've been seconds, it could've been minutes – but it felt like years were spinning by and I couldn't get off the carousel.

Art smiled, showing rows of straight, white teeth with a little gap between the front two around the size of a penny's cross-section. "I thought this might happen." He reached below his chair and on sitting up swung his arm in a flamboyant arc to the ceiling before bringing down on his head a miniature yellow party hat shaped like an ice cream cone, peaked with a cloud of fluorescent pom-poms. "Happy first date day!" he sang, his arms stretching wide in celebration. I laughed, spitting puce across the table and then covering my face with my hands, as if denying I had a mouth at all. He pulled a second hat from beneath his seat, this time shaped like a canoe with long strings dangling from the front and back like a horse's tail. He thrust it towards me. "I thought it might break the tension. Join me?"

Terrified, I took it by the tassel and didn't know what to do. Wasn't everyone in the restaurant already looking?

"I–"

"Come on, put it on!"

In the end, I did it not because I wanted to, but because I thought it might showcase us as a real couple, celebrating a birthday, or anniversary. The other diners would whisper, "Well, they *must* know each other already. Why else would they dare to be so ostentatious?" I grinned back at Art as if it was all for him, only letting a hint of self-consciousness shine though. And you know what? As soon as I pulled the hat over my eyes, something changed. I couldn't even see if anyone was looking anymore, and that slight act of outrageousness overshadowed mine and Art's feeble history. Now, we were set apart from everyone else in a positive way. We were the loud ones, the ones everyone deliberately tried to ignore. It was genius. We had our first funny story. *Remember the hats, darling? Tell them about the hats!*

Art moved his portfolio aside to the edge of the table, leaving it closed, and I didn't even take mine out of my bag. The whole thing felt surprisingly organic, and we moved through the night at the same pace, holding hands through time. He told me a little about his family in Wisconsin, how he'd moved to New York in his early twenties to get away from the crowd he left behind. He was vague about the details, and when I asked him about it he just shook his head and took a drink. It wasn't that he avoided it, but I picked up that he saw his life in the US as a chapter which had very much ended. At this point he'd only been living in the UK for a few months, but it sounded like he was determined to cut ties with everyone back home. He said it was "simpler". So, I was going to be taking on Arthur alone, no extra baggage, which pleased me. Nice and clean.

I watched him all the time. While he talked, he had an odd little tic of pulling on the fleshy bit of his ear as he tied off sentences, and he often looked at me sideways when I talked for more than a couple of minutes. When he ate, he never touched the cutlery with his lips or teeth, and simply dropped the food into his mouth. He opened his eyes particularly widely when listening, as if he heard more with the whites.

Our little table was positioned in front of a huge aquarium, which reached up to the ceiling and across the wall. The glass looked thick as brick, and made a dull *clunk* when Art tapped a knuckle on it. At head height, between the waving reeds, a shoal of guppies flickered with long, flashy tails, and fish with dalmatians' spots cut through the gloom to follow my finger across the glass. We each picked our favourite fish. Art chose a white guppy with a blue sheen which he named Albatross, and I chose the little brown catfish, which snuffled around on the sand with her feline whiskers and otter-like mouth. She was the only one that moved slowly enough for me to make out the tiny stitches holding her together, the bulging seams.

The right time never came to show our portfolios, so we decided to exchange them at the end of the night, taking them home to read before discussing them at our next date. I was even more thrilled about this than I let on, as this seemed like a far less mortifying way to share the inevitable. If only we all could be absent when we're standing in the centre of someone else's room for the first time, naked.

Surprisingly, deciding what to include in my portfolio hadn't been as difficult as working out what to wear that night. Easton Grove had sent me their official protocol list, but I didn't need it. I seemed to just know what would be required of me, and putting this on paper was always easier than living it in the flesh.

I included my CV, which mainly recorded my career history beginning with my teenage job in the bakery and ending with my insurance job at Stokers. I tried to make the most of my responsibilities, keen to make myself seem like a "catch", but it was obvious to anyone reading the facts that I was more of a "cog". Once I realised that, it seemed better to be frank about it upfront after all. My job was to process small insurance claims. I never spoke to the clients myself – my part was to sit in the middle and transform loss into bankable assets – but I sometimes watched their appointments with the suits and ties through the glass walls of the meeting room. Basically, I saw everyone's misfortunes, and turned the gears enough for a few pennies to come out somewhere down the line. Though how much dropped into their purse, whenever it did, was never enough. Their eyes said it, even if their lips didn't.

On its own though, my career history seemed pitiful, so I also included a photograph of the house I grew up in on the Northumberland coast – the rows of houses behind all painted in their pastel colours, prints of two of Mum's paintings (one of me sitting at a little table with a book and the other of a sea, split by the leap of a blue whale), and a USB stick, containing a file of Edith Piaf songs. I had ummed and ahhed about the music, something about it seemed a bit... *pretentious*. But I knew the rise and fall of the melodies by heart, and though I didn't know what the lyrics meant it didn't matter, because the notes made my blood flow in quixotic waves. I hope Art would understand that, even just a little bit.

This all would've been fine on its own, but my portfolio *still* lacked the spark that made me, me. This disturbed me, because the gaps say more about you than what's between the pages. I tried writing something, a poem, a few lines of meaning, but it went nowhere and meant nothing. So after a few increasingly frustrated evenings of scribbling, I scrapped my futile attempt at creativity and instead slipped inside an old photo of a seagull that I'd picked up at an antiques market years before. I wished I still had the feathers in the egg-cups. How significant it would have been to fold something so irrefutable between my pages. But they were all gone now.

By the time I got home from La Folie, the Shiraz was bubbling back up my throat. I locked the door to my flat and threw myself on the sofa, face-down. The room shuddered and swayed, the walls pulsing with the beat of Art's voice, every word he'd spoken. It was late and my flat was silent, yet it was so very, very loud.

I turned on the TV to drown it out, and unzipped Art's leather folio on the coffee table. He'd included his CV, ironed crisp, detailing his journey from his first job as a junior copywriter to full-time authorship. Here was a list of his published novels, and I counted seventeen, including the one currently in progress. Scanning the list, I hadn't read any of them, but I'd heard of one or two of the titles, and could remember one or two of the covers. They were all crime novels, not my sort of thing but the sort of paperback people snap up at the airport for holiday reading. I would never have told him this, but I looked down on them. These were lives written to templates, and it made my skin crawl that the main character – though so flawed in all the usual ways – claimed to never see the ending coming.

But looking at Art's list of successes was still enviable, and with a sickening jolt I realised that he would be looking at my own paltry resumé right now. I let the CV waft back onto the table and picked up one of the two novels he'd included. The title *Frame of Impact* groaned in heavy blue and black. I turned it over and on the back was a greyed-out picture of Art sitting in a library, the desk in front of him messy with open volumes and stacks of old hardbacks, as if playing a detective himself. He didn't look like the Art in the party hat. This was Arthur McIntyre, who didn't laugh or smile. His eyes were smaller, concealed behind thick-framed acetate glasses that he might've found in a fancy-dress shop.

There was a photo in the folder too: Art when he couldn't have been more than five or six, standing beside a couple wearing the protective green overalls, wide-brimmed hats, and veils of the scatterers. Behind them stood a row of sealed white tents and chemical sprinkler pipes. Above the awnings and half out of shot, I could just about make out the edge of an iron cage suspended in mid-air – a tractor, or harvester of some sort. Through the mesh, the woman grinned from ear to ear with the same straight and square teeth Art had. The same wide, white eyes, but set into a face that had lost a lot of weight. Skin hung loose beneath her chin, her neck a slim column of blue tendons. The man, who must have been Art's dad, stood head and shoulders above the woman, and wore a sharp grimace. One arm pinned the woman close to him, while the other held Art's wrist. Art was half-standing and half-sitting, as if his legs had buckled and the photographer had captured the exact moment he'd started to fall. He was looking away to the right, at something beyond the edge of the snapshot, with his mouth gaping, his eyes angry and small. I propped the photo up against a cup on the coffee table.

Back to the folder. Next up was a pile of letters, folded carefully into envelopes which were badly crinkled at the corners. I knew what these were. Art had been telling me about a pen-pal he'd had in his early teens who lived in England, a girl the same age named Wendy. They'd been matched up by a school programme and written to each other for four years, comparing their day-to-day lives and sharing ambitions that transfigured with every letter. They never met in person. Art said that as the years went by he'd get a thrill when a new letter arrived in his mailbox, and he'd rush straight upstairs to his bedroom to read Wendy's news. But when it came to writing back he'd hit a blank, and end up repeating the same stories, hating himself for his laziness and the banality of what his life must sound like. So he started to make things up, but when he received further replies from Wendy he was surprised to see she wasn't as captivated as he'd imagined she'd be. She just wrote about herself.

His stories became more and more elaborate and unrealistic until he ended up writing stories for himself, rather than Wendy. This way, he could live a thousand different lives without lying to anyone. But he kept Wendy's letters, and when the opportunity came (years later) to move to the UK he snapped up the chance, this being the only other home he felt he knew.

The final piece of himself Art had included in the folio were a pair of purple socks, spotted with red. They were obviously well worn, the heels thin and threadbare. When the voices began to settle and I could raise my head again, I carried the socks to my bedroom, closed my eyes, and threw them towards the bed. They lay at the foot on the right hand side. I stared at them for some time before stripping and crawling under the covers on the left side, trying to forget that the socks were new and convincing myself that having them there was utterly, utterly normal.